TEN YEARS
BEYOND
BAKER STREET

TEN YEARS BEYOND BAKER STREET

Sherlock Holmes matches wits with the diabolical Dr. Fu Manchu

CAY VAN ASH

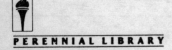

PERENNIAL LIBRARY

Harper & Row, Publishers, New York
Cambridge, Philadelphia, San Francisco
London, Mexico City, São Paulo, Singapore, Sydney

Grateful acknowledgement is made to Dame Jean Conan Doyle for permission to use characters created by Sir Arthur Conan Doyle.

The character "Fu Manchu" and other characters from the works of Sax Rohmer are used by permission of The Society of Authors and The Authors League of America, Inc., owners of the copyrights in these works.

A hardcover edition of this book was published in 1984 by Harper & Row, Publishers.

First PERENNIAL LIBRARY edition published 1988.

Library of Congress Cataloging in Publication Data

Van Ash, Cay.
  Ten years beyond Baker Street.

  "Perennial Library."
  I. Title.
PR6072.A55T4   1988   823'.914   82-48687
ISBN 0-06-080947-7 (pbk.)

88   89   90   91   92   OPM   10   9   8   7   6   5   4   3   2   1

for
OKCHON,
who thinks
there are just not enough
Sherlock Holmes and Fu Manchu
stories

CONTENTS

FOREWORD

If, in the first years of the present century, Sherlock Holmes was the most celebrated criminologist, the name of Fu Manchu ranked equally among the infamous. Since both were active in England during the same period, it seems strange indeed that these two titans of what is loosely called right and wrong should never have crossed swords. Thus, even after the passage of so many years, it comes as no surprise to learn that they once did.

It was in the early months of the year 1914 that Mr Sherlock Holmes, ex-Baker Street, had his first encounter with the sinister Dr Fu Manchu.

Some further word as to dates will here be appropriate. At this time, Holmes, long since retired, was assumed to be living the sedentary life of a bee-keeper on the Sussex Downs, untroubled by any hazard more perilous than an occasional bee sting. Even his friend and biographer, Dr John H. Watson, thought so.

Such, however, was far from being the case. As the world has since learned, Holmes had, some two years earlier, been summoned from his retirement at the direct request of the Prime Minister, to destroy the espionage network headed by the German master-spy Von Bork. To equip himself for the task, and to establish himself in the rôle of the disaffected Irish-American 'Altamont,' he had subsequently spent a year or more in Ireland and the USA, returning to England during the latter part of 1913. Thenceforth, having gained the confidence of Von Bork, he was working as a double agent, assiduously feeding misinformation to the Kaiser's intelligence service.

Dr Petrie, who chronicled the activities of Fu Manchu prior to the First World War, never dated anything. Despite this, it is now clear that Fu Manchu's first 'mission' to England began with the summer of 1911 and ended in the autumn. Somewhat less than two years later, he was back again and responsible for a new series of outrages, interrupted in October 1913 by his presumed death. It must have been at about the same time that Sherlock Holmes himself returned from his travels, in the guise of Altamont, and commenced his operations against Von Bork. Meanwhile, alarming incidents in November had shown that Fu Manchu, though seriously wounded, was very much alive. Under his direction, the nefarious business of his dreadful organisation, the Si Fan, was resumed, and was still going strong in February of the following year. At this point, then, Holmes found himself involved in that series of strange and terrible episodes which, until the present day, have remained undisclosed.

Holmes, as we now learn, had ostensibly returned to his bee-keeping occupation. To maintain a dual identity was clearly a wiser move on his part than to pose consistently as Altamont while Sherlock Holmes remained mysteriously absent from his Sussex retreat, and the very nature of his work would have made actual meetings with Von Bork relatively infrequent. Consequently, it was possible for him to give some attention to the Fu Manchu case, and doing so was, perhaps, useful as a further reassurance to his German confederates that Sherlock Holmes was actively engaged elsewhere.*

The reasons why the tale of this Homeric encounter has never previously been told are simple in the extreme. If Dr Watson knew anything about it – which he may not have done – he evidently considered that the tale should be told by Petrie, who, by his own statement, felt that it should be done by Watson. Only when no such record had been made public by the time of the latter's death, in July 1929, did Petrie undertake the task – possibly inspired by the renewed activities of Dr Fu Manchu in the previous year, though, rather curiously, he does not

---

* A glance at the text (*His Last Bow*) shows that Von Bork was fully aware of Holmes's existence and wary of him as a potential adversary.

mention this. Nevertheless, he still refrained from immediate publication, thinking that an account might be included among the papers in the famous tin box deposited in the vaults of Cox & Co., which, by the terms of Dr Watson's will, was not to be opened till fifty years later. When, however, the stipulated period had elapsed and the box was duly opened, in August 1979, it proved to contain no particulars of these events.

These, then, were the circumstances in which Dr Petrie's manuscript came into my hands through the courtesy of Mrs Fiona Jefferson, of Palm Springs, California. From the covering letter which arrived with it, I gather that Mrs Jefferson is the daughter of Alan Sterling and Fleurette, who, of course, was Dr Petrie's daughter.

In a somewhat lengthy preface, which I think it unnecessary to quote in full, since it deals chiefly with matters already well known, Dr Petrie states as follows:

I owe an explanation and an apology to astute readers who have noted a discrepancy in the record previously given to the public. Seven relatively short episodes in which we were involved in clashes with agents of the Si Fan are listed from mid-November, when Nayland Smith and I were summoned post-haste from Egypt to resume our struggle against Fu Manchu, to the time when personal affairs compelled me temporarily to leave London. How, then, you will ask – unless there had actually been some break in this seemingly continuous sequence of events – could it have been *April* when I returned after an absence described as 'brief'?

The truth of the matter is that there had been two such breaks. I have said, and intend to say, nothing of how we spent Christmas – of the hideous business of the Six Snowmen, and the unspeakable end which threatened Ursula Trelawney, for these were events of so shocking a nature that I should not be justified in bringing them to the notice of my readers. The second break, covering a period of several weeks, occurred when the business which had caused me to leave London was itself interrupted, and during which I had the unique and rewarding privilege of working with Mr Sherlock Holmes. I admit to a deliberate equivocation in using the adjective 'brief' (which, in strict truth, referred to the conclusion of my legal affairs *after* the said interruption) and my excuse is a simple one: I had hoped that some account of my adventures in the company of that great and remarkable man might be written by a hand more worthy than mine.

Dr Petrie's record is of a particular interest in that it gives us a view of Sherlock Holmes seen through eyes other than those of Dr Watson. From the present-day reader's point of view, he was, perhaps, unnecessarily reticent in self-expression and matters pertaining to the opposite sex, though on this occasion, the nature of the people whom he dealt with compelled him to be trifle less so than usual. At all events, apart from a few footnotes added to his own, I have made no attempt to interfere with his style, which best represents the spirit of the age which it portrays. I regret only that I am unable to enhance his narrative with the literary expertise of Sax Rohmer or Sir Arthur Conan Doyle. For the rest, let Dr Petrie speak for himself.

C.V.A.

PART I

1

THE EMPTY APARTMENT

Legal business, connected with the estate of a distant relative, deceased, necessitated my sudden departure from London, within twenty-four hours of the events just narrated. . . . *

With my key still resting in the lock, I drew back suddenly, aware of a resistance to the inward movement of the door, so slight as to be almost imperceptible, and a faint, scuffling sound in the darkened hallway – for these were days in which it required but the slightest hint of the unusual to set my pulse racing.

An upward glance at the unlighted windows of our apartment, as I crossed the small court giving access from Fleet Street, had already informed me that Nayland Smith was not there. I stood still, listening intently; but the curious sound was not repeated. I found the switch and depressed it – then, laughing self-consciously at my unreasoning alarm, saw at once what had occasioned it.

A sizeable stack of folded newspapers, which had piled up against the door, lay scattered across the parquet flooring of our tiny entrance hall. It was evident, then, that Smith had not been in residence for some days.

Retrieving my key and the travelling bag which I had set down in the passage, I passed through into the sitting-room. The atmosphere was stale, like that of a room unoccupied for a week, and heavy with the fragrance of the big sandalwood coffer in one corner. Colonel Bickerstaff – an old acquaintance of Smith's, from whom

* *The Hand of Fu Manchu*, Chapter XXX.

3

we had taken the place, furnished – was an inveterate collector, and, save for the necessary but incongruous addition of a typist's desk and chair, we had done nothing to interfere with his arrangements.

On the off chance that my friend had left some note for me, I went over to the writing table, where, usually, such messages were pinned down under a small statuette of Ganesha. But to-night there was none. Indeed, there was no particular reason to expect any, since Smith had not known the exact date on which I should return.

I crossed to the window and closed the curtains, noting with approval that the precautions discussed between us on the eve of my departure had been put into effect. The sash was now screwed firmly to the frame, so that it could no longer be opened even from the inside. The chill of the unheated apartment was displeasing, but to light a fire scarcely worth the effort, as I did not intend to sit up late. Retaining my overcoat, I helped myself to whisky from the sideboard, then, staring into an empty fireplace, sat turning the glass idly in my hands while I pondered the mystery of Nayland Smith's absence – if mystery there was.

To-day was Friday the thirteenth – a date easy to remember – and I had been away nearly a fortnight, due to the death of a wealthy but eccentric relative who, for reasons best known to himself, and quite without my knowledge, had named me as executor of his will. Unwelcome though the task was at such a time, it offered a substantial reward which, in the parlous state of my finances, I could not afford to neglect. But, hoping to have done with it in a few days, I had soon discovered that it was likely to occupy me for at least as many weeks.

Somehow, with total disregard for any coherent system, my benefactor had amassed a considerable fortune. He had kept no record of anything. Every paper he had ever received – bills, letters, or receipts – he had thrown down wherever he happened to read it, eventually to be piled up on shelves and thrust into cupboards by his half-demented housekeeper. Apparently, he had

4

owned a great number of small and medium-sized properties distributed all over the county, each of which he had purchased through a different firm of solicitors, with whom the deeds were deposited, and most of which we should know nothing about till the tenants turned up to pay their rent.

I sent a postcard to Smith, apprising him of the situation, and, much as I expected, received no reply. But on the Sunday night, I had been called to the telephone at my hotel and, lifting up the instrument, was glad to hear his voice. Now, sitting in our deserted apartment, I reviewed our conversation almost word for word, seeking vainly for some clue to his subsequent actions.

'Smith!' I had exclaimed. 'If I stay here much longer, I shall become as mad as the madman whose affairs I am trying to sort out! He has left loose sums of money all over the house. They say that he never settled an account until someone came to demand payment, and then he would rush about the place collecting up coins and notes till he had found enough, and pay it without further question. The tradesmen must have swindled him a hundred times over. But the house has never been burgled – for no burglar would have any better idea where to look than I have!'

Smith's short, boyish laugh had answered me. 'I gathered all that from your card. But console yourself, Petrie. You are at least occupying yourself more usefully there than I am here. I called to-night merely to remind you that you are supposed to attend some sort of gathering of physicians on Saturday. You had not forgotten?'

'No, I had not. Chalmers Cleeve was insistent that I should tell them something about the Flower of Silence.'

'The Flower of Silence is a subject on which silence would be better kept.' Nayland Smith's tone was disapproving. 'But presumably no harm will be done, so long as you are careful to give them no particulars of how we came into contact – or, rather, *avoided* contact – with the accursed thing.'

5

'I shall be with you as soon as possible,' I replied, 'though I may have to come back here afterwards. You have no other news for me?'

A long silence. Then:

'Nothing of any significance, I am afraid. All I have done since you left is to obtain fragments of a certain conversation . . .'

Again he hesitated. 'Well, I prefer not to discuss it on the telephone, and, frankly, I can make no sense of it, anyway. I doubt if you can either. But if it pleases you to try, I will send you a note of the affair.'

With that and an exchange of farewells, Smith had hung up, in no way suggesting that he planned to be elsewhere when I reached London. I had heard nothing more from him since. The promised, or half-promised, note failed to arrive, and I assumed that he had changed his mind about sending it, evidently deciding that it could wait.

Where had he gone, and why? I could find no answer to either of those queries, but, belatedly, I realised that I had a simple means of knowing *when*. Going out again into the hall, I gathered up the scattered newspapers, and carried them back into the sitting-room. In all, they numbered a round dozen – two morning editions and an evening paper for each day – the earliest marked Tuesday 10th February. Nayland Smith must, then, have left our apartment on Monday evening.

But upon what errand? What had happened during the period of roughly twenty-four hours between his telephone call to me and his departure? Why, four days later, was he still absent? Had he gone off on some new line of inquiry and met with disaster?

Such incidents had occurred in the past. Yet, I reflected, despite his independence, even Smith had now grown wiser than to set off on the trail, leaving behind him no word of his intentions.

Weymouth, if anybody, would know. To-night he would no longer be on duty, but I had the telephone number of the quaint little cottage in Dulwich Village, where dramatic events had been staged early in the game, and where he and his wife still lived. Again I returned to the hall, and had my fingers upon the instrument when the distant sound of Great Paul striking out the hour from the south tower of the cathedral reminded me that it was late.

I drew back my hand reluctantly and re-entered the sitting-room. I was unjustified in disturbing Inspector Weymouth, whom I could see in the morning, merely on account of an anxiety which, in all probability, was no more than the instinctive uneasiness which Smith and I had come to feel whenever we were out of one another's sight.

There could be no peace of mind for us while we lived in the shadow of Dr Fu Manchu.* Setting down my half-emptied glass upon a brass-topped table, I glanced absently about me at the heavy teakwood furniture, intricately inlaid cabinets, and perforated screens – the walls hung with tapestries from the looms of Agra, the light gleaming here and there upon the curved and wedge-shaped blades of ancient weapons. From Fu Manchu my thoughts inevitably turned to the beautiful Egyptian slave-girl whom I had wrested from his hands – whom twice he had taken back from me. Kâramanèh ... Where was she now? In what vile captivity was she held? Here, in this Orientally appointed room – in which, ironically, she had never stood – I seemed to see her now with terror in her lustrous eyes, tears sparkling upon the long black lashes, her slender arms outstretched to me in an entreaty which I was powerless to answer – and now I thought that her red lips parted tremulously in an appeal not for herself but for another.

'*Save him! Save Him!*'

I started upright, wondering if for a moment I had slept or if it had been but a waking vision. My nebulous fears for Nayland Smith were becoming mixed up with my fears for Kâramanèh. If I allowed myself to go on

* In those days, I used to write his name as 'Fu-Manchu,' but eminent Sinologists have since assured me that the hyphen is unjustified. [P.]

like this, I should be a nervous wreck by morning. I stood up grimly, gulped down the remainder of my whisky at a draught, and, gasping at the foreseeable result, went angrily to bed.

I cannot say that I slept well that night, and when I got up, the situation was unchanged. Smith had not returned. The wan sunlight of a mid-February morning shone dismally upon the unsightly clutter of warehouses on the South Bank and the oily swell of the river as, too impatient for inaction, I set off to walk the length of the Embankment. I knew that Detective-inspector Weymouth would not be in his office before ten. Halfway to my destination, and still early, I paused to stare up through the leafless branches of the plane trees at the granite obelisk from Heliopolis, the ancient signs graven upon its surface vainly proclaiming the glories of Thothmes III to the illiterate throng and the tramcars rattling heedlessly by. It was a gloomy prospect, which well reflected my bleak mood of depression.

Big Ben was tolling the hour as I passed under the archway into the precincts of New Scotland. Here, however, I was lucky. Weymouth had arrived. Moments later, I was in his room and conscious of a strange sense of relief as I saw the bulky, square-shouldered man facing me across the desk, for there was something in his very solidity which was reassuring.

He rose as I entered, but I asked my question without even a greeting.

'Weymouth,' I said, 'where is Nayland Smith?'

'Smith?' he repeated, as if surprised. 'Well, in Devonshire, I suppose. Didn't you know?'

All my vague apprehensions had, then, been for nothing! I sat down feeling physically weak at the knees and, all at once, a trifle foolish.

'I have had no word of him since Sunday. But in Devon, you say? What has happened, then?'

Inspector Weymouth laughed shortly and gruffly. 'Nothing, Doctor. Fu Manchu's been lying low for the past fortnight and our friend Smith is simply taking a few days' leave. He has relatives there, hasn't he?'

'Yes,' I said. 'He has. But it is unlike Smith to take leave at a time like this, surely?'

'Why shouldn't he?' demanded Weymouth. 'No man ever earned it more than he has, and there's nothing for him to do here. He left on Tuesday, and he'll probably be back in a day or two.'

'Did he tell you of this himself?' I persisted, for I still felt uneasy. 'Did you talk to him before he went?'

'No, ' he admitted, reseating himself at his desk. 'As a matter of fact, I didn't. But Mr Smith doesn't need to ask permission from me. He just sent me a note to say that he had gone and to give me an address where we could get in touch with him if anything urgent came up.'

'How could you be certain that this note really came from him?'

'No reason not to be.' Weymouth laughed again, and his blue eyes twinkled. 'Oh, I see what you're getting at, but there's no cause for alarm. It was just a note, not a proper letter, and it wasn't signed – but then Smith rarely does, and it was typed on your own machine, which is better than a signature! That museum piece of yours is unmistakable. I copied the address onto a filing card, but I think I still have the original, and you can see it for yourself.'

He opened a drawer, took out a stack of documents, and began to thumb through them, but without immediate success.

'I'm almost sure that Fu Manchu has left London,' he went on, 'and Ki Ming is probably hiding out in the Chinese Legation. We are completely at a standstill.'

'Smith told me as much on the telephone,' I said. A fresh thought came to me as I watched Weymouth sifting through his disorderly papers, and I added: 'But he also made a hint about some sort of a conversation he had overheard – or somebody else had overheard – '

'Oh, yes! The business with Johann Grendel.'

'Who is he?'

'Johann Grendel was the Swiss waiter who served us with coffee at the Café de l'Egypte.' Weymouth paused

9

in his search and looked up. 'You'll remember our visit there, I imagine?'

'I am unlikely to forget it!'

'And so am I – my eyebrows are still singed! Well, after Fu Manchu fired the place, and nearly incinerated the three of us, we had all the staff in, of course, and questioned them pretty thoroughly. No result, except this: the man Grendel admitted that he had sometimes served in the premises at the back, though he denied knowing that drugs were sold there. We had to let him go, but he was such a bag of nerves that we felt pretty sure he knew something.'

'And did he?' I asked.

'Not much, and it was the devil of a job to get it out of him.' Temporarily abandoning his attempts to find Nayland Smith's typewritten note, Weymouth leaned back in his chair. 'We followed him around for a while, but no one got in touch with him, and he never went anywhere but to a public house, where he got drunk every night. That seemed a bit suspicious, since he was out of a job, and unless somebody was paying him off, we didn't see how he could afford it. In fact, he couldn't! He was desperate and living on his savings. Smith struck up an acquaintance with him, pretending to be a newspaper reporter, spent several evenings buying him drinks, and found out that Grendel was in fear of his life because he had been questioned by the police.'

'Which meant that he *did* know something!'

'Or that somebody thought that he did! Well, in the end, by hinting at big money for a story, and reassurances that nobody would ever know where it came from, Smith got to the bottom of it. You remember how that place upstairs was tricked out like an Arabian Nights palace, with divans and those long fretwork partitions at the back?'

'Yes,' I said. 'You see a lot of it in Egypt. It's called *mushrabîyeh*. They use it in front of windows, instead of glass.'

'Oh, do they? I wouldn't know. I've never been to

10

Egypt.'* Weymouth thought for a moment, and continued: 'Anyway, it appears that some two or three days before we went there, this man, Grendel, had been passing behind one of these screen affairs in the normal course of his duties and found himself suddenly in a position to hear the conversation of two people seated on the other side – an aristocratic-looking Chinaman, and a fat Greek. . . . '

'Ki Ming!' I exclaimed. 'And Samarkan!'

Weymouth nodded and grinned. 'Exactly. The Mandarin Ki Ming, and M. Samarkan, who had just *died* in Wandsworth Prison! Innocent as he pretended to be, Grendel must have known the kind of people he was dealing with, for he promptly froze and stayed there in a blue funk, too scared to come out for fear that they might think he'd been listening to them. Promising, eh? But here comes the snag. Firstly, they were talking in French, and Grendel's mother tongue was German. Secondly, he swore he was trying *not* to listen! Thirdly, by the time he was drunk enough to tell his story, he was too drunk to do it. All that Mr Smith got for his pains was a few scraps and isolated words which meant nothing.'

'But,' I objected, 'didn't he think it worthwhile to try again later, when the man was sober?'

'He had no opportunity,' replied Weymouth grimly. 'Johann Grendel was found dead next morning, lying in his own back garden with his face in a goldfish pond less than a foot deep.'

'My God! Surely, not an accident?'

'There was no evidence to show otherwise. We've had drunks drowned before now in a puddle. But . . .' He shrugged.

I sat silent for a moment, staring past him and out of the window to a distant view of the river, where a string of barges was passing under Westminster Bridge – eastwards, towards Limehouse. Weymouth, recalling his

---

* Little as he anticipated it, Weymouth is now Superintendent of Police in Cairo! [P.]

11

promise, began once more turning over the papers on his desk, and, at the same time, resumed speech.

'Nayland Smith was disgusted with the whole affair, and blamed himself for the man's death. Things had turned out badly here, and then, on top of it, it seems he got this telegram from Exeter, saying that his brother was in hospital – ' Weymouth broke off suddenly as he saw the look on my face. 'Why, what's the matter?'

'Dr Fu Manchu's intelligence department is formidable,' I said hoarsely, 'but it is not infallible. Smith's brother was a ship's officer aboard the *Titanic*, and went down with her nearly two years ago.'

Inspector Weymouth leaped to his feet. 'What! Then Smith's note to me was – a forgery?'

'Obviously,' I replied bitterly, and felt myself bowed down under the weight of all my fears confirmed. 'The Si Fan have taken him again. And this time . . .'

I have no very clear recollection of the events which directly followed. Weymouth, in company with two CID officers whom I did not know, visited our chambers off Fleet Street. The note allegedly from Smith, ultimately found, proved beyond all doubt to have been typed on my own typewriter. Thus it was clear that agents of the Si Fan must somehow have gained entry, despite all our defences, which, in turn, suggested that Smith had been attacked and taken forcibly from the premises. But we could find no proof of this.

A telephone call to the Exeter police revealed that the forwarding address contained in the false message had indeed been that of Smith's brother, but the house had been sold after his death and no member of the family now lived there.

How I passed the next few hours I have no idea, and my state of mind may easily be imagined when, at length, I began unwillingly to prepare for the meeting which I had come up to London to attend. The business no longer held the slightest interest for me and I felt more than half inclined to give it a miss. On the other hand, I had no sound excuse; Weymouth and his subordinates were doing all that could be done, leaving me to do literally nothing. Therefore, soon after five, I changed into dress clothes – since the affair was to be followed by dinner – and made my way along the Strand to the New Louvre Hotel.

Here, in a conference room of this palatial new building, the meeting was to be held. I wondered if Chalmers Cleeve, who knew something of our affairs, had made the choice deliberately with a grim sense of humour. Here it was that I had seen a man die by the fiendish agency of the Flower of Silence – the innocent-looking blossom which, at a touch, paralysed the muscles of articulation and killed by asphyxia in seven minutes – and here now I was to address the London Neurological Society as guest speaker on the same subject.

To-night the deliberations of that learned body and the distinguished company in which I found myself left me unmoved. Seated at one corner of the square formed by four long tables arranged about the room, I stared down blankly at my notes, not even glancing at the faces of my colleagues, whilst a famous endocrinologist expressed his views on 'Neural Inhibition of the Eosinophilic Cells.' Other speakers followed. When my own turn came, I arose, spoke without interest, drew a few desultory diagrams on the blackboard, and sat down amid scattered applause, leaving my audience little wiser than when I had begun.

Soon afterwards the formal proceedings ended with votes of thanks, and we all drifted into an adjoining salon, where we stood around talking in small groups. Two waiters moved silently among us, offering cocktails. Chalmers Cleeve of Harley Street, who, somewhat to Smith's annoyance, was responsible for my presence, came across to me and tendered cordially insincere congratulations on my performance. For a few moments, we continued talking; then, as my gaze roved listlessly and focussed on the broad back and shoulders of a man standing at the remote end of the room, my heart bounded.

I had seen him but two or three times, spoken to him only once, but I was almost certain. I set down my glass

13

untasted and hurried across, the blood pounding through my veins as I realised that Providence had placed in my hands the means of gaining access to the one man in all Europe who might be of assistance. He turned at my approach, and though he was greyer than I remembered him and had put on weight, I knew that I was right.

'Dr Watson!' I exclaimed breathlessly. 'I'm afraid you may not remember me, but – '

'Dr Petrie, is it not?' he asked, smiling. 'Good Heavens, man – you're looking a bit under the weather! Not wanting to consult me professionally, I hope?'

'In a sense, I am,' I said urgently. 'I need your help desperately.'

He stared at me, obviously surprised by the strangeness of my manner. 'What is it, then? Are you in trouble of some kind?'

'I am at my wits' end! Fu Manchu is here again, and Nayland Smith has vanished – kidnapped, perhaps murdered, for all that I know – and the police are helpless. . . .' I hesitated an instant. 'Will you – will you help me to get in touch with Mr Sherlock Holmes?'

'Ah!' said Watson, and his brows drew together in a frown. 'You are ten years too late, I'm afraid. In those days, we could have called a cab and I would have had you in Baker Street in twenty minutes. But Holmes is retired and no one, I fear, will persuade him to change his mind – certainly not I. Why, it is all of two years since I last set eyes on him myself. Recently, he has taken to travelling again – '

'Then he is away?' I asked, disappointed.

'No. I believe he was in America for quite some time, but he is back now in Sussex, devoting himself to his bee-keeping' – Watson laughed gruffly – 'though what a man of Holmes's intelligence can see in the creatures to fascinate him so much, I'm sure I don't know.'

'His farm is in Sussex?'

'Yes, not far from Eastbourne. If you go, you will find him there, and I don't think he will refuse to see you. But he's an obstinate fellow, you know, and I'm very much afraid that it will be no good.'

14

'At least I can try!' I insisted.

Dr Watson sighed heavily, shaking his head. 'Well, if you are determined, let us go into the lobby and I will write you a note for him. But I shouldn't like to raise false hopes. I have never had any influence over Holmes – no one ever has. You can try it, if you like, but I doubt whether even the Prime Minister could prise him loose now from his beehives!'*

* Watson, as usual, was wrong. The Prime Minister already had! [Ed.]

2

THE SUSSEX BEE-KEEPER

Nine o'clock next morning found me seated at the wheel of a Vauxhall tourer, heading cautiously into the traffic stream on the south side of Westminster Bridge. Possessing no car of my own, I rarely drove, but I had decided that to do so on this occasion might be advantageous to my plans. These, simply enough, were to seek out Sherlock Holmes and carry him off with me.

Weymouth, who knew of my intentions and approved, though doubting their feasibility, had obtained the car for me – whether by hiring or borrowing it, I did not inquire. I had not known how to go about it at short notice and on a Sunday morning, but I felt obstinately convinced that a car I must have. From Dr Watson I had learned that Holmes's bee-keeping establishment was situated some five miles from Eastbourne, to which there was a good train service. But from Eastbourne onwards, no regular local transport existed. It seemed to me, therefore, that I should stand an altogether better chance of persuading Holmes to accompany me back if I had a car waiting at his door.

Thankful, then, that I had at least learned to drive in the early days of setting up my small suburban practice – though the anticipated need and means to purchase a car had failed to materialise – I set off boldly enough, soon discovering, however, that it was no light undertaking for a tyro to drive through the crowded narrow streets of South London, originally planned for horse-drawn vehicles. Beset on all sides by a feverishly hurrying legion of Unic taxicabs and huge double-decked buses, and dodging tramcars which rumbled past as immutably as the planets in their courses, I thanked Heaven that it was not a weekday, when the whole noisy confusion would be aggravated by trade vans, brewers' drays, and lumbering

16

steam-traction engines. In ten years, the gaslit London of hansom cabs and four-wheelers had vanished utterly. To Sherlock Holmes, it would be another world. . . .

In the outer suburbs, the traffic thinned somewhat, but it was not until I had reached Sutton and turned off from the main Brighton road that I was able to increase speed appreciably. With coastward trippers at a minimum in the bleak days of winter, I now had the road virtually to myself – not that the journey became by any means comfortable. My Vauxhall four-seater, like the current majority of privately owned vehicles, was an open car intended primarily for pleasure jaunts in suitable weather. In February, it was a mechanised version of Dante's icy inferno. Enveloped in a heavy overcoat, with a woollen muffler around my neck and a cap pulled down low upon my forehead, I nonetheless felt the freezing gusts thrown up by my own boisterous passage stinging my cheeks, penetrating subtly below my knees, and stiffening my feet on the pedals.

As days go, in that inclement season, the morning was bright and fine, but I drove through a deserted countryside of dead fields and leafless trees, with never so much as a single horse and cart to contest the right of way. The suffocating fogs of November were gone now from the streets of London, but here the land lay shrouded in a pale ground mist rising from the frosty earth and drifting in eerie streamers across the road.*

Church bells were ringing cold and clear in the distance as I crossed the steep north slope of the Downs. Here I had come upon a more pleasing prospect of long, rolling hills, eternally green with a carpeting of tough, short grass, crowned with occasional clumps of trees, splashed here and there with shell-shaped patches of startling white, where the walls of some disused quarry exposed the chalk. Drawing nearer to the coast, I glimpsed the sea and the towering mass of Beachy Head, and knew that I had not much farther to go.

---

* Only sixteen years later, I find it rather odd to recall that a drive of sixty-five miles was still something of an adventure. [P.]

A signboard directed me to Fulworth. I turned off into a complex of byways and, without entering the village, searched for the unmarked lane of which Watson had told me. Presently I found it, or thought that I did, and, a moment later, saw that I was right when I passed a large house called the Gables – a boys' school, so I understood, a half mile distant from Holmes's premises. Glancing at my watch, I noted to my annoyance that I had grossly underestimated the time necessary for my journey, and it was already close upon midday.

The little-used lane was rutted with ancient cart tracks, and the tyres bounced incessantly, jerking my hands off the wheel. To my right, the way was bordered by a thick hedge just high enough to prevent me from seeing what lay on the other side. Suddenly, it opened up in a gap barred by a simple wooden gate, and I pulled up alongside. No name was written, but this, I was sure, was my destination.

Sherlock Holmes had no telephone – which, at least, provided me with an excuse for calling upon him unannounced. This was just as well, as I had no intention of inviting a refusal.

Climbing out stiffly from the car, I pushed open the gate to find myself standing at the foot of a gentle slope that rose to a ridge above which only the dull grey sky was visible. An onshore breeze, bringing with it a strong iodine smell of seaweed, hinted at the sea beyond. At the top of this acclivity stood a house built of Sussex stone and covered by a mansard roof from which three dormer windows peeped. Watson, I remembered, had said that Holmes referred to his property as a 'villa' rather than a farm, and, indeed, it more closely resembled one. As I made my way up the winding, flagstoned path from the lane, I realised that what I now saw was the back of the place, the front, or principal, side facing the sea.

The path curved in an S-bend, skirting an apple orchard, disappeared between fruit bushes and evergreens, and came out again directly before the house and a neat row of Langstroth hives. As my gaze fell upon them, I knew that I had not gone astray – and, in the same moment, felt my confidence evaporate. This monkish seclusion suggested a retreat from the world, a renunciation of all its problems. Could anything I might say draw him out of it?

I encountered my first check at the door. I had been given to understand that Holmes's former landlady, Mrs Hudson, had followed him into retirement and now fulfilled the rôle of his housekeeper.* Therefore it surprised me to be met on the doorstep by a thickset, red-faced man with bristling side-whiskers, who looked like an ex-coachman, and who stared at me with undisguised hostility.

'Mr 'Olmes don't see nobody without an *h*appointment,' he announced, 'and an *h*appointment be mighty 'ard to come by!'

'I have a letter from Dr Watson,' I said, holding it out. But the guardian of the gate seemed loath to take it and continued to stand squarely in front of me, as though fearing that I might attempt to push my way past. 'Dr Watson!' I repeated. 'If you will just tell him that Dr Watson . . .'

Still the man hesitated. But at that moment there was movement within the house and a sharp, high-pitched voice cried, 'Watson? Did I hear the name of Watson?'

Out of the shadowy interior a tall figure emerged, towering head and shoulders above the man in the doorway, and I knew that I stood in the presence of Sherlock Holmes. Curiously, in the half light, his gaunt height and high, domed forehead reminded me of Fu Manchu.

'Ah!' he exclaimed, with a trace of disappointment. 'So it is not Watson, but a messenger. Well, well – come in! An emissary from Watson is nonetheless welcome.'

He led the way along a short passage to a large, square room on the right-hand side, airy and comfortably furnished – though whether as a study or a sitting-room, I

---

* Correct. But Holmes had already placed her in the household of Von Bork, where she was acting as his agent. [Ed.]

was unable immediately to decide. A log fire blazed on the hearth, imparting a comfortable warmth, while here, on this side of the house, floor-length windows looked out upon a broad green slope extending down to a ragged edge of cliffs, beyond which the waters of the Channel heaved in a long, uneasy swell, grey and ominous.

Taking the envelope from me, Holmes tossed it upon a side table by the fireplace and turned to his bewhiskered servitor, who had followed us to the door and stood regarding me with the disappointed air of a bulldog called to heel.

'Benjamin,' he said, 'take our visitor's hat and coat.'

I surrendered my things and, glancing around curiously, sat down as directed in one of the worn leather armchairs drawn up before the fire, while Holmes dropped down into the other. My first impression was of an order which contrasted oddly with what I had heard of his characteristic untidiness. The books and files which once had lain scattered about his consulting room now were ranged neatly upon shelves, and the acid-stained table with its load of chemical glassware was conspicuously absent. A few old-fashioned portraits, sepia-toned and vignetted, hung upon the walls, and the silver-framed photograph of a lady dressed in the style of the 1980's stood upon the mantelpiece.

Searching further, I saw his violin case leaning up against a bookcase, and there, on a sideboard, was the antiquated, hourglass-shaped gasogene – a dangerous-looking contraption covered with a fine mesh of metal-work, presumably to protect the user from the risk of explosion. Holmes, pausing in the act of slitting open his letter with an Italian stiletto, looked up at me.

'Yes,' he said, 'you will find a few souvenirs of Baker Street, if you look for them. I am not a sentimental man, but I see no point in discarding items which continue to perform their function.' Stooping, he picked up a Persian slipper from the floor and held it out to me. 'This simple object still serves me excellently for the storage of my tobacco. Since I see that you, too, are a pipe smoker, perhaps you would care to try it?'

I accepted with interest, having often wondered how he prevented his smoking mixture from becoming dry in such a receptacle. In practice, it proved to be contained in a large oilskin pouch tucked into the toe of the famous slipper. Extracting it and recalling as I did so that Nayland Smith used just such a tobacco pouch, I experienced almost a sense of panic as the urgency of my mission swept over me afresh. Sherlock Holmes had received me courteously, even warmly. But could I persuade him to do more? Subduing my impatience, I filled my pipe carefully, lighted it, and, while he read his letter, sat studying him covertly. Sherlock Holmes had seemed so much a figure of the Victorian era that it was difficult to remember that he had retired at the early age of fifty – that it had all happened so short a time before.

'By the way,' I said thoughtfully, 'may I ask how you knew that I was a pipe smoker?'

He chuckled and I knew that he had anticipated the question.

'Firstly, by the fact that the classic symmetry of your features is marred by a deeply etched line at the right corner of your mouth, where you always hold your pipe. Secondly, by the discoloration of your left index fingertip, with which you press down the hot tobacco. Thirdly, by the several small holes in the material of your jacket, just below the right shoulder, burnt by occasional sparks – an invariable symptom of pipe smoking, which infuriates the smokers' wives.'

'I see,' I said. 'Thank you.'

'Ah!' he exclaimed, and laughed. 'You are a prudent man, Doctor. You are surprised, but you do not afford me the satisfaction of crying "Amazing!" like the good Watson.'

I shook my head. 'No. What would be amazing in another is commonplace for Sherlock Holmes.'

Holmes, I remembered, was accessible by sincere flattery, and I was glad to see that the answer did not displease him. He laughed again, rubbing his hands together in an oddly exuberant gesture, then became serious once more.

21

'Well, well! But you did not come here merely for the vulgar curiosity of seeing if the old dog could still do his tricks. Watson, in his usual florid fashion, implores me to assist you. Alas, Doctor – I am no longer in a position to assist anybody.' He picked up the letter again, glanced at it, and set it down, frowning. 'You are, I presume, that same Dr Petrie who was concerned in the Fu Manchu case?'

'I am still concerned in it – more deeply than ever.'

Holmes raised his eyebrows. 'Indeed? Your published account of the affair – which I have here on my shelves – stated that Fu Manchu died by his own hand in a burning building, more than two years ago.'

'Would that he had!' I said bitterly. 'But he escaped and has been back here since early last summer, committing one outrage after another, and supported by a gang of fanatics stronger, if anything, than before. It has been kept from the press, but – ' I hesitated. 'But you have heard nothing of all this?'

'Nothing,' he replied, staring at me, his stern features set in an expression of concern altogether deeper than I had expected. 'Lestrade and Gregson are long since gone, and I no longer have any contact with Scotland Yard. But there have been some curiously veiled incidents in the newspapers, and I admit that I have sometimes wondered . . .'

Rising abruptly to his feet, he turned towards the windows and stood there with his back to me, staring out across the white-capped waves to the leaden grey nothingness beyond which lay the coast of Europe. I saw his hands clenched so tightly that the knuckles of his thin fingers stood out like those of a skeleton, and for a long moment he said nothing. Then:

'Has England not enough enemies already on her doorstep,' he muttered, 'but that this Chinese maniac must come here again with his band of cut-throats?'

'Unfortunately,' I said grimly, 'it would seem not; and at present the odds are on his side. Six weeks ago, he succeeded in kidnapping Kâramanèh, the girl I was about to marry, and he is holding her hostage – '

22

Holmes turned quickly to face me. 'And it is for this that you have come to seek my help?'

'God knows, I should be glad of it,' I replied fervently. 'But the situation is more desperate even than that, for now Smith, too, has fallen into his hands.'

'Smith?' he echoed. 'So you have lost your leader, and now you come to me!' His high voice rose all at once to a pitch of exasperation. 'Why? To find him for you? To take his place? I cannot do either.'

His sudden anger took me aback. Yet I had the curious feeling that it was directed against himself rather than at me. Making what seemed to be a conscious effort at control, he walked slowly across the room to the sideboard, took a cut-glass bottle from the tantalus, and withdrew the stopper.

'Well, Doctor,' he said, in the same quiet tone as before, 'you have had a long and cold journey. A glass of spirits will not come amiss, and at least I will not send you back unheard. Let us make ourselves comfortable, and you shall tell me the rest of it.'

He poured two liberal portions, added aerated water from the gasogene, to the accompaniment of much hissing and spluttering, and, with a glass in each hand, returned to the fireplace. Passing one glass to me, he resumed his seat in the chair opposite, took an enormous calabash from the pipe rack, and commenced to load it from the Persian slipper.

'Continue!' he directed.

Thus encouraged, I launched forth rapidly into my tale, giving him only the barest outline of past events – since to have done otherwise would have required several hours – and going into a minute description only of what had occurred more recently. Sherlock Holmes leaned back in his chair, the calabash fuming between his teeth, his eyes closed, and his fingertips pressed together – lost, I thought hopefully, in nostalgic memories of Baker Street. He did not speak again until I mentioned the forged note received by Inspector Weymouth, whereupon his eyes opened and regarded me sharply.

'How was it delivered?' he demanded.

23

'By post,' I replied. 'The envelope has been destroyed. But, luckily, Weymouth has an excellent memory for details, and is also in the habit of looking at the postmark before opening his correspondence. It was despatched from Charing Cross on Tuesday morning – the day after Smith's disappearance.'

'There were no other notable features?'

'Only one. Weymouth noted that the postage stamp had been stuck on sideways, which he thought somewhat peculiar. . . .'

'And this did not arouse his suspicions?'

'He considered it unusual, certainly,' I said. 'But, at that time, there was no reason for suspicion, and he concluded that Smith had been careless and in a hurry.'

Holmes shook his head sadly. 'Whereby valuable time was wasted! Evidently, Doctor, neither Inspector Weymouth nor yourself realises that a native of the Far East, who writes his language vertically, turns the short side of his envelope to the top, and places the stamp in the lefthand corner. Thus, laterally, it would appear sideways at the right. The man to whom this task was entrusted typed the address correctly, no doubt as he had been told, but he did not know how to affix the stamp.'

'Which proves that there were Orientals concerned in this business!'

'Quite so. But, since you never doubted that, we are no better off.' Sherlock Holmes stirred restlessly in his chair. 'Well, you have already told me of what you found – or failed to find – when you came home, and Inspector Weymouth has since looked into the matter. Have no further facts come to light?'

'None, I am afraid. We are sure only that Nayland Smith vanished at some time between six o'clock on Monday evening and five o'clock the next morning – from the evidence of the uncollected newspapers found on the premises. We do not even know whether he was attacked there or outside.'

'And it will probably not help you much when you do know! However, if it is simply a matter of whether or not

Mr Smith had gone out, that should not be difficult to determine. Presumably, you have checked the contents of his wardrobe?'

'Yes. There is a grey suit missing – '

'It is not a matter of what is missing,' interrupted Holmes impatiently, 'but of what is *there*. His overcoats?'

'You mean,' I replied, 'that he would be unlikely to go outside without an overcoat? In fact, both the raincoat and the long greatcoat which I have often seen him wear are still in his room. But' – I hesitated – 'I cannot say for certain that he did not have another.'

'H'm!' commented Holmes, giving me a look of disapproval – though why he should expect me to possess an exact knowledge of my friend's wardrobe, I could not altogether see. 'Yet, if I am not mistaken, you tend rather to believe that the attack was made there. May I ask why?'

It was a question which I found difficult to answer.

'Perhaps,' I said slowly, 'only because the note to Weymouth was typed on my machine, and agents of the Si Fan must have entered to have done that.'

'True! But if they have Mr Smith, we may reasonably assume that they also have his keys. Apart from this, you have noticed nothing about the state of your rooms which is in any way unusual?'

'So far as I can see, nothing,' I replied, and sighed. 'I confess that I cannot explain it. It is just a feeling – an impression. . . .'

Holmes leaned suddenly towards me, his eyes watchful but less cold.

'No, Doctor,' he said quietly. 'It is more than just that. There are things which you have seen unconsciously – things which you know to be wrong. But you lack the training to make them conscious and interpret them.'

'*You* would see them, and you would know!' I answered. A clatter of dishes and a smell of onions from some adjoining room warned me that lunch was imminent, and I had not much time. I made my plunge recklessly. 'Come with me, and see the place for

25

yourself. I have a car outside. We can be in London in two hours, and, if you wish, I will guarantee to have you back here this evening.'

Holmes stared at me with an expression which I found it hard to analyse, as though he was struggling with conflicting emotions.

'It could serve no purpose!' he retorted. 'Will a knowledge of the circumstances in which Mr Smith was abducted tell you where he is now?' His thin lips snapped shut like a rat-trap, and an age seemed to pass while I sat silent and disappointed, watching him. And then, just as I had begun to feel all hope was lost, his face changed again and the hard, angry fire died out of his eyes, leaving them almost sad. 'No!' he said softly. 'That was less than an honest remark, and I had no right to make it. In the absence of any other line of inquiry, an investigation must inevitably commence at the scene of the crime. We may seriously doubt that it will lead anywhere, but until it has been made, we cannot *know* that it will not.'

'Then you will come?' I cried eagerly.

Holmes, making no immediate answer, looked away from me and down at the letter lying on the table beside him.

'Watson, Watson,' he murmured. 'You have much to answer for!' Then, with one of the rare impulsive gestures characteristic of him, he leapt upright, strode to the door, and, throwing it open, shouted across the passage. 'Benjamin! Bring Dr Petrie's things! And, if she will eat it, give my lunch to the cat!'

Turning back slowly to face me, he smiled.

'Such fare as my man prepares is not worth the delay,' he said. 'Let us go now, and have something to eat on the way.'

3

THE EXPERT AT WORK

'I have some domestic instructions to leave with Benjamin,' observed Holmes, as he accompanied me out to the porch. 'Go ahead, Doctor, and get your car turned around. I will join you in a few minutes.'

I nodded, walked down the flagstoned path to the waiting Vauxhall, and re-started the engine. Turning in the narrow lane was not an easy operation, and I felt secretly relieved that he was not there to see me do it. The manoeuvre accomplished, I sat looking back towards the house till, in due course, Holmes appeared – attired in the long, caped overcoat and deerstalker cap familiar to me from so many pictures.

He climbed in beside me, bringing with him a strong smell of mothballs, and met my somewhat startled glance with a glare.

'I am not dressing the part of Sherlock Holmes to create an impression!' he snapped. 'I simply have no more suitable clothing for a journey in a conveyance of this sort.'

Arranging the long skirt of his overcoat carefully about his knees, he added:

'I suggest that you also refrain from attempting to impress me. I know that the car is not yours. It bears Somerset number plates, and you have twice backed it into my hedge. Well, well – pull the necessary levers, and let us be going.'

Since the lunch hour had begun ere we started, we drove only as far as Uckfield before finding a hotel to cater to our needs. Here we enjoyed a simple but well-cooked meal, enlivened with a half bottle of Bordeaux, which Holmes darkly suspected to be smuggled. Having consented to accompany me to London, he now showed no impatience and lingered over the wine, talking like one who had long been deprived of an audience. But, declaring that it was unsound policy to speculate upon insufficient data, he refused to discuss the business upon which we were engaged, treating me instead to a discourse on the numerical table of Zarlino based on the Ionian mode, while I maintained a respectful silence of ignorance. I believe that it had something to do with music.

When we resumed our journey, conversation languished. Although we sat side by side, the roar of the engine and the constant bursts of wintry air hurled up from the windscreen made hearing impossible without our shouting. Holmes spoke only once – after the intemperate approach of a family car handled even less skilfully than mine caused me to curse, brake violently, and stall the motor.

'A horse,' he remarked sagely, 'no matter how poorly managed, would have more sense than to run head-on into another!'

I smiled and said nothing, finding his antipathy to motor cars very much as I had expected. But time was slipping past with every mile. I knew that my mendacious estimate of two hours to London – which might have been true as far as the county border – would prove well short of the mark.

It was nearly five o'clock when ultimately we reached Fleet Street. Rain clouds were gathering and the light was already gone. As we passed through the arched opening in the high blank wall and entered the small courtyard giving upon our premises, Sherlock Holmes glanced swiftly around.

'Is this the only way in?' he demanded.

'No,' I said, and pointed to the cloisteresque arches on the opposite side. 'You can get through to the Embankment from there, but the route is a trifle complicated.'

Turning to the right, and leading the way upstairs to the door of our apartment, I went through the involved process of unlocking it, which required three full turns of the key in one direction, and two in the other.

'We have made the place into quite a fortress,' I observed. 'This is a lock which would defy Houdini.'

'H'm!' replied Holmes doubtfully.

I crossed the narrow hall, switching up the lights, and, following, he stood for a moment in the sitting-room doorway, staring about at the array of ivory Buddhas, ebony elephants, grotesque, multi-limbed gods and seductively nude goddesses.

'You appear to live in a museum of Indian curiosities!'

'Yes, but they are not ours. These rooms belong to Colonel Bickerstaff, who has spent half his life in India, and although he is retired from the army, he is there again now on some sort of civil appointment, I believe.'

Holmes nodded, took off his cap, and tossed it upon a chair. He did not, however, remove his overcoat – no doubt because the room was cold, but also, I thought, as an indication that he did not intend to stay there very long. His keen eyes roved ceaselessly over the exotic furnishings, the ornaments, but, for the moment, he touched nothing.

'Who looks after the place?' he inquired.

'Mostly,' I said, 'we look after it ourselves. There is a cleaning woman who comes in on Wednesday mornings, but we have to let her in, since she has no key. We have not allowed anyone to have a key – not even the porter downstairs. Since Smith was not here last week, she will not have been able to get in.'

'Good! Then nothing has been disturbed.' Sherlock Holmes walked across to the incongruous desk and lifted the cover from the typewriter. 'It was this which was used for the note sent to Inspector Weymouth?'

I nodded and watched him fit a sheet of paper into the machine – a timeworn veteran which I had purchased in Thieves' Market at the modest price of ten shillings. Together with the greater part of my worldly goods – such as they were – my faithful portable still rested in the house on Gezirah Island which I had hoped soon to share with Kâramanèh. We were to have been married by the Consul at Christmas. . . .

Holmes struck the keys in sequence and turned up the

sheet to reveal an erratic line of lettering in a peculiarly unpleasant shade of indigo.

'Yes,' he said. 'I think we may take the inspector's word for it. This would be hard to imitate.'

Thereupon, moving away from the desk, he began methodically to examine the room and its contents, going from each item to the next with the air of a person who knew what he was looking for and where to find it – though the object of his search was not altogether plain to me. He picked up the smaller ornaments one by one, glanced at them, ran his finger along the edges of the furniture, and stooped to inspect chair and table legs.

'For my own taste,' he remarked presently, and with apparent irrelevance, 'I choose my tobacco pipe to match my mood. I use seven. Mr Smith, I believe, has only one?'

'Yes,' I said absently. 'It seems to me to have been always the same – though I suppose he must at some time or other buy a new one.'

'At some time, certainly. But, even if it is ill-used, a good quality briar will survive for several years.' Holmes shot out his hand, palm upwards. 'Here it is!'

'Good Heavens!' I exclaimed, staring down at Smith's cracked and blackened briar. 'Where did you find it?'

'In an ash tray, where doubtless you have seen it so often that you failed to notice it,' he replied dryly. 'A confirmed pipe smoker may, of course, occasionally forget his pipe when he goes out – but not often. Put it in your pocket, Doctor. We must give it back to him as soon as possible.' With a quick smile of encouragement, he handed it to me, and added: 'Now, where are the boots kept?'

His abrupt changes of topic were sometimes a trifle bewildering, but I was growing used to them.

'In the small cupboard in the hall,' I said, guessing, or thinking that I guessed, what he had in mind. 'But I am not sure how many pairs Smith had.'

'Nevertheless, I will take a look.'

Sherlock Holmes went out into the hall, where I heard him rummaging around for a few minutes, and returned holding a pair of carpet slippers in his hand.

'Yours?'

'Yes. I have not worn them since I came back to London, but – '

'They are the only pair in the cupboard,' he said significantly. 'Where, then, are Mr Smith's? Is he in the habit of going outside in his slippers? Look around for them, while I complete my work here. But I doubt if you will find them.'

I obeyed and, while Holmes resumed his slow, painstaking circuit of the room, searched assiduously under the armchairs, the settee, and the desk. Failing to discover anything, I went into Smith's bedroom, and having searched there, likewise without avail, re-entered the living room to find Holmes standing on tiptoe against one wall, with his nose flattened against the plaster. He turned at my approach, and, offering no explanation of this unusual exercise, pointed to the sideboard.

'There was something standing upon that? A vase, perhaps?'

'I don't know,' I said wearily. 'There may have been. But, really, there are so many of these things here, and, since they don't belong to us, I have never taken any special notice of them.'

Holmes shook his head and frowned, but said nothing. Then, taking a small lens from a wash-leather case, he went down upon his knees, muttering something about rheumatism – which, frankly, I did not believe – and carefully examined a sizeable area of the carpet directly in front of the door leading in from the hall, with the aid of an electric pocket lamp held close to the surface. Finally, he stood up again, crossed to the desk, and, laying down his lens on a pad of paper beside the typewriter, turned once more to face me.

'Any further search would be pointless,' he said gloomily.

'What!' I cried, disappointed. 'You mean you can find nothing?'

'I mean,' said Holmes, glaring like a basilisk, 'that I have found all we need to be sure that Mr Smith did not leave this room of his own accord. Of course he did not!

31

How can you ever have doubted it? There has been a battle royal in this apartment, and although a major attempt was made to clear the place up afterwards, the traces of it are everywhere. Most of the lighter furniture has been overturned, chipped, and scratched. Many of the ornaments were thrown down and replaced in slightly different positions.'

Striding across to the fireplace, he took up a small, elephant-headed statuette from the mantelpiece.

'This, for example, did not formerly stand here?'

'No!' I exclaimed, recognizing it. 'It was on the writing table. We used it as a paperweight.'

'Just so,' said Holmes, nodding. 'Fortunately, you are poor housekeepers, and your charwoman neglects her duties. Hence there is dust under all those objects which were moved, and none under those which were not.' He walked back to the door, took the lamp from his pocket, and shone it down upon the floor. 'Look! If your eyes are sharp, you can see it without troubling to go down on all fours. A large part of the carpet around here has been washed. They had no proper carpet soap, so they used the soap from the bathroom, and it has left sediment upon the threads. They were also unable completely to remove a few small bloodstains –'

'Bloodstains!' I repeated, aghast.

'Oh, there is no occasion to alarm yourself,' replied Holmes indifferently. 'An encounter of this nature could hardly have taken place without some loss of blood. But the wounds were superficial, and may equally well have been suffered by either side.' He fell silent for a moment, frowning thoughtfully. 'There must have been a good deal of noise. Why, I wonder, was it not heard?'

'The apartment beneath this is untenanted,' I said, 'and the young couple who have the rooms opposite keep late hours. They are rarely home before midnight.'

Holmes nodded again. 'We may assume, then, that the assault took place during the evening – probably not long after Mr Smith came in. He had put on his slippers, but not yet lit a fire in the grate.'

'How did they get in?' I asked. 'Even if they could

have climbed up from the court, or down from the roof –
which, I might add, is the sort of thing Fu Manchu's
people not infrequently do – the windows have been
permanently secured to prevent any such attack.'

'They entered by less dramatic and more conventional
means. In other words, by the door!'

'But,' I objected, 'Smith would have been on his guard
– particularly since I myself was caught in a trap of that
nature only the day before I left London. Smith was
cautious. Even in the daytime, an unexpected caller was
obliged to shout his name and business through the door
before he would open it – and even then he usually had a
pistol in his hand. He would not answer less prudently to
anyone but Weymouth or myself – '

'Or, possibly,' said Holmes quietly, 'to one other? A
woman whose voice he knew? Did you not tell me this
morning that your fiancée had fallen into the hands of Dr
Fu Manchu?'

I stared at him blankly for an instant and then, as the
full import of his words came home to me, felt a hot flush
rise to my cheeks.

'Kâramanèh?' I said, forcing myself to speak calmly.
'Once, when she was his slave in fact as well as in name,
he could have made her do it. But not now. Nothing – no
form of coercion – could persuade her – '

'It was unnecessary to persuade her,' rejoined
Holmes. 'But she was here! This useful carpet has
yielded several excellent specimens of hair too long for a
man's, and I do not think they came from the head of
your slovenly charwoman. It is simple to reconstruct
what must have occurred. The girl was brought to this
building and conveniently allowed to escape. What
would she do but rush precipitately to your door and
beat upon it, calling for help? Smith sprang up to answer
the summons, and no sooner was the door open than she
did what any woman does in such circumstances. She
flung herself upon him, so hindering his movements that
when, an instant later, the others burst in at her heels, he
was unable to defend himself.'

Leaving me still shocked into silence, he turned aside

and went into the kitchen, to re-appear not long after with a broom in his right hand and something apparently clutched in his left.

'A part of my theory is confirmed,' he said. 'We will see if it is possible to test the other.'

With a jerk of his head, beckoning me to follow, he approached the ornate sideboard and stood beside it while continuing to talk.

'The pistol was hurled from Mr Smith's grasp before he could use it. Here is the mark where it struck the wall behind this piece of furniture, after breaking the vase which then stood upon it.' Opening his clenched hand, he showed me a fragment of brightly coloured pottery. 'The pieces I have just found, neatly deposited in the kitchen rubbish bin. And now – '

Stooping down upon one knee, he raked beneath the sideboard with the broom handle – and out upon the carpet came a Browning automatic pistol!

'Ah!' said Holmes, rising. 'I doubted if they would have bothered to recover it, since it was out of sight, even if they saw where it fell. See! The safety catch is off, but it has not been fired. Two men grappled with Mr Smith. A third seized the girl by the hair, and no doubt chloroformed her. Does your fiancée favor high-heeled shoes?'

I thought wistfully of the little red shoes I had some-times seen upon her feet, and nodded.

'Yes,' I said. 'When she wears European dress.'

'I thought that she might. It is impossible to be sure, but there is a deep indentation here in the carpet, heavy enough to damage the pile, probably made when she tried to stamp upon the man's foot. But, having subdued her, he carried her outside while his companions dealt with Mr Nayland Smith. It was a tough fight, but eventually they were successful. They were powerful fellows, these two, but rather an ill-matched pair who must have been somewhat conspicuous if they went about together. One was as tall as myself and the other unusually short.'

Again taking the lamp from his pocket, he pressed the

button, casting a circle of light upon the wall at the spot where I had seen him standing.

'Do you see that large, greasy smear? That is where the tall man hit the back of his head when, at one stage in the fray, he was thrust back against the wall. His hair was thickly plastered with a preparation of camellia oil, popular among the Far Eastern peoples. It has a characteristic odour – '

My expression of amazed respect as I listened to this dissertation must have lapsed into something like incredulity at this point, for Holmes laughed shortly, shaking his head.

'Oh, of course, it is very slight now,' he said. 'But, fortunately, I have a nose like a bloodhound. Can you imagine how seriously I was once inconvenienced by catching a cold during an important investigation? I have also obtained from the carpet a few strands of this man's hair – or it may be his comrade's – which are equally informative. You will find them there on the desk behind you.'

Glancing down at the pad of typewriting paper upon which he had put his lens, I saw that there were three or four hairs weighted beneath it. Holmes, coming up beside me, plucked a single strand from his own sparse, neutral-coloured hair, and placed it with the others.

'Compare them through the glass,' he directed. 'As a medical man, you may possible know already that the hair of an Asiatic is notably coarser and stiffer than that of a European. You are satisfied? And now look here. . . .'

He was pointing to a set of three large and handsomely bound volumes sandwiched between carved bookends.

'This no doubt valuable history of Indian art was thrown upon the floor and later restored to its place. But who other than an Oriental would think to arrange it so that the sequence runs from right to left?'

'As Watson has so often remarked,' I said wonderingly, 'it all sounds simple when you explain it. But your reasoning has the simplicity of genius.' Holmes flushed with pleasure, and I added: 'By the way, how do you know that the second man was short? I realise, naturally, that you deduced the height of the taller by the mark on the wall, but . . .'

'The chair!' he answered, seizing the back of the adjustable chair and drawing it away from the desk. 'While the other did the cleaning up, he occupied himself with the typing. He has raised the seat of this chair so high that it is difficult to insert one's knees under the desk. Why, he could scarcely have been more than five feet in stature! A Japanese, perhaps, or a native of Cochin China.'

Walking back to the fireplace, he sat down on the edge of an armchair and remained there unspeaking for a while, with his elbows on his knees and his long chin cupped in his hands, his attitude reminding me, somewhat disrespectfully, of a particular gargoyle on the towers of Notre Dame.* Then:

'We know now how the attack took place,' he said slowly, 'and we may easily surmise the reason for it. Mr Nayland Smith said little when he spoke to you on the telephone, but he said too much. Do you suppose that it is hard for Dr Fu Manchu to place some kind of listening device upon the wires? I would wager that everything you say is both heard and inscribed on one of Mr Edison's wax cylinders. Mr Smith told you that he believed he had a possible clue to the activities of the Si Fan and promised to send you a copy. Though he himself considered it incomprehensible, this was sufficient to bring them down upon him at once.'

'I suppose so – and, unfortunately, whatever it was that he proposed to send me, I never received it.'

'No. Evidently he did not write immediately, and they moved too swiftly. What happened afterwards? Having secured Mr Smith, and presumably drugged him, how did they convey him out of the building? The girl with the awkward name – your fiancée, I mean – '

---

* As Dr Petrie does not mention the goatee beard which Holmes wore in the character of 'Altamont,' this must have been artificial, even though the text (*His Last Bow*) tends to suggest otherwise. [Ed.]

'Kâramanèh,' I said. 'She is Egyptian.'

'Ah, yes! Kâramanèh. Is that right?'

I nodded, and Holmes continued:

'Well, then, Kâramanèh, having unwittingly played her part, was doubtless assisted, semi-conscious, into a waiting car. No one takes much notice of a fainting woman. But the handling of Mr Smith would have presented more difficulty. They ran little risk in carrying him down the stairs. But outside? Both Fleet Street and the Embankment are relatively populous even in the middle of the night. . . .'

Standing suddenly, he gathered up his discarded cap from the opposite chair.

'There is nothing more to be learned here,' he declared. 'But, before I leave, it is possible that we may gain something by a visit downstairs.'

4

A SACK OF COALS

As we came to the foot of the stairway, Holmes turned to the door of the apartment situated directly beneath ours, and laid his hand upon the knob.

'You said, I think, that these premises were vacant?'

'Yes,' I replied. 'They have been so ever since we moved in here. But the porter may have a key – '

'It will not be needed,' said Holmes.

He pushed and, to my surprise, the door opened. Groping for and finding the light switch, he operated it, and, to my further surprise, the lamps which should have been turned off at the fuse box became lighted.

'It was easy to force the lock,' he observed, 'but it would have been less easy to secure it afterwards. They did not bother themselves with it.'

Following him across the hall, I looked into a sitting-room identical in size and shape with our own. As the place was destined to be let furnished, it was summarily equipped with a table, two armchairs, and a settee, but there were no smaller or personal items.

'We are trespassing,' remarked Holmes. 'But I doubt if we shall be prosecuted.' He walked around the room, subjecting the few appointments to a rapid scrutiny. 'This was their base. It was here that they waited for Mr Smith to come home – here that they subsequently held him until they were ready to move him elsewhere. There are no curtains; they must have brought something to cover the window so that no light shone out into the court.'

The settee standing against one wall was shrouded in a dust sheet, but I saw that those which had formerly been draped over the armchairs were heaped beside them on the floor.

'They made themselves comfortable,' I said grimly.

38

Holmes smiled. 'They were here for some hours, and made no attempt to clear up afterwards, since they expected no one to come in here. They smoked a good deal, and left the ash lying about everywhere.'

So much was evident. They greyish patches here and there upon the dark carpet were plainly visible even to me.

'So I see,' I replied, and, remembering his celebrated monograph on the subject of tobacco ash, could not resist adding: 'To which of your hundred and forty varieties does it belong?'

'None of them. It is *hashīsh*.'

'*Hashīsh*?'

He laughed shortly. 'You are surprised because you are familiar with *cannabis* only as a powerful drug which produces nightmarish hallucinations. But the plant in its crude form is regularly smoked in many Eastern countries as freely as tobacco and probably with no more injurious effect. Mr Nayland Smith was, of course, drugged with something else – an injection of some kind which would render him unconscious for a considerable period.' Turning back to the settee, he inspected it more closely, fingered the dust sheet, and nodded. 'I think this is where they laid him. The cover is creased and disordered. But there are no bloodstains.'

I said nothing but continued to stand in the doorway, watching him while he examined each of the armchairs in turn, again making use of his lens and pocket torch.

'Ah!' he exclaimed triumphantly. 'So it was our tall friend who sat here – his greasy hair has left a mark on the back – and it was he who was wounded, evidently in his right hand or forearm. There are a few blood spots on that arm of the chair.'

As he straightened up and turned, his foot caught and disturbed the discarded dust sheet, disclosing a bright patch of colour beneath. Holmes saw it in the same instant as I, and pounced.

'Good Heavens!' he muttered. 'What are these things doing here?'

He pulled the sheet completely to one side, and,

39

approaching, I stared down at a small heap seemingly composed of multicoloured scraps of rubber and a number of short tubes. I could not immediately identify them, and, ridiculous though it may seem, felt the warning pulse of fear which invariably accompanied the finding of anything bizarre in a place entered by agents of Fu Manchu.

'What are they?' I asked.

'I can see what they are,' rejoined Holmes irritably. 'But I cannot imagine why they should be here. They are toy balloons, and all of them have been burst.' Stooping quickly, he extracted one from the heap and stretched the material between his fingers. 'You see? The necks are knotted, so that they were not meant to be re-used. They could be deflated only by breaking them. But why? What could these people have used them for?'

Throwing the fragment aside, he began to pace restlessly about the room, shaking his head, and talking rather to himself than to me.

'Why did they come back here after they had finished upstairs? Why did they keep their victim here? How did they bring him out into the street, and why could they not do it sooner?'

In the near distance, the bell of Great Paul pealed out the hour of six. As though at a signal, Sherlock Holmes ceased his pacing and stood for a moment close to the settee, with his chin sunk upon his breast. He scowled down at the floor, then suddenly went down upon hands and knees, sniffed the carpet, rubbed his fingers upon it, inspected their tips, and stood up.

'This is coal dust!' he snapped. 'You have coal fires upstairs, but this apartment is fitted with electric radiators. Why should there be coal dust here?'

I shook my head blankly. Holmes, relapsing into silence, frowned at his soiled fingers and cleaned them perfunctorily on his handkerchief. Then:

'Where is the coal kept?' he demanded. 'And how do you get it up to your rooms?'

'There is a cellar,' I said, 'and the porter brings it up in scuttles, as we require it.'

'Does he live in this building, or in the other across the court?'

'He lives here, in a basement at the back.'

Holmes nodded. 'I think,' he said, 'that I will go and have a word with this porter of yours. Wait here. I may be able to do this better on my own.'

He departed forthwith, leaving me to stand peering aimlessly across the court through the uncurtained window. Yellow patches of light from the block of flats opposite glittered upon driving spears of rain. Even my temporary elation at securing the assistance of Sherlock Holmes had deserted me, for I knew that I had come back to London too late – too late by five days.

Holmes was absent for some fifteen minutes. Then, hearing his brisk tread across the hall, I turned to see him enter, beaming and rubbing his hands.

'Well, well!' He chuckled. 'There are times when it is some advantage to be a legendary figure. Your porter took me for a phantom, and when I had convinced him of my reality, fell over his own words in his eagerness to supply information to Sherlock Holmes. He even offered to come around to Baker Street.'

Laughing outright, he sat down in the nearer armchair and continued more seriously, but still with a hint of mirth in his voice.

'There was, so it appears, a curious incident here at about eight o'clock on Tuesday morning, when the porter's breakfast was interrupted by the arrival of a coalman bearing a hundredweight sack on his back. This, the coalman announced, had been ordered by a Mrs Wainwright. The porter had some difficulty in persuading him that no one of that name lived in any of the apartments and that, in fact, no one had ordered coal. However, he finally succeeded, and the coalman went off, blaspheming, to lug his sack out into the street again.'

'And you think . . .?'.

'There is no *thinking* about it. Surely, the facts speak for themselves. Mr Commissioner Nayland Smith was taken from here, in broad daylight, crammed into a sack

41

and lugged on the back of a supposed coalman. Fortunately, he was unconscious and knew nothing about it.'
Holmes's lips curved in a grin of sardonic humour, which I quite failed to share. 'I may say,' he went on, 'that this coal heaver who played his part so well was *not* an Oriental. He was a European, and probably a Londoner.'

'There are Europeans who do not scruple to work for the Si Fan,' I replied harshly. 'But still I do not completely understand. Why did he deliberately go and make himself known to the porter?'

'What?' cried Holmes. 'Where is your sense of artistry? Could a coalman be seen carrying a full sack *out* of a residential building without some reasonable explanation to offer, in the event of inquiry? Since, likewise, it would have been equally unusual to enter with an *empty* sack, it was stuffed with the balloons to make it appear full when it went in.'

'But why not, then, fill it with coal?'

Holmes laughed again. 'Really, Doctor! Apart from the unnecessary labour of lugging a hundredweight of coal in from the street, what could they have done with it? If, by some mischance, the porter should later have discovered that this apartment was unlocked, he would no doubt have concluded that it had been left so by accident, and, since there is nothing here to steal, have taken no more than a superficial glance around. But if he had found a vast heap of coal piled up somewhere in here, he would have started to wonder.'

'Yes! Undoubtedly he would!'

'Well, then – hence the balloons, which could be easily disposed of.' Holmes frowned and shook his head. 'However, since they were so careful in this respect, it was a cardinal error to leave the furniture uncovered and the electricity turned on. Obviously, this business was planned by an intelligence superior to that of the rascals who carried it out.'

There was an odd clip of finality in his tone as he finished speaking. He paused, looked carefully around, as though to assure himself that nothing had been forgotten, then rose slowly to his feet.

'I have done what I came to do,' he said, taking his thick woollen gloves from a pocket in the caped over-coat, 'and, as I warned you would no doubt be the case, you are no better off. Nothing we have learned here provides us with a clue as to where Mr Smith is now, or offers any useful lead. The most significant point in the whole affair was known to you before you came to me.'

'And what was that?' I asked.

'The forged note received by Inspector Weymouth. You knew from the outset that Mr Smith had not been murdered, since we are dealing with a group of terrorists who advertise rather than conceal their slayings. They would not have removed the body. The bare possibility that Mr Smith had been murdered outside and his body not yet discovered was negatived by the forged note. Why was it sent? Why did they go to such lengths to conceal their handiwork upstairs? Did it matter to them that you should know he had been abducted, any more than if he had been murdered?'

'Perhaps not. Have you some explanation?'

'Yes,' Sherlock Holmes was drawing his gloves over his long, artist's fingers. 'One which I could have given you this morning. They wished to cover their tracks for a limited period – no more than a few days, since the note ostensibly written by Mr Smith must have been proved false as soon as anyone tried to get in touch with him at the given address. There is only one reason why they should have desired this. They were taking him to a temporary hiding place which they feared might be discovered by a prompt search.'

'Then you think there may still be hope?'

'No. They have had as much time as they bargained for. By now they have removed him to the later destina-tion, which, it appears, was not immediately available. As to that, two hypotheses are possible. Either this place of greater security was not then prepared, or they intended to convey their captive a considerable distance and lacked suitable transport.' He smoothed down his gloves and adjusted his quaint, ear-flapped cap. 'And now I must really be on my way home.'

Disappointed, but realising that there was little else to be expected, I accompanied him out into the street. Rain was falling steadily but not heavily, and I saw that we would not need umbrellas for the short walk back to the car.

'You will not go farther with this matter?' I inquired hopefully.

Holmes shook his head decisively. 'There is nowhere for me to go with it. All that can be done now is to comb all the known haunts of these Asiatic fanatics, or to seek some witness who may have seen the coalman leaving with his burden. The police are excellent at this kind of thing and have all the necessary facilities; the London which I could once cover with a gang of street arabs, my Baker Street Irregulars, vanished with the nineteenth century. You may, perhaps, institute inquiries about a cart stolen from a coal merchant's. But it is just as likely that the self-styled coalman really *was* a coalman. There are plenty of his kind who would have done it for a five-pound note.'

He might, I thought, be right. Perhaps there was nothing more that he could do – nothing that any of us could do. Yet I remained unsatisfied as we walked briskly on through the rain towards the garage where I had left the Vauxhall to be refueled and serviced – fed and watered like a camel for its third trek across the wintry desert of the Sussex Downs.

'Thers is no need for you to make another excursion,' said Holmes, as if reading my thoughts. 'You may simply drive me to Victoria Station, and I will take the train.'

'No,' I said obstinately. 'You have carried out your part of the bargain, and I will do mine. I will take you back to your door.'

Holmes glanced at me and shrugged. I had an idea that he would distinctly have preferred the train, but I was still determined not to let him out of my sight till the last possible moment.

'Very well,' he said shortly. 'As you will.'

We reached the garage and stood beside the car while

two helpful mechanics raised the canvas hood and lighted the headlamps.

'If we turn up new evidence,' I said boldly, 'may I come to you again?'

'My dear Dr Petrie!' burst out Holmes, in a high, exasperated voice. 'Even if I were prepared to involve myself in this adventure – which, frankly, I am not – I have not the ability. I cannot, at my age, go climbing walls and jumping over rooftops, while as regards China, I know only as much as anyone may learn from a common encyclopaedia. Why must you ask me?'

'I appealed to you this morning,' I said, choosing my words carefully, 'because I had confidence in your great reputation. But now that I have met you and watched you at work, my confidence is in *you*.'

He acknowledged the compliment with a wistful smile and a bow, but my diplomacy failed otherwise to move him.

'My retirement is complete,' he replied firmly, 'and must remain so. I, too, have my commitments – '

'Commitments?' I demanded, my voice trembling with disappointment and indignation. 'To what? To your bees?' It was out before I could check myself and instantly I was ashamed.* 'I am sorry,' I said. 'That was intolerably rude.'

'Let us say no more about it,' answered Sherlock Holmes, opening the rear door of the car and placing one foot upon the running board. 'You are thinking that if it had been not Smith but Watson who had been taken, my response might have been otherwise.'

He climbed into the back seat, making it clear that he desired no further conversation, while I took my place disconsolately at the wheel.

It was a cold, miserable journey which lay before us, and one not altogether free from danger, since, to tell the truth, I had never previously driven at night. The

* Years later, when I knew how deeply he was committed to his country, I bitterly regretted my angry words and the hurt which they must have inflicted upon him. [P.]

canvas roof above our heads protected us from the rain, but the sides of the vehicle remained open to the elements, and I was not surprised that Holmes, seated silent behind me, would readily have chosen the comfort of a steam-heated railway carriage. Yet in his silence and deliberate isolation I sensed no resentment. Rather it seemed to me that he was embarrassed by his rejection of my entreaties, for although I had known him only a few hours, I saw already that his cold-blooded mask of aloofness hid a sensitive nature.

Outside the metropolis and the range of street lights, I found night driving an eerie and exacting experience, my world limited by the glare of the acetylene headlamps and the throbbing pulse of the engine. My right sleeve was rain-soaked, and the constant rivulets tracing serpentine trails upon the windscreen blurred and confused my vision. Every now and then, the lights of an approaching car would spring up suddenly above the crest of a rise like the glowing eyes of a wild beast, to bear down upon me, expanding with enormous rapidity, till they swept past in a maelstrom of noise and turbulence, leaving me buffeted and blind. Sacrificing speed to caution, I drove as carefully as I could, praying that I might avoid an accident – that the car might not break down, stranding us in the middle of nowhere.

Godstone and East Grinstead were passed in safety, and a few miles farther on, the rain stopped. A stiff breeze sprang up, sending the clouds scudding across a pale, watery moon, fitfully disclosing and obscuring the landscape in a drifting patchwork of light and shadow. Then, in the maze of minor roads beyond Uckfield, I made a wrong turn and presently found myself out on the coast, somewhere near Seaford. Holmes, making no complaint, leaned over my shoulder and directed me so that, after much twisting and turning, we eventually came into the bumpy narrow lane, passed the big house on the right, and pulled up before the gate of his premises.

I switched off the engine and sat with my arms folded on the wheel, feeling physically and mentally drained.

Dimly, I heard Holmes getting out. He came around to my side of the car and leaned over the door.

'You cannot go back to London like this,' he said seriously. 'It is past ten o'clock, and you are exhausted. Come up to the house and share a meal with me. Benjamin's ideas of the culinary art are crude but substantial.'

I nodded dumbly, obeying rather than accepting the invitation. Extinguishing the headlights, but leaving ths sidelights burning for the benefit of any unlikely passer-by on this remote road, I followed him through the gate and up the flagstoned path. The salt scent of the sea was strong and the restless murmur of the waves curiously near.

'I have, unfortunately, no accommodation to offer,' continued Holmes, as we groped our way up the un-lighted path. 'But there is a reasonable enough inn at Fulworth, and if you take my advice, you will put up there to-night.'

The winding route between the bushes was pitch black, but he seemed able to see in the dark. I looked up at the house silhouetted against the night sky of shifting clouds, and noted that a window left of the door was illuminated. Evidently, it was that of the kitchen. As we drew nearer, I could make out the figure of the man, Benjamin, seated at a table and apparently reading by the light of an oil-lamp placed upon it.

The toe of my right shoe caught suddenly in a crevice, and I stumbled badly. Holmes seized my arm, and, betraying a strength quite beyond expectation, suppor-ted my full wieght for a moment before I regained my balance.

'The stones are uneven,' he said, 'and need seeing to. Here – take my torch and shine it down by your feet.'

I felt the hard, flat shape of it thrust into my hand, grasped it, and pressed the button, muttering a word of thanks which was never completed – for at that same instant, from out of the darkness behind us, came a high-pitched *whirring* sound, followed by a crash of glass and a dull, sullen explosion like the sound made by the lighting of a large gas oven. My eyes still turned towards the house fifty yards distant, I saw the kitchen window dissolve in a burst of silvery splinters, saw the man inside leap up from the table, and heard his startled cry of alarm transposed into an inhuman scream of agony such as I pray I may never hear again.

The torch slipped from my fingers and clattered at my feet, spilling its light across the flagstones. Speechless and paralysed with shock, we saw the door of the house flung open and the gross figure of Benjamin come lurching out upon the path in a dreadful, shambling run, his arms swinging helplessly like the limbs of a rag doll, while from his throat poured a continuous moaning, gurgling sound neither human nor animal. Heading towards us, he vanished into the curtain of shrubbery and we heard the sound of a crashing fall.

Holmes sprang forward. Stooping, I snatched up the torch, and its rays, sweeping at random, momentarily outlined him in the act of kneeling beside the stricken man, who lay ten paces ahead of me on the path. I saw Holmes stretch out his hand, then start to his feet with a gasp of pain and go plunging into the bushes to one side.

'Don't touch him!' he shouted, in a high, strained voice. 'For God's sake, don't touch him!'

5

HORROR ON THE DOWNS

From the direction of the lane came the roar of a motorcycle engine bursting into life, fading into a whine of rapid acceleration, but it registered upon my consciousness only as an impression to be afterwards remembered. Holmes, for the moment, was nowhere to be seen; I was vaguely aware of a faint splashing sound, away to my right, where, as I later learned, he was rinsing his hand vigorously in a rainwater butt.

Still dazed with shock, and wondering at the meaning of his warning, I rushed up the path to the fallen figure of Benjamin, and, as I bent over him, found my eyes watering and my nostrils stinging with the acrid, sulphurous fumes of a chemical laboratory. I turned the light full upon him – and recoiled, shaken afresh. Nothing that I had seen, either in hospitals or among the horrors conceived by Fu Manchu, had prepared me quite for this. Twitching feebly at my feet lay the body of a man seemingly drenched from head to foot in a corrosive solution of such virulent potency that the whole visible surface of flesh and clothing seethed in a spongy mass that bubbled, smoked, and *hissed*.

Only an inchoate sobbing, choking sound now issued from between his teeth, for the terrible stuff which he had inhaled was acting upon larynx and trachea, causing rapid necrosis of the mucous membrane and pulmonary oedema. Even as I stood there, helpless and trembling with a deathly sickness, his tortured frame was racked by a convulsive shiver and he was still. Sherlock Holmes came bursting through the shrubbery.

'It – it is over,' I said hoarsely.

'Thank God!' he murmured. 'There was nothing that we could do for him. But now we must look to ourselves.'

He snatched the torch from my grasp and swung the beam towards the house. From the broken window and the open door, trails of vapour were boiling out into the garden, like liquid oxygen, lit from the rear by the oil-lamp still burning in the kitchen. I saw tendrils of it touch the nearer bushes – and where they touched, leaves withered and stems writhed and drooped. The lamp in the kitchen flared horribly and went out.

'Quick!' shouted Holmes, grasping my sleeve. 'Back to the car!'

Together we stumbled down the path to the gate and out into the lane, in desperate flight from the formless menace at our heels.

'Don't try to turn it!' he snapped. 'Drive on! You must make do with the sidelights. It's a straight road for the first half mile.'

Somehow I managed to get the motor started. Holmes piled into the seat beside me and, with a wicked grinding of gears, we moved off, jolting and swaying as I tried to keep to the middle of the narrow, cart-rutted lane. Leaning out on his side, Holmes played the light of his torch on the nearside verge, calling out directions as though he were conning a ship in to the quayside.

'Left! Left a bit! Steady as she goes! Stop, stop! We are at the corner.'

I pulled up. Here, at least, we were safe, if only, perhaps, for a few minutes. The expansive power and deadly effect of that terrible white vapour were unknowable. Leaping out, I hastily re-lighted the head-lamps, though not without difficulty, since the metal was still hot. Holmes, I noted, was clasping the fingers of his right hand in his left.

'You are hurt!' I said, and went to the back of the car to get my bag – for, in those days, I had learned never to go far without my medical bag handy and a pistol in my pocket.

'It is nothing,' he answered shortly. 'I have had more than a few such burns in the laboratory. Very well – if you must. But hurry!'

His injuries were, as he said, not serious, but he had skinned three fingertips.

'Poor Benjamin!' he muttered, as I applied a salve and adhesive plaster. 'He had done nothing – nothing to earn such an end as this! In Heaven's name, what was it? A volatile liquid having the properties of concentrated nitric acid! Only a perverted genius could devise such a weapon, and only a fiend would employ it! Can it, in some way, have combined with the nitrogen in the atmosphere? No, no – surely that is impossible. . . .'

Having dressed his wounds, I once more took my place behind the wheel and drove on at his instructions till the lane presently emerged upon the coast road skirting the tiny bay and village of Fulworth. Here our immediate concern was to visit the constable's cottage.

'We have no idea how far that fearful stuff will spread,' observed Holmes solemnly, 'or to what extent it must disperse before it becomes harmless. Probably no more than a few hundred yards. But I must telephone Stackhurst at the school, warn him to keep his doors and windows closed, and let nobody go outside to-night.'

He went in, leaving me seated in the car, and came out again in less than ten minutes.

'Anderson is a good man,' he said. 'He will see to it that no one enters the lane from this end. But he cannot cope with an affair like this. We shall have to go on to Lewes. It will be about fifteen miles, if you go via Newhaven. Can you do it?'

'Yes,' I said firmly. 'I can.'

All tiredness had left me with the call to action, but I felt no pleasurable thrill of excitement. The onus of the tragedy which I had brought upon Sherlock Holmes and his household lay too heavily upon my conscience. I knew – had always known – that to pursue Dr Fu Manchu was to take one's life in one's hands, but that my unsuccessful attempt to bring Holmes into the business should lead to so swift and hideous a reprisal still shocked and amazed me.

'I have no words to apologize for this,' I said, turning towards him. 'I had never dreamed – '

'And nor had I!' he interrupted. 'But I am responsible, not you. I underestimated both the resources and the incredible ferocity of these people. I entered your premises dressed up like a caricature of myself, and taking it for granted that the place was no longer watched. They identified me, and set up their counter-attack even before we left London. Their man was no doubt sent down by train – unless they have someone locally. You heard the motorcycle, of course? He was waiting for us, farther down the lane, and we survive only because the savages who execute the orders of this ruthless demon are fools. He saw the car, and seeing the light in the house, thought that we had already gone in.'

Compared with the journey back from Fleet Street, it was an easy run to Lewes, but I was unfamiliar with the roads, and so was Holmes. I lost my way more than once, but at length we found ourselves in the long, sloping high street of the county town, which now, silent and bathed in moonlight, looked to have changed little since the days of stagecoaches and sedan chairs. Passing half-timbered houses, I glanced up at a large clock suspended above the pavement and saw that the hands registered eleven-twenty.

A reception committee awaited us at the headquarters of the East Sussex Constabulary, presided over by a somewhat disgruntled inspector, who had been called back to duty while eating his supper. Neither his digestion nor his temper was improved by our news, and had the speaker been any other than Sherlock Holmes, I think it might have gone hard with us. Introducing me only as a friend who had driven him down from London, he described the terrible incident at his villa simply as a bomb outrage using a corrosive vesicant of astonishing strength.

We had agreed to say nothing of Fu Manchu until we could say it to Inspector Weymouth. Asked about his suspicions, if any, Holmes shrugged and answered that he knew of at least fifty men who might desire his death, several of whom might recently have been released from prison. As to the fantastic means employed, he shrugged

52

again and made vague hints about the late Professor Moriarty.

'The important point now,' he said urgently, 'is that men must be sent out from Eastbourne to seal off the area. No one must attempt to go near the place till it is light, and special equipment will be needed.'

Leaving out the Si Fan background, we had really little more to tell, but our story was so extraordinary that it had to be told over and over again. Midnight came and went. The police brought us sandwiches and coffee while we continued to answer questions and dictate statements. We drank the coffee, but had poor appetite for anything more.

I spent the rest of that night in a cell – not that I mean I was arrested. By the time we were through with it all, it was too late to think of a hotel, if we wished to make an early start after dawn, so the officers kindly made up beds for us in the cells.

In the event, however, we started back for Holmes's premises later than we had expected. Delays were encountered in obtaining the apparatus needed for such an emergency, and it was decided that no one, including ourselves, should go in until the villa and grounds had been inspected and declared safe. Thus it was about nine o'clock when Holmes and I once more climbed into the Vauxhall, this time accompanied by the inspector and a plainclothes CID man whom we had not previously met.

We arrived to find the place swarming with men in uniform, the lane blocked with official cars, taxicabs, and two red-painted vehicles of the Eastbourne Fire Brigade. As Holmes had predicted, the deadly vapour had not spread beyond his property, but we found ugly yellow blotches of it on the hedge as far down as the lane, while the bushes near the house were scarred and striated as though by the searing blast of a flame thrower. The persistency of the stuff was incredible. Everywhere that traces of it lay, it remained viciously active and dangerous to the touch. Brass-helmeted men from the fire brigade were still going around cautiously, spraying the affected areas with some sort of chemical foam.

I cannot write of what we found on the path – nor would any sane reader wish me to attempt it. Holmes, whose nerves were stronger than mine, stood for a moment by the pitiful remains with his head bowed and his cap in his hand, and I saw his lips move fiercely – not, I thought, in a prayer for the deceased but in a curse on his slayers.

'This is monstrous!' he exclaimed, some moments later, when we were standing out of earshot of the others. 'My life has been attempted more than once – efforts have been made to intimidate me, to prevent me from taking up a case. But this! This is the arrogant contempt of a man who sets his heel upon an insect simply because it runs across his path!'

We walked up to the house. The state of things in the kitchen was appalling beyond belief, everything dripping with the soapy neutralising agent used by the firemen, the paper hanging in slimy strips from the walls. When we touched the table, it collapsed as though the legs were honeycombed with dry rot. Every scrap of wood was similarly affected, every item of metal, from the silverware to the stove, pitted and corroded as if it had lain outside for a decade. Only objects of porcelain and glass were unharmed. Among the broken pieces from the window, we discovered curved fragments which, from their size and shape, might have formed part of a sphere about six inches in diameter.

'They used some kind of mechanical device,' said Holmes, examining them closely, 'and flung this thing from the lane. They could not see who was in here.'

The whole room, obviously, would require complete reconstruction. But, fortunately, though there had been damage to the wallpaper and woodwork in the passage, no other rooms had suffered. We went outside again, Holmes literally trembling with a cold rage, his eyes hard as agate.

'A wanton destruction of property and life,' he muttered, 'and not only human life, but six colonies of bees! The hives were directly in the path of the main cloud, and at this season bees cannot fly.'

He went to talk briefly with the inspector from Lewes, shook hands with him, and came back.

'We are free to leave now,' he reported. 'They say, of course, that we shall be required for the inquest. Though,' he added grimly, 'Heaven knows what kind of a post mortem they can perform!'

I nodded, shuddering.

'I cannot stay here,' continued Holmes, after a moment. 'It will take a major rebuilding operation to make the place habitable. Will you wait for me while I pack a bag? I suppose I may count upon you for transport?'

'Certainly,' I replied. 'I will take you wherever you wish to go.'

He thanked me with a brusque nod and went into the house, leaving me standing in the ravaged garden. The early morning sun glittered on the helmets of the firemen moving about between the trees of the orchard, and I saw ambulance men coming up the path with a long, basketlike contrivance. . . .

The CID man, who had managed to find an untreated patch and burnt a hole in his coat sleeve, came up to me in no very good humour, and engaged me in conversation. He seemed to have taken it into his head that the disaster must have resulted from some outlandish chemical experiment conducted by Sherlock Holmes. I did my best to disabuse him of this idea, till, at length, I got rid of him and he moved off, dissatisfied.

Holmes returned, carrying a large suitcase almost completely covered with British and Continental hotel labels. I told him of the incident with the CID man, and he laughed harshly.

'Yes,' he said. 'I still undertake experiments occasionally – but not in the kitchen!' He smiled rather wanly. 'You know, Doctor, the deplorable state of things in Baker Street, to which Watson has given quite unnecessary publicity, was chiefly due to the fact that we had only the one room in which to do everything, apart from our bedrooms.'

We made our way back to the car.

'Where shall I take you?' I asked, putting his suitcase into the back. 'To the village inn?'

'No,' answered Holmes unexpectedly. 'To London.'

Turning to face him, I saw that his lips were set in a firm, hard line and his eyes feverishly bright.

'There is a score to be settled,' he said quietly. 'By neglecting the most elementary precautions, I have the blood of an innocent man on my hands. Well, you sought the help of Sherlock Holmes, and now you shall have it. Can you put me up at Fleet Street for a few days?'

6

SHERLOCK HOLMES OF
FLEET STREET

Seated, that evening, with his slippered feet extended towards the fire, a pile of newspapers beside him, and a dressing gown over his shoulders, Sherlock Holmes looked so much at home that it was hard to believe that this was not Baker Street – that it was I and not Watson who sat watching him from the armchair opposite. Indeed, so marked was the impression that, throwing down the last of the papers which he had been studying and catching my eye at the same moment, he burst into a laugh.

'Upon my word, Doctor!' he exclaimed. 'To look at you, one might think that you were listening for cab wheels on the street and hurrying footsteps on the stairs, bringing a fresh case to our door, rather than that we had one already. Yet, in a certain sense, you may be right. Nothing has changed since I was last here. We have had an unpleasant adventure, but it has brought us no nearer to tracing Nayland Smith.'

I noted with some slight amusement that, since joining forces, he had dropped the 'Mr.' Holmes's ideas of decorum remained, in some respects, oddly Victorian.

Since our arrival, early in the afternoon, nothing of significance had occurred. Temporarily, we had parted company, Holmes to undertake personal shopping while I went to Scotland Yard to report to Weymouth. As it chanced, however, Weymouth had been out harassing the East End in his relentless but vain quest for Smith. Therefore, leaving word for him, and arranging for the return of the Vauxhall tourer – which, as I now learned, belonged to the Assistant Commissioner – I came back to Fleet Street, pausing on the way only to buy a few household necessities for our stay.

Now, again bending over the newspapers beside his

chair, Holmes picked up one which he had laid aside from the rest. These were the same which I had found piled up in the hall on my initial homecoming, and he had asked to see them, saying that the London evening editions had not been available to him in Sussex.

'There is nothing here which offers any assistance,' he remarked, 'but you will find an item of interest in this one published on Monday the ninth – the night of Smith's disappearance.'

He held out the paper, marking the place with his thumb, and, taking it, I read:

Vandals in Fleet Street

Passing through Fleet Street late last night, Mr John Courtney, of Lincoln's Inn Fields, was startled to observe smoke pouring from a Post Office pillar box. With praiseworthy presence of mind, he ran to nearby editorial offices at which staff remained on duty, and obtained assistance, whereby the fire was extinguished by pouring water through the letter slot. The conflagration was at first thought to have been caused by the careless insertion of a cigarette end together with correspondence. When, however, the box was later opened by Post Office officials, it was found to have been started deliberately with burning newspaper. Thanks to Mr Courtney's prompt action, a part of the mail was saved, though much had been destroyed.

'So now you know what happened to your letter,' commented Holmes, as I finished reading. 'Smith *did* write to you, directly after he had spoken to you on the telephone. But, as we may now be sure, his call was intercepted, and when he went out to post his letter, he was followed. The follower was unable to prevent him from posting it, and therefore took emergency measures. The spectacle of a group of public-spirited gentlemen endeavouring to pour jugs of water into a pillar box has an undeniable element of comedy in it, but it again illustrates the extravagant lengths to which Fu Manchu's people will go. They could not know that Smith had anything of value to communicate – he himself thought that he had not – yet they set fire to the entire contents of a postbox.'

'It is maddening,' I said reflectively, 'to think that Smith must actually have had this newspaper in his hands. He had brought it in, but evidently did not read it before the attack was made on him soon afterwards – otherwise, he might have been prepared.'

'Quite so. Once again, we are wiser after the event, but it leads us no farther.'

Sherlock Holmes stood up and, reverting to Baker Street habits, kicked the pile of newspapers partially out of sight under his armchair. Neither he nor I had at that moment the faintest idea that the incident of the vandalised postbox was yet destined to lead farther than we expected. Taking up a curved briar which he had laid down half-smoked on the mantelpiece, he re-lighted it and continued:

'Until something new comes along, there is only one possible move to be made. We must identify the man – or one of the men – who watches this building, and hope that, through him, we may be able to trace his employers. It is a thin thread, and one which will likely enough break in our hands – for he probably makes his reports in some roundabout manner, and may not even know who employs him. But we cannot afford to neglect it.'

'I agree,' I said eagerly, for any action was better than none. 'But how shall we achieve it?'

'That you may safely leave to me. And now I suggest that we walk over to that small Italian restaurant where, as you told me, the *lasagne* is excellent, and partake of a meal, after which we will make an early night of it. We are both short of sleep, and may need our energies for tomorrow.'

'Very well,' I replied, standing up also. I crossed to the door of my bedroom and paused, turning back. 'By the way, before I forget it, I had better give you a key to this apartment. We have a spare, safely tucked away in a jar of sugar in the kitchen cupboard.'

'A commendable hiding place,' murmured Holmes, smiling mischievously, 'but, surely, a trifle superfluous? If the Si Fan could get in without a key – which, in fact, they did – why should they need to search for one? Moreover, since they now have Smith's key, do you not realise that they can get in when they like?'

'Good Heavens!' I cried. 'I had completely forgotten that! However, now that you have reminded me, there is something we can do about it. Our complicated lock works like that of a safe, and by unscrewing a panel at the back, I can change the sequence of turns needed to open it.'

'Then I recommend you to do it before we go out.'

While I occupied myself with a screwdriver, Holmes disappeared into the bedroom which, until now, had been Nayland Smith's, and presently returned wearing a polo-necked sweater, curiously reminiscent of his light-weight boxing days. He was twice my age, yet, noting how the tight material outlined the muscles of his deceptively slender arms, I wondered if I could go three rounds with him.

'After we come back from our dinner,' he said briskly, 'I shall be glad if you will type up a deposition of last night's events for the coroner's court. We will both sign it, and Inspector Weymouth will see to it that we are excused from attending. I trust that we shall have more urgent things to do. In the meantime, I must try to bring myself up to date on Dr Fu Manchu and the Si Fan. At present, I know little more than I have been able to gain from your highly coloured narrative of his earlier activities, which pays a great deal of attention to dramatic incidents and atmosphere, but very little to facts. Have you anything in writing as regards more recent developments?'

'Yes,' I said, somewhat nettled by his criticism of a work which had proved popular. 'I have a completed record up to last autumn, when we again thought we had done with him – when, with my own eyes, I saw him shot in the head – and the rest I have in the form of notes – ' I broke off suddenly. 'That is, I *think* I have!'

Walking quickly to the desk, I jerked open a drawer and took out a number of folders, containing, in all, some five hundred pages of type-script.

'Good!' I said, after a cursory inspection. 'It is all here. I wonder why the Si Fan did not take it?'

'No doubt,' he said tartly, 'they have the same opinion of its documentary value as I have.'

When I arose shortly before eight the next morning, I found that Sherlock Holmes had already breakfasted and gone out, leaving behind him a great stench of burnt bacon in the kitchen and a cryptic note on the table.

'Use the telephone,' it read. 'Make the first call at 9 a.m., the next at 9.10, and thereafter at intervals increased by 3 minutes – i.e., 9.23, 9.39, etc. Call anyone and talk about anything. Time your calls by the clock on the mantelpiece.'

The purpose of these directions was not readily apparent, but I knew that I could expect explanations from Holmes even less than from Smith. Therefore, I proceeded to carry them out. Having few acquaintances in London whom I could ring up and converse with on subjects of no importance, I at first found this a severe tax on my ingenuity. Presently, however, it dawned upon me that my calls must, in some way, be intended to confuse the enemy, so I made spurious inquiries about sailings for Egypt and the prices of tropical clothing. Likewise it occurred to me that the object of the staggered intervals was to prevent an eavesdropper from suspecting them as contrived – though, in that case, I could not quite see why I had not simply been ordered to make my calls at random.

In this way, two hours passed, during which I found my curiosity giving place to some anxiety. Still Holmes had not returned. How long, I wondered, was this ridiculous telephoning business to go on? We were expecting Weymouth at eleven. Our telephone being considered unsafe, a messenger from New Scoland Yard had been sent the previous evening to advise us that he would be calling at this hour. Holmes was aware of this, but, when eleven came, and Weymouth duly arrived, he yet remained absent.

'Where's Mr Sherlock Holmes?' was the inspector's first question.

'Heaven knows!' I said. 'He went out early this morning, and I was expecting him back before now.'

'What!' he exclaimed. 'Don't tell me we've lost him too!'

I shook my head and was about to make some reply when a faint sound in the hallway caught my attention and I stiffened.

'Listen!' I said. 'There's someone out there!'

We both turned to face the door as the sound came again – now unmistakable: a shuffling step and a tapping sound which reminded me horribly of the dragging gait of Dr Fu Manchu, half-paralysed by the bullet lodged in his skull. But, due partially to my own unwilling efforts, Fu Manchu was no longer paralysed. . . .

Slowly, the door began to open. The tip of a white-painted stick emerged from behind, and following it came the bent figure of a man clad in shapeless rags, with a lettered card and a tin cup slung about his neck, dark spectacles, and long, straggling locks of dirty grey hair.

'Blind!' he croaked. 'Blind!'

'Who are you?' snapped Weymouth. 'How did you get in?'

But the decrepit visitor, casting about with his stick in an unpleasantly purposeful manner, continued his advance towards us.

'Stop where you are!' I ordered, and reached for the pistol in my pocket.

The man dropped his stick, threw up his hands, and cowered back.

'What?' he quavered. 'You wouldn't shoot a blind old man?'

'Humbug!' shouted Weymouth. 'If you're blind, how do you know what he's doing?'

A peal of laughter answered him, as the stooping figure straightened up and the dark glasses were thrown off to reveal the twinkling eyes of Sherlock Holmes.

'Well!' he said. 'At least one of you has his wits about him! Inspector Weymouth, I presume?'

'Mr Holmes!' roared the inspector. 'I might have known!' Covering the distance between them at a bound, he seized Holmes's hand and wrung it as if they had been old comrades long parted. 'Glad to have you back with us, sir!'

'Thank you, Inspector,' said Holmes, smiling. 'And thank you for the sixpence which you gave me when you came in.'

Weymouth started. 'Eh? Why, of course! It was you sitting there under the arch!'

'Yes, and a cold job it was, too!' Picking up his blind man's stick from the carpet, Holmes walked away across the room. 'Excuse me while I change into something warmer and more presentable. Dr Petrie will tell you about our adventures in Sussex, and then I will tell you both about this morning.'

'And I'll have my sixpence back!' Weymouth called after him, as he vanished into the bedroom. Turning back towards me in his boisterous, open-hearted fashion, he clapped me upon the shoulder. 'I never thought you would,' he said, 'but you've done it! You've got him! The question is, can we keep him?'

'I believe so,' I replied.'I rather fancy he's enjoying himself.'

'I'm sure of it!' Weymouth shook his head, scowling ferociously. 'What! A man like that, cooped up miles from nowhere with a swarm of bees? It doesn't make sense – even though some of the fools at the Yard used to say he had one in his bonnet!'

I smiled appreciatively. Weymouth, as big in heart as he was in body, was not the man for petty professional jealousies.

'And now,' he continued, seating himself in an armchair, 'you'd better tell me what's been going on. I gather, from the note you left in my office, that you've had a lively weekend, and the old man's lucky to get his car back.'

'You're lucky to get *us* back!' I said grimly.

Whilst he listened, unspeaking, I gave him a terse account covering the ground from my first meeting with

63

Sherlock Holmes to the atrocious incident at the villa and the terrible death of his manservant.

'I have seen some pretty ghastly sights,' I concluded, 'since I first heard the name of Dr Fu Manchu. But I honestly believe this is the most dreadful thing he has ever done.'

'Remember the fungus cellars, where we lost eight of our men?' asked Weymouth. He rubbed his chin reflectively. 'He has these bursts of fiendishness, from time to time. And the queer thing is, I think he's sorry afterwards.'

Holmes came in from his bedroom, freshly shaved and attired in a well-cut lounge suit. Ignoring us for the moment, he went over to the desk, typed a few words on a sheet of paper, and brought it across to Weymouth.

'Here,' he said, 'is the name and business address of a man who is spying on these premises and listening in to our telephone calls.'

'What!' I exclaimed. 'You have found him?'

'You may say that I had found him yesterday. My little performance this morning was merely to secure confirmation.'

Holmes took up a position by the mantelpiece, resting one elbow upon it, and stared down at Inspector Weymouth.

'My first act on arriving here was to look into this matter which I had so foolishly neglected on my previous visit. I thought, initially, that this building might be watched from one of the other apartments. However, a brief conversation with the porter, who regards me with a sort of religious fervour, informed me that all of them have been occupied for more than a year. Thus it became evident that it was the entrance to the court which was under surveillance from the street outside.'

He paused, as if inviting comments, but as neither of us had one to offer, went on immediately:

'Well, then – it is a matter of elementary optics that anyone who stands in the archway and looks out into Fleet Street can see every point from which he himself can be seen. Therefore, it required less than a minute for me to ascertain that the only likely vantage point was an office building nearly opposite. I made some discreet inquiries, and learned that only two suites had been recently let, and one of these has no windows facing the street. The other is tenanted by a Mr Jacob Morley, described as a tax accountant.'

Taking from his pocket the dark glasses which had formed part of his disguise, Holmes tendered them to Weymouth.

'If you care to examine my glasses,' he said, 'you will find them less dark than they appear. In fact, they admit more light than ordinary spectacle lenses. They were made for me by the Carl Zeiss Works, incorporating principles first recognised by the pioneer Dennis Taylor, and are slightly telescopic. No, Inspector – you cannot see the effect from there. You will have to take them over to the window.'

Weymouth stood up obediently and crossed to the window, where he remained for a few minutes, holding Holmes's glasses up to his eyes and staring out into the court.

'There are small focussing screws, just behind the hinges,' said Holmes. 'Having adopted an advantageous, though distinctly draughty, position under the arch, I focussed my glasses on Mr Morley's window. He has his desk drawn up alongside it, and seems to have no work to do but peer across the street. Dr Petrie, meanwhile, played his part admirably – '

'I did nothing but act as you instructed me!' I said, gratified but surprised.

'Precisely! That is just what I mean. Well, it was a little difficult for a blind man to keep one eye on a relatively expensive Swiss pocket watch without exciting some suspicion, but I managed it. Within thirty seconds of the times at which I had arranged for Dr Petrie to use the telephone, Mr Morley also held a telephone receiver to his ear.'

Turning again to the mantelpiece, Holmes picked up his briar, examined the bowl critically to see if the contents were worthy of re-lighting, decided they were not, and knocked out the ashes into the grate.

'I have had an amusing morning,' he declared, 'and I quite see now why a gentleman in whose interests I once acted found it more profitable to pose as a beggar than to pursue his legitimate trade as a journalist. In less than three hours, I have earned twenty-three shillings – at the price, however, of being half frozen. A cup of coffee with a little fortification would be welcome, I think.'

'An excellent suggestion!' I said. 'We will all have one.'

I went into the kitchen, poured milk into a saucepan, and set it on the stove. But as I reached up to the shelf for a tin of coffee, the doorbell rang loudly, followed by a peremptory double rap, and, putting down the tin, unopened, I hurried back into the living room.

'I will go,' said Sherlock Holmes, heading for the hall. 'We are anticipating no danger, but cover me.'

He crossed the hallway and began to unfasten the outer door, while Weymouth and I hastily took up positions to either side of the door in the sitting-room. We heard the lock click and a muttered colloquy of voices.

'Postman,' said Weymouth.

Holmes re-entered carrying a medium-sized manila envelope and passed it to me.

'For you, Doctor.'

Taking it, I saw that it was headed with the printed letters 'O.H.M.S.' and had been re-addressed to me from the hotel where I had stayed during my absence from London. Also, it was endorsed with a rubber-stamped impression which read: 'Found damaged and officially re-sealed.' I ripped it open quickly and found within it a second envelope – or, rather, the left-hand half of one, the torn edge charred and uneven, and a part of the address gone.

'Your missing letter from Smith!' said Holmes jubilantly. 'Or, at least, half of it! God bless His Majesty's Post Office! Your name, fortunately, is a short one. '"Royal H – "could only be "Hotel"' and sufficient of the address remains to be identifiable. But, as the stamp has been destroyed, you have threepence to pay.'

'Open it!' urged Weymouth. 'Let's see what we have.'

I fished inside the damaged envelope and drew out a similarly damaged sheet of notepaper. We all bent our heads over it, and, as we did so, a sharp crackling sound came from the kitchen.

'Dear me!' remarked Holmes, shaking his head sadly. 'The milk has boiled over!'

7

NEW HORIZONS

'I am afraid,' I said slowly, 'that the main part is missing.'

The sheet which I held in my hand had been folded and inserted in such a manner that, whereas the right half of the envelope had been burned, it was the left side of the text which was wanting. Apart from a few, obviously personal, phrases at the beginning, the surviving portion appeared as follows:

> the little enough there is to
> man was as drunk as an owl,
> eems there is a chinese ship
> be hanging around off the west
> Si Fan is bringing up rein-
> something about a <u>worm</u>, and
> <u>thirty thousand bicycles</u> (!)
> a <u>trap</u> to be set for <u>Morgan</u>
> deal with <u>Gillian Rochester</u> (?)
> what you can of it!

'On the contrary,' said Holmes, peering over my shoulder, 'I think we have most of it – though what we may gain from it is another matter. First, the man who supplied this information was drunk – yes, we already know that. Next, there is apparently a Chinese ship hanging around off the west something – '

'The West Indian Dock?' I hazarded.

'No, no! The word "off" would not be appropriate to a dock. We shall find that it is the west coast of somewhere. A fairly wide choice – England, Scotland, Ireland, or some country in Europe. . . .'

'We can check on the arrival of ships from the Far East,' suggested Inspector Weymouth.

Holmes dismissed this impatiently. 'A vessel on a regular schedule could not be "hanging around" anywhere. This must be some privately owned boat – and a large one, if it has come all the way from China.'

'The coastguard service can look into that,' said Weymouth, but without much enthusiasm. 'However, if she keeps outside the three-mile limit, they won't be able to do much either.'

Taking the letter from me, Holmes crossed to the fireplace and sat down, frowning. 'Smith has been told, or guesses, that the Si Fan is bringing up reinforcements – we presume by means of this Chinese ship. We have only the first four letters here, but the only alternative I can think of is "reindeer," which seems less likely. But for what purpose is the ship "hanging around"? To land them in some obscure spot, or to take something off?'

Neither of us ventured an opinion, and he was silent for some time, sitting with the sheet of notepaper spread out on his knee and scowling down at it.

'The rest,' he said at length, 'consists of isolated words picked out from the slurred speech of a drunken man, and, in conclusion, Smith invites us to make what we can of it. Well, then, let us see what we can. A *worm?* H'm! What kind of a monstrosity have we to face there, I wonder? And what in the name of sanity could the Si Fan do with *thirty thousand bicycles?* Then, there is a *trap* – that, at least, is clear enough – followed by the names of two persons against whom some action is presumably to be taken. But *Morgan* is the name of every sixth or seventh man in Wales, and might be either his surname or his Christian name. *Gillian Rochester* is certainly more distinctive, but – '

'Good God!' burst out Weymouth. 'May I see that for a moment?' Coming rapidly to Holmes's side, he picked up the letter fragment and peered at it closely. 'It *must* be!' he muttered. 'Not "Gillian Rochester," but Sir Julian Rossiter! He was murdered early this morning.'

'What!' I cried, jumping up, while even Holmes looked startled. 'Who is – or who *was* – this man?'

Weymouth shook his head doubtfully. 'I don't really know. Some sort of local industrialist, I believe. I never heard of him myself till this morning.'

'Where did he die?' inquired Holmes. 'In London?'

'By no means! Miles outside some mining town in Glamorganshire.'

'Good Heavens!'

'Well,' said Weymouth, almost apologetically, 'you said something about Wales, and then I re-membered. . . . I heard about it at the Yard – not directly, you understand. I know nothing about it, but there's poison in it, and evidently more than that. The local inspector seems to be puzzled and in two minds about asking the Chief Constable to call in Scotland Yard, so he rang us up first to get a bit of unofficial advice.'

'Will you go out there?' I asked quickly.

Again Weymouth shook his head. 'I can't, Doctor. You know Scotland Yard won't interfere unless we're invited – and even if we are, it's not likely to be my job. I'm supposed to be covering the Fu Manchu case in London: I haven't got Mr Smith's special powers to go chasing him round the world.' He turned briskly towards Holmes. 'But there's nothing to prevent *you* going!'

'I?' exclaimed Holmes, starting.

'Isn't that what you came here for?' Weymouth faced him truculently. 'You wanted a lead on Fu Manchu, didn't you? Well, now you've got one.'

'But I have less authority even than youself!'

'As a private citizen,' retorted the inspector, 'you can go anywhere you please. After that, it's up to the locals in charge.' His stern features relaxed suddenly into a smile. 'Times have changed, Mr Holmes! I know there was a bit of rivalry and bad feeling between you and the police in the old days. But take my word for it – you won't find a man on the force now who isn't proud and delighted to work with Sherlock Holmes!'

'Shall we go?' I urged, eagerly.

Holmes hesitated for a long moment, staring into the fire. Then:

'Yes,' he replied shortly. 'We will go. We have no choice.'

'Splendid!' said Weymouth enthusiastically. 'I knew you'd do it! If you take a train just after lunch, you can get to Cardiff by about six, or maybe seven. Somebody will be there to meet you. As soon as I'm back at the Yard, I'll get in touch with the local inspector and tell him to leave everthing as it is. And I can ask him for details. . . .'

'No,' answered Holmes, with an emphatic shake of his head. 'We will have the details when we arrive. Until then, I will keep an open mind. And there is one thing more, Inspector: I should be obliged if you would take immediate steps to apprehend Mr Jacob Morley, who is keeping a watch on us.'

Weymouth looked thoughtful. 'Wouldn't it be wiser, perhaps, to keep a watch on *him?*'

'I think not. His reports are almost certainly made by telephone, and since they will all be made to the same number, you can easily discover it – not that I think it will lead you anywhere. Mr Morley is not a member of the Si Fan, but simply an outside employee.' Holmes smiled grimly. 'However, I should prefer to have him gone before we leave this building. Judging by our recent experience, I wouldn't put it past them to wreck the train!'

'All right, then – we'll nab him. How about the Embankment side? Do you suppose there's anybody watching from there?'

'That entrance is rarely used, so they may not have thought it worthwhile,' said Holmes reflectively. 'I have really had no opportunity to look into that. Yes, certainly – there *is* a pavement artist who draws suspiciously bad pictures sitting some way down from Blackfriars Bridge. You might check up on him, perhaps, but you will probably find that the poor fellow is just clumsy with his chalks.'

After Weymouth's departure, he continued for a while

71

to sit moodily at the fireside, and some minutes elapsed before he spoke again.

'I had not counted on going so far afield,' I heard him mutter, seemingly to himself. 'It may be awkward. . . .' He shrugged, and , like a man who has all at once made up his mind, leapt to his feet. 'Let us make our preparations, Doctor! I shall take everything with me, and you, too, had better pack for a considerable stay. I doubt if we shall come back here before this case is concluded one way or another. If Fu Manchu is in Wales, you may be sure that he is there to do more than to murder some obscure industrialist.'

When, in due course, we carried our suitcases out to the waiting taxi, I glanced up at the building opposite and noted that a blind was pulled down over the office window of Mr Jacob Morley. Holmes smiled in grim satisfaction, and a few minutes later we were traversing the Strand, bound for Paddington and the west. Our route lay along Marylebone Road, and, despite his avowed contempt for sentimental attachments, I saw my companion's eyes switch momentarily to the left as we passed the corner of Baker Street.

The dull sense of helpless apathy had left me, and I felt better than I had for days. There is a stimulus, a call of action, in the purposeful noise and bustle of a London terminal, and now that some action was at last possible, I could respond to it. Pretty you might not call it, yet there is a sense of spaciousness in Paddington, with its lofty glass roof and passenger facilities strung out along one platform, rather than cluttered about the entrance – a promise of the open countryside to which it is the gate. Holmes paused at the bookstall to make a purchase, and as we took our places in the train, tossed a slim *Guide to Wales* down upon the seat beside me.

'Read it on the way,' he directed. 'One of us must know something about the place!'

At the expense of travelling first class, we had a carriage to ourselves. Holmes settled down into the corner seat opposite mine in a characteristic pose, looking like, and yet oddly unlike, Sherlock Holmes – no longer clad in his caped Inverness, but wearing a belted leather coat of distinctly military cut, and a soft felt hat with a turned-down brim. Seen thus, he somehow looked younger than in his pictures of fifteen years ago. He met my gaze, conscious of my appraisal, I think, and, as the train pulled out, smiled.

'So, once again, the game's afoot!' he remarked. 'Fate and Fu Manchu have made us partners for a while. Therefore, I shall be happy if you will do me the favour of henceforth calling me plain "Holmes." Your "Mr Holmes" reminds me of a policeman.'

'Gladly,' I said, smiling in my turn, 'assuming that you will cease to address me as "Doctor."'

Holmes nodded. Looking at him as he sat there opposite me, I could not help but remember how often, at the outset of such adventures, he had sat opposite Watson – and how often I had sat opposite Smith.

'Strange, isn't it,' I said reminiscently, 'that Nayland Smith and Sherlock Holmes should both be accompanied by writers who are also doctors!'

To my chagrin, however, he stiffened abruptly and frowned.

'I do not find it strange,' he said, with a certain haughtiness. 'Doctors may make themselves useful, adjust their working hours as required, and find time to write. And, in any event, I beg you not to equate me with Nayland Smith, whose behaviour is hardly that of a detective!'

'Smith is not a detective,' I replied indignantly. 'His position as a Burmese Commissioner of Police is that of an administrator, and he is here now in an advisory capacity only because he has had previous contact with the Si Fan and knows something about them.'

'Which is precisely my point! Smith is qualified for this work, and I am not. What is there for an investigator to investigate? What is the point in seeking to establish methods and motives when the identity of the culprit is known before we begin? It is merely a question of laying hands upon him.'

Holmes turned his face to the window and sat for some

minutes peering morosely out at the vista of suburban west London sliding past at gradually increasing speed. Seen in profile, his hawklike features made me think of the head of a Red Indian carved in ivory. Presently, he sighed, lifted his hands in a peculiar gesture of resignation, and faced me again, with a wry smile on his lips.

'We shall do well to avoid comparisons,' he said quietly. 'I am not Smith, and you are not Watson. I shall find you impatient, impetuous, and emotional. You will find me indolent, morose, ill-tempered, and often downright rude. We must make the best of each other.'

'With all my heart!' I said, and held out my hand.

He took it and grasped it warmly enough, but with a quizzical smile in his eyes which told me that this was just the sort of demonstrative gesture which he despised. Then, standing up, he took his suitcase down from the rack, unstrapped it, and drew forth the thick wad of typescript which I had given him the night before.

'For the next few hours,' he said, 'occupy yourself with your guidebook. Pay special attention to the geography – we may need it. In the meantime, I shall try to learn something of the Si Fan from your colourful record.'

Settling himself again in his corner, he produced and lighted a cherrywood pipe which filled the carriage with an unpleasantly fruity odour. With the exception of a meerschaum, the size and shape of a small saxophone, he had apparently brought along the entire contents of his pipe rack. The cherrywood was not one which I liked, and I came to dislike it the more when I found that it betokened Holmes in a black mood. Brows drawn together, he sat thumbing through my manuscript, muttering, occasionally rolling his eyes heavenward in disapproval, turning down pages, and scribbling comments in the margins, till I saw that the whole thing would have to be re-typed before it went to a publisher – if, indeed, it ever did.

I opened my newly acquired guidebook and attempted to emulate Holmes, turning a blind eye to seductive descriptions of pastoral charm, imposing mountains, and spectacular seascapes. So far as I could make out, the area north and west of Cardiff was one vast workshop of industrial valleys devoted to the production of coal and iron. But at twenty miles inland from the coast at any point, the map of the entire principality was a patchwork of huge blank spaces outlined by widely separated highways, crossed only here and there by narrow, erratic roads linking hamlets and villages. For one accustomed only to southern England and the Midlands, it was difficult to imagine such an empty immensity of virgin highlands. Here, I though, Fu Manchu might hide an army, if he had one and any means to supply it.

But was Fu Manchu there? Even if he was, were we, perhaps, leaving Nayland Smith shut up in some secret dungeon, all unsuspected, beneath the teeming streets of London? And where now was Kâramanèh?

Tortured by these uncertainties, I found it hard to concentrate on my reading, and impossible to cope with a host of place names literally unpronounceable by English orthography. It occurred to me that, though it might not be necessary to learn the Welsh language, we should have a major problem in asking for directions, if we had to do any great amount of travelling. At length, weary, and half-stifled by the noxious fumes of my companion's pipe, I closed the book with a snap, put it down beside me, and was about to speak when Holmes suddenly laid aside my manuscript and spoke first.

'You are even more poetic than Watson!' he said gloomily.

'We agreed,' I murmured, 'to avoid comparisons.'

He looked at me sharply, then burst out laughing, his ill humour gone in an instant.

'Good, Petrie!' he exclaimed. 'We shall get on. Yes, we shall get on!'

Didcot and Swindon lay behind us now and the last rays of a glorious sunset cast tinted shadows over the rolling expanses of the beautiful Cotswold hills – a fairy tale landscape conceived on a more generous scale than that of the home counties, wooded here and there, the fields hedged around with cunningly piled ramparts of stones, and offering occasional glimpses of thatch-roofed farmhouses. Silent for a time, I sat staring from the window till the light was nearly gone, seeing in this tranquil panorama of rural England a gentle prelude to the windswept mountains and stark drama of Wales, of which, so far, I knew nothing.

'I have been thinking . . .' I said slowly.

'Really?' inquired Holmes.

But I was not to be ruffled by his sarcasms as easily as Watson.

'Yes, I do sometimes!' I said promptly. 'I have been thinking about the awful business at your place in Sussex, and wondering. It was unnecessary, hasty, and ill-advised – '

'Ill-advised, indeed,' he commented, 'since the net result has been to put Sherlock Holmes on their track!'

I smiled, allowing him his vanity.

'It seems to me unlike the work of Fu Manchu, and I am now inclined to believe that it was not he who gave the order, but the Mandarin Ki Ming.'

'Ki Ming? Ah, yes! He is the other villain who has recently appeared on the scene, is he not?'

'Yes. Unlike Fu Manchu, he has a recognised status in international diplomacy. But he is also one of the so-called Council of Seven which controls the Si Fan, and a diabolically accomplished hypnotist – a skill which, as I know to my cost, he exercises for criminal purposes. Smith says that he is a graduate of the Tibetan monastery of Rachë Churân – '

'If Smith says that, he is mistaken, or, at least, not quite accurate,' said Holmes unexpectedly. 'Rachë Churân is not a monastery but the name of a sub-sect of Lamaism which practises alleged magic.' He met my surprised look with a smile. 'I was in Tibet for some time.'

'What!' I cried. 'And you say you are not qualified?'

'Neither am I. My studies there were of a purely philosophical nature, concerning the character of Tibetan Buddhism. Dr Fu Manchu is no Buddhist. He worships older and darker gods.'

'Still,' I said thoughtfully, 'the fact that you were once

76

there may explain something. Your name is undoubtedly upon their list of potential enemies who know too much. Therefore, your death was determined upon the moment you were seen in my company. Nayland Smith believes that there is competition between Fu Manchu and Ki Ming for leadership of the Si Fan. They are working for the same ends, but independently. If Fu Manchu is in Wales, he may well have been there for some time – in fact, we have not actually set eyes on him for at least a month – and Ki Ming will have a free hand in London.'

Sherlock Holmes made no immediate answer but seemed, I thought, to be giving serious consideration to my words – which was something of a rarity.

'You may be in the better position to judge,' he said finally, 'since you have had dealings with these persons. According to your theory, it might, then, have been Ki Ming who was also responsible for Smith's abduction?'

'I hardly think so,' I said doubtfully. 'Ki Ming would have killed him on the spot: he has made at least two recent attempts to do so. For reasons which are not altogether clear, Fu Manchu would apparently prefer to take him alive.'

Darkness had fallen while we had been talking, and now our discussion was abruptly terminated as the train rushed into the greater darkness of the Severn Tunnel. For the next ten minutes, we sat confined as though in a submarine, seeing nothing, yet awesomely aware of the thousands of tons of water above our heads as we crossed the natural frontier between England and Wales. While the carriage lights flickered eerily and smoke billowed past the tightly closed windows, I wondered what it would feel like to those possessed of an imagination, if the tunnel between Dover and Calais were ever constructed. Then, in a flash, the noise and the sense of pressure vanished, and once again we were out in God's air, in the disputed border county of Monmouth.

Holmes stood up, took down his suitcase, and re-packed my manuscript.

'You may be right,' he said, as though no interruption had occurred. 'But the best way in which we can serve

Nayland Smith is to forget about him for the moment, and devote ourselves to the solution of what is, to all intents and purposes, a fresh case – the murder of Sir Julian Rossiter, about whom we as yet know nothing.'

Our train was making good time – or, in other words, was only half an hour in arrears of the printed schedule. We stopped briefly at Newport; then, at a reduced speed, continued south along the coast, passing through a chain of small industrial towns or oversized villages – a dreary, disconcerting prospect of ill-lit streets, with slate-roofed houses built of some yellowish kind of stone. Our first view of Wales was not prepossessing. Holmes sat staring fixedly out from the train window, his chin resting upon one upraised hand.

'Strange as it may seem,' he said soberly, 'though I have been to Lhasa, I know as little of this country and its people as I do of China. I think we may need to remember that Wales is not England.'

8

THE TWICE-MURDERED MAN

We had scarcely set foot on the platform at Cardiff station when we were accosted by a short, stocky man in police inspector's uniform, who greeted us with a complete lack of formality.

'Mr Holmes? I'd have known you in a million, sir, with that nose of yours and your pipe in your mouth.' Grasping Holmes's extended hand firmly in his right, he reached out simultaneously with his left and clutched my arm above the elbow. 'And you'll be Dr Petrie, of course! I'm Owen Beynon, from Merthyr Tydfil.'

I recognised the name of a principal mining town mentioned in my guidebook, but not particularised for its attractions. If memory served me correctly, it had not so long ago been the scene of shocking riots involving stone throwing and baton charges.*

'Is that where we have to go?' I asked.

'Some way out from the town, the house is,' answered the inspector, 'and not too near anywhere. We'll have a cup of tea and a chat first, and then I'll take you out there.'

'Another train journey?'

'No. There's a fine car Sir Julian had, and I've commandeered it, along with his chauffeur.'

He seized our two heavy suitcases, one in either hand, and led the way towards the station refreshment room. There, seated side by side at a marble-topped table, we waited while our new friend collected steaming cups of tea from the counter and, setting them before us, took his place opposite.

'I'll give you just the gist of it. I know your methods,

---

* Dr Petrie's memory did *not* serve him correctly. It was Tonypandy. But it is not very far away. [Ed.]

79

Mr Holmes – read every word about you that's ever been written.' Beynon removed his official cap, revealing stiff auburn hair which closely resembled the bristles of a scrubbing brush. 'They say there's more reading done in the valleys than anywhere in the British Isles – and some of the men you'd think couldn't hardly write their own names. We know about this old devil of a Chinese doctor too, and here it is we don't want him.'

'Tell us, first, about Sir Julian Rossiter,' suggested Holmes, with a faint smile. 'Who, or what, was he?'

'He was owner of the Pentrefdu mine.'

I started slightly, finding this ready answer not quite what I had expected.

'But he had some connections with the Far East?' I inquired. 'I mean, had he lived out there? Could he, perhaps, speak Chinese?'

'Him?' exclaimed Inspector Beynon, staring at me. 'Never been beyond Porthcawl that I know of. And as for Chinese, why,' he continued disgustedly, 'he couldn't even speak Welsh!'

'And no member of his family had any such connections?'

Beynon shook his head doubtfully. 'I believe there was once a cousin, or something, who went out to India and hanged himself in a potting shed. . . .'

'When?'

'Oh, about 1850, I think.'

'I hardly think that is what we are looking for,' said Holmes dryly. 'There is then, nothing about this man's death which you would regard as, let us say, Oriental?'

'No . . .' replied Beynon, and added somewhat naïvely, 'excepting it was queer!'

'Queer? How did he die, then?'

The inspector hesitated, drawing his bushy eyebrows down into a scowl.

'Well, the facts are simple enough, but they take a bit of explaining. At about two o'clock this morning, Sir Julian Rossiter rushed out of his bedroom, screaming like a madman, ran down the passage, went base-over-tip down the stairs, and fractured his skull. Queer enough, you might say – but there's queerer yet. The doctor says he was poisoned! He has other injuries, which he couldn't have got by falling down the stairs – as if he'd been slashed repeatedly with a knife. But there's no blood anywhere excepting in the hall, and no trace of anything wrong in the bedroom. Why should he jump out of bed in the middle of the night and race off as if Satan was on his heels, without stopping to put on a dressing gown or slippers, or switching on the lights?'

Sherlock Holmes nodded thoughtfully. 'We shall have to look for those answers on the spot. Would you say that this man had enemies?'

'Hundreds of them, I should think!' said Beynon promptly. 'There's good owners and there's bad, and he wasn't one of the good. The Rossiters were landowners from way back – land that Oliver Cromwell took away from them that sided with the King, as most of the folk round these parts did.'

'Sir Julian was a baronet, then?' I asked, and, as the inspector continued to look blank: 'I mean, he had the title from his father?'

'No, he didn't. He got it for himself, somehow.'

'So he was a knight,' snapped Holmes impatiently. 'Go on!'

'Anyhow, most of their land's sold and built on now,' said Beynon. 'It was Sir Julian's grandfather that started in the mining business – and a wicked old man he was, too. Had girls of seventeen working three-parts naked at the coalface along with the men, and kids maybe eight or nine years old dragging loads through tunnels about two feet high – they being small enough to get through easy, you see. Well, things aren't that bad nowadays, but they're not all that much better neither. It's a filthy, backbreaking job, with dust in your lungs and your eyesight gone at the end of it. Starvation wages was what he paid, and no more spent on making the work safe than he had to. There won't be any of his men sorry to be rid of him. But why should they murder him? What could they get out of it?'

What, I wondered, could Fu Manchu get out of it?

Sitting there, sipping cautiously at the worst tea I had ever tasted and vaguely conscious of a confused background of station noises, I began to feel doubts. Had we, after all, come out here on a wild-goose chase? Were 'Gillian Rochester' and 'Julian Rossiter' no more than a coincidence?

'Who inherits the property?' demanded Holmes.

'His wife, Lady Elinor – and a right bitch she is. Twenty years younger than him, only waiting to see the end of him, and doesn't care who knows it.'

'But,' I objected vaguely, 'if she takes the title from her husband, shouldn't she be called "Lady Rossiter"?'

'Leave it!' said Holmes irritable. 'Let her call herself what she will. Are there no children?'

'No,' answered Inspector Beynon, shaking his head wisely. 'There's a merciful God in Heaven! Only just the two of the, him and her, and they hadn't shared a meal or a bed for ten years or more. I'd reckon she might have done it, if I could only see how.'

'Servants?'

'Well, it's not a big place, and there's but three – four, counting young Rhys, who's outside freezing his' – Beynon choked, gulped loudly at his tea, and resumed hastily – 'in the car. There's Howell – the butler, I suppose you'd call him – who does all the work. He was the first to come down and find Sir Julian when all the row started. The only sensible man in the house. His wife looks after the cooking. She came down too, a couple of minutes after her husband. Lastly, there's Gwennie, the housemaid, who never came down at all, and who's shut up in her bedroom having the bawling hysterics because we won't let her pack and run off to Merthyr.'

Holmes glanced at his watch and stood up. 'We can hear the rest of it there.'

We did the remainder of our journey seated comfortably enough in the back of an opulent Rolls-Royce, enclosed by a collapsible hood and windows fastened with a strap, like those of a railway carriage. Inspector Beynon, who sat in front with Rhys – a personable young man in a grey uniform – was not so enclosed and less comfortable.

'Really,' I said to Holmes, as we took our places, 'I fail to see what all this can have to do with Fu Manchu.'

'That is what we have to find out!' he snapped.

After that, he would say no more, leaving me to sit staring out of the window, from which very little was to be seen. Once outside Cardiff, we passed abruptly into complete darkness, for, as I now realised, the coal came from higher up, where the spurs of the mountains reached southwards like the spread fingers of a hand, while the long, narrow valleys between served uniquely as a means of access from the coast. Now and then, a cluster of lights appeared briefly, and the twin beams of the headlamps played across the walls and grey slate roofs of squalid little houses, as we ran through some tiny village; to right and left there was nothing but the inhospitable slopes of the encompassing mountains.

Holmes lay back in a corner of the car, closed his eyes, and, I believe, went to sleep, numbering among his accomplishments the ability to sleep when and where opportunity was afforded. Our northward passage continued for the better part of an hour, in the latter part of which Rhys spun the wheel right-handed, taking us away from the main road and into some tributary valley where the sides rose so steeply that I could no longer see even the sky. The going, smooth at first, became gradually worse till we were lurching over the uneven surface of a lane little superior to that which approached Holmes's premises in Sussex. Another abrupt right-handed turn followed, and suddenly we stopped broadside on to the façade of a house with lighted windows and porch.

The residence of the late Sir Julian – somewhat larger than I expected, and standing in some nine or ten acres of ground – was an ugly modern two-storied building of Portland stone. A small motor ambulance stood drawn up to the entrance, and Inspector Beynon gestured towards it as we descended from the car.

'They were just going to take away the body when Inspector Weymouth telephoned and asked me to hold things up,' he said. 'So they've made an easy day of it, the lazy devils.'

He rang the bell and we were admitted by a grey-haired, middle-aged man of dignified appearance, who, although he wore no livery, evidently fulfilled the functions of a butler in this loosely run household. Rhys, the chauffeur, brought in our suitcases and dumped them down behind us. The atmosphere inside the house was warm and stuffy, with a characteristic odour of hot metal, hinting at a central heating system. Glancing about me as I took off my hat and coat, I saw that we stood in a spacious hall with a tiled floor, not unlike a hotel lobby, and divided by a wide staircase. Around this, as I later learned, the various apartments of the house were located more or less symmetrically – a convenient arrangement, as it happened, in an establishment which had for so long been partitioned between man and wife.

A heavily moustached man in the uniform of a police sergeant rose from a chair to greet us.

'Lloyd,' said Inspector Beynon, 'this is Mr Sherlock Holmes.'

'*Iesu Gris*!' said the sergeant, proffering nervous fingers. 'Never dreamed I'd live to shake hands with you, sir!'

'He won't bite you, man!' snapped Beynon. 'Anything happened while I was away?'

'No, sir. Nothing.'

'Good. Where's Edwards?'

'Upstairs, at his post, sir.'

'Both had something to eat?'

'Yes, sir.'

'Ha!' said the inspector. 'Well, that's more than we have. What about the St. John's men?'

'Out in the kitchen, sir, drinking beer and playing cards.'

'Wish we were!' Beynon turned, laid a hand on Holmes's arm, and pointed to a group of reddish-brown stains at the foot of the stairs. 'That's where he fell, see?'

Holmes nodded. 'Yes, I see. None on the steps?'

'A few, Mr Holmes. Seems like he fell from the top. But there are no stains anywhere else. Let's go and have a look at the body.' Inspector Beynon led the way across the hall, following a sparse trail of blood spots revealing the direction in which Sir Julian had been carried. He paused for a moment at an arched doorway and spoke over his shoulder to the butler, who stood silently waiting. 'You'd best come with us, Howell. Mr Holmes will want to hear what you've got to say.'

'Very good, sir.'

We entered a lounge furnished expensively but without taste, like the rest of the house. On a settee, close to the door, lay a sinister shape draped with a sheet, the top of which Beynon drew down to disclose the head and shoulders of a man in pyjamas. He appeared to have been in his late fifties – a once powerful man who had run to fat.

'Your job, Petrie!' said Holmes.

I approached and bent over the body, shuddering a little at the wide-open, twisted mouth, and staring eyes which seemed still to reflect an expression of ultimate horror. A heavy contusion above the left eyebrow showed where Sir Julian had struck his head upon the tiles, and it required but a moment's examination to satisfy me that the skull was deeply fractured.

'Did it kill him?' demanded the inspector.

'It could have done,' I replied. 'Probably, it did.'

'Quite. That's what the divisional surgeon said. Now look at this!'

With a dramatic gesture, Beynon threw back the lower half of the sheet, revealing the pyjama trousers and bare feet of the victim. The source of the bloodstains was immediately apparent. How inflicted I could not imagine, but the sole of the right foot was criss-crossed with long, clean cuts as though by a sword blade. A few similar cuts appeared on the left foot, close to the heel. The flesh around them and up to the ankle was peculiarly discoloured and hideously swollen.

'Poisoned, of course,' said Holmes, nodding.

'Yes,' I said, 'but with what I cannot be certain. It may

have caused his death. But unless it was something in the nature of cyanide – or something known only to Fu Manchu – it could hardly have taken effect so rapidly. Only a post mortem, and, perhaps, not even that, will tell us whether it was the poisoning or the fall which actually killed him.'

'Nor does it matter much!' he rejoined, shrugging. 'Obviously, the poison was intended to be fatal. They could not know for certain that he would fall.'

'But how could he have come by these wounds?' cried Inspector Beynon.

'What do you think, Petrie?' asked Holmes, smiling at me rather mischievously.

I shook my head. 'Frankly, I have no idea. One such cut might have been made by someone who lay in hiding with a knife or a sword, but so many . . . Unless he had been drugged, or tied down on his bed . . .'

'In which case, there would have been blood all over the bedroom, and we have the inspector's word for it that there is not. Surely, then, there can be only one explanation?' Holmes turned suddenly to face Howell, the butler, who had followed us in, obedient to Beynon's instructions. 'But before we speculate upon that, let us have things in order. You, I understand, were the first to appear upon the scene. I shall be glad, therefore, if you will tell me exactly what occurred.'

'Yes, sir,' answered Howell, speaking quietly and easily in the impassive manner of a professional servant. 'It was shortly before two o'clock in the morning. My wife and I had retired to our bedroom only some twenty minutes previously – '

'How did you come to be up so late?'

'We are a late household, sir. Sir Julian never retired before midnight, and sometimes not until two or three. He suffered from insomnia and, even after getting into bed, he usually read for at least half an hour.'

'At what time did he retire last night?'

'I'm afraid I can't say, sir. I last saw him in his study at about midnight, when he was working on some accounts. My wife and I were occupied for some time afterwards with household duties which are more usually carried out in the morning, in other establishments – '

Howell broke off as the door re-opened to admit a woman clad in a long housecoat, lank, corn-coloured hair falling to her shoulders. Her pale, angular features, which retained a faded prettiness, offset brightly rouged lips set in a fixed smile of contempt. I judged her age at thirty-five, and realised that this must be the self-styled Lady Elinor.

Taking no notice of us, she crossed the room to the far side and took a cigarette from a cedarwood box.

'I should be obliged, madam,' said Holmes sharply, 'if you would not smoke in here for the present.'

She turned, regarding him with a surprised, petulant look. Inspector Beynon cleared his throat awkwardly.

'This is – '

'I know who he is,' interrupted Lady Elinor, 'and I'll not take orders from him in my own house. Nor from you, Inspector!' She sat down on the arm of a chair, crossing her legs, so that the housecoat parted above her knees, and lighted her cigarette defiantly. 'Go on with your little story, Howell.'

The butler inclined his head gravely and continued, unruffled.

'My wife had already got into bed, sir, but I had not yet undressed when, a few moments before two, we heard a crash from the other side of the house. It was made by Sir Julian's bedroom door striking against the wall as it was hurled violently open. Directly after, we heard him screaming in terror as he ran down the passage – so loudly that it aroused both her ladyship and the housemaid, who were asleep – and then a much louder crash – '

'Just a minute, Howell!' interjected Beynon. 'How could you know whether he was screaming in terror or in pain?'

'I know, Inspector,' replied Howell quietly. 'I served with the Volunteers in South Africa, sir. I know when a man is hurt and when he is frightened.'

'Good man!' approved Holmes. 'What did you do?'

'I hurried down the hall, where the sound had seemed to come from, switched on the lights, and saw Sir Julian lying face downwards at the foot of the stairs. I ran to him and found that he was unconscious, but still breathing. At that moment, my wife came down, having thrown on a dressing gown, and, since we could not move him ourselves, I told her to go out to the chauffeur's lodge and fetch Rhys.'

'How did you and your wife come down? By the same staircase?'

'No, sir. By the servants' stairs at the back of the house. While I was waiting for my wife to return, Lady Elinor also came down. She stood for a moment on the stairs, and said . . .'

For the first time, he hesitated, and Lady Elinor glanced across at him impatiently.

'Why don't you tell them what I said?' she challenged. 'I said, "So the drunken swine has done for himself."'

Holmes switched his eyes towards her, his expression unreadable. 'Do you mean that your husband was habitually drunk?'

'No. It was said in anger because I thought he was drunk then. He drank fairly heavily, and was sometimes drunk, but not often.'

'By which staircase did you descend?'

'The main staircase – the same that he had fallen down.'

Holmes nodded and turned back to Howell. 'Is there anything further you can tell us?'

'Not much, sir. My wife came back with the chauffeur, and together we carried Sir Julian in here. We laid him upon the settee, where he lies now, and when we examined him we then found that he was dead.'

'None of which helps us,' said Beynon impatiently, 'to explain how he got those poisoned cuts on his feet!'

Sherlock Holmes stared at him, treating him to the look of pained surprise which, I imagined, Lestrade and Gregson had so often suffered in the past; turned his regard upon me, much as the dying Caesar must have regarded Brutus, and shook his head sadly.

'Dear me! Do you still require me to answer that? But it is simply a matter of negative deduction – or, if you prefer, elimination. The man's feet were *not* cut when he reached the top of the stairs, but they were when he reached the bottom – '

'What!' shouted Beynon incredulously. 'You mean it was done while he was flying head first through the air?'

'Not precisely,' murmured Holmes, smiling. 'Observe that the wounds are almost wholly upon his right foot. It was the infliction of that injury which *caused* him to fall. In no other way could it have happened. Something in the nature of a rubber mat to which slivers of broken glass had been stuck – and, of course, poisoned – was placed upon the second or third step from the top. When a man descends a staircase, rapidly or otherwise, he puts his feet on alternate steps. Sir Julian trod squarely upon this fiendish device with his right foot, tripped, and caught the heel of his left upon it as he fell.'

'But we found no such thing afterwards!'

'Of course not. It was put there at some time after he went upstairs, and must have been removed – probably by means of a line attached to one corner – directly after it had done its work, since his wife descended safely a few minutes later.'

A short silence followed while all of us considered this, with differing results.

'But, sir,' protested Howell, diffidently, 'if there was an intruder in the house, how did he get out? Someone has been in the hall continuously since the alarm was raised, and all the windows are fastened. I checked them myself after leaving Sir Julian for the night, and they are still fastened.'

'Might he,' I suggested, 'have come down by the other stairs and escaped by a back entrance?'

'There is only one, sir. It is locked at night and cannot be opened without a key. As a rule, I open it in the morning, but because of what happened last night, it has remained locked all day.'

'H'm!' said Holmes, fingering the bridge of his long nose. 'Very interesting!'

'So I suppose you think it was me!' Lady Elinor stood up stiffly and threw her cigarette into an ash tray. 'There could have been no one upstairs, so it must have been me! You're wrong, Mr Holmes – I did not hate my husband. I merely disliked him, and we were strangers to each other. Sir Julian was not a man who could live with any woman for longer than six months. I knew that when I married him. Afterwards, when I had ceased to be attractive to him, I left him free to amuse himself as he pleased, and managed his house for him in return for adequate support and the understanding that all his property was willed to me. He was content with that; he had no one else to leave it to.'

'Thank you for your frankness,' replied Holmes quietly. He glanced sideways at Beynon. 'Apart from the question as to how this unknown person entered and escaped, there is a still more curious aspect of this affair. By what conceivable means could the victim be thrown into such a state of abject panic that he would flee from his bedroom, just as he was, and fall into the trap set for him? There are no witnesses, since he was alone – '

'He wasn't always!' said Lady Elinor viciously. 'He often had girls in for the weekend from Merthyr and Cardiff. But never the same one twice.'

'However, there was no one with him last night?'

'There have been no visitors of any description inside the house for the past ten days, sir,' answered Howell.

Again, and for a longer period, there was a silence among us, while the discarded cigarette in the bronze ash tray sent up acrid pencils of smoke in a ghastly travesty of incense offered at a tomb. Lady Elinor whirled suddenly upon Beynon, her face flushed.

'What does it matter how he died, or who killed him?' she cried passionately. 'All of this should have been over and done with hours ago, yet you must go on and on with it, and have Sherlock Holmes down from London. . . .' She stabbed a forefinger savagely towards the shrouded form on the settee. 'I want *that* taken out of here, and all of you out of my house!'

Inspector Beynon looked uncomfortable, but the outburst had no such effect upon Holmes.

'I think, madam,' he said smoothly, 'that it would be better for us to remain until we have found what your husband saw in his bedroom, because, you see, it is still here – and we don't know what it is!'

Seconds passed while they faced each other, and I saw the fear kindled in her eyes. Lady Elinor faltered and drew a deep, sobbing breath.

'You bastard!' she said faintly, then pivoted on her heel and flounced out of the room.

Sherlock Holmes laughed.

'Well,' he remarked, 'we shall have the less reason to fear deceit among people who speak their minds! I think that the ambulance men may remove the corpse now, and, in the meantime, we will go upstairs.'

9

THE HOUSE OF FEAR

At the top of fatal staircase, Holmes halted and pointed to a narrow door set back in a recess.

'What is that?' he asked.

'Only a cupboard, sir,' replied Howell, who, at Holmes's instructions, had accompanied us up the stairs, while Inspector Beynon lingered below, talking to the ambulance men.

'Ah! I thought we should find something of the sort.'

Holmes jerked open the door, and taking out his pocket lamp, shone it into the dark interior. Nothing seemed to be there but a few old coats and some cleaning materials. Leaning forward, and thrusting in his head, he sniffed suspiciously.

'Does your wife use garlic in her cooking?'

'No, sir. Never.'

Holmes withdrew his head and re-closed the door.

'This,' he said, 'is undoubtedly where the assassin concealed himself after placing his diabolical contrivance upon the stairs. My nose tells me that this cupboard has been inhabited by a man who customarily ate quantities of garlic – which, in Britain, is a somewhat rare taste.'

'But, I believe, equally rare in China,' I commented.

'No doubt,' said Holmes, frowning at me. 'But you should know better than I that Fu Manchu's men are not, for the most part, Chinese.' He turned once more to the butler. 'Show us Sir Julian's study – where you last spoke to him.'

'This way, sir.'

We passed through a short corridor and entered a medium-sized room which appeared to me to be appointed rather as an office than a study, the more conspicuous items being a large, roll-top desk, a workmanlike swivel chair, and a steel safe, although there were also armchairs and a small bookcase. Part of a table in one corner was occupied by a gramophone with a huge horn shaped like the flaring petals of a convolvulus, and a number of wax discs piled up alongside.

'A coarse, insensitive man, even in his aesthetic pleasures,' said Holmes, with disgust. 'Look! He has stacked his records one on top of another without their covers, so that the surfaces are scratched.'

Turning his attention to the desk, he took out some of the papers from the pigeonholes, found all of them to concern the mining business, and thrust them back.

'Sir Julian was seated there when I left him,' volunteered Howell.

'Why did you come in?' inquired Holmes absently, flicking over the pages of a ledger. 'Had he called you?'

'No, sir. I came merely to ask if he required anything further for the night.'

'Which he did not. What I am anxious to establish is how soon afterwards he retired – or, in other words, how long he was in his bedroom before the event which caused him to leave it.' Holmes picked up an ash tray from the desk. 'Did you, by any chance, notice whether this was empty last night?'

'It was, sir, since I emptied it before leaving. I knew that Sir Julian might be up for some time, and so it was my custom to do that.'

'Excellent! Was he actually smoking then?'

'No, sir. He was not.'

Holmes gave a brusque nod of satisfaction. 'In that case, it is clear that he smoked two cigars after you left him. Each would have taken about forty minutes. Hence he could not have gone to bed before, let us say, one-fifteen.'

'Holmes,' I said eagerly, struck by an inspiration, as I thought, 'if two cigars were smoked, may there not have been two persons here? He might have had some secret visitor, whom he admitted after Howell had gone to his room.'

I was rewarded only by a look of annoyance.

'Do you suggest,' said Holmes tartly, 'that he had an

assignation with some woman who smoked cigars? And if the visitor was a man, for what purpose did he come?' He thrust the ash tray under my nose. 'Surely, you can see for yourself that the ends of both these cigars were bitten off in the same way, and presumably by the same man? And, again, if two persons had smoked, would they have used the same ash tray, which is awkwardly situated on the desk? Really, Petrie, I wish you would not find additional mysteries for us to solve!'

He turned aside and I retreated, abashed, to a remote corner of the room. I was beginning to realize that Holmes, unlike Nayland Smith, did not encourage initiative. All he required was an extra pair of hands to do his work.

Whilst he continued to examine the papers and books on the desk, I devoted myself to the bookcase just behind me, and on inspecting some of the volumes which it contained, discovered them to be cheap novels of a nature which I prefer not to describe. Seemingly, Sir Julian had read nothing else. I wondered idly what he had done to obtain his knighthood, and remembering that we stood in the legendary resting place of King Arthur and his Knights of the Round Table, wondered what kind of reception might await him at that ghostly board.

Heavy footsteps sounded in the passage and Inspector Beynon came in to join us. At the same moment, I heard Sherlock Holmes say, 'What is this doing here?' and looked round to see him pointing at a pot-bellied and slightly rusty oil stove standing directly in front of one of the long iron radiators.

'Sir Julian was using it last night,' replied Howell, 'because the central heating system was out of order.'

'It's working now,' growled Beynon.

'Yes, sir,' replied Howell, turning to face him. 'If you remember, sir, it was you yourself who asked me to light the furnace.'

'That's right – so I did! The house was cold when I came in early this morning, but I thought then that you probably let the fire go out at nights.'

'No, sir. We keep it banked up. The boiler had been repaired during the afternoon, but the plumber said that it should not be used for at least twelve hours.'

'The plumber?' asked Holmes sharply. 'I thought you told us that no one had been in here for the past ten days.'

Howell glanced at him in some surprise. 'I meant no *visitors*, sir. Of course, there have been tradesmen – the milkman, the butcher, and so forth.'

'Yes, of course – but none of them came inside, whereas the plumber obviously did!' Holmes sat down upon the desk chair, putting his hands on his knees. 'I think you had better tell us about this!'

'Well, sir,' said Howell, with a puzzled expression on his face, 'when I got up yesterday morning, I found that the pipes were cold. Sir Julian, naturally, was very angry about it. I went down immediately to the cellar and discovered that a considerable amount of water had leaked into the furnace, so I thereupon telephoned to Ross Brothers, in Merthyr – ' He looked at Beynon. 'You know them, I expect, sir?'

'Yes, I know them.'

'I asked them to send someone as soon as possible, and a man came soon after lunch.'

'Did you know this man personally?' demanded Holmes.

'No, sir. But he must have been from Ross Brothers, since I had telephoned them myself. He made an inspection and found that the supply pipe in Sir Julian's bathroom was leaking – '

'Ah!' exclaimed Holmes. 'Adjoining his bedroom, of course! How long was the man up there?'

'Nearly three hours, sir. He had to take down some of the panelling to get at it.'

'No one was with him during this time?'

Howell shook his head. 'I remained with him for a while, sir. But I had other duties to attend to, so I left him to complete his work and come down to the kitchen when he had finished – which he did.'

Holmes said nothing for a moment.

'Obvious!' he muttered. 'Obvious! But, unfortunately, the shop must be closed now. . . .'

'Yes, but it's a family business, Mr. Holmes,' said Inspector Beynon, catching his meaning before I did. 'They live on the premises.'

'Good!' replied Holmes, and stood up. 'Where is the telephone?'

'Downstairs, in the hall,' said Howell, flushing, 'and, if you doubt my word, sir, you will find their number on the pad, where I wrote it yesterday morning.'

'Your word is not in doubt. All the same, I propose to telephone.'

Holmes hurried out of the room, leaving the door open. We heard the clatter of his footfalls on the stairs, and his voice drifted up faintly from the hall. Then, in less than five minutes, he was back, rubbing his hands, and evidently in high spirits.

'The telephone again, Petrie!' he said triumphantly. 'An instrument which, like most of our modern devices, may serve the criminal at least as well as it serves the police! Out here, where the wires are above ground, one has only to put on workman's clothes and climb a telephone pole – and what is there for a passer-by to see but a Post Office engineer going about his lawful business?' He turned to the butler. 'Ten minutes after your call was made to the shop, a second call was received, from a woman who said that the cause of the trouble had been found and that a plumber would not, after all, be needed. They assumed,' he added, with a significant glance in my direction, 'that she was a foreign housemaid.'

'Kâramanèh?' I asked, attempting to keep my voice level. 'No, I don't think so. In any case, her accent is very slight.'

'Probably you are right. Well, Fu Manchu has other women in his household – one at least.'*

'But – but, sir!' stammered Howell, who looked

---

* In fact, there were two. In addition to Zarmi the Eurasian, he had his daughter with him, though we did not then know of her existence. [P.]

stunned. 'I still don't understand. There *was* water in the furnace!'

'Pah!' answered Holmes contemptuously. 'There is a stovepipe outside the house, of course; nothing easier than to pour a few gallons of water down it. I take it, by the way, that this spurious plumber who arrived later was not a foreigner?'

'No, sir. But I don't think he was a Welshman.'

'What do you suppose he did while he was here, Mr Holmes?' inquired the inspector.

'One thing he did was to admit a confederate – no doubt by means of a rope ladder lowered from the window – the man who remained here, and later hid in the cupboard.'

'Do you think he was there all the time?'

'Unlikely, I should say. He may have hidden in some other place or changed his hiding places several times during the evening. However, the point is, Inspector, that they would scarcely have resorted to so elaborate a scheme merely to admit an agent who might more simply have broken in. What else did their plumber do while he was in the bathroom? Let us take a look at it.'

With Howell again in the lead, we traversed a second corridor and, at the end, came to a large bedroom, overfurnished with a massive wardrobe, chairs, a chest of drawers, and a low dressing table with a long mirror, clearly intended for feminine use. A double bed stood with the headboard against one wall, the sheets and blankets being tumbled upon the carpet, so that only a corner of the mattress was now covered. In a chair close to the door by which we had entered sat a police constable, with his helmet resting on his lap.

'All in order, Edwards?' asked Inspector Beynon.

'Yes, Inspector. But I think I'm getting the jumps.'

'What do you mean by that? Something happened?'

'Not exactly, sir,' replied PC Edwards uneasily. 'Only, about an hour after you went off to Cardiff, I thought I heard a very faint scratching noise. But it stopped after a few seconds, and then, a couple of hours later, when I was starting to think I'd imagined it, I heard it again. I don't like this place, sir!'

'Think it means anything?' queried Beynon, glancing at Holmes.

'H'm! It may, or it may not.'

'This is the bathroom, sir,' said Howell, from the other side of the room, pointing to the only other door which it contained.

Holmes and I crossed and entered a small and unpretentious bathroom with partially tiled and matchboarded walls.

'He has had a part of this off,' said my companion, examining a section of the matchboarding which presumably covered the pipes. 'But he has nailed it up again pretty thoroughly. Try the taps, Petrie.'

I did so, turning the bath taps on and off, followed by those over the wash basin.

'Everything works,' I reported.

'As it should, since nothing was wrong in the first place.' Holmes frowned, biting his lip in perplexity. 'What did he do here? I thought, at first, that it might have been something to do with the hot water system, but he seems not to have interfered with it. Why was he anxious that the boiler should not be used till the following morning?' With an irritable shake of the head, he walked out again into the adjoining bedroom. 'Inspector Beynon! Is everything in here exactly as it was when you first arrived?'

'Yes,' replied Beynon. 'Only that the top light is now on as well as the bedside lamp, which was the only one in use when we came in.'

As he said it, it seemed suddenly strange to me that there should be electric lighting in a house so distant from the town. However, I was later to discover that where, in England, oil-lamps would have served, electricity was often available here in quite remote areas – the only benefit, perhaps, which industrialisation had brought to those who dwelt in this ruthlessly exploited region.

Seating himself on the edge of the disordered bed, Holmes picked up a lurid-covered book which lay directly beneath the lamp and displayed it to Howell.

'You have a good memory for details,' he said. 'Was this same book here on the morning before Sir Julian died?'

'Yesterday, sir? Yes, it was.' Howell permitted himself a slight smile. 'One could hardly mistake it, I believe, sir.'

Holmes opened the covers to a bookmarked page and pointed.

'Look! He has read only twenty-three pages, and if he did that the previous night – it being, as you say, his custom to read every night – he cannot have read it at all last night. Therefore, he had been in bed no more than a few minutes before the apparition took place.'

'Apparition!' I exclaimed.

Holmes laughed shortly. 'I use the word in its literal sense of something which appeared. A man lacking both sensibility and imagination, such as Sir Julian, would not be frightened out of his wits by rattling chains and dancing skeletons. And it appeared in a reasonably well-lighted room!'

'Might he have seen something at the window?'

'Since the curtains were drawn, he could not see the window! No, Petrie. It was here, in this room – something material, and so threatening in its aspect that the only possible escape was by instant flight. But where did it come from, and where did it go?'

'And what in Heaven's name was it?' cried Beynon.

Standing up again, and switching off the bedside lamp, Holmes walked across and opened the curtains, disclosing an ordinary sash window.

'I can think of five or six things which it might have been,' he replied. 'But nothing which fully covers all the facts.'

He examined the window catch, assured himself that it was fastened securely, and turned away, leaving the curtains open. Then, drawing a heavy chair across the carpet, he shifted it into a position near the door leading into the passage, and sat down in it.

'I should be grateful, Inspector, if you and Dr Petrie would kindly move that dressing table about eighteen inches left from where it now stands.'

Beynon looked at me and I at him, but neither of us ventured to ask why. We laid our hands upon the low table with its weighty mirror, and, with some effort, lugged it several times back and forth in response to Holmes's instructions until, seemingly satisfied, he stood up.

'Thank you, gentlemen,' he said. 'If Constable Edwards will be good enough to stay here a little longer, I think that the rest of us may go back downstairs.'

Holmes and I bringing up the rear, we retraced our steps along the corridor down which Sir Julian had fled to his death. With this, what I might term the first phase of Holmes's investigation appeared to be concluded. But we were come only halfway to the stairs when, suddenly, he halted and seized my arm.

'What is it?' I asked.

Holmes took the torch once more from his pocket and, switching it on, knelt upon the polished floorboards.

'Look!' he said grimly. 'Are these not bloodstains?'

Kneeling beside him to examine the spot at which he was pointing, I saw three or four dark patches, each no bigger than a sixpence, grouped close to the wall.

'Yes! Indeed they are!'

'It was only by the merest chance that I noticed them.'

I sat back on my heels, looking at him in bewilderment.

'But Sir Julian's feet were injured *after* he had passed this point!'

'Quite so!' said Holmes, frowning and gnawing at his lower lip. 'Could I have been wrong? No, surely not. Those cuts must have bled profusely. . . .' Leaping upright with an exclamation, he struck the heel of his hand furiously against his forehead. 'Confound it! I have let them go. . . . But perhaps it is not too late. . . .'

He thrust past me and went rushing down the passage. Following at a more leisurely pace, I descended the stairs to join the others in the hall, and in time to observe two men in the black uniform of the St John's Ambulance

Brigade carrying a loaded stretcher back into the lounge under Holmes's urging. But, as I reached the lowest step and turned to follow, my attention was arrested and diverted by a low wailing sound from a distant part of the house.

'Damn!' said Inspector Beynon. 'It's that bloody housemaid! She's been going on like that, on and off, since six o'clock this morning. See here, Doctor – can't you go upstairs and give her something to make her shut up?'

'Yes,' I said unwillingly. 'I suppose so.'

Restraining my curiosity as to what Holmes was doing, I went to my suitcase, which still stood where Rhys had placed it, and took out the small medicine chest which I carried on my travels.

'This way, sir!' said Howell.

He guided me through a number of passages to a back staircase, and up to the bedroom of the vociferously tearful Gwennie. Here, while he remained tactfully outside, I spent an awkward ten minutes, coping with a large-limbed, hoydenish girl in an advanced state of hysteria, who clutched me by my coat lapels the moment I bent over her. Having eventually subdued her struggles (by the desperate expedient of sitting on her) long enough to administer an injection, I rejoined the bland-faced butler and we returned to the hall, where my companions were waiting. Beynon pulled out and consulted a pocket watch.

'It's ten o'clock already,' he announced. 'We shall have to find somewhere for you two gentlemen to stay, though there isn't much of anything in Merthyr.'

Holmes shook his head decisively. 'No. With your permission, Inspector, we shall remain here. The essential part of our work is still to be done.'

'Oh!' said Beynon, looking surprised, and then, in a slightly ludicrous fashion, drew himself upright and squared his shoulders. 'Very well, Mr Holmes. Give us our orders!'

But again Holmes shook his head. 'I have no authority to give orders.'

101

'Eh?' cried the inspector. 'Don't talk so daft, man! You're Sherlock Holmes!'

'I must insist,' replied Holmes, smiling, 'that Sherlock Holmes, who is not even a constable, cannot give orders to police officers. However, if you wish, I may give you some advice.'

'Give us your advice, then,' said Beynon, with a broad grin. 'And if any man of mine doesn't take it, he'll have me to reckon with!'

'Then my advice is this. We should ask Mrs Howell to find some food for us in the kitchen, since we have had nothing since midday and may have a strenuous night ahead of us. Meanwhile, Sergeant Lloyd must relieve Edwards, who has been at his post too long. We shall need no one down here for the time being. If transport can be found for him, Edwards can go home. But I should like a word with Lloyd first.'

'Lloyd!' snapped Beynon. 'Come here!'

Sergeant Lloyd, seated by the stairs as we had first seen him, stood up at once. 'Yes, sir!' he said briskly. 'What do you want me to do, sir?'

'I want you to stay upstairs for about an hour, till Dr Petrie and I come up to take over. While you are there, walk about a bit, and make some noise. You may smoke, if you like, and it might be better if you did. Be careful not to move any piece of furniture, and . . . yes – keep your helmet on. Do you understand?'

'Yes, sir!' answered Lloyd promptly. 'Though I don't understand why.'

'Why?' Holmes smiled somewhat impishly. 'Well, to tell you the truth, Sergeant, I am none to clear about it myself. But, finally, when we come up presently, say nothing, and take no notice of anything we may say. Simply leave the room and come straight downstairs. If you do as I suggest, I think you will be all right, but I should warn you that there *is* a slight element of danger.'

'Danger?' echoed Beynon.

Holmes turned towards him and nodded soberly.

'Yes,' he said. 'We now know that a dangerous man was here last night, and you have assured me that there is no way by which he could have got out again. Therefore, he is still on the premises – together with something equally dangerous, which he is here to recover.'

10

THE APPARITION

'Upon my word, Petrie!' exclaimed Holmes, pushing his empty plate away from him. 'If we eat any more, we shall never be fit for a night's work. No, really, Mrs Howell – despite the tempting aroma of your apple pie, we must decline dessert. But a cup of strong coffee would be acceptable.'

Grouped around the kitchen table, the three of us had partaken of an excellent repast, learning, to our amazement, that a full three-course dinner awaited us in place of the scratch meal we had expected. The butler's wife – a rosy-cheeked woman who looked exactly like a cook in a fairy tale – had, it seemed, begun preparations as soon as it was known that we were leaving London, apologising for the fact that 'it had to be stew, because I wasn't quite sure when you'd be coming, like.'

Inspector Beynon leaned back in his chair with a sigh of inner satisfaction, the top button of his tunic undone, and permitted himself the luxury of an off-duty cigarette. For the sake of digestion, as Holmes remarked, we had suspended discussion during our delightful meal, but when coffee had been served, it was recommenced.

'There are no secret rooms or passages in a house like this,' declared the inspector. 'There isn't even an attic. So if there's a man hiding here, I can't imagine where.'

'I can!' said Holmes. 'However, I might be mistaken, so I will not take the risk of misleading you. Time will tell. If Dr Fu Manchu is really at the bottom of all this – and I incline to believe that he is – something of a deadly nature was introduced into Sir Julian's bedroom last night. Whether it is alive or something mechanical, I am not strictly sure, but, sometime after the house becomes quiet, our man will come out of hiding to retrieve it – which, for some reason, he could not do immediately.'

'Why doesn't he just leave it?' grunted Beynon.

'Well, it presumably has some value,' returned Holmes, laughing. 'After all, even Fu Manchu's arsenal is not unlimited. If they had meant to abandon it, his agent would have made off by the nearest convenient exit directly after Sir Julian's death. But, as Dr Petrie here well understands, it is also a matter of policy. The victims of the Si Fan must die in some bizarre and spectacular fashion, so as to discourage opposition to their demands. The terror of the inexplicable is their most potent weapon, and once the trick is known, it cannot be repeated.' He paused, glancing in my direction. 'It is in this, perhaps, that you have scored your most notable successes, by depleting the enemy's resources. Let us hope that to-night we may rob him of another.'

Beynon squirmed in his chair a trifle uneasily. 'Your idea is, then, Mr Holmes, that we should sit up there in the dark and wait for some Chiness bugaboo to come dropping down our necks? I'm blessed if I fancy that!'

'Dr Petrie and I will post ourselves in the bedroom, Inspector. You must leave that end of it to us, since we have both had some experience. You and Sergeant Lloyd will stay downstairs in the hall.'

'To do what?'

'To act as our rear guard, and cut off the retreat of our quarry if he tries to escape that way.' Sherlock Holmes pushed back his chair from the table and stood up. 'It is time for us to make our preparations and take up our positions. Howell, will you come with me, please?'

He walked out of the room, followed by the butler, leaving Beynon and me to sit looking at each other across the table. A silence followed, broken only by a rattle of dishes in the scullery, where Mrs Howell was washing up.

'Brave as a lion, and clever as a fox!' said Beynon suddenly, his hero-worship natural and unashamed as a schoolboy's. 'By damn, Doctor, there's nobody like him!'

Nearly fifteen minutes had passed when Holmes and

the butler returned, the latter, as I saw with some surprise, carrying our hats and coats.

'Are we going outside?' I inquired.

'No,' answered Holmes. 'But we are going to put on our coats, and also our hats.' He turned towards Beynon. 'In the unlikely event that our man should try the back stairs, we will give him a taste of his own medicine. I have fixed up a trip wire and taken down the light. Howell and his wife will go up to bed by the front stairs to-night.' Putting on his overcoat, while I did the same, he appeared lost in thought for a moment, then spoke again to the butler. 'And now, Howell, since you evidently ride a bicycle – '

Howell's expression of open-mouthed astonishment was so ludicrous as to cause an interruption.

'There is no mystery about it!' snapped Holmes impatiently. 'I can see the grease mark from the chain, just above your ankle. The point is, can you lend me a pair of cycle clips?'

'Yes, sir,' said Howell, quickly recovering his imperturbability. 'I have them right here, sir.'

He opened a small drawer in the kitchen dresser and searched.

'Good!' said Holmes. 'You don't have two pairs, I suppose? Well, never mind. Give them to Dr Petrie, and I will make do with my socks.'

Putting his right foot on the seat of a chair, he set about tucking the turns-ups of his trousers into his socks.

'Holmes,' I said, mystified beyond further tolerance, 'This is too much! We are to wear our overcoats, although we are not going out, and now I am to put on cycle clips. . . .'

Holmes paused in his operations and looked at me gravely.

'Have you forgotten,' he asked, 'that in your very first encounter, Dr Fu Manchu employed a venomous centipede? Do you want some such horror scuttling up your trouser leg? We don't know what is in that room, and, short of having every stick of furniture out, we cannot search it – while, as Inspector Beynon has aptly remarked, the danger may equally well come from above. Hence our overcoats and hats.'

'Good Heavens!' I cried, shuddering at the thought. 'Of course, you are right! It may be a snake; he used one once. . . .'

'Which is an excellent reason why he will not use one again.' Holmes shook his head grimly. 'No, it is not a snake. Well, if you are ready, let us go to our posts.'

As we trooped out into the hall, he took a weapon from his jacket pocket and transferred it to the right-hand pocket of his overcoat, whereat I observed, with some curiosity, that he had at some time or other exchanged his old-fashioned revolver for a flat automatic of American manufacture.

'Have your pistol ready,' he said. 'When this man comes, he will be dangerous. But a word of warning, Petrie . . .' His hand dropped lightly upon my shoulder and he leaned towards me, speaking quietly, as though unwilling that Inspector Beynon should hear. 'We do not have the unique privileges of Nayland Smith, who is free to act much as he no doubt does in Burma. Unless this scoundrel is armed and attacks us, you may not fire upon him, or we shall have trouble with the law.'

Leaving the inspector below, we once more climbed the stairs, and, at the top, Holmes halted momentarily to issue final instructions.

'When we have entered, sit in the chair by the door. I have left the bathroom door open, and with the dressing table where it now stands, you will be able to see inside by looking in the mirror. It will be a nerve-wracking business, I'm afraid, but if our man is where I think he is, he can't be very comfortable, and we shall probably not have to wait very long for him.'

'Lead on,' I said. 'I'm ready.'

Holmes gave me a quick nod of approval, took out a key which he had evidently obtained from Howell, and strode off along the corridor. I followed and we entered the bedroom, greeted by the somewhat odd spectacle of a helmeted police sergeant seated on the edge of the bed with a clay pipe in his mouth and Sir Julian's deplorable choice of reading matter open in his hand.

'All right, Sergeant!' said Holmes loudly. 'This room can be locked up now till to-morrow morning. Switch off the light, and bring the key with you.'

Sergeant Lloyd stood up, put the book down hastily, and, with a somewhat red-faced expression, hurried silently out of the room. Holmes pointed to the chair which I was to occupy, and, as I slipped quietly into it, extinguished the light, closed the door with a bang, and locked it noisily on the *inside*. In the semi-darkness which ensued, I had a dim vision of his tall figure tiptoeing across to the bed and sitting down on it.

Thus our vigil commenced. We were old hands at this game, I thought, but it was never a pleasant one. So it had begun for me on that memorable night of which Holmes had reminded me, now almost three years past, when Fu Manchu was as yet but a name to me – before I had first looked into those baleful, cat-green eyes and felt their awful power. And so, I thought solemnly, one night it might end; we should not always be lucky.

In the silence of the house, I heard the Howells coming up the stairs to bed, earlier than usual, as Holmes had ordered. A door closed distantly and again there was silence. Gradually, as of old, my eyes were becoming accustomed to the gloom, so that now I could pick out the shapes of the furniture and that of Sherlock Holmes seated upon the bed with his hand on the switch of the table lamp. Soon I could distinguish the pallor of his face from the contrasting darkness of his clothing. In the mirror, I could see the square patch of light formed by the bathroom window and a glimmer on the tiles.

A grandfather's clock in the hall chimed the half hour, and inevitably my thoughts reverted to that first night when Smith and I had crouched in my darkened bedroom, waiting the advent of the thing which caused death and the red mark of the Zayat Kiss. Then it had been the clock across the common. But, as I realised with a sudden chill, to-night was *not* the same. We were not waiting for something to be brought, but for something which was already in the room.

What was it? What *could* it be – this thing so menacing that it had driven a strong, brutish man headlong to his death? I felt no fear of the other – the Burmese dacoit or Indian strangler who might come in search of it. I thought all at once of the disjointed phrases of Smith's half-destroyed letter – 'something about a *worm*' – and felt the hair prickling on the base of my neck.

The Westminster chimes rang faintly below: midnight. We had been here an hour. With the improvement in my sense of sight, hearing had likewise sharpened and now I detected the tiny, furtive sounds always to be heard in a sleeping house: unexplained creakings and rustlings, a soft bump – a cat, perhaps, jumping on the roof – now and then a dry, scratching sound – a rat? – the same, possibly, that PC Edwards had heard. Outside, a fitful breeze stirred the branches of the trees growing close to the house; a night bird screeched and, very far off, a dog barked.

The radiators were turned full on and, in my protective armour of hat and overcoat, it was stiflingly hot. I felt the perspiration trickling down inside my collar and a subtle drowsiness stealing over me, no doubt engendered by my over-indulgence at dinner. Striving to keep my eyes open, I fixed my gaze upon the window, where the light of a waning moon made silhouette shapes of the surrounding trees. Out of them seemed to come something with burning eyes and great, flapping wings – a thing of the Pit, which swooped at the window and scrabbled at the glass with savage claws and beak. . . .

My chin thumped upon my chest, and I sat up with a jerk, knowing that my waking fears were drifting into nightmare. Out in the garden, all remained tranquil. I switched my regard to the mirror. Something in its limpid depths seemed curiously different, and, for an instant, I was puzzled, till, belatedly, it dawned upon me that I could no longer see the upper part of the bathroom window. Starting fully upright in my chair, I perceived that a square flap had swung downwards from the ceiling, and in the same moment, a pair of legs appeared beneath it; a lithe figure dropped apelike and noiselessly to the floor.

Crouching briefly, the man straightened and came forward, his reflection looming up in the foreground of the mirror. My heart beating wildly, but no longer afraid, I turned my head quickly and saw him emerge from the open doorway, passing thence between me and the window of the room in which we sat. Though, as yet, I could discern no details of his appearance, I saw that he had something large and cylindrical tucked beneath one arm – something which glittered as he moved.

'*Now*!' shouted Holmes.

The switch clicked under his fingers as we sprang up and flung ourselves from opposite sides upon the intruder. In the soft light of the bedside lamp, I had one fleeting glimpse of a short, swarthy-skinned man with slitlike eyes, and yellowed teeth bared in a snarl, clad like an athlete in singlet and boxer shorts, a striped towel bound around his forehead. We had taken him utterly by surprise – yet the effect of that surprise was only to trigger a co-ordinated action of such incredible agility as I had never witnessed.

Ere we could close with him, the man dropped his burden with a metallic crash upon the carpet and whirled. How can I describe it? It was all done in a single turn, performed with the speed and precision of a tumbling act. His right arm shot out straight and rigid. The edge of his extended hand took me across the chest with the agonising force of an iron bar and sent me sprawling. Even as I fell, I saw his left foot swing up high above the shoulder, and Holmes go staggering back, off balance, to avoid a kick which, had it landed under his chin, must have lifted the head from his body. In the same instant, the turn was completed, and our opponent, leaping high off the floor, hurled himself feet first through the window in a shower of splintering glass.

Still gasping for breath, I heard the front door go crashing open and the raised voices of Beynon and Lloyd, as they rushed outside. Holmes picked himself up from the bed, upon which he had fallen, hurried to the window, and peered down.

'They won't catch him,' he said. 'A drop of twenty feet is nothing to *that* man.'

I struggled painfully to my feet and staggered across to join my companion at the broken window, but could see no sign of either fugitive or pursuers.

'A Korean, I think,' commented Holmes. 'See how neatly he placed his feet? There's scarcely a shred of glass left in the frame, and I'll swear he hasn't a scratch on him. We were armed and ready – but no match for an adept in the martial art of *taekwondo*.' The admiration in his voice was undisguised, and, more or less as an afterthought, he added: 'Are you hurt?'

'Just winded,' I said shakily. 'It was only a glancing blow, or I believe he would have smashed my ribs.'

In the excitement of the encounter, I had forgotten the purpose with which our assailant had come. But now, with a thrill of apprehension, I remembered. He had brought something. *What?* I spun around from the window, my eyes searching anxiously – then laughed in nervous relief at the harmlessly absurd sight of half a dozen white mice scampering frantically in a large wire cage. But as my gaze turned to the wardrobe and I saw that which had crept out from behind it, the laugh died on my lips.

Half hidden in the angle of shadow between the wardrobe and the wall lay a thing like an enormous slug, nearly two feet in length, its beady skin banded and patterned in blotches of blackish brown and yellow. It waddled out into the light on ungainly legs, switching a short, thick tail, and raised a blunt-snouted reptilian head with eyes like beads of jet and a questing tongue.

'Hold still, Petrie!' said Holmes quietly.

With soft, gliding steps, he moved across the carpet, stooped, and, to my consternation struck at the creature with his forearm. In a flash, clumsy though it seemed, it darted, closing viselike jaws six inches above his wrist and holding on. Holmes bounded upright, threw up his arm with the fearful thing dangling from it, and dashed its bloated body three times against the window sill, till it fell broken and writhing upon the floor.

'My God! Has it bitten you?' I cried – for the very look of it convinced me that it was poisonous.

'Well, it has damaged a good overcoat,' replied Holmes calmly, unfastening his cuff-link. Pulling up his shirtsleeve, he inspected an ugly red mark on his arm. 'Good! The skin is not punctured. I did not think it would be able to penetrate a leather coat and a Harris tweed jacket, or I should not have ventured to tackle it as I did. It is a Gila monster, a native of the Arizona desert, and, as you saw, it is tenacious. It *chews* to inject the poison, and, although its bite is rarely fatal, it might have had me on my back for some days.' He rolled down his cuff and re-fastened it. 'They put it in his bed, of course. But they could not rely on it to kill him.'

I stared with loathing at the garishly hued shape twitching feebly on the carpet, and Holmes, glancing at it likewise, gave a shudder of disgust.

'It is still alive,' he muttered distastefully. 'But even a venomous reptile should not be left to suffer.'

He drew his pistol and, to the detriment of our eardrums, fired a shot at close quarters – a curious sidelight on the character of a man whom many might have thought callous.

'Let's go downstairs,' I said, finding to my shame that I was trembling. 'I've had enough of it up here.'

Holmes nodded silently and unlocked the door. We walked along the passage and, at the top of the stairs, met Inspector Beynon pounding up, recalled to the house by the sound of the explosion.

'What's going on?' he panted.

'I have shot a lizard,' answered Holmes shortly.

Leaving our Welsh colleague to make what he might of this useful information, he descended to the hall and collapsed into an armchair, all the nervous energy drained out of him.

Sergeant Lloyd appeared at the open front door.

'No luck,' he reported sorrowfully. 'I think he had a motorbike hidden somewhere. I heard one.'

'Well, come in, then, and shut the door,' said Beynon philosophically. 'It's getting chilly. Where the devil did he come from, Mr Holmes?'

'From the bathroom.' Taking out his cherrywood and his tobacco pouch, Holmes began preparations for his first pipe since our arrival. 'Their plumber – who was actually a carpenter – took down one of the plaster boards, and hinged it to make a rudimentary trap-door. The Korean has been up there all day, crammed into the narrow space between the ceiling joists and the roof slope – and still he had all that strength! You tell the inspector the rest of it, Petrie.'

Whilst he filled and lighted his pipe and lay back in his chair, eyes half closed, in an attitude of recuperation, I did my best to narrate our adventures upstairs. But when I had done, much remained lacking, and I turned back helplessly to Holmes.

'They put the lizard under the sheets at the foot of the bed,' he said wearily. 'It is a tropical creature and hunts by night. It would stay there torpid, so long as the room was cold, until Sir Julian touched it with his foot, whereupon it bit him, of course. The rest was a foregone conclusion. Finding himself gripped by the teeth of a monstrosity such as he had never seen, and probably never heard of, what would any man do but tear himself loose and run for his life?

'The Korean was at that time hiding in the cupboard. If, on returning to the bedroom after Sir Julian had fallen, he had been able to secure the lizard immediately, he would no doubt have done so and escaped. But by then, as he had expected, it had crawled behind some piece of furniture, and would not emerge until the room became warm and its peculiar sensory apparatus – which is not yet fully understood – told it that food was available. Hence the mousetrap, in which the mice were the bait!'

Pausing to re-light his pipe, which had gone out during this recital, Sherlock Holmes fixed me with a wintry eye.

'Your examination of the body was adequate from a

medical standpoint, but superficial. I should have checked it myself. But I admit that, until we came upon the bloodstains in the corridor, it had never occurred to me that the victim might have received a *third* injury. Luckily, the body had not been removed, and I was able to rectify my error while you were ministering to the housemaid. In addition to the deep cuts on the right foot, made by a sharp-edged instrument, I found jagged wounds close to the heel, as if he had been bitten by a small dog. Discounting the dog as impossible in the circumstances, I could think of only one likely suspect, and I was right – though, in view of your insistence that Fu Manchu has creatures unknown to Western science, I retained an open mind.'

He ceased speaking and glanced around at our faces, like a lecturer inviting questions, but we shook our heads – a silent but approving audience of two police officers and myself. Despite the noise of the fracas upstairs and Holmes's pistol shot, neither the staff nor her ladyship chose to put in an appearance. They had, I surmised, had more than enough excitement the previous night.

'By damn!' said Inspector Beynon in an awed voice. 'I never heard the like of it!'

'Well, I suppose we have taken the first step,' replied Holmes morosely. 'At least, we now know that we are dealing with Dr Fu Manchu. But, apart from that, I'm afraid we have accomplished nothing but to learn how Sir Julian died – which interests not even his widow – and destroy a fine specimen of *Heloderma* which the Regent's Park Zoo would no doubt have appreciated.'*

* 'Venomous lizard or Gila. Remarkable case, that!' This remark is ascribed to Holmes during his handling of The Sussex Vampire mystery, which occurred in 1896 but was not made public until the mid-1920's, so that I think Watson has it out of context. [Ed.]

11

PENTREFDU

'Confound it!' remarked Holmes, contracting his eyebrows in a prodigious scowl. 'I have been studying those two men at the next table for the past ten minutes, and still I am unable to tell what their profession is. Of what use is my work on the influence of a trade upon the hands, in this machine age, where there are no trades? If I deduce from the flattening of a man's right thumb that he spends his life pressing a button, how am I to know what the button does?'

Some hours had passed since our adventures at Sir Julian Rossiter's house, and we sat now over the remains of a combined breakfast and lunch in the dining room of a commercial hotel in Merthyr Tydfil. Here, to the discontent of the management, Inspector Beynon had deposited us at four o'clock in the morning, and we had slept till midday, our further investigations having produced only the murderous device stuffed into the Korean's hiding place above the bathroom ceiling. This, almost exactly as Holmes had predicted, proved to consist of a piece of strong canvas armed with razor- edged strips of broken glass, sticky with a vegetable poison, which, later, defied analysis.

Sherlock Holmes, saying little throughout our somewhat indifferent meal, had lapsed into a mood of self-critical depression – his usual state after an inquiry which had ended less successfully than he had hoped.

'Even you cannot be omniscient,' I said, endeavouring to arouse him. 'Forget those two over there, who are of no possible significance to us, and try the man on our left. He looks harmless enough too, but I notice that he glances persistently in our direction.'

Holmes turned his head briefly and sniffed contemptuously.

'Oh, he is not looking at us, but at the clock on the wall behind us. He is a ledger clerk, scared of being back late at the office because he has spent part of his lunch hour in buying birthday presents for the twins.'

'Capital!' I said, smiling. 'And now tell me how you know it.'

He burst into a laugh, and I saw that my stratagem had been effective.

'Well, of course, the man carries two fountain pens. Only in book-keeping does one need both red and black ink in large quantity, and he cannot hold any more senior position than that of a ledger clerk, since he is nervous of his employers and poorly dressed. His right coat sleeve is worn below the elbow, where he brushes it on the edge of the desk, and it has been neatly darned, which suggests a peaceful domestic life. The two small parcels on the table beside him, tied with ribbon and wrapped with the printed paper of a local toyshop, can only be presents for children. One would hardly give presents in February other than for a birthday, and why two identical parcels from the same shop, unless they are for twins?'

Having cleared the air, so to speak, by this preliminary exercise, Holmes plunged a hand into his pocket and produced a pipe – this, I was happy to note, being the well-worn briar. He loaded it carefully, struck a match, and, without further prompting, continued:

'The question which we have now to consider is *why* Sir Julian Rossiter was killed. Fu Manchu is a madman who aims at nothing less than the destruction of the British Empire – more even than that, the elimination of all Western influence from Asia. His organisation, the Si Fan, is unlike the majority of secret societies, which murder for profit and revenge. The Si Fan seek to kill only those who possess some knowledge dangerous to their ends, and kidnap those possessed of specialised skills which they wish to acquire. Nayland Smith appears, recently, to have been added to the latter category. But Sir Julian belonged to neither. He was, by all accounts, an obnoxious man. But why was he obnoxious to Dr Fu Manchu?'

116

'I confess that I cannot imagine.'

'If he held some dangerous secret, he can only have learned it by accident, and probably remained unaware of it himself. Hence it will be doubly difficult for us to learn.'

The lunch hour was rapidly drawing to a close, and I became aware of a concerted movement towards the door. Holmes, noticing it also, took it as a cue, and folding his napkin, threw it on the table.

'Let us postpone further discussion,' he said. 'I have some telephoning to do, and I propose to do it from the post office, where the wires go straight into the main cable. I doubt whether Fu Manchu yet knows exactly where we are, but we will take no chances. That slippery Korean acrobat will certainly have reported us.'

'Do you intend to get in touch with Inspector Weymouth?'

'Yes. We must find out what – if anything – has been happening in London. At the same time, since we now feel sure that Fu Manchu is here, Weymouth must see to it that every police officer west of the Severn is warned to keep a sharp lookout for suspicious-looking Orientals, and, particularly, the doctor himself – if he is ever unwise enough to show himself on the street.' Holmes smiled a trifle satirically. 'A tall, green-eyed Chinaman must be something of a rarity. What is your classic phrase, Petrie? "A brow like Shakespeare and a face like Satan." Dear me!'

'He wears tinted spectacles and disguises himself as a European,' I said. 'You are as tall as he is, and your forehead is nearly as high.'

'Nearly?' countered Holmes, with a frown. 'Well, I suppose, in the case of Fu Manchu, some exaggeration is to be looked for. And, after all, Petrie, Shakespeare was bald!'

With this parting shot he left me and I sat for a while staring idly at my coffee cup, smiling a little at his colossal vanity. In any other man it would have been the merest conceit, yet his superiority in all that he claimed was so far indisputable as to have made humility ridiculous. Leaving a shilling for the morose waiter, who was now clearing up ths débris of lunch and clearly wanted the place empty, I transferred myself to the adjoining parlour – a musty-smelling room, forlornly appointed with chintz-covered furniture.

By a process of trial and error, I selected the least lumpy of the armchairs and sat down, having no more to do, for the present, than to wait for Holmes's return with as much patience as I could command. A tall clock behind my left shoulder ticked loudly and solemnly, marking off the irrevocable seconds of my life – seconds while Nayland Smith and Kâramanèh lay prisoners in the hands of Fu Manchu and I did nothing. The local newspaper with its gloomy predictions of another coal strike failed to hold my attention. Drawing an envelope from my pocket, I took out of it the fragmentary remains of Smith's letter and, for the hundredth time, studied the words he had underlined.

Obviously, they were garbled and out of sequence. I wondered vaguely if the horror we had seen last night could have been the *worm*, and decided that it could not. The *worm* was yet to come – to say nothing of the *thirty thousand bicycles*. Time slipped into the past while I sat staring stupidly at those few typewritten phrases – the last I had had from my old friend, and the last, perhaps, that I should ever have.

The mournful clock emitted a hideous gobbling sound and struck the hour. Sherlock Holmes had been absent longer than I expected, but a few minutes later came in, glanced at the paper in my hand, and shrugged.

'Put it away,' he said, and sat down beside me. 'We have enough on our hands already.'

'You have spoken to Inspector Weymouth?' I asked.

'Yes. They have got nothing useful from the man Morley, who was watching us in Fleet Street. He is a so-called private investigator – one of those blackguards who defile the profession I created – and does not know who engaged him. Morley has the nerve to claim that it is not illegal to look out of one's window – and he has been paid through the post.'

'But how did he make his reports?'

'By a means which even I had not anticipated.' Holmes laughed shortly. 'By a small wireless transmitter, operated by an assistant, whom I could not see from the road – a young man who is, in fact, a licenced amateur. Neither, of course, has any idea where their messages were received. But here is something even more fantastic: *Nothing* was connected to your telephone wires! Somehow, your calls were picked up likewise on some kind of wireless set. * They have it at Scotland Yard, but have not been able to make anything of it. Morley, by the way, says that the watch was kept only during daylight hours and denies any knowledge of the incident which led to Smith's abduction. At night, I suppose, the Si Fan had relays of their own men on the job, probably working from the street.'

He paused for a moment, then turned towards me with a significant gleam in his eyes

'However, Inspector Weymouth has been active in other directions. Listen to this, Petrie! He has found a ticket collector at Paddington station who actually remembers the arrival of a curious trio last Monday afternoon – a tall man and a short, oddly misshapen man, both of them Asiatics, accompanied by a woman covered from head to foot in traditional Moslem garments, who seemed to be ill.'

'Kâramanèh!' I exclaimed. 'And the two men whose presence you detected in our apartment! Then this must be where they came from!'

'From the west, anyway, and the inference is plain. Fu Manchu was here then, and a report of Smith's telephone call to you was submitted to him – quite likely by wireless, since they seem to use this medium – acting upon which, he immediately despatched his task force. He may even have done so in order to forestall action by Ki Ming, if, as you say, there is some rivalry between them.'

* Fu Manchu evidently anticipated the Watergate incident by sixty years. [Ed.]

'Do you think that they brought Smith back here?' I asked quickly.

'There is at least that possibility,' he replied cautiously. 'If so, that might explain why they were anxious to gain time. They could not transport him by train, and to carry an unconscious man two hundred miles by road would probably have to be done in several stages, with judicious changes of vehicles on the way. Furthermore, since they were acting in an emergency, they were not prepared for such an operation.'

Despite the tentative manner in which he spoke, I felt a sense of relief, knowing that Holmes was rarely optimistic. Not the least of my worries had been that while we searched for Fu Manchu in one part of the country, Smith might lie captive in another, but now – unreasonably, perhaps – I felt confident that we were on the right track.

'Now for some less satisfying news,' continued Holmes, giving me a peculiarly self-conscious look – an expression which I thought quite foreign to him. 'The fact is that certain matters which have no connection with this case make it imperative for me to go back to London at once.'

'Go back?' I exclaimed.

'Oh, I am not deserting you!' he answered hastily, and still, it seemed, with some embarrassment. 'I shall go up by the night train, and be with you again – let me see; to-day is Wednesday – by Saturday morning at the latest.' He hesitated, then added slowly and in a curiously low voice, 'You have my word for it that I will not withdraw from this case before Smith is set at liberty, but, meanwhile, it may occasionally be necessary for me to attend to personal affairs. I beg of you to ask me no more, Petrie, for I cannot answer you.'

Startled, I looked directly into his eyes, and, for the first time, understood much that had puzzled me: the odd little details which, somehow, had seemed incongruous in a man ten years retired from practice.

'That is good enough for me, Holmes,' I said firmly, and, ignoring his distaste for such dramatic gestures, grasped his hand.

'Thank you,' he replied simply, and the mask of gravity

vanished from his face. 'Well, during my absence, you will remain in the field, and there is no need for you to be idle. I suggest that you stay here to-night, and to-morrow morning assist our friend Inspector Beynon to make out his report – which he finds himself quite unable to do. In the afternoon, you will go to Pentrefdu.'

'Where is that?'

'The village where the late Sir Julian's coal mining business is situated – which, by the way, is nowhere near his house but in another of these wretched valleys. There you may carry out a reconnaissance until I am able to rejoin you.'

'What am I to look for?'

'For anything of a suspicious nature in connection with this mine. I am convinced that there were no secrets in Sir Julian's private life – he was, on the contrary, disgustingly frank in all his misbehaviour. Therefore, any connection with Fu Manchu can only be, in some way, through his business.'

'But how?'

Holmes smiled sardonically. 'That is what you must try to ascertain! Work which goes on literally under-ground surely lends itself to suspicion. Beynon is making arrangements for you. There is an inn, but no accommo-dation, at Pentrefdu, and, in any case, no ordinary tourist would go there. You will stay with the local police constable – ostensibly as a cousin visiting him from England. Walk around the place, keep your eyes open, and get into conversation with the villagers. But, above all, be circumspect. Ask nothing and do nothing which a casual visitor might not do. If Fu Manchu has interests there, the least slip on your part could be fatal.'

So it was decided and, for the time being, we divided forces. Holmes departed on his 'personal' business – the true nature of which I was not to learn until years later – and the following morning, I spent two hours at the police station with Owen Beynon, attempting to compile an officially acceptable report from such unlikely mate-rial as poisoned glass, a superhuman Korean, and a venomous lizard. We lunched together and then, with my suitcase once more in my hand, I set out for my next destination, not altogether sorry to leave Merthyr Tydfil behind me. My experiences in Wales had, so far, not been pleasant, and, I might add, conspired to give me a false impression of a people whom I soon came to know as among the most generous and warm-hearted I have ever visited.

The nature of the terrain made it necessary to approach Pentrefdu by a circuitous route, involving a change of buses. It was late afternoon, and the narrow valley lay half in shadow, when the second deposited me at the lower end of the solitary village street. My first impressions were still somewhat unfavourable. Apart from a church with a squat stone tower, a general store, and an inn called The Three Feathers, the place consisted of two parallel rows of slate-roofed hovels built wall to wall, so that they rose in a series of steps on either side of the steeply sloping street – the whole effect that of a city slum transplanted in the country.

Meeting no one on the way – for the village seemed deserted – I climbed the hill and, at the top, found a somewhat larger cottage, detached from the rest, with a neat garden in front. I approached, knocked, and had the door opened to me immediately by a man of about my own age, in shirtsleeves and police uniform trousers. He glanced quickly at my suitcase and smiled a welcome.

'Why, it's Tom, isn't it?' he cried. 'How's Mary and the three kids?' – which, I thought, was overdoing it a bit. 'Clara!' he shouted. 'Tom's here!'

Grinning broadly, PC Jones dragged me inside with a muscular arm, and the next ten minutes went by in a turmoil of family hospitality such that I began to wonder if he really though he had a 'cousin from England.' I was introduced to his wife, thrust into an armchair, slippers found for me, and a teacup put into my hand. A large cat ambled up, sniffed interrogatively at my trouser legs, and settled itself on my lap. Whilst Clara – a cheerfully plain woman whose buxsom condition suggested an anticipated addition to the Jones clan – bustled about laying the table for tea, my host sat opposite me and talked about football, leaving me to broach the subject of my mission.

This I felt strangely reluctant to do in the pleasant sense of somnolence induced by the fire blazing in the grate and the cat purring on my knees. However, when at length I voiced suspicions about mining operations at Pentrefdu, Jones shook his head.

'It's coal, all right,' he said, and, picking up a brass poker, pointed. 'There it is. Good stuff, too.' He stabbed with the poker, and a burst of sparks went up the chimney. 'See how it burns? Dry and fiery, it is – the best in Europe, and dangerous as the devil. You'd be safer working in a powder mill than down there where that comes from.'

I nodded, vaguely recalling newspaper reports of a disaster which, not so long ago, had shocked all England.

'You had a bad business up here last year, didn't you?'

'Senghenydd, you mean. Yes – nearly five hundred lives they lost there.' PC Jones stared reflectively into the dancing flames. 'But it's Nant Gareth, five miles up the road, that we remember here. Fifteen years ago, that was, and only a hundred and seventy-eight gone that time – but not a family in this village now that didn't lose somebody.' He was silent for a moment, then added quietly, 'My father was one of them.'

Thus commenced what I might call my introduction to life and death in the coalfields of South Wales. I did not go out again that evening, but spent most of it talking to Jones, and a part of it with my thumbs up, assisting Mrs Jones to wind wool. My acquired relatives retired early and I followed suit, to sleep in the Sybaritic luxury of a huge feather bed which, together with a wash stand, occupied nearly the whole floor space of their tiny spare room.

The sun was shining brightly when, after a hearty breakfast, I walked down the hill next morning. Perhaps it was the weather, or perhaps the genial hospitality of my hosts, but, whatever the cause, my reactions to my surroundings were undergoing a subtle change and I felt almost light-hearted. I noted now that the horrible little houses on either side of the road were impeccably clean, each with a well-scrubbed doorstep and a glowing brass knocker.

At the foot of the hill, I found the ladies of Pentrefdu gathered about the bus stop and the general store. Several of them were speaking Welsh, and if anything further had been needed to give me the impression of a land far distant from my native England, their overall appearance would have provided it. All wore scarves over their heads and two carried babies as I had never seen babies carried before – bundled up against one hip and bound firmly to the bearer by a shawl swathed diagonally from the opposite shoulder.

Entering the store, on the pretext of buying cigarettes and matches, I experienced no difficulty in starting a conversation with the shopkeeper, and whilst I lingered, pretending to examine postcards, some of the house-wives joined in. A terse paragraph in the Cardiff daily paper had announced the death of Sir Julian Rossiter, attributed simple to 'a fall.' Rather unexpectedly, I discovered that none of the people to whom I talked had ever seen him – apparently he had visited his property only upon rare occasions. No one expressed either sorrow or satisfaction at his demise. It was generally assumed that his successor – I knew this to be Lady Elinor, but did not say so – would continue to operate the mine as heretofore.

'But, maybe,' one of the younger women said hopefully, 'they'll listen to reason and won't have no more to do with his wicked ideas.'

This sounded a shade more promising, but before I could find a discreet means of inquiring what Sir Julian's 'wicked ideas' might have been, a bus came in bearing a sign which said that it was going to Cwmbwlch (how did they pronounce *that*, I wondered), and she rushed out of the shop to get on it.

A half mile beyond the church and the last of the houses, I came upon the entrance to the colliery. From the road, nothing more was to be seen than an iron gate and a sort of sentry box tenanted by a gatekeeper. Remembering Holmes's injunction to be, above all, circumspect, I made no attempt to enter – for I could think of no plausible excuse for such a visit. Instead, I continued on for a few hundred yards, searching the steeply rising ground to my left for a footpath which would bring me to the top of the ridge, whence I might look down upon the premises. Soon enough I found one, and, toiling up through a screen of pine and fir trees, presently found myself on a narrow strip of tableland skirting one wall of the canyon – since such it was – in which Pentrefdu was situated.

My immediate object was achieved, but, to my surprise, there was actually little to see. The visible portion of the late Sir Julian's mining concern consisted only of a few buildings grouped about the skeletal steel towers and huge wheels of the winding gear. Knowing nothing about the subject, and never having really thought about it until now, I became only gradually aware that, apart from some hand sorting and cleaning, there was nothing more to be done with the coal once it reached the surface. All the real activity was going on belowground.

Sitting down on a flat outcrop of rock, I lighted my pipe and watched for about half an hour, during which I saw two or three heavy trucks driven in empty and driven out loaded. That was all. I stood up, and, telling myself that since there was nothing of a more detailed nature to be learned I would do better to gain a more general picture of the locality, turned my face north and continued to climb.

For all my earnest intentions, my walk was turning into the kind of country holiday that it was supposed to be. The weather was delightful and it seemed to me that spring was already here. PC Jones had told me that the climate in these parts, generally milder than that of southern England, was even less predictable, often with flowers blooming unseasonally in December, while, occasionally, March might end in a tropical heat wave surpassing the later temperatures of July. The higher I climbed, the harder it became, when I looked back, to think of this as a centre of industry. To the stranger, the panorama of steep, often densely wooded hillsides appeared to be virgin land, with here and there the cultivated fields of a few small farms.

It was difficult to believe that the hand of Fu Manchu lay upon this outwardly fair prospect – difficult to remember that beneath it all (how far beneath, I had then no idea), men slaved and sweated for a pittance, in dirt and danger, gambling health and lives in a toil fit only for convicts.

I cannot pretend that I accomplished anything more useful that day, or that I much endeavoured. Before me, in the distance, rose the summits of the Brecon Beacons – low enough in comparison with the Swiss Alps, yet rugged and unreal-looking to one accustomed only to the gentle hills of the south-east, like a painted backdrop in a theatre. I gave myself over to their lure and tramped on northwards, not that I seemed to come any nearer, since they seemed to retreat as I walked, leaving me always amid grassy, rock-strewn slopes where black-faced sheep grazed and wandered at will.

After a bread-and-cheese lunch at a fortuitous inn, I continued my walk all that afternoon, returning to Pentrefdu only as the shadows were falling. Here, as I trudged up the hill to the police cottage, I saw my first miners returning home from a day shift, clad still in their rough pit clothes, basin-shaped helmets on their heads, and their faces as black as those of the sheep on the hills above. I thought with a shiver of what my host had said the previous night: '. . . the coal dust – it gets into your clothes, and your skin, and your hair, and no way to get clean but a tin bath in the living-room and kettles boiled on the fire.' But, oddly as it appeared to me, though they looked weary, these grimy toilers seemed quite cheerful, their broad grins and flashing teeth lending them an extraordinary resemblance to black-face minstrels in a seaside show.

Even the constable's cottage possessed no bathroom. Having washed off the travel stains of the day with the aid of the china jug and bowl in my cupboardlike bedroom, I sat down to an evening meal with my Welsh friends – already, I found it impossible to think of them otherwise – and rested for a while. Relaxed and comfortably tired from my long walk, I felt rather disinclined to go out again, but duty called. Sherlock Holmes had promised to be back with me by the following morning, and, so far, I had nothing of any value to report to him. I doubted, in fact, if there was anything to be learned – the mine seemed clearly enough a legitimate operation – but to-night at The Three Feathers would be my first and only opportunity of making contact with some of the men who worked underground.

The evening was still reasonably warm, and, abandoning my overcoat in favour of a sweater, since I did not want to appear to well dressed in such a place, I re-descended the hill, finding my way by my pocket torch and the guiding lights of lace-curtained windows to either side. A blanket of low cloud hid the stars, and distantly, beyond the crests of the mountains, an eerie red glare spread upwards from the blast furnaces of the Dowlais ironworks. I heard voices ahead and followed in the wake of two men bound for the same destination as myself. At the foot of the hill, where a lantern crudely painted with a fleur-de-lys hung above the doorway of the local hostelry, they turned in and I entered a pace behind them.

A babel of noise greeted me, for the place was crowded. I remembered suddenly that Friday was pay-day. Although no more than thirty or forty people were there, the room was barely large enough to accommodate them, the atmosphere was thick with tobacco smoke and reeking with the stale fumes of fourpenny ale. So far as I could see, no women were present. Apart from two benches against the walls, there seemed to be no furniture, and the drinkers were mostly standing – all of them big, tough-looking men with the leathery skin and unnaturally pale faces of miners.

Assuming, since I could not see it, that the bar was behind them, I pushed my way through, doing my best to avoid stepping on toes and jogging elbows. Directly in front of the counter, where the press was greatest, a tight knot of half a dozen with their backs to me barred further progress. With a word of apology, I persevered, and, squeezing in between them, found to my astonishment that they surrounded a girl who sat on a high stool with her brightly striped skirt draped audaciously over the back, so that it hung down nearly to the floor. She wore an embroidered blouse with short, wide sleeves, and a mass of frizzy black hair covered her shoulders.

I gasped and stepped back, attempting to retreat, but already too late – for, at the same moment, she turned her head and I stared full into the beautiful, evil face of Zarmi the Eurasian.

12

A CARESS FROM SALOME

Recognition was instant and mutual.

'*You!*' she snarled. 'Why you follow me about?'

'I was *not* following you – ' I began, thrown momentarily on the defensive by the sheer effrontery of her challenge, then broke off as the absurdity of the situation dawned upon me. 'You have no right to make complaints,' I said curtly. 'You know as well as I do that you are wanted by the police.'

Zarmi's lips curled in a scornful smile, and she shrugged with the lazy, feline grace of a cat arching its back.

'You got your policemans here?' she inquired pointedly.

'Here, what's this?' demanded a rough voice at my elbow, and a hand seized my arm.

I turned, attempting without success to wrench myself free, and saw that I was hemmed in by the men behind me, some of whom had apparently been talking to her before my arrival. Their faces were angry and hostile, and I realised then that Zarmi had not come here alone. Five or six, at least, were her companions, and what her relations might be with the rest in this crowded room I had no means of knowing.

'Take your hands off me!' I said hotly, clenching my fists, but, even as I did so, recognising the futility of the gesture.

Help came from an unexpected quarter.

'Yes – leave him go!' snapped Zarmi. 'I take care of myself, see!'

With a quick flip of her skirt and a flash of ivory thigh, she snatched out the Malay *kris* of which I had dreadful memories, tossed it high in the air, so that it turned over and over as it fell, the lamplight glittering on the serpentine blade, and caught it deftly by the hilt. The innkeeper, whose nose it had narrowly missed, started back visibly.

'Hey! You put that thing away!' he muttered.

Zarmi laughed softly and huskily. 'Nobody get hurt. We all good friends here.' Displaying her black silk stockings to advantage, she slipped the knife unhurriedly back into its shagreen sheath, and cast a glance around the circle of her champions. 'You push off now, while I talk my friend. Later, maybe, I dance for you. You like, eh?'

Grumbling, but obedient as sheep dogs, they retreated a few paces to merge with the general throng, and she turned towards me, her almond-shaped eyes lustrous with Satanic amusement.

'You want to be friends? All right – I buy you a drink!'

She was intoxicated, I thought – though less with alcohol than with the joy of knowing herself inviolate, knowing that she held this band of simple, hard-bitten men in her thrall, fascinating and, perhaps, frightening them a little, as surely as I had seen her dominate the dregs of London's waterfront at John Ki's. Here I was alone and a stranger. Here I had no raiding party of Thames river police awaiting my summons. This was no Limehouse den of half-caste gamblers and opium smokers – yet what chance did I have of making these people understand that this woman was a trusted lieutenant of the Chinesse fiend whose shadow, unbeknown to them, lay upon their peaceful valley?

Zarmi extracted half a crown from a purse of hand-worked Egyptian leather, and banged it down on the counter.

'Rum and water!' she shouted, and laughed in my face. 'That what you drink at the joy-shop, eh? my big, strong sailorman!'

It pleased her to make fun of me by recalling the disguise in which I had visited that unsalubrious establishment. Controlling my temper with an effort, I endured her raillery, and wondered if, by guile, I might not even yet gain something from her recklessness. The man behind the bar – a corpulent individual in a striped apron and greasy waistcoat – pushed a glass across to me, eyeing us warily. I picked it up and, confronting Zarmi with a forced smile upon my lips, raised the glass in a mocking salute.

'*Fîh sahittik*!' I said. 'Old friends, or old enemies – what does it matter here?' I sipped a little of the potent spirit, regarding her fixedly, then added suddenly: 'Where is Nayland Smith?'

She started, evidently taken aback, but recovered herself quickly.

'Why I tell you anything?' she retorted.

'Why not?' I said lightly. 'Since you hold all the cards, what can you lose?'

Zarmi frowned, biting her lip. She snapped open her purse and, from a lacquered case, took out one of the thick yellow cigarettes which I had seen her smoke before. From what Sherlock Holmes had said, I guessed now that they contained *hashîsh*.

'Give me a light!' she ordered.

I struck a match and held it, remembering her pleasant trick of blowing smoke in one's eyes, and keeping my face averted. But, attempting nothing of the sort this time, she sat smoking silently for a moment, inhaling deeply and expelling the smoke lazily through her nostrils.

'I don't know where he is,' she said sullenly. 'I don't see him.'

'Very well,' I said, disappointed, but determined to continue the attack. 'Then tell me about Kâramanèh.'

'Oh, I see *her*!' Zarmi laughed wickedly with vicious enjoyment. 'She make big fight in train coming back – bite through Wang Lo's ear. But 'Ali, who is once master of the *harêm* in Istanbul, make plenty sorry later. She get the *mikra'ah** – here and here.'

She raised her hands suggestively and I flushed with outrage. At that moment there was nothing I would have liked better than to seize her by the throat and choke the

---

* The dried stem of a palm leaf, traditionally used for corporal punishment in the Middle East. [Ed.]

smile from her face, but, at the same time, I realised that I had gained something. I knew now that Kâramanèh had been brought back from London, and, even though mistreated, was alive.

'But you know nothing of Smith?' I insisted.

'You never see him again,' came the curt reply. 'He go China.'

China! For one timeless instant, the smiling face of Zarmi, the room and all its occupants, faded from my sight and, with a visionlike clarity, I saw only those few typewritten words: 'a Chinese ship . . . hanging around off the west . . .' Had they already taken him aboard? Had the ship already sailed?

A renewed hubbub in my immediate vicinty brought me back to my senses. Zarmi's entourage, impatient and mistrustful of our conversation, were clamouring about her again, demanding her attention and urging her to dance – though where she was to do it in this room packed to capacity was more than I could imagine.

'All right!' she yelled. 'Shut up, you noisy fellers! I dance, and then we go home.'

She leapt up, threw her cigarette on the floor, ground it out with her heel, and kicked off her shoes. Then, seizing me by the arms, she pushed me down upon the stool she had just vacated.

'Sit there and watch!' she commanded. 'You mind this for me!'

With a quick grab, she jerked up the hem of my sweater and thrust her leather purse down deep under my belt, to the accompaniment of raucous jeers from her henchmen. Someone thumped me violently on the back and roared beery pleasantries in my ear. Zarmi turned, placed her hands flat on the counter, sprang lithely upon it, and stood upright with her head only inches removed from the smoke-blackened beams of the low ceiling. Administering a monstrous kick to a half-emptied tankard at her feet, she sent it sailing across the room, where it struck a man in the chest, to the loud delight of all but the recipient and the man whose pint it was. Amid further delight, she began to remove her stockings.

'You'll 'ave the law on us!' complained the corpulent innkeeper uneasily. 'Somebody put the bolt on the door!'

'*Plisman* Jones better keep his long nose out of here!' roared back another voice, and more laughter followed.

Zarmi, having disposed of her stockings and other somewhat personal items,* unfastened her blouse, clapped her hands smartly, and started to dance, at the same time singing in the harsh, nasal Arabic of the desert.

> *Habayibna-lli hebbouna*
> *A'emelou qahwah w'a'ezemouna.*
> *A'ezemouna wa segouna!*
> *Habayibna-lli yehebbouna!*

Twice she repeated the same simple refrain, and on the third repetition, the whole room burst into song, whether imitating her words or inventing words of their own, I have no idea. They might never have heard it before, yet, with the ancient genius of their race, these rough, labouring men who knew nothing of formal music orchestrated her song in four-part harmony and improvised cadences till the crude Bedawi melody was transformed into a paean of glory such as Handel might have composed, had his sympathies lain with Islam.

This, indeed, was a far cry from the Cafè de l'Egypte, where I had watched Zarmi dance, lithe and luresome, to the wailing reed pipes and throbbing *darabukkeh*, and had thought of el-Wasr. Through the smoke-laden atmosphere, I looked up at her now, whirling on her narrow stage like Nouronihar in the Halls of Eblis, her face half-hidden in the cloud of her long black hair, her skirt swirling about her waist, her blouse flying open. The light of the oil-lamps gleamed on the dusky pallor of her skin and struck fire from the jewelled hilt of the knife strapped above her knee. Over the chanting voices, I heard the slap of her bare feet on the counter

---

* Dr Petrie's discretion sometimes borders upon the absurd. Presumably, her panties. [Ed.]

and the metallic chink of the bangles on her arms. I looked around at the circle of eager faces and burning eyes and thought, not of el-Wasr, but of some pirates' cave in Tortuga.

Adapting herself to her audience, Zarmi was dancing with the audacity of a *Gitane* rather than the languorous allure of a *Ghazeeyeh*, her rapid movements alternately revealing and concealing. To a bedlam of catcalls and shouts of enthusiasm, she aimed kicks at the ceiling, and bent backwards till her hair swept down over the counter's edge. Turning away from the room, she raised her skirt deliberately, and danced the length of the bar, offering insolent glimpses of her tigerish figure in the cracked mirror behind the shelves of glasses and bottles.

After the first few stanzas she left the song to her talented admirers, who no longer needed her lead. Over and over again they sang it, clapping their hands and stamping their feet. In Cairo, I have heard the same monotonous refrain of sixteen bars repeated for half an hour, but Zarmi's dancing did not go on that long. Coming suddenly to a standstill directly in front of me, she thrust back her disordered hair, and, with a piercing scream of ecstasy, like a *djinn* released from a bottle, launched herself off the bar – to come crashing down astride my knees with such force that, but for the press of the crowd at my back, I should have been hurled to the floor.

In the same instant, locking her hands behind my neck, Zarmi pulled me towards her and crushed her lips hard against mine. Shouts and laughter rocked the room. Still holding me fast in her embrace, the hot, suffocating perfume of her hair playing havoc with my senses, she slid her lips up to my ear.

'You follow me now,' she whispered, 'and they kill you!'

She leaned back, groped for her purse – which, frankly, I had forgotten – found it after subjecting me to further embarrassment, and stood up. Then, resuming her discarded apparel, she elbowed her way through the tempestuous throng, slapping off hands and spitting in faces, and went out, accompanied by her retinue.

It was impossible for me to see who, or how many, went out with her.

I doubted whether I was in any danger, but I felt equally sure that if I attempted to go after her, I should be good-naturedly but firmly prevented. With a face-saving show of nonchalance, I took out a cigarette, lighted it, picked up my drink – the same that she had paid for – and remained seated as I was, pretending unawareness of the grinning countenances and mis-chievous murmurings behind me. The harrassed inn-eeper produced a wet cloth and swabbed the counter top where Zarmi's immoderate efforts had brought down a fine powdering of soot from the ceiling.

Keeping an eye on my watch, I allowed five minutes to pass, then finished my drink and stood up. My fellow drinkers made way for me as I headed for the door and someone called a derisive 'Good night!' Outside, the night was black as pitch, save for the lighted windows leading up the hill, and, of course, there was no sign of Zarmi or her companions.

I stood for a moment in the circle of light beneath the lantern bearing the sign of The Three Feathers, thrusting my hands into my pockets and breathing deeply. As I did so, I became aware of approaching footsteps and glanced quickly to my right. The footsteps drew nearer, and a tall figure emerged out of the darkness.

'And what have you been up to now?' asked Sherlock Holmes.

MR QUIMBY OF WHITEHALL

'Holmes!' I exclaimed. 'I was not expecting you till the morning. Where have you come from?'

'From Brecon,' he replied. 'Jones told me that you had gone to the inn, and I came down after you. What has happened?'

As the light of the lantern fell fully upon him, I saw that his appearance had been altered by the addition of pince-nez and a small moustache, though insufficiently to render him unrecognisable to one who knew him. He wore a neat black overcoat and pin-stripe trousers, as if dressed for the City. But, without pausing to ask him the reason for these changes, I hastened into an excited recitation of my adventures inside The Three Feathers.

Holmes dashed his right fist into his left palm, in a gesture reminiscent of Nayland Smith.

'I had a feeling that something like this would occur! Our first real chance to make contact with the enemy, and you have lost it! Why, in Heaven's name, did you let her see you?'

'I was too close to her before I had any idea that she was there.'

Holmes groaned. 'I knew that I should not have left you alone! That is why I took the bus over here to-night, to have a word with you as soon as possible. If I had arrived only ten minutes earlier, I could have followed her.'

'Well, it can't be helped,' I said wearily. 'At least we know now that Fu Manchu must be somewhere near.'

'Near, perhaps – but she is not directly in touch with him. Remember that she was as much surprised to see you as you were to see her.' He took out his pocket watch and glanced at it. 'Walk over to the bus stop with me. I have a room in Brecon, and I must catch the last bus back.'

We crossed the road and stood in the shadows with our

backs to the shuttered window of the general store. No one else was waiting and we were able to continue our conversation without fear of being overheard.

'Our suspicions are confirmed in one respect,' remarked Holmes. 'There is something going on here, and it is something to do with the mining business. This impertinent woman is not one of the Doctor's more insidious weapons, but she is the manager of what we may call his casual labour force. She knows how to secure and control men for rough jobs. Clearly enough, she has been here before to-night. But, unfortunately, now that she knows you are here, she will not come back again.'

Three men emerged unsteadily from the doorway of the inn, and, arm in arm, went blundering up the hill, their voices raised in a reprise of Zarmi's song.

'Have you any further news from London?' I asked.

'No. I have had no opportunity to see Inspector Weymouth. As regards events in Sussex, I hear that the inquest on poor Benjamin has been held and an open verdict returned. What else could they do? Poor fellow! Thank Heaven he was as lonely as I and leaves no family to mourn him. He had been with me only six weeks. . . .' Holmes fell silent and I could visualise him shaking his head in the darkness. 'The builders are in the house,' he added, 'and have a thousand questions to ask, but I cannot be bothered with all that now. Brother Mycroft will have to see to it.'

I heard the click of a cigarette case, and the flare of a match lighted up Holmes's angular features, reminding me.

'Why have you adopted a disguise?' I inquired.

'It is not a disguise,' he replied, 'but only a change of identity. I am Mr Percival Quimby, a Government inspector of mines. Luckily, I had just sufficient time to obtain credentials from Whitehall.'

'You propose to visit Sir Julian's property?'

'Exactly. I had intended to do it in the morning, but I think now that I will leave it till the afternoon. We will try the inn at lunchtime, when the place will be quiet, and see if we can get any further information about the girl and her associates. You may expect me at about eleven.'

Shortly afterwards, the bus came in. Sherlock Holmes climbed aboard and departed, leaving me to walk back up the hill to PC Jones's cottage and a second night in my feather bed. But I passed it less peacefully than the first, my sleep haunted by nightmares which now included the blood-red lips and savage eyes of Zarmi the Eurasian.

True to his word, Holmes was back with us by eleven, and soon after midday we were tramping down the hill, bound for The Three Feathers, after deciding upon a simple plan of approach. Holmes, in his guise of the visitor from Whitehall, was to be a chance acquaintance not unnaturally intrigued by my story of Zarmi's immodest behaviour and anxious to learn if a repeat performance might be anticipated.

'You must do most of the talking.' he instructed, as we neared the entrance. 'But you know what to say.'

I nodded, and we went in.

At this hour of the day, we found ourselves the only customers. The same man, in the same greasy waistcoat, stood behind the bar and, over a glass of his own beer, proved quite willing to communicate.

'Ah, the gypsy girl!' he said – this being, evidently, how he interpreted Zarmi. 'In 'ere last week, she was – prancin' around up 'ere, an' no more on 'er than a string o' beads!'

This I took to be a poetic exaggeration.*

'Does she come in often?' I asked.

'No, praise be to the Lord, she don't,' came the quick answer. 'I never seen 'er but the three times – an 'the week before last, that was the first.'

'Do you know where she come from?' put in Holmes.

The innkeeper shook his head vigorously. 'Gypsies don't come from nowhere – an' I 'ope she soon goes back there. Dancin' shameful, an' singin' 'eathen songs

* Not necessarily. Dancing girls often performed naked in the palace of the Abbasside caliphs. [Ed.]

138

– an' 'oo knows what they might mean? Get my place a bad name, she will, so's respectable folk won't come 'ere.'

'Well,' I said reflectively, resisting the temptation to ask him when any ever had, 'I think she was singing something last night about drinking coffee.'

'Was she, now?' Regarding me with a puzzled and slightly suspicious air, he took a long drink from his tankard and removed the froth from his moustache with the back of his unoccupied hand.

'But she has friends here, doesn't she?' said Holmes quickly. 'The men who were here last night?'

'Aye, six of 'em, there was – six last night she brung 'ere, six last week, an' six the week before. Only I reckon they wasn't all the same ones, but I know they was six because they 'ad six pints, an' none of 'em don't come from around 'ere.'

'You don't know any of them, then?' I pursued.

'Well, I know two, an' t'others I never seen before, but there was Ivor Thomas an' Dan Fuller, an' a bright pair they are! Out of a job, an' not lookin' for none neither. Ivor's got a wife that takes in washin', an' 'ow 'is mate gets on, I'm sure I dunno.'

'Are they miners?'

'They was once, but not these past three years. Don't see much of 'em as a rule, but they both been in a lot lately. Got some money from somewhere, but I dunno 'ow. Been up to Bryn Coed an' thieved somebody's pig, I shouldn't wonder.'

Such was the extent of the useful information which we obtained at The Three Feathers. We stayed talking with the landlord for a while longer, and then made our retreat.

'More or less what we expected,' commented Holmes, as we came out into the sunlight. 'She is assembling a fixed number of workers for some job in the vicinity, which is probably done at weekends. But,' he went on severely, 'you should not have alarmed the man by letting him know that you spoke Arabic.'

'I don't,' I said gloomily. 'I have been trying to learn

some – you can guess why. But God knows if it will ever be any use.'

I suppose I looked so disconsolate that Sherlock Holmes ceased to reproach me and favoured me instead with one of his rare smiles of encouragement.

'You must not lose heart,' he said. 'The fight has only just begun. Who is looking after your property in Cairo?'

'Kâramanèh's brother, Azîz.'

'Good. Then you have nothing to worry about on that score, and we will have you there doctoring sunstrokes and sick stomachs before the season ends.' Holmes patted the official-looking briefcase which he was carrying, and laughed roguishly. 'Now I must go about Mr Quimby's business, and see what I can get out of them at the mine. I cannot take you with me, so you had better go back to the cottage and play draughts with Mrs Jones – or, better still, get out your Arabic grammar, if you have it with you, and study quadrilateral verbs. I will see you there presently.'

Back at the top of the hill, I found Clara Jones with her sleeves rolled up and her plump arms white with flour, busily preparing Christmas puddings for *next* Christmas – an operation, she explained, which should be done with the loving foresight of a vintner stocking his cellar.

These interludes when I had nothing specific to do were invariably the worst. I sat by the fire, trying vainly to lose myself in her homely talk, and ignoring Holmes's advice not only because I had packed no books but because, for nearly two months now, I had read nothing either for study or for entertainment.

Through the window, I saw PC Jones wheeling his bicycle up the garden, on the way back from his daily duties – consisting of what, I had little idea. As he sat down opposite me and began to unlace his boots, I glanced idly at the ornate silver chain on the helmet which he had put down on the dresser, at the other unfamiliar details of his county police uniform, and reflected on the wisdom of Great Britain in avoiding the kind of unified national police force which has so often become an instrument of political terror in other countries.

This being the first opportunity which I had had, I gave him a full account of the past night's doings at The Three Feathers and also of what we had just learned there. He replied that he knew both the men mentioned by the landlord – 'Wrong 'uns, both of them' – and tentatively suggested that we might put a watch on them in the hope that it would lead back to Zarmi.

'Possibly,' I said. 'But she has very likely thought of thah too, and will not employ them again.'

'Well,' said Jones, with a deep, Celtic sigh, 'if she's looking for desperate men to do some dirty work for her, she'll find them as easy around here as in your London's East End. Can you blame them? There's thousands of them worse off than slaves.'

'At least they have their freedom,' I protested. Kâramanèh was a slave, bought and paid for in the slave market at Mecca. . . .

'Freedom to starve!' he retorted contemptuously. 'When a slave owner loses a slave, he has to buy another one. A mine owner can throw a man out on the street, jobless and without a penny, get somebody else in, and not a brass farthing to lose by it.'

I smiled faintly. My host was a well-read man, with a bookshelf ranging from Marcus Aurelius to *The Wealth of Nations*, and a staunch supporter of Lloyd George, whom he confidently predicted as our next Prime Minister.

'But they have some insurance now, don't they?' I asked.

'Maybe enough to starve a bit slower – if they can get it!' PC Jones stared around at his books and shook his head sadly. 'And if they get more, where's it to end? If they ever get enough to make the job worth the risk, the price of coal will go sky high, and there's the finish of their jobs, and Cardiff docks into the bargain.'

A knock sounded at the door, and Mrs Jones hurried to open it. Sherlock Holmes stepped into the room, answering our greeting with a nod and a smile. He appeared to be in excellent spirits. Removing his townish overcoat, he threw it across a chair, took off his gold-rimmed pince-nez, and rubbed his nose ruefully.

'I wish I had chosen some other form of eyeglasses,' he remarked. 'These things are really quite agonising on a nose as thin as mine. No, no, Constable! I will not rob you of your chair.' He thrust PC Jones back into the armchair from which he had half risen. 'I will sit here.'

Pulling a deal chair out from the table, he turned it around and sat down between us. Clara Jones snatched up the ubiquitous teapot and made a bee-line for the kitchen.

'Well,' asked her husband, looking at Holmes, 'have you solved it?'

As the sole representative of local law and order, PC Jones was something of an independent, and treated him with the easy familiarity of a detective-inspector.

'Yes!' said Holmes, unexpectedly. 'It is not Pentrefdu. It is Nant Gareth.'

'Nant Gareth?' Jones looked surprised.

The name was vaguely familiar to me – and then, meeting his gaze, I remembered. This was the nearby mine of which he had told me on my first night in the village – the mine where his father had been killed.

'Nant Gareth has been closed for fifteen years,' he said slowly.

'But what has this place to do with Sir Julian Rossiter?' I inquired.

'He bought the property three months ago.'

'What!' cried Jones. 'He intended to re-open it?'

'Yes. Pentrefdu is no longer a profitable concern. They are down to working seams less than two feet wide.'

My Welsh 'cousin' nodded thoughtfully. 'There's coal enough in Nant Gareth,' he said, 'and like to stay there, too. He couldn't have realised the difficulties. The reputation of the place alone would make it – ' He broke off, shaking his head.

'How is it that you have not heard about this before now?' queried Holmes.

'People around here are what we call tactful,' answered Jones, smiling. 'If there was going to be trouble, they'd see I was the last to know. Did you talk to Cliff Langley?'

'Yes. I followed your advice.' Holmes turned his head briefly in my direction. 'Mr Langley is the works foreman, or whatever they call him, at Pentrefdu. My Whitehall papers were adequate to get me inside, but I doubt if I could have sustained the imposture for very long, or, at any rate, learned anything useful by it. Fortunately, it was not necessary.' He turned back towards Jones. 'Supposing me to be a Government inspector, Mr Langley asked me immediately if I had come to see him about Nant Gareth. My impressions of him confirmed your assurances, and, after a short talk, I put my cards on the table. I confided my identity to him, and he gave me the full story.'

Clara Jones bustled up, pre-empting the conversation with teacups. Holmes suffered the interruption gracefully, accepted milk and sugar, and, balancing the saucer on his knees, continued:

'Mr Langley has long been in the difficult position of acting as Sir Julian's confidant and as a buffer between his employer and the men, with whom he sympathises. It was impossible to prevent them from learning what was contemplated, but Mr Langley was hoping to dissuade them from any overt action, at least until there was some real likelihood of the plan being put into effect. Sir Julian always held the whip hand. He employed only non-union labour, and no strike at Pentrefdu has ever been successful.'

'But,' I broke in, feeling a little puzzled, 'why should his men object to his re-opening this other place?'

'Because it's a death-trap!' cried Jones. 'Everybody knows it!'

'Well, in that case, would anybody take the job?'

'You don't understand,' answered my friend sadly. 'Likely enough, there'd be few desperate enough. But that's not how he'd work it. What he'd do is transfer his own men to Nant Gareth and, if he meant to keep it

143

going, take on others to replace them at Pentrefdu. Men may be desperate to get jobs – but never so desperate as a man is to keep the job he's got.'

'So Mr Langley explained it,' said Holmes, nodding. 'The men were scared of being sent there, but even more afraid of losing their jobs if they didn't go. Sir Julian was already having more trouble than he had expected. Of course, if his wife had taken any interest in his business, she could have told us all about this when we were at the house. But, as things are, we have had to come here and get the facts from his foreman. Apparently, the Government does now make some attempt to regulate these matters. It was necessary for Sir Julian to secure official approval for his project. He anticipated no difficulty over this – quite frankly, with the aid of some bribery. But all kinds of obstacles were put in his way, and, at first, he supposed this to be due to organized opposition by the labour union. These legal problems were not, however, the only obstacles. When a survey team was eventually sent out from Cardiff, it was met halfway and falsely informed that the order had been cancelled. A second team met with more serious trouble. Their vehicle was waylaid and overturned by a band of masked men, and members of the party assaulted with pick handles.'

Setting aside his teacup, Holmes took his pipe from his pocket and plumbed the bowl with one fingertip. Satisfied that it was yet smokeable, he expended three matches in getting it alight – why he enjoyed the harsh flavour of half-smoked tobacco, I could never understand – and leaned back in an odourous cloud, the pipe crackling and wheezing asthmatically.

'The situation,' he went on, again addressing himself directly to me, 'is now plain enough. The Si Fan have been using this abandoned mine working for some purpose of their own – very likely, for years. They are unwilling to give it up, and even less willing that their operation should be discovered before they have time to get out. This is more than just a surmise, Petrie. Sir Julian told Mr Langley that they had actually threatened him. But, despite this, Dr Fu Manchu seems to have been prepared to settle the matter peaceably. Some two weeks ago, a girl was sent to see Sir Julian – not Kâramanèh or Zarmi, but a Chinese girl – one of the Si Fan's part-time employees, I imagine, and probably a university student. Having regard to his character, it was clearly easiest for a girl to obtain access to him, and she brought him an offer to re-purchase the property. Sir Julian not only rejected it, but also misused the girl. Afterwards, he boasted of this episode to his foreman, saying that he was not to be bought or frightened off by "cross-eyed Chinamen." His fate was sealed from that moment, and Fu Manchu, who had thus far held his hand, determined that he should die in a fitting manner.'

'And I'm not so sure that he didn't!' said PC Jones candidly. 'Don't tell the inspector I said so, Mr Holmes, but he's sent more men to their deaths than your Dr Fu Manchu.'

'You are entitled to your opinion,' replied Holmes, smiling. 'Well, fortunately, we are not seeking to avenge the late Sir Julian but to track down Fu Manchu for other crimes, and, principally, to rescue the persons whom he now holds captive.'

At this juncture, and to the relief of the rest of us, his pipe went out. Holmes looked at it sorrowfully and put it away.

'So what is our next move?' I asked.

'Nine o'clock to-morrow morning,' he answered, and stood up. 'I shall spend the night in Brecon, and join you again here after breakfast. To-morrow will be the Sabbath, and Mr Langley has agreed to forgo his devotions in order to take us into Nant Gareth – which, I gather, is quite an expedition. We must find out what the Si Fan are doing there.'

14

FIREDAMP

Cliff Langley turned out to be a man of some fifty years of age and small of stature, his hands knotted and gnarled, his skin desiccated and etched with a fine tracery of wrinkles like that of an Egyptian mummy.

He arrived at the police cottage in a light Ford truck belonging to the mine, and in which, ten minutes later, we were on our way out to Nant Gareth, Holmes electing to sit among the impedimenta in the open back, while I sat in front with the driver. The spell of fine weather remained unbroken and, unlike the yellow fogs of Limehouse, there was nothing in the atmosphere to hint at the sinister business upon which we were engaged. Langley, I discovered, believed it impossible that anything could be going on at the abandoned mine, where he himself had actually worked until the disaster which brought about its closure, but he accepted philosophically, and without opposition, Holmes's determination to visit the place.

A few hundred yards from our starting point, all attempts at road surfacing ceased. The truck jolted and swayed, the solid tyres hammering painfully on hard-packed earth dotted with stones and dented with potholes. At each successive jerk, I was flung either against the side of the cab or against my companion, and I hoped fervently that Sherlock Holmes, clinging to a precarious support in the rear, would not be bounced out upon the road.

'There's nothing but a few farm wagons been up here for fifteen years,' said Langley, wrestling with the wheel. 'After the mine was closed, it never led anywhere but to a couple of farmsteads up in the mountains, and I don't believe anybody lives there now.'

The valley narrowed and became more winding, the

rough track over which we were making our way climbing ever more steeply along one side till we looked down upon treetops and a mass of tangled vegetation where, from time to time, the morning sunlight flashed upon the silvery thread of a stream. Three or four miles farther on, we passed above a ghostly village of derelict houses of which only parts of the walls remained, the slates having been stripped from the roofs and re-used for building purposes elsewhere, just as the ancient builders plundered the ruins of Pompeii. This, I realised, must have been the habitation of the miners, a third of whom had been lost in one night. The survivors had moved into Pentrefdu, or found employment farther afield.

Several minutes after we had left the last of these forlorn relics behind us, the going improved temporarily as we traversed a stout stone bridge, and, looking upwards from my side of the cab, I saw a deep cleft in the mountainside down which a torrent foamed over a staircase of boulders.

'Nant Gareth,' said my companion and, as I failed immediately to understand, lifted a hand from the wheel, pointing. 'The stream – that's what they call it . . . named, so it's said, after Gareth the Shepherd, who drowned himself and his whole flock of sheep in the lake up top when Owen Glendower was defeated by the English.'

I made no reply, feeling slightly guilty – not so much because I was English, but because I had only the vaguest ideas about Owen Glendower. My gaze still turned to the same side of the road, I noticed a broken iron gate set between roughly shaped pillars of rock.

'Is that the way in to the mine?' I asked.

'It was,' answered Cliff Langley. 'But we can't use it now. It's blocked.'

Offering no further information, he drove on for a few minutes longer, then abruptly stopped. I got out, following his lead, and walked quickly around to the back, relieved to find that Holmes was still with us.

'Upon my soul,' he remarked, scowling as he climbed

down stiffly beside me, 'that was a bone-shaker! You can have my place on the way back, Petrie!'

'There's worse to come yet,' promised Langley, with a malicious grin. 'Hope you're both fit. I'll have to take you in by the old mineral line – if I can find it.'

To one side of us, the ground fell away steeply into the valley. To the other, where it rose less steeply towards the distant hills, the road was bordered by a dense growth of woodland in which no opening was visible. Langley searched up and down in either direction, bending close to the trees and probing between them. For almost ten minutes, his search was without avail; then, with a cry of triumph, he straightened up and beckoned. Approaching, I saw that he was pointing to the rusted ends of two steel rails half hidden in the undergrowth.

'That's it!'

Leaving us where we stood, our guide returned briefly to the truck and came back lugging three army-pattern knapsacks, which he distributed among us.

'I've brought everything just as you said, Mr Holmes,' he observed. 'But I don't know what good it's likely to be. You won't be able to get in.'

Holmes shrugged and made no comment. I strapped on the pack which Langley had handed to me, finding it more bulky than heavy, and wondering what it contained. Warned in advance of the kind of journey which lay before us, we had both put on our sturdiest tweeds and dispensed with overcoats. Holmes, I might add, had likewise disposed of 'Mr Quimby' and was now himself.

Cliff Langley led the way, armed with a long-bladed cleaver of the type used for splitting firewood, and swinging it like a *machete* as he set about clearing a path for us. It was heavy work, every yard of our passage contested by brambles and bracken. The trees to either side of the track were not large, but they grew close together, spreading a net of branches before our faces. Here and there, saplings had grown up between the rails themselves, and the wooden tie beams on which we walked lay half-buried under a mass of decayed vegetation, and were awkwardly spaced so that they were less than two comfortable paces apart, whilst to step across each involved the risk of tripping over the next.

'We used to run the coal trucks down to the road – ' Langley explained spasmodically, between swings of the axe. 'They came down easy enough, because of the gradient, and then we hitched them up to a steam traction engine. The men came in the other way, half a mile up the road, but we couldn't get the steamer up there. It was too heavy for the bridge – '

'What bridge?' I asked. 'The one we came over?'

'No, not that one. There's a point halfway up to the mine where the stream – the same that you saw – runs deep, right across the lane, and there was a bridge over it. But it's down now, and that's why we can't go in that way this morning. . . .'

Conversation lapsed and Langley's articulations subsided into gasps and curses as he hacked at the thicket. In another few months, when the grass was up and the trees clothed with leaves, progress would doubtless have been impossible. Thorny tentacles of briar clawed at our arms and legs, and set snares for our feet. More than once, when I followed too closely on the footsteps of our leader, the supple branches which he had trust aside whipped back and lashed me painfully across the body. Sunlight filtered dimly through the network overhead and the atmosphere was musty with a dank, unwholesome smell.

We had only a mile to go, but it took us an hour to do it. Towards the end of our arduous journey, Langley halted for a few minutes to regain his breath, drew out a large spotted handkerchief, and mopped at his streaming brow.

'You can see for yourselves,' he panted, 'that your damned Chinamen don't use this route!'

'Then they use some other,' replied Sherlock Holmes tersely. 'In my opinion, we should have tried the lane first. Are you sure that the bridge is down?'

'I saw it go.' Cliff Langley blew his nose violently in the same handkerchief and stuffed it back into his pocket. 'Have you seen a pit disaster, Mr Holmes? No – and you won't want to neither. The women all standing there weeping, and the kids clinging to their skirts . . . the ambulances, and the stretchers covered with blankets, and the rescue men going down looking more like devils with the cylinders on their backs and masks on their faces . . . When it was all over, we never tried to salvage anything. Left the lot – picks, shovels and everything – just as it was, we did. Old Jem Griffiths, who used to run Nant Gareth, was the last out. Two sticks of dynamite he put under the bridge, and down she come into the ravine. . . .'

'Did the original owners never consider re-opening the place?'

'The Beaumont family? No – they had other interests. Five years later, the old man died and the property came to his children; three of them, there were, a son and two daughters. The son had already gone out to Australia and got into some mining concern out there; the daughters both married and moved away. Now there's only one left, and it's from her Sir Julian got the place, for next to nothing. But he made a bad bargain and I told him so to his face. He knew a lot about the coal market, but nothing on the working side. Always wanting impossible things done, he was, and couldn't understand why they couldn't be.'

Now that we had stopped moving, it was chilly under the trees and I felt the perspiration cold and clammy on my skin. I shivered.

'Let's be going,' I urged. 'It can't be much farther, can it?'

Langley nodded, spat on his hands, took a fresh grip on his axe, and recommenced his attack, forging valiantly ahead while we stumbled along in his wake. For ten or twelve minutes more we continued in this fashion; then, suddenly, the trees thinned out, and we emerged upon the rim of a huge, saucer-shaped depression several hundred yards in diameter, enclosed by steep and frowning hills. Save for isolated clumps of weeds and thistles, nothing grew upon it. Much of the whole area had once been cemented over, the surface now streaked with cracks, as though by an earthquake, and blotched with yellowish patches, so that, for a moment, I had the impression of standing within the crater of an extinct volcano.

The sense of desolation was appalling. Heaps of stones, roughly shaped beams of wood, tarnished utensils and hand tools, lay scattered about everywhere. The narrow-gauge track upon which we stood curved away to a spur line with a string of squat iron trucks, a few of them overturned, two still piled high with great lumps of coal, amid which blades of grass stuck up like whiskers. A group of ugly, red brick buildings occupied the centre, their windows empty of glass, the walls so covered with creepers, fungi, and lichen that they appeared almost like monstrous natural formations, rather than the handiwork of man, putting me in mind of what Smith had told me of the ruined city of Ayudhya. Above the broken roofs, the framework of the winding gear stood out stark against the sky, resembling enormous bicycle wheels supported by a lopsided structure like two strokes of a letter N.

Nothing about the whole aspect of the place suggested that anyone had been there for the past decade. Cliff Langley, standing beside me, raised his arm and pointed vaguely, his eyes distant and troubled.

'That's where they were,' he said, and, though I could not make out the exact spot at which he was pointing, I knew that the scene was indelibly clear in his mind. 'Laid out in four rows, they were. A hundred and nine they brought up, and sixty-nine there is down there as will never come up, under a thousand tons of rock. By God's mercy, I was on the night shift that week, or I'd be there with them.'

'What was it?' I asked. 'An explosion?'

'Yes.' He nodded soberly. 'Firedamp, we call it. It comes out of the coal, and a spark from a man's pick striking against a flint can set it off.'

'Methane gas,' said Holmes quietly. 'Five percent is enough to make an explosive mixture.'

Langley nodded again. 'When I was a boy, we used to think it was only that. But it's not. It's the coal dust in the air, and the firedamp touches it off like a blasting cap. And then it turns into something else that strangles all the rest there are left.'

'Is that why the miners don't want this pit re-opened?' I inquired. 'The fear of another explosion?'

'No, it's not just that. There's firedamp wherever there is coal, and so long as the ventilation is good enough, we can handle it. The real danger isn't the big affairs that make the news, like Senghenydd. It's the rock-falls that kill maybe two or three at a time – and anything up to three hundred a year, over the whole country. Nant Gareth was always a killer. There's good coal down there, and it comes out easy, but the roof's rotten.'

'We shall get nowhere if we stand here discussing the hazards of mining!' interjected Holmes, with an irascibility intended, I think, to conceal more charitable emotions. 'We came here to find out what the Si Fan have been doing. Let us go and see.'

He set off towards the central group of buildings.

'I don't see what anybody could want here,' said Landly doggedly, catching him up, 'if it's not coal.'

Holmes made no reply. Still following the rails, but walking now alongside them, we crossed the intervening space, and, in a few minutes, found ourselves standing within the shadow of the verdure-encrusted walls. From six feet above, the gaping mouths of two square steel chutes pointed down at us, reminded me uncomfortably of defences set in a castle wall to precipitate stones on the heads of would-be invaders. Holmes glanced swiftly about him, then, muttering something unintelligible, moved away, staring down at the broken cement surfacing and the patches of earth between. Taking a tape measure from his pocket, he knelt, applied it to the ground, and stood up, turning to regard us with an expression of little satisfaction on his face.

'We have wasted our efforts!' he said irritably 'They

have found some way to restore the bridge. These are the tyre tracks of a heavy motor vehicle – a four-ton Leyland, I should think – and it has been here recently, at least four times.'

Cliff Langley looked blank. Shock and incredulity were plainly written on his features, but he ventured no argument. Performing a curious shrugging movement, he turned diplomatically aside to an opening in the wall from which an iron staircase led upwards.

'I'll go and take a look,' he said. 'Don't come up till I call. Everything in this place is dangerous.'

He ascended the stairs gingerly, testing each with his foot.

'Holmes,' I exclaimed, 'you never cease to amaze me! You have been in retirement for ten years, yet, during that time, you have familiarised yourself with types of motor cars and learned to identify tyre tracks. Why did you bother?'

'The habits of a lifetime are not discarded with impunity,' he answered, smiling a trifle wanly. 'If I had not kept up my store of knowledge, I should probably have become an imbecile.'

Langley's voice floated down to us. 'Come up! It's safe!'

We climbed the staircase, our boots ringing hollowly on the perforated metal treads, and came out on a sort of staging enclosed on right and left by the weathered brick walls of the taller buildings. Directly above us towered the upper part of the weird steel framework and the two giant wheels. Cliff Langley stood with his back to us on an oblong iron platform, the farther side guarded by a rusted handrail. I went to join him, and as I made to peer over, he reached out a warning hand, grabbing a fold of my jacket.

'Don't lean on it!' he said. 'It may give way.'

Bending cautiously forward, I found myself looking down into a well. It appeared deep, but how deep I could not tell, for the daylight penetrated only for some twenty or thirty feet and then was swallowed up in unfathomable blackness, the dark walls of this noisome hole casting few reflections. As Holmes came up beside us, Langley turned to him.

'This is it!' he said. 'I don't know what else there is to see. This was the main shaft.'

I straightened up, tearing my gaze away from the uncanny fascination of those unseen depths, and stared out over the littered wasteland of Nant Gareth at a point near the fringe of the property, where a tangle of steel girders and a great wheel lying upon the ground hinted at the collapse of a structure similar to that under which we stood.

'There were two shafts, then?' I asked.

'There are always two. I told you – there's got to be ventilation. But Number Two's gone. That's where the explosion was.'

Sherlock Holmes continued to peer over the rail, shaking his head in the baffled manner of a terrier which has lost the scent.

'Whatever they are doing, the answer is there,' he muttered. 'Is there no way down?'

'Oh, there's a way *down*,' said Langley, with grim humour. 'But no way up again! This isn't a bloody gold mine or something you can just walk in.'

'How deep is it?' I inquired.

'Fifteen hundred feet,' he answered indifferently.

The reply was so unexpected that I gasped and stared at him foolishly. In my innocent ignorance, I had visualised something in the nature of two or three hundred feet, but my imagination boggled at a depth half as much again as the height of the tallest building in the world.* Even Holmes looked slightly taken aback.

'In that case,' he said thoughtfully, 'I suppose there could hardly have been any stairs.'

'There was an emergency system of ladders in Number Two, seventy-five of them, but they've gone with the rest of it.'

'What has become of the lift which used to go up and down this shaft?' I asked vaguely.

---

* At that time, the Tour Eiffel, in Paris. [Ed.]

'You're standing on it!' said Cliff Langley, and laughed as I recoiled a pace instinctively. 'Don't worry – it won't move. Everything's rusted solid.'

'Is it?' snapped Holmes. 'I would say that all these things appear to me in suspiciously good order.'

Langley shrugged again and was silent. Regardless of his assurances, I had retreated to the rear edge of the platform, and, as I looked aimlessly about, chance permitted me, for once, to be the first to make a discovery. There, within inches of my right foot, lay the stub of a thick yellow cigarette. I stooped, snatched it up, and held it out triumphantly to Holmes.

'Zarmi!' I said.

Holmes smiled, gave me a nod of approval, and turned briskly to Langley.

'Where is the machinery which drives this thing?' he demanded.

Langley jerked his thumb towards an open doorway in the adjacent building. Beyond it, we came into a large square room with holes high up in one wall through which heavy wire hawsers ran down at a steep angle to what was evidently some sort of winch, hidden under a rust-streaked housing. Rubbish lay about the floor. Part of the roof had gone, admitting trailing vines, and there were birds' nests in the crevices of the broken masonry which had supported it. Holmes reached up, closed a hand over one of the hawsers, and opened it to exhibit a dark smear on his palm.

'Grease!' he said significantly, and looked down at the rusty iron cover which concealed the winch. 'But I see no kind of engine. How was it operated? By steam?'

'Nothing so modern as that,' replied Langley, shaking his head. 'All the power in Nant Gareth came from a water wheel. There's a conduit down from the lake – '

'Then, if the sluices were opened, it would run, wouldn't it?'

'Yes, if they *could* be opened, and if the wheel hasn't fallen apart!'

'There is an easy way to determine that,' said Holmes curtly. 'I suggest we go and try it!'

Langley sighed, took off his cap, scratched his head, and put his cap on again. His scepticism had been rudely shaken during the past few minutes, but, with Welsh stubbornness, he continued to make a show of patient disbelief.

'It's your party, Mr Holmes,' he said resignedly. 'If you want to go dragging up there, we'll go. But I warn you it's rough. We'd better leave our packs down here.'

Having become accustomed to its weight, I had almost forgotten the knapsack strapped to my shoulders. I took it off and set it down beside the winch, while my companions did likewise. Then, re-descending the iron stairs, we came outside again and, under our guide's direction, set out for what seemed to be a gap in the hills surrounding three sides of the mine precincts.

Since leaving Pentrefdu, I had completely lost my bearings. This rugged countryside of hills and valleys was bewildering in its rapid and unexpected changes, where rivulets flowing down the hillsides cut gorges and cross-valleys. One might follow the banks of a shallow stream meandering peacefully through fields, and emerge from a hundred yards of copse to find oneself all at once enclosed by the precipitous walls of a ravine with a cataract boiling at one's feet. The environs of Nant Gareth were no less unpredictable.

Passing through a detached group of semi-demolished buildings and tin-roofed sheds, we reached the foot of a flight of narrow stone steps winding up alongside a deep channel which seemed, at least in part, to be artificial. There were no less than a hundred of them, moss-grown and slimy, and some half-crumbled away.

'Watch yourselves!' cautioned Langley, and started up.

We toiled up after him. On our left rose a wall of natural rock; on our right, a wooden guardrail, in part missing, alone protected the edge of the steps. I was conscious of depth and a sheer drop, but a thick screen of bushes prevented me from seeing what lay at the bottom. Treading with extreme care, and keeping myself pressed close to the grey limestone wall, I followed three paces behind Holmes.

'What an infernally long way to go, just to open a sluice gate!' he remarked irritably.

'When the mine was working, it was open night and day,' answered Langley, over his shoulder. 'It wasn't necessary to come up very often.'

Although we had been steadily ascending from the commencement of our journey, we were yet far below the crests of the surrounding hills. At the top of the steps, a narrow stone causeway bordered one edge of a placid sheet of water which stretched away to the horizon in a V-shaped fold of the mountain, so that, save that it was still, it looked more like a river than a lake. The slopes on either side were green, and, in the distance, I could make out a cluster of white dots which must be sheep.

'Llyn Gareth,' said Langley.

Holmes was already out upon the causeway, walking with quick, sure strides towards the three horizontal wheels which controlled the sluice gates. We saw him lay his hands upon the nearest and try to turn it, saw him change his hold as the wheel moved, and heard the unmistakable sound of water falling from a considerable height.

'It works!' he shouted. 'Come and help me with the others!'

We obeyed – Langley with his face set in an expression of comic incredulity – and hurried out to join him, Holmes moving on to the farthest wheel so that we should not have to pass him. It was a dizzy operation, like walking along the top of a harbour wall. Standing with my back to the blue surface of Llyn Gareth, and poised on the brink of a dark pit half-concealed by overhanging branches, I seized the wheel which Holmes had abandoned and exerted my strength upon it. It required not a little force, but turned smoothly, and as the long black screw lengthened and rose from its centre, the gate came up with it, releasing a great jet of water into the pit. When all three had been fully opened, we returned to the steps.

'I don't believe it!' spluttered Langley, as we began the descent. 'It's impossible! After fifteen years . . .'

'Nant Gareth was not left undisturbed for fifteen years

– and probably for no more than five or six,' replied Holmes. 'So far as we know, Fu Manchu first appeared in England in 1911, but the Si Fan had obviously been setting up facilities for quite some time previous. They may not have used this place very often, but they have been keeping it in working order.'

For what purpose? I wondered. As he spoke, I remembered Fu Manchu's fondness for subterranean premises – the forgotten cellars below Limehouse, and the vaults under Hampstead Heath. Now, my imagination running riot, I peopled the corridors and galleries of Nant Gareth with slinking shadows, and furnished them with the splendour of an Abbasside palace – a vast complex of workrooms, laboratories, and exotic apartments. But I had no more than mentioned the thought to Holmes when he shook his head brusquely.

'No, it is nothing so extensive as that. He would not establish a headquarters in a spot so remote as this. But we shall soon enough find out just what it is, I think.'

Our way back to the shaft was uneventful, though I have nightmarish recollections of that climb down the treacherous steps with the pent-up waters of the lake crashing behind us and splashing noisily but invisibly through the spillway under the concealing tangle of greenery below. I did not see the wheel, nor have I any idea where it was situated or how its power was transmitted to the machinery. I am no engineer. We reentered the winch room to find all as we had left it, and, with no more ado, Cliff Langley threw over two levers. Little sound followed, but the thick wire cables commenced at once to bounce and vibrate in a way which showed them to be passing through the ports cut in the brickwork.

We hurried outside. Overhead, the two huge wheels were spinning. The iron platform upon which we had stood had vanished, so that the cavernous opening at our feet was now expanded to double its former width. Several minutes elapsed; then, almost silently, an identical platform came gliding up out of the darkness, and stopped on the far side of the shaft.

'There are two hoists, of course,' explained Langley,

'so that they counterbalance. When one goes down, the other comes up.'

With an inspiration of hope yet tinged with a chill of apprehension, I clutched suddenly at my companion's arm.

'Holmes!' I cried. 'Smith may be down there!'

'If he is,' said Langley, with a contemptuous sniff, and before Holmes could answer, 'he's a dead man! Nobody could live more than a few hours in an atmosphere like there must be in those tunnels – maybe only a few seconds.'

'We cannot be sure what the conditions are,' retorted Holmes. 'We do not know what the Si Fan may have done. I doubt whether they are holding Smith there, but it is nevertheless a possibility.' He turned to me with his jaw thrust out in a pugnacious fashion which, for an instant, gave him a curious resemblance to my missing friend. 'There is only one way to make certain. I am going down.'

15

THE BLACK LABYRINTH

'Go down?' echoed Cliff Langley, his lined face creased in a mask of consternation. 'It would be madness, Mr Holmes! Just plain suicide!'

'Nonsense,' said Holmes stiffly. 'The Si Fan do it, so why cannot I?'

'But the atmosphere . . . '

'It must be breathable, or the mine would be useless to them.'

'It is not only the mine itself,' I said doubtfully. 'If Fu Manchu has some secret buried down there, it may be as full of traps and pitfalls as an Egyptian tomb.' I looked down and tried not to shudder. I was afraid – horribly afraid – but pride spurred me relentlessly on. 'You are not going down there without me.'

'And neither of you is going without *me*!' shouted Langley. 'You'll kill yourselves for certain!'

Holmes looked at him thoughtfully and with surprise. 'You are prepared to attempt it, then?'

'If you're determined – yes.' Langley nodded grimly. 'I don't want to, but I can't let you go groping around in a mine you know nothing about. You'd get lost, even if nothing worse happened.'

'But,' said Holmes, smiling, 'if we all go, who is to operate the machinery up here?'

'So long as the brake's off the winch, we can work it from the hoist.'

Without another word, Langley turned on his heel and strode off into the room we had just left. Having made up his mind, he seemed anxious to get the business over. As we followed, he motioned us to pick up the packs which we had left on the floor, and conducted us through into another, and larger, room. Here there were benches and a number of crude wooden lockers, some with the doors hanging open and some still housing mouldering rags of clothes.

'Take your choice!' he said tersely, indicating the lockers.

Opened, our knapsacks proved to contain three sets of pit clothing, made of some stiff serge material, together with the basin-shaped helmets I had seen in Pentrefdu. In addition, there were three square electric lanterns similar to those used by the Metropolitan Police, which gave a more intense beam of light than our pocket torches; and, finally, three neatly wrapped packets of sandwiches made up by Clara Jones. We changed and hung up our things in lockers which were still serviceable. In a corner of the one I used, I found a copy of the *Cornhill Magazine* dated March 1899, the cover faded but legible, and felt a pang of sympathy for the unknown man who had never come back to read it.

Cliff Langley, seated on a bench, was lighting an odd, cylindrical oil-lamp with a metal gauze shield to enclose the flame.

'Our lanterns will give a better light than that,' I said.

'It's not meant to give light,' he replied, with a tight-lipped grin. 'It's to test for firedamp.'

Arrayed in his working outfit, he looked cool and professional, with the solemn, composed expression that I have seen on the faces of life-boatmen. His fear of Nant Gareth was almost a superstition, and I recognised that he was braver than I, since, unlike myself, he knew what there was to fear, yet chose to accompany us. Feeling awkward and ridiculous in my borrowed clothes – and Holmes looked just as bad – with the unfamiliar weight of the helmet on my head, I brought up the rear as we passed once more through the winch room, where Langley paused to check the position of the levers.

All seemed satisfactory. We were committed, now, to the test. Going outside, and around to the opposite side of the staging, we took our places on the hoist which we had summoned up from the shadows. Like the one we had sent down, it was a simple affair possessing neither roof nor walls, but only a handrail on the side facing inwards to the shaft, and joined to the supporting cables merely by an elongated horseshoe of heavy black metal. I gathered that it was designed not for the comfort of passengers but to bring up loaded coal trucks, which had then only to be wheeled off and the contents tumbled into the chutes.

Langley reached up and seized a dangling rope – a dangerously primitive-looking device – and looked around at us.

'Ready?' he challenged.

Holmes nodded, and Langley hauled upon the rope, which, in some way that I did not understand, engaged the machinery. Instantly, and with no more than a slight jerk, we were slipping rapidly down the shaft. I drew a deep breath, feeling my chest tight and constricted, and switched on my light. The pallid beam revealed nothing but the hewn rock drifting upwards. Already the square of daylight above had dwindled to the apparent size of a postcard. I fixed my eyes upon it, watching it shrink to a postage stamp, and feverishly wondering if it was the last I might ever see. Holmes, less affected than I, did not look up but stood placidly with his arms folded.

'After all these years,' said Langley, in a hoarse, dry voice, 'there must be enough firedamp down here to blow up Cardiff!'

'Yes,' rejoined Holmes calmly. 'But methane gas is not particularly poisonous. It is carbon monoxide that we have to fear, but I assume that the Si Fan have taken all necessary precautions.'

As I later calculated, our rate of descent was about three hundred feet per minute. Thus our journey into the bowels of the earth occupied five minutes. At the halfway level, the other car appeared, passed us, and vanished above in a darkness now as profound as the darkness below. The hoist shook slightly and rattled. At the end of another two minutes – though it seemed vastly longer – it thumped heavily against the soles of my feet and stopped.

We stepped off into a fairly wide passage along which ancient rails ran, the walls black as pitch and the air redolent with the sour smell of a gasworks. The atmosphere was anything but healthy, but at least it was possible to breathe, and, as we made our way down the passage, I became conscious of a faint draught on my face.

'They've put in some sort of fan system,' said Langley, speaking in quick, nervous tones. 'But it wouldn't be good enough for working in.'

'All the same, it is safe,' responded Holmes. 'The team they first sent here to survey and set up the place knew what they were doing. Why not? Marco Polo reported coal mines in Cathay in the thirteenth century.'

The powerful rays from our electric lanterns lit our immediate surroundings adequately, but, in the absence of reflection from the walls and roof, carried no farther than a few yards, so that the effect was something like walking through a dense London fog. We could see where we were, but not where we were going – an eerie sense of isolation, as though we were no longer part of the material world. At some considerable distance from the hoist, a corridor likewise equipped with a railed track, but somewhat less wide, came in at right angles to the first.

'This is the main gate road,' announced Langley, directing us to turn down it. 'It runs through to the coalface.'

Here, the ceiling was lower, and there were pit props at frequent intervals. The air became worse, the acrid odour catching at my throat. The yellow flame of Langley's safety lamp elongated in a peculiar fashion. He stopped, raised the lamp above his head, and blue witch fires danced within the gauze cylinder.

'Dear God!' he muttered. 'Look at that!'

'There is no risk, so long as we are careful,' said Holmes impatiently.

I nodded silently, understanding the threat, yet unwilling that my voice should betray a more acute, if less reasoned, fear of my own – for now we had entered a labyrinth. From one side of the corridor, a seemingly endless series of narrow openings led off into the eternal night of Nant Gareth – low, square-cut passages, reminding me horribly of the dark catacomb beneath the step pyramid of Saqqara, into which I had once ventured with my father, many years before.* Though I have a fair head for heights, I have a claustrophobic dislike for underground tunnels, whether natural or artificial, and, for me, this was the worst part of the whole mad undertaking, since these we were fated to explore.

In the first, we made a curious discovery – a large wire cage, divided into sections, and populated by a horde of white mice. Our lights failed to alarm them, and, peering closely, I realised with a thrill of horror that all of them were blind.

'They breed them down here to ascertain the presence of dangerous gases,' said Holmes, 'which are difficult to detect otherwise. But Heaven knows how they feed them.'

We penetrated the tunnel for some further distance, but found nothing more, so retraced our steps and tried the next. This also yielded nothing, as did the one beyond, but marks in the thick carpet of dust which covered the floors indicated that weighty objects had stood there, while everywhere were the footprints left by heavy boots. In the fourth that we entered, Holmes gave a cry of triumph and hurried forward, casting his light upon a stack of wooden boxes piled up against one wall. They were of varying shapes and sizes ranging from twenty to thirty inches in length, and furnished with rope handles.

In another moment, the secret of the Si Fan was ours – though a simple one it proved to be. Seizing the nearest box, Holmes attacked the lock with his clasp knife, forced it, and threw up the lid to disclose strangely shaped items of chemical glassware couched in velvet. The second which he opened was filled with soft cylinders of some aromatic substance wrapped in rice-straw

* Dr Petrie, who tells us nothing of his antecedents, is said to have been a son of the celebrated British Egyptologist Sir Flinders Petrie. [Ed.]

mats. A third contained books in unfamiliar bindings lettered in Arabic and Chinese – ancient volumes such as I had more than once seen in the clawlike fingers of Dr Fu Manchu . . .

'It is a storehouse!' declared Holmes jubilantly, desisting from his efforts. 'Here – and doubtless in other equally inaccessible locations – they have cached the paraphernalia for their operations. Fu Manchu travels light, with few followers – yet, Petrie, you have often remarked on the bizarre and elaborate equipment which he possesses, much of which he has lost. Has it never occurred to you to wonder where he gets it, how he transports it?'

'He sends his luggage in advance!' I said, with a grim laugh. 'So much is evident. He has been working out of makeshift quarters ever since we destroyed his last major premises, nearly six months ago. Now he is drawing upon his supplies to set up some new base.'

'Yes – there are only these few things left. If Sir Julian Rossiter had waited only a week or so longer, they might have let him live. But his impatience – and, more than that, I think, his open affront to the Si Fan – condemned him.'

Cliff Langley, who had stood watching us in silence, shuffled his feet uneasily.

'What is all this stuff?' he grunted.

'The wherewithal to terrorise a nation,' answered Holmes.

He slammed the boxes shut and heaved them back into place.

'Let us go on,' I urged. 'There is still a chance that we may find Smith.'

We did not find Smith. Nant Gareth was a storehouse – though, perhaps, something slightly more. In the adjacent tunnel we found no boxes, but walls and ceiling were covered with gigantic fungi unlike anything I had ever seen, as black as the coal surface from which they sprang. Holmes eagerly broke off a few pieces and stuffed them into his pockets. We persevered, and halted in the entrance to the next, astonished and not a little alarmed by a dull glow which waxed and waned in the darkness ahead, slowly alternating from deepest magenta to the hue of a red-hot iron. Advancing cautiously, we found the walls hung with a thick tracery of vines from which gourdlike excrescences depended. The temperature of the passage was tropical, seemingly induced by the weird contrivance on the floor – a metal frame some three feet high, enclosing two glass globes of unequal size, placed one upon the other like the halves of a cottage loaf. Within them, the baleful light swelled and dwindled, accompanied by a low, throbbing sound.

'H'm!' said Holmes, approaching his face closer. 'I wonder how it works?'

'Come away from it, Mr Holmes!' panted Langley. 'There's nobody else but Satan made that thing!'

Beyond this point, our search ended abruptly – and so, very nearly, did we. Our seventh tunnel terminated at twenty paces in a heap of broken rock. We attempted another, but had penetrated it less than a few yards when our nostrils were assailed by the disgusting odour of hydrogen sulphide.

'Stinkdamp!' gasped Langley, and we came reeling out, choking and retching.

'Fortunately, it soon makes itself felt,' I said shakily. 'One part in a thousand is fatal.'

'There's no sense going on,' said Langley, still coughing and spitting. He shone his lantern up the corridor at a wedge-shaped tip-truck standing on the rails just ahead. 'The blighters pushed the trucks up here to get them out of their way and never went any farther.'

'Very likely,' replied Holmes. He advanced a short distance, examining the floor and finding the dust no longer churned up by recent footfalls. 'Let us go back, then.'

Cliff Langley gave vent to a sigh, relieved, I think, that Holmes did not insist upon continuing, and our journey was resumed in reverse. Leaving them in the lead, I walked close behind, a prey to mixed feelings: thankful that the business was over, elated in that we had scored a point against Fu Manchu, but at the same time disappointed because we had found neither Nayland Smith nor any clue to his whereabouts.

'We had best leave things as they stand,' remarked Holmes, addressing me over one shoulder, 'though I should dearly like to help myself to some of those books! As soon as we reach the surface, we must arrange for a squad of men to take over this place.'

As he spoke, we had already come to the junction and were turning into the cross-corridor. We traversed half its length and then, ere we had taken a step more, occurred the most dreadful development, heralded by a metallic, rattling sound.

'My God!' screamed Langley. 'It's the hoist!'

He ran forward, the beam of his lantern dancing in front of him, and we hurried after. The iron platform on which we had descended was gone! Langley clutched at his forehead in a frenzied gesture and stood peering up the empty shaft.

'It's the bloody Chinamen!' he cried. 'They're coming down to murder us!'

'Back!' ordered Holmes.

Stumbling in our haste, we retreated at a run. We had no immediate object but to elude pursuit for a scant few minutes more and make such plans as we could. My senses reeled at the thought of a battle in the stinking darkness of that hellish maze. Yet what else could it come to? We were trapped like rabbits running blindly through a warren invaded by ferrets. I missed the corner of the crossway and would have gone plunging on, but Cliff Langley seized me by the coat-tails, hauling me back.

'Not that way!' he shouted. 'It's blocked a hundred yards up. There's no way but the way we came!'

We turned off, and, again passing the tunnels which held the remaining property of the Si Fan, reached the line of tip-trucks at which we had previously halted. Squeezing ourselves in between them, we turned at bay. Even Langley did not know what lay in the network of passages beyond. At a terse command from Holmes, we extinguished our lights, including even the safety lamp, and waited in the impenetrable darkness of a rock tomb deeper by far than any of the Valley of the Kings. Allowing for the time taken by the descent of the hoist, we had a respite of no more than five minutes.

'We are idiots!' said Holmes, in a low, angry voice. 'This is what comes of acting on an impulse. We should not have come down here without a rear guard. Like a fool, I told myself that Zarmi and her gang of miners would not risk coming here again after they had seen you at the inn, and I was wrong.'

'They have come back for the last load,' I said, trying desperately to think. 'But they must know now that we are here. They must have seen that the machinery was running.'

Holmes was silent for a moment, apparently considering.

'Yes . . . ' he muttered. 'But, excepting for the girl, they do not belong to the Si Fan. They are just labourers. Will they fight?'

'Make no mistake about it!' answered Langley. 'Chinamen or Welshmen, they'll slit our throats for a ha'penny if they think they can get away with it.'

His voice trembled and I knew that, courageous as he was in his own perilous profession, he was no fighting man.

'We can give a good account of ourselves,' I retorted. 'Zarmi will have her knife, but the others will be unarmed, while we have our pistols – '

'You damned stupid fool!' snapped Langley, in a tone bordering on hysteria. 'If you fire a pistol down here, you'll have the whole place in on top of us!'

'Quiet!' warned Holmes. 'They are coming!'

Lights had appeared at the remote end of the corridor, springing up one by one out of the darkness, until there were seven. They moved in an oddly erratic fashion, cutting this way and that across the walls, and, as they drew closer, I saw that, unlike ours, they were attached to the wearers' helmets.* The party advanced slowly, in

* I was later told that this pattern was unpopular at Pentrefdu, due to the weight of the battery pack. [P.]

168

a singularly casual manner, I thought, for men engaged upon a desperate venture, and, to my further surprise, made no attempt to search the first three empty tunnels, as we had done. They walked in single file, talking in rough, loud voices – sometimes laughing – and the lights behind her revealed Zarmi in the lead.

At the entrance to the tunnel which contained the boxes, she halted and turned, standing with her back to us. Scorning pit clothes, she wore the black, form-fitting costume of a ballerina – a veritable imp of the infernal regions in the shifting rays of the headlamps, as her followers passed in before her, still laughing, and talking apparently in Welsh.

'Cut the gabble, you no-good johnnies!' she shouted, her dry, husky tones carrying clearly to my ears. 'You think I stay all night in this rathole?'

Ere the fourth man had entered at her bidding, the first came out again, bent down under the weight of a box, and plodded away down the corridor.

'This is extraordinary!' whispered Holmes. 'They seem to have no idea that there is anyone down here! Can you understand what they are saying?'

'Yes!' replied Langley, and (I believe) blushed invisibly. 'They're making dirty jokes about the girl!'

Inexplicable though it was, we seemed to be in no danger of attack. We watched each of the six men enter, and, soon after, go off burdened towards the shaft. Zarmi, without entering, stalked off after the last, her slim, tigerish figure boldly outlined in silhouette, and, characteristically, carrying nothing. The headlamps of the first two men, coming back for a second load, reappeared and passed.

'Of course! It must be!' Sherlock Holmes's voice came to me in a hoarse whisper through the darkness. 'These are all *new* men, or she would not have come down to guide them. They are a slipshod lot, and they must simply have thought that the others who came here last had neglected to shut off the machinery!'

'You are probably right,' I answered, and then, a new thought crossing my mind, found it impossible to keep my voice level as I added: 'But if *they* shut it off when they have finished, we shall be buried down here forever!'

Holmes made no response, and Langley gave something like a groan.

Zarmi did not return. We watched the procession of lights approaching and receding, the intervals between trips lengthening by the time taken in loading the wooden boxes upon the hoist.

'Supposing,' I said desperately, 'that we immediately get on the car that comes down when theirs goes up – can we not make it go up again?'

'No,' said Langley. 'Even if they don't close the sluices, it will take them only a minute to put the brake on the winch, and the hoist will stop halfway up the shaft.'

'Then there is only a single chance for us,' declared Holmes suddenly, in a stronger, more confident tone. 'We must seize the last man, and one of us must take his place. I had better do it. Langley is a real miner, but I am the better actor. It is dark in the shaft, and they will probably not detect me till we reach the surface. Then I can either dodge them, or hold them at pistol point, and bring up the hoist.'

It was an audacious plan, and one which had the simplicity of desperation, but none of us could think of a better.

'How shall we know which man *is* the last?' I asked. 'There were about two dozen boxes, so each man will make about four trips. . . . '

'We must get back into that passage and ambush him there,' said Holmes. 'How far can we go up it, Langley?'

'Half a mile, if you like!'

'Fifty yards will do. Now watch – and as soon as the next man comes out, in we go!'

All this last had necessarily been conducted in an undertone. I felt my throat aching with the effort of speaking in whispers and the saline taste of methane. One of Zarmi's helpers was nearly at the end of the corridor, on his way back to the hoist, and another had just gone into the fourth passage. We waited till his light re-appeared, then edged out of our cramped hiding place, keeping pace with him and feeling our way along the wall past the entrances to the intervening tunnels – past the one in which the baleful red light still glowed fitfully, and the next, where the black fungus thrived. The headlamp of the man coming up appeared round the corner, though too distant for the beam to reach us, as we dived into the passage they were clearing. Holmes flashed on his light.

'God! We are only just in time!'

Only one box remained upon the floor! Like hunted animals, we bolted on into the shadowy depths beyond the range of the last man's lamp, for we did not intend to confront him face to face, but to take him from behind. Holmes switched off his lantern and utter darkness engulfed us once more till, within the space of a few seconds, the cold round eye of the miner's headlamp shone in at the opening. We could see nothing of the man who carried it, save that, fortunately, he was not conspicuously shorter than Holmes.

He entered, unsuspecting, took nine or ten steps towards us, and stopped. By the way in which his light swung downwards and dropped, he seemed to have sat on the floor, in no apparent hurry to pick up his load. Minutes passed – or, perhaps, they were but seconds – during which he sat there and appeared to grope about aimlessly. It is difficult to see much about a man or his movements when the only available light is carried on his head. Eventually, however, he stood up and, lifting the last box by its two rope handles, turned back towards the entrance, stooping over his burden.

We had made no plan for assault, but none was required. Holmes glided silently forward and pounced like a leopard. His long arms shot out straight, his fingers closing around the back of the man's neck and pressing expertly on the carotid artery. The heavy box fell with a crash. Langley and I rushed to join in the attack, but our help was unnecessary. Making scarcely a sound, the victim sagged in Holmes's grasp and went limp.

Holmes seized him under the armpits, dragged him a

few paces back and let him fall, bent, tore the helmet from the man's head, and clapped it upon his own.

'Quick!' he ordered. 'Bind him – use your belts – and gag him! He will be unconscious only a minute or so.'

Snatching up the fallen box, he rushed out into the corridor, leaving us to secure the prisoner. Nayland Smith having long since schooled me in the useful art of tying people up, this was a task which fell principally to me. By the time I had completed it, the man was beginning to stir, and I was thankful it was no sooner, for he was an ugly brute. Langley stuffed his big spotted handkerchief into the man's mouth, and bound it into place with my necktie.

'What now?' I asked breathlessly.

'Back to the shaft!'

I got to my feet, looking down uncertainly at the man on the floor, who was rolling about and arching his body like a stricken insect. His eyes bulged, and his bearded face seemed purple with rage. It was surely inhuman to leave him there, but I knew that we could not manage him.

'Let him stay here till the police come,' said Langley savagely. 'We've troubles enough of our own.'

There was nothing else to be done. I nodded, and we went out into the corridor. Now able to risk using our lanterns, we traversed it to the end but switched off before turning the corner and crept the rest of the way in the dark, listening all the while for an altercation which would indicate that Holmes's imposture had been discovered. But, evidently, it had not. At the base of the shaft, we found that the loaded hoist had already gone up, and the other was down in its place. We scrambled aboard, and Langley tugged impatiently at the rope. Nothing happened.

'They have put on the brake,' I said. 'It is up to Holmes now.'

Langley slumped down beside me, squatting on his heels in the peculiar fashion of his colleagues.

'Oh, Christ!' he murmured. 'Oh, Christ!' – and I knew that it was not an oath but a prayer.

I, too, was frightened – terrified – but his fear was sharper and more real than mine, for he had lived with it all his life – the miner's fear of being entombed. As for me, while we waited there helplessly in the tiny circle of light cast by our lanterns, I dared not even let myself think. Five minutes passed, and then ten. With my watch in my hand, I stared as though hypnotised at the second hand creeping around the dial and counted. Langley rested his head upon his knees and began softly to sing 'Rock of Ages' – a poor choice, I felt.

'Brace up!' I said shortly. 'We're not done yet.'

'There's no harm in being ready!' he answered gloomily, and went on singing.

The hoist bucked and, to my unspeakable relief, commenced to rise. Cliff Langley sprang upright, and we stood side by side, peering up at the tiny speck of daylight far above. At an infinitely slow rate, it broadened to a clearly defined square and grew larger. Light streamed down the shaft, picking out the iron framework of the hoist and the hewn rock. The metal platform rose level with the surface and clattered to a standstill. We leapt off and stared into the anxious face of Sherlock Holmes, black with coal dust, and his lips parted, exposing ivory teeth in a miner's grin.

'Thank Heaven it worked!' he said.

Too overcome to speak, I stumbled past him, making for the steps. We descended, and, with one accord, hurried far back from the ruinous brick buildings. I looked up at the midday sun till it hurt my eyes, and drew great breaths of cold, clean air deep into my lungs. Never had plain air tasted so good. When, at length, I came sufficiently to my senses to glance around and take stock of my surroundings, I saw that the compound was as deserted as when we had entered.

'Where are they?' I asked.

'Gone,' replied Holmes. 'I dared not try to stop them and chance a fight while you were still down there.'

'What – what happened?' inquired Langley, still gasping like a fish. 'How – how did you manage it?'

Holmes laughed, choosing, as usual, to make light of much, once it had been accomplished.

'It was easy! I got on the hoist, bent double over my box, sat down in one corner, and had a coughing fit into my handkerchief till we reached the surface. Out here, they had a motor van waiting. Incidentally, I have the number. I put one box into it, making myself the last off the hoist, then walked around the van and made off for the stone steps, as if I was going up to the sluice gates. The girl shouted something after me – telling me not to bother, I think – but I pretended not to hear and went on. No one attempted to stop me, and I took cover behind the first shed that I came to. As soon as they had finished loading the van, the men climbed into the back, and they left. Zarmi drove.'

'Yes,' I said. 'I know she can drive. She once impersonated a taximan. But surely they noticed that one of their number was missing?'

'Well,' replied Holmes, shrugging, 'I told you they were a careless bunch of rascals. I daresay they can count up to six, but the girl no doubt thought that all the others were in the back, while they thought that the missing man was in front with her. But the point is, rather, what are *we* to do about him? We cannot very well leave him down there – '

Coincident with his question came a terrible answer, as the ground literally shook under our feet. There was a low, grumbling sound, as of distant thunder, and a vast column of smoke spouted up from the mine shaft. The wooden staging collapsed, bringing down with it the two square chutes and gouging holes in the cement. Veiled in the same dense pall of smoke, the tall steel uprights of the winding gear swayed drunkenly and tottered.

'God forgive us!' whispered Cliff Langley. 'We've killed the poor devil!'

Nant Gareth had claimed its final victim.

Holmes, for once nonplussed, stood staring at the tangled mass of wreckage about the shaft.

'An explosion was always possible,' he said slowly. 'But – an accident? That is hard to believe.'

'It was not an accident,' I replied, still shivering at the narrowness of our escape, and now remembering – but too late to save a man's life. 'Fu Manchu almost invariably destroys the premises he vacates. Now I understand why our unhappy prisoner was struggling like a madman. He had just set the time fuse!'

Little more remains to be written of our escapade at that haunted spot. We left by the same route that Zarmi's truck had followed, and arrived at the ravine of which Langley had spoken, to find that it was bridged – though not quite as we expected. A large part of the original bridge remained, including the massive stone supports, but there was a gap of some ten or twelve feet in the middle. Across this had been laid two steel girders, each about eighteen inches wide, over which, with sufficient skill and considerable nerve, it was possible to drive a motor vehicle. We thought that they had probably been removed when Fu Manchu's storehouse was not in use, and re-laid when occasion demanded. Cliff Langley explained to me how this could have been done with the aid of the truck, but I did not understand it very well.

Crossing these narrow catwalks, with the stream running a hundred feet beneath, was another hair-raising business. Holmes, I need hardly say, danced across one as lightly as a tightrope artist and stood waiting on the other side while Langley and I crawled laboriously over. It was as well, in the end, that we had not come in by that road, for we should have had to leave our truck – the girders being spaced too widely apart for its wheels – and the Si Fan gang would have found it there.

We re-joined the Ford half a mile up the road, nothing having happened to it in the meantime, and drove back to Pentrefdu. Langley went home with his grizzled grey hair a shade whiter than when he had departed, leaving Holmes and me at the police cottage. We cleaned up as best we could without resorting to the conventional tin bath in front of the fire, and prepared to leave, Holmes having decided on Cardiff as our next and immediate headquarters. I packed my things, said goodbye to the

Joneses with genuine regret, and we walked down to the bus stop.

There were lights in the simple stained-glass windows of the church, and from it emerged the noble strains of 'Pen Calfaria' sung by massed voices. From the plaintive melody of the first two stanzas it swelled thunderously to a leaping cascade of sound, wave upon wave, triumphant and exultant. We stood and listened spellbound, willing to swear that no less than a cathedral choir sang within that crude stone building. Yet these, I knew, were the same who had sung and applauded while Zarmi danced in a whirl of flying garments on the counter of The Three Feathers – some, perhaps, were those from whom we had fled in the black labyrinth of Nant Gareth.

'The Celtic heritage!' said Holmes sorrowfully. 'Our writers come from Ireland, our poets from Scotland, our singers from Wales. What, I wonder, has England to offer?'

'Well,' I said, laughing, 'of course, we have Sherlock Holmes!'

16

THE CHINESE SARCOPHAGUS

We reached Cardiff two hours after leaving Pentrefdu; forty-eight hours later, we were still there, having in the meantime accomplished nothing of any significance.

Sherlock Holmes spent a considerable amount of time at the county police headquarters, putting the finishing touches to the affair of Sir Julian Rossiter, and reporting our adventures at Nant Gareth. Nothing, however, could be done about the unfortunate death of our prisoner, since his identity was unknown and recovery of the body impossible. The vehicle used by the Si Fan, of which Holmes had been quick to obtain the registration number, was soon traced. It had been hired a month previously from a garage in Swansea.

'I hope they demanded a sufficient deposit,' observed Holmes, with a sour smile, 'for I don't suppose they will see it again.'

With commendable diplomacy, he had left further inquiries regarding the two men named by the landlord of The Three Feathers to be handled by PC Jones as a village matter. We expected to get nothing much from them, and there was little with which they could be charged other than trespass on Sir Julian's property. They lay low for a few days and our friend's report did not come in until after the events yet to be related, but I may as well mention it here. It served merely to confirm much of what Holmes had suspected.

In return for an assurance by Jones that proceedings would not be taken against them, the two vagabonds were easily persuaded to part with their information. Each had made three trips to the mine. They believed – or, at least, had been told – that the boxes they were shifting contained stolen goods. Zarmi drove the van, picking up her gang at an agreed rendezvous and dropping them there on the way back, so that they knew neither where she lived nor where the van was unloaded. On the last occasion – the morning after my appearance at the inn – it had been driven by a man who seemingly spoke no English, and who subsequently paid them off. Zarmi, I imagine, was meanwhile spending a busy day assembling a fresh labour force for the final effort, no doubt cursing the luck which had led to our meeting, and unwilling to employ the same men, since she was not sure how many I could identify.

Still later investigations produced the information – too late to be of any service to us – that the van had been garaged in Brecon, where Zarmi had been staying at an ordinary boarding house.

Breakfast on Wednesday was a silent meal as we sat facing each other across a table in the eminently respectable, but unhomely, hotel in which we were now installed. Holmes, when he could not be surrounded by his books, test tubes, and relics of crimes solved in the past, seemed to prefer an impersonal environment which offered no distraction to his thoughts. I, for my part, was already regretting the warm family atmosphere of PC Jones's stuffy little living room, with the eternal kettle singing on the hob.

'I wonder if we are wasting our time here?' I remarked anxiously. 'For all we know, Fu Manchu may have gone back to London.'

'I think not,' replied Holmes. 'The trouble with Sir Julian would not have been sufficient to bring him up here, leaving his rival, Ki Ming, to profit by his absence. He is after bigger game, though we have yet to discover what.'

I sighed listlessly, and toyed idly with a piece of toast, breaking off charred fragments which powdered between my fingers like coal dust. . . .

'A strange coincidence,' I said absently. 'We started with a coalman, and we have finished up in a coal mine.'

Holmes, on the verge of attacking his third egg, paused, and shook his head.

'Much which people mistake for coincidence is, in

reality, cause and effect – in this case, the simple association of ideas. Fu Manchu was preoccupied with Nant Gareth when he was unexpectedly called upon to plan the abduction of Nayland Smith. There is nothing more natural than that the idea of using a coalman should come first into his mind – ' Abruptly, he ceased speaking and stared at me with a most peculiar expression on his face. 'Good Heavens! Is it possible?'

Leaving the egg unmolested, he leapt to his feet and, with no further word, rushed out of the room.

He did not come back. I finished my breakfast and waited. But when, after another fifteen minutes, he had still failed to return, I went in search of him, and found him seated in the lounge with his nose in a magazine, having apparently forgotten my existence.

'What have you been doing?' I asked.

'Eh?' he said, looking up as if startled.

'Why did you leave so suddenly?'

'Oh! An inspiration, or perhaps no more than an idle fancy. I have called Weymouth on the telephone, and his reply may help me to determine which it is. But it may take some time to obtain the information. . . . ' Holmes switched his eyes back to the magazine. 'Don't bother me now, Petrie! Here is a remarkable account of something called *pennillion*, in which the performer plays a traditional melody upon the harp and, at the same time, improvises a separate air to harmonise with it. Fascinating! Sit down quietly somewhere, like a good fellow, and translate the Lord's Prayer into Arabic, or something.'

There was no more to be got out of him for the time being, and I knew better than to try. Taking a seat at a discreet distance, I occupied myself for the next hour or so in some fashion which I no longer remember, while my companion, frowning over his text, tapped his fingers on his knee, simultaneously humming and occasionally singing *sotto voce*. This I found far from entertaining, for, despite his musical accomplishments in other fields, Holmes had the voice of a corncrake. Finally, unable to put up with it any longer, I went out for a walk.

The day was cloudy and cold, and my mood unoptimistic. The stolid grey city, which exported nineteen million tons of coal annually to the hungry furnaces of Europe, I found purposeful but uninspiring, the pavements encumbered by a turgid stream of pedestrians, which flowed sluggishly, impeding the passage of the less patient, rather than sweeping away those who would linger, like the febrile, bustling current of London. It was easy, I thought, to understand how earthbound Cardiff had stood firm in the cause of Parliament against the heroic but futile assaults of the King's men pouring down recklessly through the valleys from distant Raglan.

It was midday when I returned to the hotel, to find Sherlock Holmes tapping and chanting just as I had left him. He glanced up at me and shook his head.

'Unfortunately,' he said sadly, 'I am unable to play the harp. I wish I had my violin with me!'

I nodded and smiled politely, feeling secretly thankful that he had not, for the spectacle of Holmes endeavouring to sing while scraping at his violin was too alarming to contemplate.

'I am hungry,' he said suddenly. 'Let us go in to lunch.'

'You did not finish your breakfast,' I reminded him.

'Oh?' he said. 'Didn't I?'

We went into the restaurant and sat down. In rare moments of ease, Holmes showed an appreciation of good food, but, at other times, he would often neglect, or forget, to eat till he was famished. We finished our soup without incident and without much conversation, but the *entrée* had only just been served when a waiter came in to inform my companion that he was wanted on the telephone. Holmes rushed out, for the second time leaving his meal to grow cold upon the table, and again failed to return till the plates had been removed and I was beginning dessert.

'Leave that,' he said impatiently, 'and come along!'

'But you have not finished your lunch!' I protested.

'That is of no importance. If we go now, he will probably not have finished *his* lunch, and we shall find him at home.'

'Find whom?'

'The man we are going to see.'

Holmes rushed out again, and I perforce followed, abandoning peaches and cream. We crossed the lobby and hurried upstairs to get our coats.

'I have ordered a taxi,' he remarked as we ascended. 'Put on your Burberry, not your overcoat. I'm afraid "Mr Quimby's" bowler hat will not fit you. . . . Well, then, you had better not wear any. . . .'

The purpose of these cryptic directions was far from clear, but I obeyed meekly. Holmes cast a critical eye over my attire and nodded.

'Yes – that will do, I think. But leave the top button unfastened.'

Outside the hotel, a taxi was already waiting. Holmes bent to address the driver. 'Do you know Skibber Vower Street?'

'Yes – down by the docks.'

'Good!' said Holmes, taking his place beside me. 'It seems I can say it well enough, though I cannot imagine how it may be written.'

Passing the imposing new building of the County Hall on our left and the old Norman castle on our right, we turned off into a busy shopping centre, passed Queen Street station, and turned off again into a maze of lesser thoroughfares leading down to dockland. Here, presently, in an area which seemed to be residential rather than commercial, we stopped.

'One and eight,' said the taximan.

We got out, paid, and stood looking around at the junction of three sordid little streets. At the corner of each, a neatly inscribed sign proclaimed its identity, but none looked remotely like 'Skibber Vower.' We glanced at each other, baffled. Behind us, the taxi was moving off.

'Where is it?' I demanded.

Our driver leaned out, pointing. 'By there!' he shouted. 'Can't you read?'

We stared up at the sign above our heads, and beheld: 'Heol Ysguborfawr.'

181

'Incredible!' muttered Holmes. 'What a wicked perversion of the alphabet!'

Heol Ysguborfawr was a street of narrow-fronted, three-storied houses built *en bloc* like those of Pentrefdu, each with a steeply pitched roof and a door opening directly upon the pavement. Holmes led the way briskly along it, peering at the numbers painted above the doors.

'Never advertise yourself by taking a taxi up to your quarry's doorstep,' he advised. 'While you are paying off the driver, he escapes through the back garden. Ah! There it is!'

He halted before a house distinguished from its neighbours only by the number '23' written on the transom, and, lifting his hand to the ugly iron knocker, paused for a final word.

'Well, we will play out our hand and see what it wins us – though if coincidence was the dealer, after all, a pretty pair of fools we shall look. Say as little as possible, keep your hands in your pockets, and try to think like a plainclothes officer.'

He knocked, but no answer came. A second, more urgent, knocking produced no different result. With a hiss of annoyance, he beat out a bombardment which echoed across the street.

'Confound it!' he exclaimed. 'He seems to be out.'

'No,' I said. 'Listen! Somebody is coming.'

Heavy footsteps sounded, and the door was flung open, disclosing the red, angry face of a massive-framed man in shirt and trousers, collarless, his braces hanging down in loops. Hostile eyes glared at us.

'Shove off!' he shouted. 'Whatever yer sellin', we don't want none!'

He made to close the door, but Holmes's foot was quicker.

'We are selling nothing. Are you Samuel Wade, master of the collier *Marquis of Bute*?'

'An' what if I am?' came the truculent retort. 'Who the 'ell are you?'

'My name is Sherlock Holmes.'

'*Gord*!' said Captain Wade, his eyes widening. 'You was dead and buried twenty years ago!'

'Then I am resurrected!' snapped Holmes. 'And I wish to have a word with you.'

The man hesitated and I thought I saw a flicker of fear cross his face.

'I don't want no truck wiv the likes of you!' he growled. 'Take yer blawsted foot outa my door!'

Holmes shrugged and turned away, glancing eloquently at me.

'Very well,' he said lightly. 'After all, it is your affair if you prefer a visit to the police station.'

The belligerent figure of Captain Wade seemed suddenly to deflate. He uttered an unintelligible response, then, desisting from his efforts to close the door, threw it wide open.

'Aw right!' he said thickly. 'Come in, blawst yer! My slate's clean, I tell yer!'

A dim passage alongside an uncarpeted staircase gave entrance to a living room garishly wallpapered and reeking with the odour of boiled cabbage, a clutter of plates and a bottle of stout on an oilcloth-covered table indicating that we had indeed interrupted the captain's lunch. On the far side, a second door communicated with a kitchen, and before this stood a middle-aged woman in a pinafore apron, who, judging from her expression of dismay, had overheard at least part of our conversation.

'Oh, Sam!' she wailed. 'Now you're in trouble with the p'lice!'

'You shut up, and sling yer 'ook!' ordered Captain Wade, in his best seafaring manner. Evidently a man who had travelled much and in mixed company, his speech ranged from Cardiff to Camberwell.

His wife – or such I supposed her to be – made a gulping sound and retreated into the kitchen. Our reluctant host sat down at the littered table, thrust away the plates, and leaned forward on folded arms.

'Now then, mister,' he began defiantly, 'I don't know what all this is about, but–'

'Inquiries made by Scotland Yard show that the *Marquis of Bute* was unloading coal at Longman's Wharf on the eleventh of this month,' said Holmes, and sat down, uninvited, while I remained standing with my hands thrust deep in my raincoat pockets. 'I have two questions to ask you,' he continued. 'What did you bring from London, and where did you land it?'

'Who says I brought anythin'? I ain't done nothin' agin the lor!'

'In that case,' I said cheerfully, speaking for the first time, 'you won't mind telling us about it, will you, sir?'

Captain Wade shot an uneasy glance at me, his worst suspicions confirmed. He cleared his throat noisily.

'There ain't no lor agin carryin' a bloody body!' he grumbled.

The words took me by surprise and I clenched my hands hard in my pockets. I saw now what Holmes had in mind, and, shocked by the reply and its dreadful implications, found it difficult to maintain my official mask of composure. Wade looked hastily at my companion, as if appealing for support.

'I 'adn't done 'im in!' he said hoarsely. 'Nobody 'ad. 'E was a old Chinee, what 'ad caught 'is death of cold, an' died of bummonia! Leastways, that's what they told me – '

'Who told you?' insisted Holmes. 'How did this matter come about?'

Captain Wade hesitated, shifting his eyes aimlessly from a filthy mark on the wallpaper to a patriotic, but outdated, portrait of the late King Edward VII. With an unsteady hand, he reached for the bottle of stout, drank copiously, and set it down on the table.

'It was Fong told me,' he said sullenly. 'Our cook, 'e was. Nine trips 'e done wiv us, an' never bin no bother. When we was up to Lunnon, 'e'd go ashore an' play *fantan*, an' maybe 'ave a pipe or two, but 'e weren't never no bother.' Again he hesitated, then went on with a rush. 'Well, the Thursday night, 'e come an' told me about this old bloke what 'ad kicked the bucket, an' 'ad to be got 'ome to sleep peaceful wiv 'is ancestors. "You yellow bat-brain!" I says to 'im. "You think I can take this coal tub out to China?" But 'e says, no, all they wants is a bit of 'elp to get the old un round quiet-like to a ship what's waitin' for 'im, because there's a 'orrible secret society what wants to steal 'is body an' saw it up so's 'e can't sleep peaceful nowhere.'

'Remarkable!' said Holmes sarcastically. 'Did he, by any chance, tell you the name of this *'orrible* society?'

'Yus. 'E said it was called the Si Fan.'

Holmes glanced back over his shoulder at me. 'It seems,' he remarked, 'that Fu Manchu has a sense of humour!' He turned again to the seaman. 'And you believed this preposterous story?'

'Course I did!' said Captain Wade firmly. 'They was payin' me, wasn't they?'

Holmes shook his head reprovingly. 'By shipping cargo for your own profit without the knowledge of the owners, you have committed the crime of barratry. You had better tell us the rest of it. How was the business managed?'

'Fong an' 'is pals done it. They got the coffin aboard the night before we left – 'eavy as lead, an' a beautiful job it was, too, like one of them Egyptian sar – sarcopof-fagusses what they keeps mummies in.' Little though Captain Wade had wished to tell his tale, the bardic strain which lies beneath the surface in every Welshman was forcing its way out. 'Beautiful!' he repeated. 'All black an' gold an' red an' green it was, an' the lid done up like a flight of steps, all knobbly an' carved about like icin' on a cake. But I wasn't goin' to be let in for carryin' no bloody coffin full of opium, so I made 'em open it, an' there 'e was – a old geezer wiv a long white beard, as old as Mefoozalum, in a nightshirt wiv peacocks an' dragons all over it.'

'You are sure that this man was dead?' asked Holmes, frowning.

'Of course 'e was dead!' roared the captain indignantly. 'If 'e wasn't dead, what was 'e doin' in a coffin?'

This logic seemed unanswerable. Holmes sighed and gave it up.

'Go on, then!' he said sternly. 'Where did you take him?'

'We was to take 'im just off Oystermouth, on the west side of Swansea Bay. They give me 'arf 'is passage money, an' the others was to give me the rest when they come an' get 'im. "An' they better 'ad," I says, "or over 'e goes, box an' all, an' 'e can sleep in an oyster bed!" We never took it below – just lashed it down on deck an' got a tarpaulin over it. I 'ad to tell the mate, but we reckoned the 'ands was better off not knowin' we 'ad a dead un aboard, some of 'em bein' superstitious-like. It was a smooth trip round, an' I fixed it so as when the time come we could heave to in the Roads.'

'Where, exactly, is that?'

'Off the Mumbles light, where the ships wait for the tide, when they're goin' into the docks.'

'Hm!' said Holmes critically. 'But since you were bound for Cardiff, not Swansea, you had no business to be there. They must have paid you a tidy penny, since you were willing to delay your ship.' Captain Wade made no answer, and Holmes shrugged. 'Well, that, perhaps, is your business. What happened next?'

Wade picked up the stout bottle, tilted his chair to an alarming angle to obtain the last drop, and put the bottle down, empty, with an expression of regret.

'I'll tell yer the truth, mister,' he said darkly. 'I didn't know what they was at, an' I didn't want to know. Two hours before dawn, Fong come up to the bridge an' made a light signal out to sea, two or three times. There wasn't no answer – if there 'ad bin, they'd 'ave seen it from the coastguard station on Mumbles 'Ead – but presently a motorboat slipped up alongside, without lights. We slung a ladder over the side, an' two men come up. Ugly as sin, they was – one of 'em tall an' thin, wiv a neck like a giraffe, an' t'other a short little hap'orth, wider across the beam than 'e was 'igh, like 'e'd been squashed.'

I started involuntarily, recognising the description.

'An' strong, they was,' went on Wade, staring vacantly into space. 'They picked up that ruddy coffin between 'em, what it 'ad took four of us to do in Lunnon. We got it on a tackle, an' down into the boat. "What about my money?" I says, an' the long un grins at me like a skull, an' chucks a leather bag down on the deck. Full of bloody sovereigns, it was, an' while I was countin' 'em, they both jabbers at Fong. I see 'e didn't want to go wiv 'em, but the short un shows 'im a knife, an' 'e went. The boat shoved off, an' I never see any of 'em agin.'

'What night was this?' snapped Holmes.

'Friday last week, gettin' on for Saturday,' said Captain Wade mournfully. 'I waited as long as I could, but Fong never come back. I 'ad to tell the crew 'e was sick in 'is bunk, but we was in Cardiff by midday, an' none of 'em noticed 'e didn't come ashore. 'E ain't bin in to the office for 'is pay neither, an' I reckon they done 'im in. A bloody good cook 'e was, too. Do up a brace of seagulls, just like they was pigeon, 'e could. The 'ands never knew what 'e give 'em, an' they never arsked, 'cause they liked it. I see 'im wiv a dog once, an' I never see it arterwards, but I never said nothin'. . . . '

'You are an unconscionable villain,' said Sherlock Holmes, standing up abruptly, 'and responsible for more than you know. But, luckily for you, the ends of justice will not be served by proceeding further with the matter.'

We walked up to the corner of Heol Ysguborfawr, leaving behind us a chastened and bewildered skipper.

'An excellent performance, Petrie!' observed my companion, chuckling. 'Really, you are a loss to the CID!'

But, rare as it was, his praise fell upon deaf ears.

'It was Nayland Smith!' I said excitedly.

Holmes nodded. 'Yes, of course. Smith in a heavy Chinese make-up, and drugged.'

'Fu Manchu has a preparation which produces the semblance of death,' I said grimly. 'My God! And to think that it was only last Saturday morning, while I was asleep in PC Jones's cottage!'

'Yes, they kept him in London longer than I expected.' Holmes frowned and made a clicking sound with his tongue suggestive of self-reproach. 'But my inspiration proved correct. The mind of Dr Fu Manchu, while it may be superior to others, works in the same way. Coal mine – coal ship – coalman . . . They were lucky to find a ship suitable to their purpose, and particularly one which carried a Chinese cook.'

We had reached the corner. In this district, no taxicabs were available, but, with an unerring sense of direction, though he had been this way but once before, Holmes set off towards the city centre.

'It is almost beyond belief!' I said bitterly. 'Does every Chinese cook and laundryman in Britain belong to the Si Fan?'

'In a sense, yes,' he replied. 'Not that they are members, or even sympathisers. You still do not see how it works, Petrie. Fu Manchu can command the allegiance of his countrymen simply by threatening the lives of relatives who remain in China – a threat far more potent than it might be elsewhere. The rigid system of family ties and obligations is both the strength and the weakness of Far Eastern society. In Korea, for example, it extends even to an acknowledged responsibility between the grandchildren of cousins!'

17

TWO DEAD SHEEP

Holmes walked with long, rapid strides, and, trudging alongside, I found it hard to keep up with him, my steps leaden and my spirits low. I no longer had any doubts about the fate of Nayland Smith.

'We have lost him!' I said, my voice dull with despair. 'They have got him aboard that Chinese ship – '

'Why should you suppose that?'

'You heard what that man told us. They transferred him to a motorboat – '

'Quite! A motorboat – which is more likely to have come from the shore than from a ship. And it is equally likely that they brought him ashore.' Holmes glanced at me severely, but tempered his severity with a smile. 'You are making too much of this Chinese ship, Petrie. We know of it only from a conversation overheard more than a month ago. If it was here then, it is almost certainly elsewhere now. The coastguards have been searching for it for the past ten days – long before Captain Wade's vessel entered these waters – and can find no trace of it.'

Coming to a standstill, he plunged a hand into his coat pocket and pulled out his well-worn briar.

'Wait a minute while I light my pipe,' he directed, 'and then I will tell you what I think about this ship.'

We had entered a street of small shops dealing chiefly in maritime supplies. Holmes used a convenient doorway to fill and to light his pipe, and emerged contributing odorous clouds to the polluted atmosphere of dockland.

'Now,' he went on, 'when Fu Manchu came back to England last summer, he probably brought with him no more than a dozen of his key men – experts in strange arts and techniques of assassination. According to your own notes, he had lost at least six of them by the autumn. Hence the need for the reinforcements hinted at in Smith's letter. We know already of four whom you have not previously encountered. There is the Korean we met at Sir Julian's house. We have several times heard of the tall man and the short man, and, thanks to the indiscretions of your lady friend at the village inn, we know that one of them – who has a badly bitten ear – is named Wang Lo. From the same source, we learn that there is also a fourth, named 'Ali, who is probably a eunuch.'

'Yes,' I said, nodding, 'and they were presumably brought direct from China by this ship.'

'Correct – but the ship was not sent solely for that purpose. Now, it was in October, was it not, that Dr Fu Manchu was shot in the head by your fiancée, Kâramanèh?'

Again I nodded.

'And it was last month when Ki Ming first appeared in London,' added Holmes. 'Well, then, what happened is clear enough. When the news reached Chinese headquarters – wherever that may be – that Fu Manchu was injured and unlikely to survive, arrangements were made to send out Ki Ming as a replacement. The ship could not have left much before the end of November, and the journey would take five or six weeks. Why, subsequently, did it remain "hanging around," as Nayland Smith puts it? Certainly not to transport him to China, since his abduction was not then contemplated. The original intention was, I think, to bring back Dr Fu Manchu, if he still lived. But, in the meantime, Fu Manchu had been operated upon by one of the finest brain surgeons in London, and, no doubt to the disappointment of his would-be successor, refused to leave.'

We had entered a more populous quarter of the city. Holmes flagged down a taxi, and hustled me into it.

'Take us to the public library,' he instructed.

During the short drive which followed, he said no more. We arrived at our destination, and he shepherded me through into the reading room. Here, stowing away his pipe – after an exchange of glares with the assistant librarian – he demanded and received a large-scale map of the Swansea Bay area.

'Now we shall see!' he said, spreading the map out upon the table. He studied it in silence for a moment, then pointed. 'There is the lighthouse off which the *Marquis of Bute* anchored. Even supposing that the Chinese ship were still here, would they risk taking Smith aboard in a district of busy sea lanes such as this?'

'But the coast seems equally frequented,' I objected. 'Where could they have landed him?'

'There!' declared Holmes, and drew a circle with his fingertip.

Looking down, I saw a narrow strip of land which, breaking away from the mainland, thrust westwards into the Bristol Channel, immediately beyond the lighthouse. The outline of the Welsh coast has often been likened to a pig's head seen in profile. Substituting the likeness of a boar, the area to which he pointed might have represented one of the animal's tusks, and on any smaller map might easily have passed unnoticed.

'That is the Gower peninsula,' said Holmes, measuring with his thumbnail. 'Length, fifteen miles, perhaps – five across at the widest point. But the coast – look at the coast. Fifty miles, or a hundred? Nothing but a continuous chain of cliffs, bays, and coves, near which no road approaches. Inland, only villages – no towns, no railways. Offshore, shoals and submerged reefs, so that any sizeable shipping must give it a wide berth. *That* is where they landed him!'

The confidence with which he spoke was infectious.

'Then let us go to Swansea!' I exclaimed excitedly. 'We are doing no good here.' Hot upon the first, a fresh thought came to me, and, ignoring the outraged glances of our companions in this municipal temple of silence, I went on loudly: 'It was from Swansea that they hired the truck! The centre of their operations is *there*!'

Holmes looked at me, shaking his head slowly, and smiling.

'There is no centre,' he replied. 'Fu Manchu is here to clear up unfinished business, and though Wales may be small enough in comparison with England, we are like beetles chasing each other about London. But if it gives you any satisfaction to prefer Swansea to Cardiff, by all means let us go there.'

So it came about that, Holmes yielding gracefully to my enthusiasm, we re-packed our bags, and, the next day, moved an hour's journey down through an industrialised stretch of coast even uglier than that which approached Cardiff from the north. Here the worship of coal, with its grim sacrifices, gave place to the adoration of iron and copper. Here, amid the huge, ungainly buildings and pyramids of slag, rose ponderous *ziggurats* of outlandish machinery like the nightmare constructions of a Babylonian madman, the whole obscured by hissing steam and billows of smoke. One enormous workshop, furnished with no less than fourteen chimneys, appeared, so far as I could see, to be engaged solely in the manufacture of fog.

I began to feel depressed again.

We secured accommodation at a comfortable, though undistinguished, hotel, near the High Street station, lunched, and came out to explore, finding ourselves, unexpectedly, in a city of old-fashioned shops and houses, built on the slopes of two hills facing the sea, the streets clean and unhindered by tramways. My depression vanished, and, somehow, an immediate affection for the place took hold on me, as I saw between Swansea and Cardiff the same difference that exists between the fantasy atmosphere of Copenhagen and the grey stolidity of Amsterdam.

We paid a courtesy call at police headquarters, and made ourselves known to Superintendent Gribbler, upon whom we were thenceforth to rely for official co-operation. He was an affable idiot who promised all the assistance he could give us – at present, nil – but found it hard to believe in the existence of the Si Fan, particularly on his territory. He was friendly enough, I must say, and apparently believed that the best demonstration of goodwill was to call us by our Christian names, which he took to be 'Peter' and 'Shylock.'

'The man must be either hard of hearing or hard of intellect!' said Holmes savagely, as we came out into the street.

At my insistence – Sherlock Holmes complaining that nothing was to be gained – we climbed up through a residential district and ultimately by a long flight of steps to a small common from which we could look down upon the whole expanse of the bay. In a material sense, perhaps we gained nothing, but I for one found the exercise rewarding. Below us, and to our right, the coast swept south and west in a broad, graceful arc, running five miles from the town to a rocky headland, off which lay two small islands, the outer crowned by the white tower of a lighthouse. Fishing boats and the triangular sails of yachts speckled the surface of the bay, while, farther out to sea, larger craft might be seen approaching and departing from the docks on our left. Nearer to hand, the rooftops of Swansea descended in multicoloured terraces to the shore.

So far as our quest was concerned, we entered now upon a frustrating period of inaction. Holmes, if not content, was at least resigned to wait. I, less patient, and with grave personal issues at stake, was driven to a near frenzy. Occasionally, we were active, but to no avail. In response to a circular issued by Scotland Yard, the county and borough police forces of Wales were co-operating energetically. We were invited to look into incidents ranging from a knife fight between two lascars in Cardiff to the theft of nine pairs of trousers from a Chinese laundry in Denbigh. Most of these problems Holmes declined, but we once went out to Carmarthen and passed a fruitless day inquiring into the furtive behaviour of an Algerian carpet seller, who, in the end, proved to be carrying on a clandestine affair with a local barmaid.

To my disappointment, after identifying the Gower coast as the most likely point of Smith's landing, Holmes blankly refused to set foot west of the lighthouse, saying that it was pointless to speculate upon which of a hundred possible sites might have been used a week ago.

Since he could not be persuaded to accompany me, I went on my own, but succeeded only in confirming his conclusions. Beyond the lighthouse island, a reasonably civilised footpath snaked around the cliff face to two attractive bays, popular in summer and easily accessible by road. Westwards of that point was a different story. The path deteriorated into a goat track winding across precipitous headlands, passing above a deep cove and many narrow inlets in which a boat might have been beached, given a calm sea. After an hour of scrambling, it brought me into another large bay, with a bank of pebbles at the rear, totally deserted, and miles from any road.

It took me hours to get back, following the tortuous course of a stream through dense woods and into a wide valley where it vanished underground, leaving me hopelessly lost. Like the coast, it was a place of wild, awesome beauty, with pits and subsidences hinting at the existence of subterranean caverns to which no entrance was known – unless, I thought, it was known to Fu Manchu. By the time that I eventually emerged on a country lane, it was nearly dark.

But, for all my efforts, when I looked later at my guidebook, I saw that I had covered only a fraction of a ragged coastline which would require literally weeks to explore in detail.

Ten days passed, during much of which Sherlock Holmes stayed in bed till all hours of the day, to the confusion of the hotel chambermaids, the floor of his room littered with books on Welsh music, Celtic handicrafts, and Chinese history. I cannot honestly say that we ever really became friends. I respected him profoundly, and knew him for a loyal and courageous comrade in emergencies, but I knew also that the sort of close companionship which I had with Smith would never be ours.* On the subjects of both marriage and friendship, his views were coldly and succinctly expressed.

* Readers who suspect a homosexual relationship should realise that Dr Perie refers to a total commitment based on the ethics and standards of his day – a kind of friendship which may now be impossible. [Ed.]

194

'To have friends and family is to give hostages to Fate. A man in my position cannot afford such extravagances.'

Such was his philosophy, and, for the most part, his work and his studies were sufficient for him. But I know that 'there were also times when he was desperately lonely.

It was on one of these rare occasions, coincident with the second Monday of our stay in Swansea, that we had walked about the town, after our daily visit to the police station, and idled over coffee while Holmes expounded to me his recently formed theories on *pennillion*, including an audacious attempt to trace the Welsh harp to Chaldea via the Phoenicians. Returning to our hotel a little after six, we found that we had a visitor.

'Sergeant Hughes, from Brynamman,' the desk clerk informed us. 'He's been waiting for you in the lounge for the last half hour.'

'Odd!' said Holmes, frowning. 'I wonder what he can want? Well, we shall soon see.'

Without pausing to remove our hats and coats, we hurried into the lounge, and found it occupied only by a single individual – a man of about forty, wearing country tweeds, but with an air of the policeman about him. He stood up as we entered.

'Sergeant Hughes?' I asked.

'Yes, sir,' he answered.

'Detective-sergeant?' suggested Holmes, glancing at his clothing.

'No, sir. I'm out of uniform because it's my day off.'

'Dear me! Are we to regard this, then, as an unofficial visit?'

'I'd take it kindly if you would, sir,' replied Hughes, rather nervously, and with a trace of embarrassment. 'The truth of it is, sir, that I've come here on my own time because I don't want to be accused of going over the heads of my superiors.'

'Well, then,' I said, smiling – for there was something in the transparent honesty of the man which appealed to me, 'since you are off duty, there is nothing to prevent us from going into the bar, where we can discuss the matter more comfortably.'

This proposal was adopted. Over a glass of beer, our visitor's nervousness in the presence of Holmes – whom he clearly regarded as equivalent to a chief constable – relaxed a trifle, and he grinned apologetically.

'It's this way, sir,' he confided. 'The inspector thinks there's nothing in it, and he won't make a report. But we've all been told to keep our eyes open for funny business where there's Chinamen mixed up in it, haven't we, sir? And I still think you ought to know.'

'Go on!' I said quickly.

Sergeant Hughes took a cautious drink and glanced anxiously at Holmes.

'When there's two queer things happen more or less in the same place and at the same time, wouldn't you think there might be a connection, sir?'

'That is a natural inference,' said Holmes encouragingly, but a little impatiently, 'even if it is not strictly logical.'

'Then I'll give it to you in the right order, sir, though now it's the wrong way round, if you see what I mean.' We did not, but forbore to interrupt while Hughes, gaining confidence, slipped unconsciously into the manner of an officer giving evidence in court, garbling his instructions. 'It was Saturday morning last, when, PC Meredith being sick, I was instructed to go up to Capel Gwynfe and see Mr Garman of Bethesda Farm, two of his sheep which, having been missing since Thursday, had now turned up dead.'

'Good Heavens!' muttered Holmes, looking at me sideways. 'Are we to go and investigate the deaths of two sheep?'

'Mr Holmes, sir,' said Hughes, in an oddly hushed tone, 'do you know of anything that could lift up a full-grown sheep and hurl it on the ground hard enough to break every bone in its body?'

It was a hit for Hughes. Holmes's eyebrows shot up to a peak.

'Short of a gorilla, I do not!' he said slowly, and became suddenly attentive. 'And both of these animals were found in the same condition? Proceed, Sergeant – let us hear more about this!'

'They were found at Carreg Cennen, not far off the riverbank,' said Hughes. 'It's a bit of a queer place, sir. Farther back, there's a great limestone crag that goes up like a cliff, with an old castle on top – but not so steep on the other side, which is the side of Bethesda Farm is. Five or six miles round by the road, from the place they was found to the place they were took from – and they had to have been took, for there's no break in the stone wall round the field they were in, and the gate wasn't left open.'

At ease now that he felt sure of his audience, Sergeant Hughes paused to drink, licked his lips, and resumed:

'And now for the other queer bit, sir. I had to go out about the sheep because Meredith, the village constable, was sick, and the reason he was sick was this, sir – on the Wednesday night, or Thursday morning, that is, Meredith was called out of his bed by a fire reported in some woods, a mile or so the other side of the farm. But he never got there. On the way, he fell in with a Chinese loony who went for him and hit him a fearful blow in his stomach. An awful-looking man, Meredith says he was, deformed, and all over blood, with a great bit of plaster stuck over one ear – '

'Good God!' I exclaimed, starting up from my chair. 'Wang Lo!'

'Ah!' said Holmes, quietly. 'So Wang Lo is the short one, then.'

Sergeant Hughes gave us a puzzled look, not knowing quite what to make of this interruption.

'Well, sir, if you think it worthwhile, I'd advise you to go and see PC Meredith, because I can only give it to you second-hand, except for the sheep. He reported it, of course, but the inspector doesn't like him and says he wouldn't know a Chinaman from a Zulu.'

'Yes,' said Holmes, nodding. 'I think we will go and see him, and also the farmer. One more thing, Sergeant

– where was this place where the constable was assaulted, in relation to the farm?'

'About two miles nearer to Capel Gwynfe, sir.'

'Then there are really three centres of interest, not two – the field from which the sheep disappeared, the spot where they were found, and the place where Meredith met the Chinaman – situated roughly at three points of a triangle, with Carreg Cennen in the middle. Is that right?'

'Yes, that would be about right, sir.'

'Good!' said Holmes. He finished his beer and stood up. 'You have helped us materially. We will say nothing to your inspector, but I will see to it that a good word is put in for you at headquarters. Now, is there anything else?'

Hughes hesitated, seeming to become once again embarrassed.

'Well, yes, there is, sir – ' he said finally, reddening, and running a finger round inside his collar. From a side pocket of his jacket he produced a small notebook. 'It's for my boy that's fourteen and up to grammar school, you see, sir. . . . If I might just have your autograph? It would mean so much to him, sir. . . . '

Our visitor departed, his desires gratified, and Holmes regarded me with an exuberant expression illuminating his pale features, chuckling and rubbing his hands together.

'We have picked up his trail!' he declared. 'Why Fu Manchu should wish to murder sheep defies the imagination – but no matter. Get out your maps and timetables, Petrie, and find out how we may come at this place.'

This, as it had often been Watson's, was a task now usually left to me. In preparation for it, I had early equipped myself with train and bus schedules covering virtually the whole of South Wales. But after searching through them for some time, I threw the lot down in despair.

'It's no good, Holmes,' I said. 'There is no bus that goes anywhere near. We simply cannot go on relying on bus services when we may be called upon to go to the most unlikely places at a minute's notice. We must have a car.'

Holmes groaned comically, and shrugged.

'Well, if we must,' he acknowledged morosely, 'I suppose we must.'

'Do you honestly dislike motor cars so much?' I asked curiously.

'It is not that I dislike them,' he replied, 'but that I recognise the danger of placing such machines in private hands. The motor car will create the car thief, who will be more difficult to catch than the horse thief. It will provide the criminal with a rapid means of escape from the scene of his crime, which he needs more often than the police need a rapid means of pursuit. But, not only that, when these murderous contraptions become cheap enough for anyone to buy, the toll of death and injury on the roads of Europe will exceed that of the battlefields.'

In the interests of an early start, we agreed to breakfast together the following day, which we had not so often done recently, due to Holmes's irregular habits. But, though lunch and dinner compared favourably with West End standards, breakfast at our hotel was always a minor disaster.

I came down a few minutes before Holmes to find the table reserved for our use laid, as usual, hours in advance, with cutlery, cruet stand, a glass jar of preserves, and a toast rack filled with slices of scorched bread, stone cold and tough as leather. A wooden-faced waiter sidled up beside me, added a teapot and cups, and went through the ritual of asking for my order – which meant that if I asked for anything but eggs and bacon, I would be told that it was 'off.'

'Well,' I demanded, 'what have you got?'

'Eggs and bacon,' he said, and went out again.

Sherlock Holmes, dressed, but still wearing a dressing gown in lieu of a jacket, joined me and sat down, yawning, to pour himself a cup of tea. Both of us preferred coffee at breakfast time, but none was available before eleven.

'Really,' he said crossly, 'I could wish for a more

auspicious start to the day. But at least we have fine weather.'

Early morning sunlight streamed into the room and a bee, entering by the partly opened window, buzzed around my head.

'A little soon yet for bees, isn't it?' I observed, fanning it away.

'No,' replied Holmes, again yawning. 'That is not a social bee. It is one of the solitary sort which breed three or four times a year, and can be seen at almost any season.'

Drawing a piece of toast towards him, he levered one of the little yellow marbles out of the butter dish and endeavoured to spread it. This was not easy, since they were straight from the ice and had a maddening tendency to roll off the table. Holmes swore under his breath, attacked with energy, and bent the handle of the butter knife. Taking advantage of his preoccupation, the bee returned.

'It is persistent!' I said.

'It is hungry,' answered Holmes shortly. 'Just leave it alone, and it won't sting you. I daresay it is attracted to the marmalade.' He lifted up the metal cover experimentally, and looked slightly surprised. 'Oh! It is not marmalade this morning. It is honey.'

'Possibly the management intends it in your honour,' I said, smiling.

'A misplaced gesture, then,' he grumbled. 'I am not particularly fond of the stuff. It is merely the behaviour of the manufacturers which interests me.'

The wandering bee, unopposed, had descended into the jar and was now gorging itself, while Holmes watched with a tolerant eye. Then, suddenly, he stiffened and leaned forward. Climbing up to the edge of the jar, the bee seemed curiously to falter. It launched itself ceilingwards, fell upon the tablecloth between us, and, agitating its wings furiously, spun like a top, rolled over on its back, and was still.

'What is the matter with it?' I gasped.

With a steely look in his eyes, Holmes picked up a

teaspoon and turned the insect over, but it did not move. He dipped the spoon into the jar, sniffed, applied the tip of his tongue, and spat into his handkerchief.

'Remarkable!' he said softly. 'I had heard of it, but never seen any. It is the deadly honey of Trebizond, gathered from a poisonous species of azalea.'

I stared at him, shocked, and still unable to comprehend. Holmes swung about in his chair, and summoned the waiter with a shout which brought all heads in the room jerking around to face in our direction.

'Who placed this pot of honey on our table?' he snapped.

'Honey?' stammered the waiter. 'But we never serve it, sir!' He peered foolishly at the glass jar, and his eyes widened. 'And – and that isn't one of our containers!'

No great amount of investigation was required. Inquiries quickly revealed that the first down to breakfast that morning had been an Indian student who had stayed overnight and left early, allegedly to catch a train for London. The container of marmalade belonging to our table was found on the floor under his.

'Not a serious attempt, Petrie,' said Holmes, with a saturnine smile. 'Just a grim jest in the Fu Manchu manner – and, but for an importunate bee, he might have had the laugh on me!'

18

MORGAN LE FAY

Rather than present the reader with an anticlimax, I should confess that our investigation in the matter of Mr Garman's sheep led to no direct conclusion, though it ended in a manner totally unforeseen.

'It is fortunate for us,' remarked Holmes, as we drove northwards through the Swansea Valley, 'that Fu Manchu wastes little effort on revenge. If he were to concentrate on our destruction, I doubt if our lives would be worth a moment's purchase.'

This was not the day which we had originally planned for our excursion, but the next, since we had found it impossible to hire a suitable car soon enough.* The model which we now had was a 'Continental' Standard tourer, similar in appearance to the Assistant Commissioner's Vauxhall in which I had first visited Holmes in Sussex. It had a collapsible hood and a spare wheel bolted to the starboard side, but was of a sturdier build – adequate, I hoped, to contend with roads likely to be as rough as any on the European continent.

The present road, though not a main one, was reasonably good, the distant horizon a vista of green-clad mountains. Up to Brynamman, where the enterprising Sergeant Hughes was stationed, it was an easy and uneventful run. Thereafter, we negotiated a switchback network of tortuous highways through wooded country divided between small farms and tracts of common land, often so narrow as to permit only a single lane of traffic. I wondered what would happen if we met anything. At the foot of a steep slope, we splashed through a ford.

* I was in no position to finance these adventures out of my own pocket, but Smith had an unlimited expense account, and Weymouth made special arrangements enabling me to draw on it. [P.]

'A "trap to be set for Morgan" . . . ' quoted Holmes suddenly. 'You remember Smith's letter? Look!'

He pointed, and, glancing to the left, I saw a signpost bearing the single word: 'Trapp.'

'Good Heavens!' I exclaimed. 'Can it be a coincidence?'

'Perhaps, or perhaps not,' said Holmes, shrugging. 'At all events, it is not far from where we are going.'

Navigating by means of a sketch map provided by Sergeant Hughes, we had little difficulty in finding Bethesda Farm. The name was roughly lettered on the gate. A dry stone wall surrounded a part of the property, and, within the enclosure, twenty or thirty sheep went placidly about their business, unconcerned by the violent end of their fellows. We made our way up to the house and discovered Mr Garman in an outbuilding, stirring an evil-smelling concoction designed to remove ticks from the fleeces of his flock.

The interview did not go well. He was a surly individual, probably at the best of times, and rendered the more so by the loss of his sheep. Worst of all, however, it turned out that he had never heard of Sherlock Holmes.

'The ignorance in these parts is past belief!' muttered my companion, as soon as Garman's back was turned.

Our request to see the remains of the deceased met with a flat negative.

'You can't. I've sold 'em to the butcher, and a good price I didn't get for 'em, they being so broke up.'

Our next suggestion, that we should go and inspect the spot where the sheep had been found, was likewise treated with disfavour, Mr Garman protesting that it was miles away. But on learning that we had a car and would take him there in it, he brightened up a little. I gathered that he had never ridden in a motor car, and that to do so would add to his local status. Whilst Holmes and I sat in the front, he occupied the back seat, sitting bolt upright with his arms folded and looking like a monarch going to his coronation.

After some ten minutes' driving, we came to the nearest point which could be reached by road. Here we descended, climbed over a fence, and crossed fields till we arrived at the bank of a shallow but swift-flowing river. A spectacular prospect lay before us. From the opposite bank the ground ran level for some distance to the base of an enormous pile of rock which towered up, almost vertical, to a height of three hundred feet – a precipice such as one would expect to find on a rock-bound coast rather than set amid cultivated land, and I wondered what geological convulsion at the world's birth might have produced it. At the summit, and perched on the very edge, stood dark castle walls.

Somewhat to Holmes's annoyance, since the dead animals had lain on the other side, we were unable to cross the river, but it proved that, in any case, Mr Garman could not identify the exact location.

'Were they close together?'

'No, they wasn't,' said the farmer gruffly. ''Bout three 'undred yards apart, they was. And whatever done it, it's PC Meredith's job to 'ave seen it weren't.'

I stared up at the imposing mass of Carreg Cennen and the grim silhouette of the ruined fortress. The conclusion was obvious, and yet clearly impossible.

'If they had fallen, or been thrown, from the castle,' I said wonderingly, 'they would have been found near the foot of the cliff. Could anything have hurled them this far?'

'Ah!' said Mr Garman darkly. 'Who can say what lives up there?'

'Anyone who walks up from the other side and looks, I should imagine!' snapped Holmes. He flexed his hands in an impatient gesture, then glared at our disgruntled cicerone. 'Is your name, perhaps, Morgan?'

'No, 'tain't!' came the growled retort. 'It's Paul.'

No useful purpose was to be served by remaining there longer. We returned to the car, deposited Mr Garman at the gate of his farm, and drove around to the north side of the castle, from which access was possible.

'What do you make of it?' I asked.

'Nothing,' said Holmes shortly. 'The motive is as obscure as the means. It could have been done as a threat – but, if so, he has no idea why he is being threatened, or what is demanded of him, which makes the whole thing purposeless.'

North of the escarpment, Carreg Cennen was a steep but negotiable green slope, upon which a few sheep were grazing, leading up to the crumbling walls and towers of the thirteenth-century castle – a sinister place, even in the sunlight. There was really no sound reason for suspecting that it had any connection with the mysterious events seemingly centred around it, yet the temptation was a natural one and too strong to be resisted.

We climbed up and entered through a complicated barbican once protected by pits and two drawbridges. It had been a formidable stronghold and, according to my guidebook – hastily consulted the night before – had played a significant part in the Wars of the Roses. But within the walls, virtually nothing was left standing. Worse, from our point of view, we could find no trace of visitors but a cigarette packet and a beer bottle, both of them months old.

'If this had been France or Italy,' observed Holmes gloomily, 'where they take better care of their castles, we might have found a *trebuchet* or some similar engine of mediaeval warfare capable of flinging the wretched animals across the valley!'

'Could they have been seized by some huge sort of bird?' I suggested vaguely. 'I have heard of eagles in Scotland carrying off lambs. Is there anything big enough to tackle a sheep?'

'You mean like the *rukh* of the *Arabian Nights*, which feeds elephants to its young?' Holmes smiled ironically, shaking his head. 'Well, the South American condor has a wing span of about ten feet, and might manage it, I suppose. But, even assuming such a creature to exist here, it is a singularly weak-minded bird which seizes a sheep, drops it, goes back for another one, drops that too, and comes down to eat neither!'

Unhopefully but determined, we pursued our exploration to the ultimate mystery of Carreg Cennen, passing through a vaulted passage lit by slots in the outer wall and created, in fact, by roofing over a dizzy path along the verge of the precipice we had seen from below. This, in turn, led to a cave and a damp, hideously contorted passage which, a hundred yards or so from the entrance, came to a dead end. We examined it minutely and with better reason, perhaps, than all our predecessors, but like them, failed to find the slightest evidence that it had ever gone any farther.

Save for the risk of striking one's head on the projecting rocks which, at every few yards, forced one to lean acutely sideways, there was no danger, but I was glad to get out again. Still we had discovered nothing. Back in the central compound, we retrieved the small picnic hamper which we had lugged up with us from the car – having been warned that there was nowhere to buy refreshments in the vicinity – and looked around for a suitable place to lunch. The sunny days of early spring had brought boisterous March winds with them, and there was a stiff breeze blowing. We sat down in the shelter of the castle wall, and, as we ate, stared out across a delightful panorama of rolling hills patchworked with fields and dappled with dark green clumps of woodland.

Sherlock Holmes, I regret to say, showed little interest, reserving his appreciation of scenic splendour for sparse moments of mental relaxation. He sat beside me with his legs drawn up and his elbows on his knees, munching moodily at a sausage roll and showing little interest in that either. But I was still thinking of the riddle of the blind passage.

'What did they use it for?' I said musingly. 'Why did they go to all the trouble of walling in the cliff path, just to have easy access to it?'

Holmes stared at me in mild disapproval. 'No doubt they kept the castle dragon in it,' he replied acidly.

'Welsh dragons have wings, so perhaps that is what we are looking for!' I said, laughing – then, as the thought prompted another, started slightly. 'You have reminded me of something which I read last night,' I said. 'This castle is supposed to have been inhabited by the sorceress Morgan Le Fay.'

'The legendary sister of the equally legendary King Arthur,' said Holmes promptly, refusing to be caught out. 'But let us exhaust the possibilities of nature – even condors, if you like – before we consider witchcraft.'

'I did not mean that!' I retorted, somewhat indignantly. 'But think – if the "trap" of Smith's letter may be the village of Trapp down below, may not "Morgan" be the castle of Morgan le Fay?'

'H'm!' said Holmes, looking a little surprised. 'One up to you, Petrie! It could be, of course, though I rather doubt if the Si Fan would have much to do with Norman-Celtic mythology. The trouble is there are altogether too many "traps" and "Morgans" in this business.' He stretched, easing the cramped position of his legs, and got up stiffly. 'At all events, there is nothing up here, so let us now go and try our luck with the constable.'

We descended the slope, threw the depleted hamper into the back of the car, and continued on our way. Although the steep and narrow roads were something of a trial, I was gaining experience and we reached Capel Gwynfe in twenty minutes. Locating the police cottage easily enough, we found that we were expected, Sergeant Hughes of Brynamman having previously telephoned. A small, mousy-looking woman, who introduced herself as the constable's sister and housekeeper, showed us into the living room.

Here we found the ailing PC Meredith reclining in an armchair, clothed in a woollen dressing gown, surrounded by a pungent aura of embrocation and clasping to his ample stomach a stone hot-water bottle wrapped in a piece of blanket. He was a heavily built man, with a walrus moustache which framed a lugubrious expression.

'Don't get up!' said Holmes hastily. 'We know that you are unwell.'

PC Meredith sank back into his chair with a look of surprised relief. As we presently discovered, he believed that Sherlock Holmes was the Metropolitan Commissioner of Police. We did not disillusion him, and, finding that he had a sympathetic audience, he told his story readily enough.

'Asleep and in bed, I was,' he explained, 'when the call come through from Mr Jenkins, that's got a telephone in his house. Ten past three, sir – I got it written down in me logbook. Excited, he was. Says he's just been down the garden, and seen a fire in the woods, 'bout a half mile from his place.'

'One moment,' interjected Holmes, frowning. 'What was he doing in his garden, in the middle of the night?'

PC Meredith looked a little uncomfortable. 'Well, sir,' he said awkwardly, 'out here in the country, there's times when people has to go down their gardens in the middle of the night. . . . '

'Oh! Very well!' said Holmes, looking equally uncomfortable. 'Go on, then!'

'I thinks it's bit early in the year for forest fires,' resumed PC Meredith, 'and not been all that dry lately. I reckons, if he seen anything, it's gypsies, but I better go and look. So I gets dressed, and out I goes on me bike. I come halfway to his place, but I never seen no fire, and if there was one, it must've gone out, for we never heard no more about it. And then, right in front of me, I seen 'im. . . . '

'Him? Who?'

'The Chinaman! Only I thought then he was an ape. I nearly run over 'im. Staggering about the road, he was, like a drunkenest man I ever seen, and his hands nearly touching the ground. I gets past him, jumps off me bike, and switches on me lantern. Ugly, he was – I never seen nobody so ugly – but the inspector can say what he likes: I seen Chinamen before, and I knows he was one. Dressed all funny, he was, too – '

'Funny? In what way?'

'All in one bit, like overalls. I reckon it's what they wears in the loony bin, 'cause that's where 'e come from. There's blood on his face, and blood on his clothes. "What you got up to?" I says, and I puts out me hand, meaning to help him, like. And then he snarls and come at me with a knife! How he missed me, I don't know – I was that took aback. But when he come round for another try, I was ready for 'im. I 'its him straight between the

208

eyes with me lantern, and down he went – out for the count.'

'This man had a piece of surgical tape over one ear, didn't he?' I asked.

'Yes, he did, sir,' replied PC Meredith. 'Only I don't remember if it was his left or his right. I only see him the once, and I couldn't take a good look at him afterwards, because when I hit 'im I broke me lantern.'

'Why not use your bicycle lamp?' inquired Holmes.

The constable's face became a shade more ruddy. 'Damn, I never thought of that!' he muttered. He shifted uncomfortably, and a spasm of pain crossed his features. 'Well, sir, I see I got a Chinese loony on me 'ands, and where he come from I don't know, but I see he got to be got back there. So I gets the handcuffs on him and slung him across me bike, and then I wheels him back up here like a sack of potatoes. A real job I had with 'im, what with keeping him from falling off, and trying to keep the pedals from banging 'im on the 'ead. He stayed asleep all the way – or I thought he did – but when we gets outside here, and I starts to heave him off me bike, he come to life like a spring busting out've a clock! He bends his elbows, and gives a jerk, and – the inspector says I'm a bloody liar, but he broke the link between the handcuffs like it was made of wool! Then round come 'is fist, and gets me below the belt like a steam'ammer. Down in the road I went, sick as a dog. And when I could get up on me knees and looks around, there he wasn't – nor me bike neither!'

'Wang Lo, undoubtedly,' murmured Holmes. 'Has your bicycle been recovered?'

'No, sir, it ain't,' said PC Meredith mournfully. 'The inspector says I'll have to pay for it.'

'Oh, I don't think so,' said Holmes reassuringly. 'But, believe me, you're lucky to have escaped with your life.'

With that, the official purpose of our visit came more or less to an end. The woman who had admitted us came in with teacups and for some further minutes we sat talking of unrelated matters. I asked the constable a number of purely technical questions about his stomach and advised him to get a proper examination at the hospital. At that moment, the telephone rang and PC Meredith sat up, groaning.

'Stay where you are, Alun,' ordered his sister. 'I'll answer it.' She moved to the window sill, picked up the instrument from its place beside a potted begonia plant, spoke, listened, and turned back to us. 'It's the police at Sennybridge,' she announced, 'and they want Mr Holmes.'

'Indeed?' queried Holmes, looking rather surprised. He crossed and took the telephone from her. 'This is Sherlock Holmes speaking. How did you know we were here? Oh, I see! What? What's that? Hold on a minute. . . . '

Taking the receiver from his ear, he stared at me with a curiously tense expression.

'Does Smith have a pigskin wallet stamped with the initials "D.N.S."?' he snapped.

'Yes!' I exclaimed excitedly.

'It has been found,' said Holmes tonelessly, 'in the possession of a burglar, who is apparently an Oriental.'

He returned his attention to the telephone, and, while I stood wondering feverishly what this new development might mean, completed a short conversation. Then, hanging up the receiver, he turned away from the window and took up his coat from the chair upon which he had placed it.

'They called Swansea first, and were told that we planned to come out here,' he explained, and I nodded. In these days, it was our established practice to go nowhere without leaving word of our intended destination. 'It seems you may have a chance to try out your Arabic,' he went on, smiling a trifle grimly. 'The man who has Smith's wallet is dark-skinned, wears a turban, and refuses to understand anything but his own language – which they think is Arabic. He was caught early this morning, attempting to break into a chemist's shop in Sennybridge, and they have him in custody.'

He switched his regard to our host. 'I gather that the shortest way to reach this place is across country?'

'Yes, sir,' said Meredith quickly. 'Go about a mile and a half up the road, away from Brynamman, and then you takes the road on your right that leads to Trecastle. There's a bit bumpy in places, but it's only about fifteen miles if you goes that way – half of what it would be if you goes up through Llandovery.'

We thanked him for his advice, and took our leave without further ceremony.

'Our friends at Sennybridge appear to be a smarter outfit than I would have expected in a country police station,' commented Holmes, as I started up the car. 'It was quick thinking to connect the intials "D.N.S." with the abduction of Nayland Smith.'

I nodded, stimulated to fever pitch by the belief that, at last, we had our hands upon one of the Si Fan who had seen Smith – who knew where he was. Already, as we turned out upon the road, I was searching through my small stock of Arabic for the confrontation, but, beyond starting with '*Ya zift!*' ('O filth!'), I could think of nothing very useful.

In a short space of time, we found the signpost for Trecastle and turned off. Our route now lay across some of the finest landscape in Carmarthenshire – for, though I did not know it then, we were passing through the celebrated Vale of Myddfai. It was wide, wooded country with mountains all around – Myddfai to our left, and to our right, the greater heights of Gareg Lâs and Carmarthen Van. The road, undulating gently, ran more or less straight, almost without habitation, and marked here and there with large whitewashed stones.

'I can only hope that this new line of inquiry will lead farther than the others,' remarked Holmes, shouting above the noise of the engine. 'Apart from wasting our time at that confounded castle – which seems, after all, to have nothing to do with anything – we now have three separate incidents, apparently unrelated excepting for the fact that they occurred roughly in a radius of twenty miles. As to why this Arab burglar should be breaking into a chemist's shop, I suppose they must be short of some drug which they urgently require.'

211

'They may need it for Wang Lo,' I shouted back: 'The constable said he was injured when he met him. Incidentally, I have a theory about that. . . . '

'Then I should be pleased to hear it,' answered Holmes, in a tone suggesting that he would rather not, 'for, personally, I have none.'

'Well,' I said determinedly, 'let us suppose that Fu Manchu has some terrible flying creature which Wang Lo handles. Hawks have been used for hunting in the Far East, just as falconry was once popular in Europe. The fire which was seen in the woods might have been lighted to guide it back to him. But, since it is clearly a savage brute, it turned upon him.'

'All things are possible,' rejoined Holmes, with a rude yawn. 'However, granting you your hell-bird, it must now be at large, and so we may expect to hear more of it before long.'

Jamming his pipe between his teeth, he cupped his hands and attempted to re-light it – which, in a moving car on a windswept mountain road, was manifestly impossible.

Distantly, though trees, I glimpsed a lake. As far as the eye could see, nothing moved ahead of us. I ventured to increase speed a little, at the expense of some added jolting, but kept a wary eye open for sheep, which, hereabouts, were apt to wander across one's path at the least convenient moments. Sherlock Holmes grunted ill-humouredly and put away his pipe.

I judged that we had now come about halfway. A mile farther on, but plainly visible through the crisp, clear air, I saw a cottage roof and barns of a small farm – the first buildings we had seen for some time. But as we drew abreast I saw that the place was deserted, the windows broken and the garden a riot of weeds. Then, fifty yards past, came disaster, heralded by a loud detonation and followed by a rapid thudding which shook the whole framework of the car. The steering became erratic. I braked frantically, fought the vehicle to a standstill at a crazy angle across the road, and switched off the engine, cursing like a pirate.

'Your mechanical horse has cast a shoe!' said Holmes sardonically.

We got out and I stood staring at a flat front tyre with the baffled expression of an incompetent driver confronted with his first puncture. Holmes shrugged philosophically, walked around to the front of the car, then, with a sharp exclamation, stooped and picked something up. Swinging about, he extended his hand and displayed a cluster of four steel spikes, each about an inch long and joined in such a way that, no matter how the device fell, one remained upward.

'Calthrops!' he said grimly. 'An ancient weapon for use against cavalry, and equally effective against motor cars. The road is strewn with them.'

He flung the thing away, and, ere I had overcome my first surprise, snatched the automatic pistol from his pocket.

'Stand by for the worst, Petrie!' he snapped. Jerking a cartridge into the chamber, he slipped the pistol out of sight, keeping his hand upon it. 'I don't know where the attack will come from, or what form it may take. That fool Gribbler has been tricked into giving away our plans to the enemy. There is *no* Arab burglar in Sennybridge – it was a ruse to bring us out here!'

Shock, disappointment, and alarm left me momentarily speechless. I glanced helplessly around, searching our surroundings for the first hint of an assault. Then:

'Look!' I said.

The door of the dilapidated cottage had opened, and a man was walking down the weed-choked garden. He wore a dark suit, and there was nothing menacing in his bearing, but, as he reached the gate and approached, I was conscious of a vague familiarity. Following my companion's lead, I grasped the butt of my pistol. The man walking unhurriedly towards us was now clearly revealed as Chinese, and as he came closer I recognised the black-rimmed spectacles and scholarly features of Li King Su, the graduate of Canton, who had assisted me in a certain operation. . . .

Halting six paces distant, he greeted us with a nod.

'Please do nothing impulsive,' he said pleasantly, 'or you will be shot down from the house. Dr Fu Manchu requests you to take tea with him.'

PART II

19

GREEN TEA

'There is no need to fear,' said Li King Su, with a bland smile. 'Please come!'

He turned on his heel and began to walk back towards the cottage.

I looked uncertainly at Holmes. 'What shall we do?'

'Do as he says!' he replied curtly. 'If they have rifles trained on us, what choice do we have?'

Reluctantly, I fell into step behind our guide, Holmes beside me. We passed through the open gateway into the forlorn garden of brambles and cultivated plants run wild. The Chinaman, seemingly confident that we were following, never turned his head.

'Do you know this man?' asked Holmes, in a whisper.

'Yes,' I said. 'He is Li King Su – the Chinese surgeon who acted as dresser when Sir Baldwin Frazer and I were forced to operate upon Fu Manchu.'

Pausing at the cottage door, Li King Su opened it and stood aside, waiting for us to enter.

'God help us!' I said hoarsely. 'We are walking into a trap!'

'Very possibly,' answered Holmes dryly and without emotion. 'But, if so, we go into it armed and forewarned.'

Preceding me, he strode boldly across the threshold and we came directly into what had been the principal room of the building. The interior was of a nature so astonishing and incongruous that, for a moment, even my fears were forgotten. Ruin was everywhere. The walls were cracked and plaster had fallen from the ceiling, exposing the rafters. All the débris, however, which had lain upon the floor had been swept into a great pile in one corner, and any furniture which might have remained there had been removed.

In its place stood, firstly, a tall Chinese screen in four sections, evidently masking an opening in the opposite wall – a wonderful thing composed entirely of an intricate filigree of carved ivory, in which birds, beasts, and legendary creatures intertwined with complex geometrical patterns. Before the screen was a lacquered table and three low tabourets colourfully upholstered in Egyptian leather, one upon the far side and the other two closer to us. Apart from these wildly unlikely furnishings, the room contained nothing whatsoever.

Closing the door, Li King Su crossed to the screen and disappeared behind it, leaving us alone. We looked quickly at each other, and Holmes made a slight shrugging movement. A minute passed in silence while we both stood with our eyes turned towards the screen. My fingers tightened instinctively on my pistol. Suddenly there came the metallic rattling sound of curtain rings drawn along a pole and a momentary darkening of the interstices in the elaborately worked panels.

From the left-hand side of the screen, Dr Fu Manchu stepped into the room.

He was attired as I had first seen him, in a plain yellow robe, the black skullcap on his high, domed forehead concealing the scar of his recent operation. The dreadful rictus of paralysis was gone now from his features, but his face was deeply etched with lines of suffering, and he moved slowly, still partially supporting himself on a heavy stick. Two paces within the room, he stopped, turned towards us, and bowed – a salutation which Holmes instantly acknowledged, whilst I continued to stand ungraciously upright. Fu Manchu regarded me for an instant and in his long green eyes I saw a flicker of contempt for the uncouth mannerlessness of the Occident.

'No harm is intended you,' he said.

Steadily, but still leaning upon his stick, he approached the stool on the far side of the table and stood beside it. Simultaneously there was movement behind the ivory screen and from opposite sides emerged two of

218

the fiercest-looking figures I have ever seen. Sherlock Holmes, standing grimly immobile at my side, flashed me a quick glance, warning me to hold myself in check.

These were not Burmese dacoits, but two huge Mongols with shaven heads and topknots – superb specimens of barbarous humanity, clad solely in loose, baggy trousers gathered in folds below the knee. Their muscular torsos gleamed as though oiled, and on the breast of each hung a jade medallion carved in the form of the Great Seal of the Si Fan. Leather wristbands, studded with brass, rose to their forearms, and they carried long, curved scimitars, points lowered to the floor. Their faces were savage and doglike, the tiny round eyes burning with hate.

'You will allow me my guard of honour,' said Dr Fu Manchu evenly, 'as I shall allow you your pistols. No conflict is possible without the death of at least one of us on either side.'

As his men took up their positions with their backs to the wall, he gestured towards the stools on our side of the table, inviting us to sit. Holmes did so at once while I followed suit, still hesitating. Fu Manchu seated himself upon the third, facing us, and balanced his stick across a corner of the table.

'You are a sick man,' I said, attempting to match his composure. 'After surgery such as you have received, you should still be resting.'

'You have some title to speak as my physician,' he replied smoothly, inclining his head slightly in my direction. 'Unfortunately, I am compelled to disregard your advice while there yet remain secrets to be shared and lips to be sealed.' He turned to Holmes. 'Forgive me for the deception which brought you here, but there are times when adversaries must meet under a flag of truce.'

He clapped his hands smartly. Again there was movement behind the screen, and, to my total confusion, Kâramanèh came into the room. I started forward with a hoarse cry, but Holmes's hand shot out to grasp my arm, thrusting me down upon the stool.

219

Hands locked upon the hilts of their swords, the two giants watched me with a bestial eagerness.

Kâramanèh was barefoot and dressed in the minimal indoor costume of *'anteree and shintiyán*,* of so fine a texture that I could see the dark marks of bruises on her fair skin. Her hair was unbound; she wore no jewellery – a slave in disgrace – save for the small diamond which sparkled on her left hand, and my heart leapt at the knowledge that she would have fought them to the death before letting them take that from her. Our eyes met and I saw her full red lips tremble in a brave attempt at a smile.

Averting her gaze, she turned aside and, from the tray which she carried, commenced to set out upon the table three small porcelain bowls and a teapot with a wicker handle, shaped more like a kettle.

'I regret that I must receive you in so humble a setting – or one which must appear so to your Western vision,' continued Dr Fu Manchu, completely ignoring her presence. 'But we of China possess the happy ability to see only that which we please. A T'ang screen, or a hand scroll by Wu Chen, and I may be at home anywhere.'

'I am honoured to consider myself as received, then, at your home in China,' answered Sherlock Holmes.

He had taken the measure of his man, I thought, and a thrill of anticipation ran through me as I contemplated the battle of those two great intellects. Kâramanèh took up the teapot and poured a pale green liquid into each of the three cups, her movements mercilessly revealing the graceful curves of her figure through her scanty attire. She placed two of the filled cups upon the tray and presented it, first to Holmes, who took one, and then to me. I hung back, still wondering if we were being offered the ritual cup of hemlock, but her eyes reassured me. I picked up the cup in my left hand, keeping my right firmly upon the Browning pistol in my pocket.

---

* A low-cut bodice and the well-known *harêm* trousers, turned up inside and tied under the knee. [Ed.]

Kâramanèh, her office performed, turned to go.

'*Khallîki shuwayya!*' ordered Fu Manchu, halting her. He fixed the baleful regard of his strange eyes fully upon my face. 'I will not deprive you of the opportunity to gaze upon her. She shall remain, but she may not speak.'

'I take it,' said Holmes, 'that this lady is Dr Petrie's fiancée, whom you have abducted?'

Fu Manchu slowly shook his head. 'I have not abducted her. She is my property by right of purchase under Islamic law.' He stared again at me. 'If I may now employ Kâramanèh only for menial tasks and must treat her harshly, yours is the fault, not mine. I cannot subject her a second time to the amnesiac which once I used upon her. It is an unsatisfactory preparation and the breakdown of its effects resulted in her attempt upon my life. But for this I accept the blame, and I will do no violence to her on that account.'

His words and the calm manner in which they were spoken roused me to a frenzy and I could contain myself no longer.

'Enough of these pleasantries!' I cried hotly. 'What have you done to Smith?'

'Mr Nayland Smith is safe,' he replied, in no way disturbed by my outburst. 'I have taken him into protective custody. Had I not done so, he would have been slain by those whom I am unable to control.'

Kâramanèh, leaving her tray upon the table, stood facing us, a little to the rear and to the left of Fu Manchu, her hands clasped modestly. There were tears on the long black lashes, and though I sought her face eagerly, she avoided looking at me. Her fingers twitched nervously. Behind her, the two giant sentinels stood impassive against the wall, like statues sculpted by a modern artist with a taste for the macabre.

Dr Fu Manchu leaned forward, took up the fragile cup, and raised it to his lips.

'In the somewhat peculiar circumstances,' he said, 'the host must drink first. You have my word that these vessels contain nothing but an infusion of unfermented tea leaves from the hill slopes of Kweichow.'

I hesitated an instant longer, then recalled that in all our various encounters his word had never been broken, and lifted my cup likewise. The translucent green beverage was bitter and refreshing. Holmes, with no previous experience of Fu Manchu, but an unerring judge of character, did not hesitate. He sipped appreciatively, holding the delicate china bowl between thumb and finger, lowered it to his knee, and smiled.

'I find your taste in tea superior to your taste in honey,' he commented.

Fu Manchu nodded imperturbably. 'You refer to my Byzantine honey – a secret known to the corrupt court of the Grand Comneni, and also to me. I thought that it might interest you to see a specimen, and I did not suppose that you would be so imprudent as to sample it.' He set his cup carefully upon the table. 'I rejoice to find you as perspicacious as your reputation suggests, for I did not wish to leave England without making your acquaintance.'

'You are leaving?' I burst out, and again he nodded.

'Soon, Dr Petrie. My work here is almost as an end. I return to China, and Mr Nayland Smith goes with me. He has much to confide in me concerning your police system, and when I have taken the necessary steps to correct his outlook, he will become my chief of staff in Burma.'

I sat back aghast, my nebulous fears confirmed now out of his own lips. It was true, then! Smith was to be carried back helpless to the monster's lair, like the prey of a poisonous spider, to be consumed at leisure – tortured, drugged, and, his brain filched of all that was useful, sent forth as a mindless creature of the Si Fan. Shocked to silence, I listened as in a trance to that unique, unforgettable voice, as Dr Fu Manchu went on speaking to Holmes, stressing gutturals and sibilants, and enunciating each syllable with the academic precision of a genius who has learnt English from a textbook without ever hearing it spoken.

'Neither did I wish to leave before expressing to you

my profound regrets for the incident in which a Strom-berg globe was projected into your residence by means of a spring catapult. It was done by my subordinates, but not with my consent or knowledge.'

'I had assumed as much,' said Holmes, and frowned thoughtfully. 'But, when you speak of Stromberg, do you mean the German chemist Helmuth Stromberg, who died three years ago? I was not aware that he had been working on such lines.'

'He completed his researches,' came the smooth reply, 'six months *after* his death, in my laboratory in Kiang-su, where I was able to offer him facilities denied to him during his lifetime. Regard me how you will, the day may soon come when you will be thankful that his secret lies in my hands rather than in those of Wilhelm II.'

Fu Manchu glanced over his shoulder at Kâramanèh, who came forward to refill the cups, first ours and then his. For a moment she was bending so close to me that I could smell the well-remembered perfume of her hair. I looked into her violet eyes and longed to speak, but dared not tempt her to answer me, knowing that she would suffer afterwards, though I contrived briefly to touch her fingers. They were as cold as ice. He saw, I think, but gave no sign.

Kâramanèh returned to her position, standing as before. Fu Manchu drank a little from his cup and again addressed himself to Holmes.

'The Si Fan is mine, but my will is not yet absolute.' He spoke softly but viciously, and, as he continued, his voice becoming ever more guttural and sibilant, the weird film came down over his eyes, giving an impression of blindness – a phenomenon which, as I saw, excited the keen interest of my companion. 'There are those who would cast me down and reap the harvest which I have sown. But I shall prevail. Ere I leave these shores, I will answer to the Seven and they shall judge between us.'*

The last words were spoken in a hiss so low as to be

* This indiscreet remark led, indirectly, to a successful raid on the meeting of the Seven, in London. [P.]

almost inaudible. Dr Fu Manchu seemed to rouse himself as though from sleep, and the veil passed from his eyes, leaving them once more green and lustrous, like those of a wild animal.

'Mr Sherlock Holmes, you have chosen at last to interest yourself in my affairs. Be warned in time, and leave me to complete my task in peace. It would distress me immeasurably to be the means of terminating so distinguished a career, but if you hinder the achievement of my aims, I will destroy you without compunction.'

'What *are* your aims?' asked Holmes calmly.

'I would bring order where you have brought chaos. For your selfish commercial ends, you have torn down the structure of the ages. India and Burma you have enslaved. Southeast Asia groans under the Dutchman's yoke, and the French hold Indo-China. The Prussian has set his heel upon the islands of the Pacific. Japan you have made your vassal and used against us. All this I would change, and restore my country to her rightful position of leadership, to which five thousand years of history entitle her.'

As I listened to his voice and looked about me at our incongruous surroundings – the priceless ivory screen, the sinister, half-clad figures with their long swords, the patched walls and broken ceiling – I was stricken by a nightmare sense of unreality. The wooden bars of the window frame and the few shards of glass which it contained split up the waning afternoon sunlight into narrow shafts of radiance, striking at odd angles across the shadowed interior like spotlights on a stage. With it came a chill March wind, ruffling my hair, and rippling the loose sleeves of Fu Manchu's robe. Kâramanèh, in her cruelly inadequate clothing of gossamer silk, was shivering pitifully.

'Having regard to the current conditions in China,' murmured Holmes, 'I venture the opinion that your aims would best be served there.'

'There is truth in what you say,' observed Dr Fu Manchu dispassionately, 'and I return with that object in mind. Soon my efforts will be superfluous here. In their insensate greed and lust for empire, the countries of Europe will tear at each other's throats in a ruthless contest beyond your capacity to imagine. Land, sea, and air will become a battlefield. Death and destruction will reign everywhere, and the heritage of your children will be a wilderness. Your shackles will rust and fall from the East, and never again shall you impose them on us.'

Holmes stared at him soberly for a moment. 'May I ask,' he said finally, 'when you anticipate that this apocalyptic event will take place?'

'It will come to pass in the eighth month,' replied Fu Manchu impassively.

He turned and spoke a curt word of command to Kâramanèh. She bowed her head, and, with a last agonised glance at me, vanished around the angle of the screen. Hard upon her departure, I was conscious of the green eyes narrowed to slits and focussed again upon me.

'For Dr Petrie I have also a word of counsel. You are young, and, as yet, have accomplished little, but I see in you the seeds of genius. Under my guidance, you could become great. Give up this foolish struggle which can gain you only bitterness. Join with me now, of your own free will, accept my leadership, and I will give Kâramanèh to you.'

I stared back at him and could make no immediate answer, prompted by soulless reason to compromise with my honour – to pledge my word and seek the first opportunity of betraying him. But I shook my head.

'So be it, then,' he said solemnly. 'If I find that I can acquire your services without inconvenience to myself, I shall do so. But do not presume too much upon my interest. Should it be necessary to remove you from my path, I shall not hesitate.'

Dr Fu Manchu clapped his hands and Li King Su entered the room. I noted that he now wore a cap and an overcoat. He crossed to the outer door, and I sensed that the interview was at an end.

225

'I trust that you entertain no similar thoughts as to acquiring *my* services?' remarked Holmes, less anxious, I thought, than piqued by his exclusion.

'Nothing would give me greater satisfaction,' said Fu Manchu smoothly. 'But your years forbid it. Age is the spectre which haunts us all – which makes a mockery of learning. For many years, I have sought a means to stay the hand of Time, and unless I am successful, all my work must come to nothing – for what I would do may not be done in the normal span of life.* But what I may do here and now, I will do, and before I sail for China I will strike a blow and set an example which this arrogant island shall remember as long as it bears the name of Britain.' He stood up and we stood up likewise. 'I think it destined that we shall meet again, Dr Petrie. To Mr Holmes I say farewell.'

He bowed, and, this time, both of us bowed back. Li King Su held open the door, and we went out into the garden. He did not follow. No move was made against us as we walked slowly back to our stranded vehicle. I felt furious and humiliated – treated with polite contempt, and forced to watch Kâramanèh tormented and paraded *en déshabillé* in front of us. It had been a victory, hands down, for Fu Manchu.

Holmes, on the contrary, appeared delighted.

'His eyes are extraordinary!' he exclaimed enthusiastically. 'That veil which obscures them when his emotions are aroused – it is, as you told me, a kind of extra eyelid, like the *membrana nictitans* of a bird. I wonder if he can control it?'

But I felt in no frame of mind to discuss the peculiarities of Fu Manchu's eyes.

'He has amused himself at our expense,' I said disgustedly.

'Not altogether,' answered Holmes. 'Like all tyrants who boast of their omnipotence, he has told us more than he intended.'

---

* He was successful, but it took him a further fourteen years. [Ed.]

In the background, I heard the sound of an engine and turned back to face the cottage in time to see a heavy lorry emerge from one of the tumbledown barns at the rear. The back of it was covered with a canvas hood, and I could not see who was driving. We watched it pass along what was apparently a narrow lane hidden by the weeds and bushes in front, come out upon the road a hundred yards from where we stood, and turn away towards Trecastle.

'The audacious villains!' said Holmes indignantly. 'That is the truck which I saw at Nant Gareth, and they are still using it. They cannot know that we have the number. In whatever fashion they may ultimately have accounted for their loss of the man who was killed in the mine, it seems they are unaware that we were ever there. Well, if they use the vehicle much longer, there is a chance that some astute police officer may recognise it. But, unfortunately, it will be some time before we can reach a telephone.' He glanced meaningly at our Standard tourer. 'A good thing for us that only one tyre was damaged, or we should really be in trouble. Have you ever changed a wheel, Petrie?'

'No,' I admitted disconsolately.

But Holmes, whom I had expected to find irritable and depressed, remained surprisingly cheerful.

'Well, well,' he said, 'I daresay it is something which two men of average intelligence should be able to figure out.'

I nodded and started to unpack the toolbox. Holmes, looking on satirically, lighted his pipe while I laid out a row of mysterious instruments on the running board, then suddenly he spoke again.

'Your fiancée is as courageous and resourceful as she is charming,' he remarked. 'You hardly took your eyes off her, of course, but did you notice the movement of her fingers?'

'She was nervous,' I said shortly, feeling it somewhat in bad taste that he should mention it.

Holmes gave a triumphant laugh. 'I thought so too, at

227

first – until I observed that her right index finger moved regularly, very much as one operates a telegraph key when sending the letter *H*. She addressed me because she knows that you cannot read the Morse code.'

'What!' I exclaimed.

My surprise was such that I dropped the spanner I was holding and it clattered loudly on the road. But in the same instant I remembered how Kâramanèh had once flashed a warning across the moors which had saved my life and Smith's. Now, forbidden to speak, she had nevertheless found a means of communication.

'She was, as you recall, standing between Dr Fu Manchu and his bodyguard,' went on Holmes, 'so that none of them could see what she was doing. As soon as I realised, I looked straight as her and blinked once for "Acknowledged." She immediately sent this message: "DAVIES OF GLYN IDRIS – WARN HIM."'

'Davies?' I queried, in a bewildered voice. 'But who is he?'

'Obviously, the next intended victim, and Glyn Idris is where he lives. We shall discover both.'

'I see,' I said slowly, understanding but conscious of a certain disappointment. 'She said nothing about Smith, then?'

'Davies is evidently the more urgent, and I doubt whether she has any exact information about Smith.' Holmes paused, looking at me and appearing curiously loath to continue. 'Well, I suppose I shall have to tell you. . . . After she had served us our second cup of tea, she tried to send a further message. It read: "SMITH HELPLESS – THEY ARE USING THE WORM – " but she was unable to go on, since it was just then that Fu Manchu looked round and dismissed her from the room. I don't know if he suspected.'

20

DAVIES OF GLYN IDRIS

There was a flurry of activity at police headquarters that evening, where books and maps were consulted and telephone calls made in an energetic attempt to locate Glyn Idris. It was not in their territory, and nobody knew in whose territory it was.

We had ultimately arrived in Swansea at about eight. As regards the conclusion of the wheel-changing episode, the least said may be the best. Sherlock Holmes sat on one of the whitewashed stones at the side of the road and offered helpful suggestions while I battled clumsily with unfamiliar tools, skinned my knuckles, and soiled a nearly new Donegal tweed suit with indelible patches of oil.* His only comment was that I should have known better than to go motoring in my best clothes, to which I retorted, angrily, that I had no old clothes with me.

'Well, you have now!' he said, shrugging.

The homeward journey was accomplished without further adventures or mishaps, and we drove straight to the police station. Our first concern was to act upon Kâramanèh's information – for we knew that a man's life was at stake. We found Superintendent Gribbler off duty, but, although we did not specifically ask, someone called him and he turned up, voluntarily, while the search for Glyn Idris was still going on. Now a new mystery presented itself. Taxed with giving away our whereabouts, his round, jovial face became lined with concern, and he hotly denied having done so.

'Now, look here, Shylock,' he protested (Holmes

* I suppose Holmes never really *told* me that he could not drive – but my sentiments may be imagined when I discovered, years later, that he had taken part in the London to Brighton Rally and, in the rôle of Altamont, worked as a mechanic in Detroit. [P.]

winced), 'I've got more sense than that! If they'd told me it was Sennybridge on the line, I'd have made sure first. But nobody called! Nobody! And it wasn't anybody else in this station, because nobody but me knew where you were going!'

For the first time in our acquaintance, I saw Holmes completely at a loss.

'Then how could he have known that we were at Meredith's cottage?' he exclaimed. 'We were not even sure when we were going there ourselves! Upon my word, Petrie – you will soon have me believing that Fu Manchu is in league with Morgan le Fay!'

He fell silent for a moment, frowning, and shaking his head.

'It was planned hours in advance,' he muttered. 'The man who spoke to me was some out-of-work actor whom they employed to impersonate the sergeant at Sennybridge. I'll swear he was a Welshman!'

Gribbler, who was less of a fool than his stupidly amiable manner and indifferent ear for names led one to suspect, told his men to discontinue their inefficient efforts at finding Glyn Idris and telephone the town librarian. This was done, and the librarian called away – with some difficulty – from his dinner, to come downtown and consult the reference books contained in the public library. Twenty minutes later, to our dismay, he had found no less than four villages named Glyn Idris – two in North Wales, one in Pembrokeshire, and another in Cardiganshire.

None was anywhere near Carreg Cennen, but, for the time being, we disregarded the two in the north, believing – or hoping, rather – that Fu Manchu's current campaign was confined to the south. As to the identity of 'Davies,' we were once again confronted with one of the commonest names in Wales, and there could be no possible way of finding out other than by inquiries on the spot.

'Kâramanèh could not be more specific,' observed Holmes, 'since she is no longer in the confidence of Dr

Fu Manchu. She knows only what she may have overheard, or seen written – in this case, the latter, since she could not otherwise have known that "Davies" was spelt with an *e*.'

'It was a terrible risk to take,' I said, shuddering. 'God knows what she will suffer if Fu Manchu noticed her signals to you.'

'Oh, he cannot do much to her,' he replied unconcernedly. 'She is too valuable to him, if only as a hostage, and she is used to a few beatings.'

On this unsympathetic note, which did nothing to ease my feelings, we left the police station and returned to our hotel. It was too late for dinner, so we had to content ourselves with a makeshift meal, soon after which Sherlock Holmes went to bed.

I suppose I was tired too, but I felt restless and disinclined for sleep, and, the night being fine, decided to go out again. At a leisurely pace, I tramped the length of Walter Road, turned off by the church, and ascended by the steep streets and steps till I reached the common overlooking the bay, which we had visited on our first afternoon in the town. A wooden bench offered itself, and I sat down to smoke a meditative pipe and to think.

Below me lay fairyland by night. Red, green, and white, the lanterns of ships riding at anchor bobbed and danced like fireflies, while, shorewards to the west, a thousand lighted windows sparkled like a jewelled net thrown across the hills. A dotted yellow line of street lamps traced out the crescent of the bay to a distant lighthouse, where an intermittent shaft of radiance scintillated across the water. I thought of what Nayland Smith had told me of the view of Hongkong from Victoria Peak, which I had never seen. . . .

I sighed wearily. Our absurd investigation into the mystery of Paul Garman's sheep had come to nothing and been superseded by an urgent summons to the defence of a stranger. As I sat there, smoking and thinking, I felt coldly indifferent to the fate of Davies of Glyn Idris. Yet in my heart I recognised my lack of concern as a betrayal of Smith. This was the work which he would do – which Holmes and I must now do in his stead.

The fantasy of twinkling lights lured with a soothing enchantment, infused with that poignant undertone of melancholy which such beauty always evokes. Staring out across the bay, I found that I could still think of nothing but my fears for Kâramanèh and for Smith himself. '*Smith helpless – they are using the worm. . . .*' Word by word, I went over that interrupted message.

'*Smith helpless. . . .*' Was he ill? Or did she mean merely that he was too closely guarded to be capable of any action? And here again was the *worm*. At the possibilities conjured up in this new context, a fresh wave of horror engulfed me. Was it, perhaps, their name for some ghastly instrument of torture? Or was it a living creature – some venomous thing which could make of him an empty shell, respondent only to the will of Dr Fu Manchu?

It was late when I came down from the hill and sought my bed. The obvious result of this exercise, while Sherlock Holmes more sensibly slept, was simply that my night's rest was haunted by abominable dreams, most of which I have happily forgotten. I recall vividly, however, that in one I saw Nayland Smith chained in a dungeon below Carreg Cennen with a black worm writhing on his forehead, and, in another, the beautiful form of Kâramanèh stretched face upwards upon a glass-topped table, while a cone-shaped machine hovered above her, emitting bolts of green light which passed completely *through* her body. . . .

We were up early next morning and out on the road again by nine. A sixty-mile drive lay ahead of us to the nearest Glyn Idris, but, save for the last few miles, we were able to use main highways, and I thought I could do it in a little over two hours. Holmes, nevertheless, had warned me to pack an overnight bag.

'If we have to go on to the second place,' he said, 'we shall probably be unable to get back to-night.'

Following the conventional bus route to Carmarthen, our journey took us through a gentle landscape of farmland, less rugged than the country we had traversed the previous day. We made good time, and stopped briefly in the town for a cup of coffee, over which I found an opportunity to voice my ideas concerning Smith. Holmes, I thought, would brush them lightly aside, but, somewhat to my regret, he chose to take them seriously.

'I admit,' he said, frowning, 'that I do not much like the sound of this *worm*. It reminds me too forcibly of a singular affair with which I was associated, some twelve or thirteen years ago – an affair in which a raving madman was found staring at an unclassified worm in a matchbox – and, unfortunately, no solution was ever arrived at.'

This, I felt, was far from reassuring.

We finished our coffee without delay and took to the road again, driving northwestwards towards Cardigan. In an hour, we came to a place called Cenarth, where there were pretty waterfalls and where, to my amazement, fishermen still went about the river in coracles, like their woad-painted ancestors in Roman Britain. From this point, crossing the Pembrokeshire border, it was all byways again through a densely wooded land of small lakes and tiny villages clustered about rough stone churches with square, battlemented towers.

At one stage, uncertain of our route, we pulled up outside a general store and I leaned out of the car to address a plump housewife in a bright print dress, who, at that moment, emerged from the doorway. She started to answer me, then, staring at my companion, was all at once overcome by an uncontrollable fit of laughter which temporarily prevented her from continuing.

'I'm sorry,' she gasped, wiping her eyes, 'and I know it's rude of me, I'm sure. But I can't help it. You look just like Mr Sherlock Holmes – really you do, sir!'

'Dear me!' said Holmes. 'Do I? How very odd.'

Whilst I was talking with her, he got out of the car and contrived to slip a visiting card into her shopping bag.

This incident had the fortunate effect of putting him in a good humour for the rest of the day.

We found Glyn Idris without further difficulty, where, of course, our prearranged point of contact was the police cottage. I am sorry to say that I have forgotten the name of the constable and his wife, for they were very hospitable and, before we left, gave us an excellent lunch. Our inquiries here produced the immediate reply that, out of a hundred, or fewer, houses in the vicinity, seven were occupied by families named Davies.

Duty required us to interview all of them. This we did, though it took us a considerable time. With a break only for lunch at the constable's cottage, we sat in one parlour after another, drinking innumerable cups of tea and asking innumerable questions about relatives and antecedents. The result was a complete blank. All were simple farmers and artisans who had no slightest connection with anything Far Eastern – no discernible features which the Si Fan could conceivably wish to suppress or to usurp.

We were forced to the conclusion that Glyn Idris, Pembrokeshire, was not the one we wanted.

Now there was nothing for it but to pursue our investigation elsewhere. But Glyn Idris, Cardiganshire, lay some fifty miles farther to the north, tucked away in a fold of the long Cambrian mountain range, the slopes of which came down to the west coast. Already it was late, and I doubted if we would get there much before dusk.

'Heaven knows where we shall sleep to-night,' remarked Holmes, 'if at all!'

His words proved prophetic.

Throughout the remainder of the afternoon, we forged steadily northwards past Tregaron and into a region of hills and vales where my road map was of little use, since it showed neither the rudimentary lanes nor the hamlets through which we were passing. But now that I was accustomed to the car, I no longer found driving an arduous task. The scenery was attractive, and had our business been less urgent, I might have enjoyed myself. Once, in a moment of enthusiasm, I ventured to point out to Holmes the obvious advantages of having one's own transport, but he shook his head.

'No man with any brains and anything to use them on could possibly wish to drive a car,' he declared firmly. 'Give me the train, where I can read, write, and think – where I can look about me and observe, without the distraction of pulling levers, stamping upon pedals, and keeping my eyes fixed on the road.'

'But you do not have to do that,' I said, smiling, 'while you have me for your driver.'

'No,' he admitted. 'But it is still impossible to read, and difficult to smoke.'

This latter was true enough, and when, somewhat later, he had had me stop the car for the fourth time to enable him to light his pipe, I was roused to a mild protest.

'You smoke too much,' I said. 'I like tobacco too, but, as a doctor, I cannot believe that it is good for you to smoke as much as you do.'

Holmes endured my criticism silently, lighted his pipe carefully, then glanced at me with a twinkle of mischief in his eyes.

'I once knew of two people who lost their lives because they did *not* smoke,' he said reminiscently, and paused to enjoy my puzzled expression.* 'Well, you see, they were locked in a room into which coal gas was introduced through a ceiling fitting. Now, in such a situation, what would you or I do, Petrie? Why, light the gas, of course! But, since neither of them smoked, they had no matches!'

Our journey continued, interrupted only for occasional pipe lightings and requests for directions at isolated farmsteads. Despite a dearth of signposts, we somehow found our way without error, and, shortly after five, reached our second Glyn Idris. It was somewhat bigger

* A curious comment in retrospect on the affair which Watson has recorded as *The Retired Colourman*. [Ed.]

than the first, boasting at least six small shops in addition to the general store.

'I expect there are fifty Davieses here!' said Holmes, scowling.

We stopped to ask the way to the police cottage from a group of three women gossiping in the street. They were speaking in Welsh, but answered us immediately in English. We had heard little Welsh spoken in Cardiff and Swansea, but in the remote country districts, it was widespread. At this era, the status of the Welsh language was anomalous – regarded as a cultured necessity such as Latin or Greek, while, on the other hand, to use it as a living language was considered a mark of ignorance by townsmen.

As we made our way up to the constable's cottage, I found time to marvel at a people so open-hearted to strangers, yet so fiercely conscious of their identity that they maintained a second language, to their own inconvenience.

The cottage occupied by PC Parry – the fourth such that I had visited – was like the rest. Inside, we found an overcrowded living room with plants on the window sill, a kettle on the fire, two repulsive china dogs on the mantelpiece, and, framed above it, a disconcerting text which enjoined us: 'Prepare to meet thy God.' Our hosts were, apparently, of a somewhat religious turn of mind, the room being further encumbered by a small harmonium.

Constable Parry, whom I judged to be less than thirty, had very blond hair and an anxious manner. He was nervous, not so much of Sherlock Holmes as of finding himself drawn into the Fu Manchu case – as well he might be, I thought. He pottered about, scratched his head, and gave a very good impression of not knowing what to do. Holmes, seating himself before the fire, prepared patiently for the inevitable rite of teacups, but, in the meantime, went straight to business. To our surprise, however, PC Parry answered that he knew few villagers named Davies.

'There's Davies-the-Fish, and Davies-the-Hearse,' he

said reflectively, 'but I don't think it could be one of them.'

We did not think so either.

Mrs Parry – a thin woman who looked to me ten years older than her husband – lifted the kettle from the fire with the aid of a piece of red flannel. She had a trick of moving about the room in a series of short darts from one piece of furniture to another, and put me in mind of a friendly wasp.

'It is possible,' said Holmes, 'that his first name is Morgan.'

'Morgan Davies?' muttered the constable. 'No, I don't think I know – '

His wife set down the teapot with a bang.

'Oh, yes, you do, Will!' she expostulated. 'Why, it's Davies-the-Heathen they want – the old man out by Ty Glas, who eats birds' nests!'

'Is his name Morgan?' asked her husband vaguely. 'Well, then, perhaps it is. I'm sorry, Mr Holmes, but he's not really in the village, you see, and not been here all that long – only about ten years.'

I wondered what they considered 'long' in Glyn Idris.

'And he has something to do with China?' queried Holmes.

'I'm not sure. I've never met him, you see.' Constable Parry's expression resembled that of a schoolboy who has failed to do his homework. 'He lives in a big old house, two miles out in the country, and a regular hermit he is. But Dai Evans, the schoolmaster, could tell you about him. I believe he goes out there and plays chess with him sometimes.'

Holmes stood up quickly. 'I think I will walk down the road and see Mr Evans,' he said. 'I'm sorry, Mrs Parry, but I would rather not have tea just now. Dr Petrie can stay and talk to you till I come back. Where does Mr Evans live?'

'It's the third house from the end, on the left-hand side,' said Mrs Parry, putting the lid on the teapot. 'If you're not sure, ask somebody for Evans-the-Stick.'

During Holmes's absence, I sat drinking tea, glad of the chance to relax and recover a little from the fatigue of a long day's driving over rough roads. Finding that PC Parry knew nothing of Dr Fu Manchu but the sketchy and inaccurate details which had earlier appeared in the newspapers, I occupied my time in telling him something of our adventures in London and elsewhere. Deliberately, since I believed that he might soon be called upon to face the active menace of the Si Fan, I stressed the fact that Fu Manchu had no respect for the police.

'He's a wicked man!' said Mrs Parry severely.

Holmes, having been away nearly half an hour, opened the unlocked door and let himself in with the casual informality of village life. His face was triumphant, and he met my inquiring glance with a brisk nod.

'Yes!' he said. 'This time, there can be no doubt of it. But he is over eighty years old! I have spoken to him on the telephone, and we are invited to dinner this evening.' He paused, shaking his head sadly in self-reproach. 'I told you I was unqualified for this business, Petrie! He is Dr T. Morgan Davies, Regius Professor of the University of Wales, and author of at least six books on Chinese literature – and I had never heard of him!'

21

THE LEARNED RECLUSE

Neither Holmes nor I had brought dress clothes, since we had not anticipated a dinner invitation, but we doubted if it would matter. We tidied ourselves up to the best of our ability, resumed our places in the car, and, with the acetylene headlamps lighted, moved off into the night. Outside the village, it was pitch black, and the road was narrow, but, since it ran straight to our destination, we could not very well lose our way to Ty Glas.

This, I gathered, was not a settlement but referred merely to an area comprising a few outlying farms, named after the old manorial property on which the professor's house stood.

'It is the sad lot of the detective usually to be called in after the event,' remarked Holmes. 'But let us hope that this time we may be a step ahead of Dr Fu Manchu.'

I nodded without otherwise answering. How often, I thought, had I heard much the same words from Nayland Smith – and how often had we arrived only to find a household in disorder and a man foully done to death. . . .

A rabbit ran across the path of the headlights, startling me. We had only a short distance to cover, but, still unused to night driving, I made my way cautiously. The sky was clouded and the road closely walled in by trees. Only by the labouring engine and the frequent necessity of changing gears could I discern that our route lay over steeply rising ground.

'Our friends hereabouts have an odd but effective way of distinguishing people by their attributes,' said Holmes, with a chuckle in his voice. 'The local fishmonger is Davies-the-Fish, because he sells it, and the undertaker is Davies-the-Hearse, because he has one – to say nothing of Evans-the-Stick! I think we shall find that Davies-the-Heathen has a Chinese servant.'

'That is not very encouraging,' I replied, 'since we know only too well what that might mean.'

Ahead of us, and to the right, a point of light appeared – an agreed signal. Slowing still further as we approached, I saw a hurricane lantern standing upon one of two stone pillars, marking the entrance to a driveway. We turned in, passing a disused gate lodge, the windows boarded up, but found the drive well kept, bordered by an avenue of poplar trees. Curving to the left, it brought us out through a dense rampart of rhododendron and hydrangea bushes to a gravelled space below a terrace, to which steps led up. Above rose the severe, rectangular façade of an old Georgian house with floor-length windows and tall square chimneys.

'Our professor is evidently a man of means,' commented Holmes, as we got out and climbed the steps. 'Confound it! It would take a regiment to defend this place.'

He jerked at an iron bell pull, and a bell jangled faintly. A short delay followed; then the heavy door swung open and there in the lighted hallway stood an old man in Chinese house dress, felt-soled slippers upon his feet, and the upper part of his body encased in a long blue jacket with looped buttons. He bowed deeply, said something which we did not understand, and stood aside for us to enter.

Closing the door behind us, he smiled gravely, indicated by a gesture that he would take our coats, and deposited them in a carved oak cabinet. He turned, displaying a magnificent queue which hung well below his waist, and guided us to a door on the right-hand side of the hall, giving access to a library. Here our host was awaiting us.

Professor Davies, clad in casual tweeds, like ourselves, was a small man with piercing blue eyes and tufted, snow-white eyebrows. His head was egg-shaped and egg-bald. He was quick and active in his movements; his handshake was firm, and, had Holmes not told me that he was in his eighties, I should have supposed him to be not much over sixty.

'Mr Sherlock Holmes?' he inquired, and I noted the lilting Welsh accent strongly marked. 'A pleasant surprise, indeed! You're a long way from Baker Street!'

'I have been a long way from Baker Street for ten years,' said Holmes, smiling.

'Have you, now? Goodness me, how time gets along!' The professor turned towards me. 'And you, sir – you look uncommonly young for Dr Watson!'

'I am not Dr Watson,' I said. 'I am Dr Petrie.'

'Dear me! Has Mr Holmes changed his doctors, then?'

'Temporarily,' replied Holmes, rather brusquely. 'But I trust that, before long, Dr Petrie and I will be able to rejoin our regular partners.'

'Oh!' said Morgan Davies, looking a little bewildered. 'I suppose,' he asked hopefully, 'that you don't speak Welsh? Or Chinese?'

We shook our heads.

'But you speak English!' I said.

'Oh, yes! I speak English, but too much thinking in it makes my head spin, you see.' He waved his hand vaguely around. 'Well, make yourselves at home, gentlemen! We'll have a glass of sherry first, and then Chao Hsing can dig up some dinner for us.'

The library in which we stood was a big, square room, comfortably furnished in the style of the eighteenth century, with a coal fire glowing in an Adam fireplace. Glancing at the tall bookcases which occupied most of the wall space, I noted that many of the volumes which they contained were lettered in Chinese. But, apart from a tabletop cabinet and two barrel stools of the Ming dynasty, which harmonised well enough with the English furnishings, there was little to suggest the Celestial Empire, other than an ink painting of willow trees and ethereal mountains. A litter of papers and books piled upon chairs indicated that this was the professor's workroom.

'Do I understand,' asked Holmes, in some surprise, 'that you and your Chinese servant live here alone?'

Davies nodded with a peculiarly shy smile. 'Yes – just the two of us now. Ridiculous, really, isn't it? What do I want with a house like this? But, there – I've got to live somewhere, and find a place to keep my books in. There were five or six servants when my wife was alive – she was Chinese, of course – but after she died, in 1908, that was, Chao could do all the looking after me that I needed.'

Despite local gossip, I gained the impression that our host was a recluse by circumstance rather than by choice, and that his eccentricity consisted simply in pursuing a life style which he preferred. As I turned from my scrutiny of the Chinese painting and passed close by a settee, a ball of brown fur in one cushioned corner uncoiled itself into a pair of handsome Siamese cats, one of which stood up. It stared at me, yawned prodigiously, and lay down again with the supercilious indifference of its breed. I was not particularly disappointed, for, though I like cats, I have always found something slightly unnerving about felines with blue eyes which shine red in the dark.

'I call them Yang and Yin,' said Morgan Davies, laughing, 'because that's what they look like when they curl up together.'

My obvious lack of comprehension caused him to laugh again.

'The male and female principles of the universe,' he said, and, taking a book from a nearby shelf, showed me the cover embossed with a design of two comma-shaped figures twined into a circle.

Chao Hsing entered, silent in his padded slippers, bearing a tray loaded with glasses and a bottle. He served us with sherry and remained standing with the tray in his hands, ready – in Chinese fashion, I suppose – to refill our glasses. Whereas his master looked less than his years, Chao looked to be at least a hundred, his lined face and wispy beard reminding me strongly of one of the Eight Immortals. Davies said something to him in his own language.

'Chao speaks only Chinese,' he explained.

'Isn't that rather inconvenient?' inquired Holmes.

'Not particularly. He has nobody to talk to except me.' The professor savoured his sherry with the air of a connoisseur and set down his glass on one of the Ming stools. 'And now, Mr Holmes, I am a non-smoker myself, but perhaps you would care to light your pipe and then tell me something more about these people who, you say, have designs upon my life. Frankly speaking, I can imagine no reason why anybody should – unless the Young China group want to murder me because I once said that Chinese literature ends with the year 1800.'

'Thank you,' said Holmes, 'but I think a cigarette might be more appropriate before dinner.' He took out his case, selected a Turkish cigarette, and lit up. 'As to the business on which we have come to you, I was hoping, rather, that you would be able to inform us. In brief, what do you know of the secret society called the Si Fan?'

'Nothing!' replied Morgan Davies promptly. To Holmes's surprise and clear disapproval, he turned to Chao Hsing and talked volubly with him in Chinese, then turned again towards us. 'No – this is the first he's heard of it too.'

'Do you think it altogether prudent to discuss the matter with a Chinese servant?' demanded Holmes, frowning.

Professor Davies smiled at him benignly. 'Chao was my houseboy when he was fifteen and I was still in my twenties.'

'All the same,' I protested, 'we have found, where the Si Fan is concerned, that length of service is not always a guarantee . . .'

The only result of my intrusion was that our host held

a further incomprehensible conversation with his servant, and they both laughed like fools.

'Chao Hsing will do me no harm,' he announced. 'We are members of the same secret society.'

'Which is not, by any chance, the Si Fan?' snapped Holmes.

'It is not,' the professor said stiffly. 'I told you that we have never heard of it.'

'The Mandarin Ki Ming claims that it is the oldest organisation in the world,' I said, somewhat puzzled.

'Old it may be,' answered Davies, glancing in my direction. 'The Hung Society dates from at least the fourth century, and maybe even earlier. Your Si Fan might be as old, but that would not necessarily make it well known. My dear Dr Petrie – there are thousands of secret societies in China, covering every occupation, every aspect of daily life, like our trade unions and friendly societies.'

'But our trade unions are not secret!' I protested.

'They were once. Less than a hundred years ago, you could still be exiled to Australia for belonging to one.' Professor Davies gave us a look which I associate with the lecture room. 'It stands to reason, gentlemen, that any organisation which exists to secure the advantage of its members is regarded as inimical to the interests of those who are not members. There is nothing especially Chinese about secret societies. There were beggars' guilds in Europe, and even a thieves' guild in Paris, at the time of François Villon.'

'But the Si Fan –' began Holmes.

'Is quite unknown to me!' finished the professor impatiently. 'What does it mean? How is it written?'

Holmes and I looked helplessly at each other.

'Unfortunately, I cannot write it,' I said. 'But Nayland Smith has told me that it is the name of a town in which the society may have originated – a place near Urumchi, the capital of Sinkiang.'

'Ah!' said Morgan Davies, sitting up sharply. 'Si Fan!' He pronounced it differently from Smith, so that it sounded to me more like 'Shur Fang.' 'I see! Now, where have I come across that recently? Something to do with some sort of an intrigue . . . Give me a minute, and let me think about it in Chinese!'

He leaned forward in his chair with one elbow propped on his knee and his bulbous forehead resting upon his upturned hand. A short period of silence ensued while Professor Davies thought in Chinese. Then, jumping up with an abruptness surprising in an octogenarian, he hurried across the room, whisked a stack of papers off a chair, and came back with them.

'It was in here, somewhere,' he declared. 'I'm sure of it. This is a load of rubbish I had last month from Edmund Backhouse, in Peking. Court letters, bits of diaries, and so forth – a sprat to catch a mackerel. He's offering to send me a mint-condition copy of the Yung-chêng encyclopaedia – ten thousand volumes of it, printed in 1726 – if I'll pay the freight charges. I don't believe there's any such edition left in China, and if I pay up I'll never see the books nor my money back.'* Whilst he talked, he was sorting through the documents, glancing at each, and discarding it at his feet. 'Backhouse speaks and writes Chinese like a native. But he's a bit of a liar and a bit out of his head, I fancy. Well, he's come to the wrong shop. I've done no more than glance at the stuff – I'm not interested in palace scandals and plots. I'm not interested in politics – Chinese, or any other sort. All nonsense, I call it, spending your life arguing about how to live instead of getting on with it.'

The pile was rapidly dwindling, and the carpet liberally scattered. With only a few left in his hands, Davies gave vent to a triumphant 'Ha!' and held up a thin sheaf of papers, folded and bound into a pamphlet by a kind of blanket stitching through the open edges. Each sheet was covered, so far as I could see, by

* Sir Edmund Backhouse (who inherited the title in 1918) was an eccentric genius. He lived in a world of fantasy which prompted him to attempt petty swindles from which he could derive little profit. (See *Hermit of Peking*, by Hugh Trevor-Roper.) [Ed.]

vertically scrawled lines of black ink which looked to me less like Chinese characters than like a child's scribblings on a wall.

'This is it, I think. There was something about the Si Fan in here. . . . '

Casting the remaining papers carelessly upon the floor with the rest, Morgan Davies uttered a brisk word to Chao, who scooped them up and returned them to the chair from which they had come. Another brief conference took place, after which he glided silently from the room.

'Gone to get dinner,' muttered the professor. Reseating himself, he spread open the pamphlet. 'Now this is supposed to be a bit out of the diary of the Grand Eunuch Li Lien-ying, who died in 1909 – the year after the old Empress. Just as likely it's a forgery, but it seems as if Backhouse did have a few shady palace connections who went groping around people's dustbins and suchlike. Well, let's see now what it's about.'

He ceased speaking and, to my frank astonishment, commenced to flip over the pages, running a finger down several lines on each, mumbling in Chinese, and seemingly reading them as easily as one might read a friend's handwriting in English.

'Yes,' he announced. 'It's what you might call a sort of counter-revolutionary plot – written, of course, before the revolution actually took place. Mostly, it's a list of agents to be infiltrated into key positions – with the assistance of the Imperial court – into foreign legations and business houses, and just about every place connected with the Republican reform movement. I don't know if it's genuine. All I can say is, if there had been such a plan, Li Lien-ying would have been the man to bring it to. He was the most powerful force in the palace for forty years or more, a reactionary, a supporter of the Boxer Rebellion, and rumoured to be mixed up in the death of the Kuang-hsü emperor.'

'In other words,' remarked Holmes thoughtfully, 'even though the revolution was accomplished, this would represent a network of subversive agents in positions to undermine the present republic, with a view to restoring the Imperial authority. Such, as we know, is a part of Dr Fu Manchu's intentions – he has been good enough to tell us so himself. I think, Professor, that we should regard this document as authentic, since the Si Fan evidently think it is. They know that you have it, and are quite prepared to murder you in order to recover it.'

'The T'ai Ping might have murdered me more than fifty years ago,' replied Morgan Davies, shrugging. 'I'm not much bothered about revolutionaries or counter-revolutionaries. But if you think this thing is so important – well, then, you'd better have it.'

He held out the roughly stitched booklet, offering it to my companion.

'No,' said Holmes. 'For the present, at least, it is best in your possession. I cannot guarantee to protect you, and it may be necessary to use it to bargain for your life. But we cannot neglect such a potent weapon for fighting the Si Fan on their home ground. Can you translate it?'

'Translate it? Yes, of course I can!'

'Then I suggest that you should do so without delay.'

The musical note of a gong sounded nearby.

'Dinner!' said the professor, and stood up. 'I trust you can eat Chinese food, gentlemen?'

'Indeed, yes,' I said. 'When it is well prepared, there is nothing better.'

'Let us go in, then, and see what Chao Hsing has for us.'

Turning towards the door, he tossed the diary of Li Lien-ying down carelessly upon the seat of his chair.

'Good Heavens!' burst out Holmes, in exasperation. 'Don't leave it there! Bring it with you, man!'

22

THE BIRTH OF THE SI FAN

The dinner party which followed was one of the few pleasant interludes in a grim business. We ate by candlelight, seated at one end of a table designed for twelve. There are no set courses in a Chinese meal. We helped ourselves at will from a profusion of dishes of all shapes and sizes which extended over half the surface of the long table. Holmes, I was glad to see, handled his chopsticks like a veteran, and behaved himself very well – in times of preoccupation, his social manners were sometimes disgraceful.

I supposed that Chao Hsing must have begun his culinary preparations soon after the receipt of Holmes's telephone call. The food was not only abundant but delicious. Among a profusion of other items, there were shrimps deep-fried in batter, succulent bamboo shoots and soya bean sprouts, sliced chicken with almonds, sweet-and-sour pork, and a kind of *ravioli* stuffed with a mixture of finely chopped meat and aromatic herbs.

'No – we don't usually have all this much,' confessed Morgan Davies. 'Five or six dishes is enough for us, as a rule. But it's a rare opportunity to have guests.'

'Where do you get all the ingredients?' I asked curiously.

'Well, we get the spices and the preserves sent up from London,' he explained. 'But Chinese food isn't really so exotic as people think. Chiefly, it's pork and chicken and a lot of vegetables – most of which we grow for ourselves. We've got some Chinese stuff planted, and it does quite well. We even raise our own bamboo shoots, and they come up nicely enough to a foot or so above ground, which is all you need for eating.'

'How large is the estate?' inquired Holmes.

He spoke casually, but I knew that he was thinking of the area to be held against the Si Fan.

'About twenty-two acres, I think,' said the professor, rather vaguely. 'I've got four gardeners coming in to look after it. The house can take care of itself, more or less – I have some cleaning women in, about once a month, to go over it. But the garden needs to be kept up regularly. Got to, you see, because the place is entailed and I can't get rid of it. Anyway, where's the point of moving, at my age? When I'm gone, it'll go to my daughter, who's married and out in America. Don't suppose she'll ever live here, but her children might. I had a son too, but he died in a boating accident, sixteen years ago.'

Our meal was a leisurely one, lasting more than an hour, during which, for a change, I asked most of the questions and Morgan Davies did most of the talking, while Holmes listened, observing, and forgetting nothing.

I learned that, in his youth, our erudite host had lived an adventurous life. His family had been concerned in the East India Company, and, in his very early twenties, he had gone out to a trading establishment in Shanghai, before the second of the so-called Opium Wars. At an era when foreigners travelled little in China, he had soon after visited Nanking – just in time to see the celebrated Porcelain Pagoda, before the T'ai Ping rebels toppled it to the ground. Caught there in the same incident, he had lived in Nanking under the rebel occupation for ten years, no doubt surviving by his sympathy for Chinese life and his happy knack of making friends with everybody. It was here, in this former capital of the Empire and ancient literary centre, that he had first become interested in Chinese literature. Again, in 1864, he had lived through the bloody re-taking of the city by the Imperial troops, when three-quarters of the buildings had been burned, and a hundred thousand of the insurgents massacred in three days, within the surrounding province of Kiang-su. Afterwards, he had gone north to

Peking, and remained there till 1881, when he had returned to his own country, with Chao Hsing, a Chinese wife, and two children, to teach peaceably at a university.

Such, in the briefest of outlines, was the history of Dr T. Morgan Davies, professor of Chinese literature, whose life was now sought by the Si Fan.

Of all that had happened since, he was largely ignorant, expressing only pity and contempt for the tangled skein of intrigues and skirmishes between Young China, the foreign powers, and the Old Buddha* which had but recently culminated in the overthrow of the reigning dynasty, and the creation of an equally unstable republic.

'Nothing of any value has been written in China since the *Hung Lou Meng*!' he declared, and left it at that.

We found, as we might have anticipated, that if Morgan Davies was unacquainted with the Si Fan, he was equally unfamiliar with the name of Dr Fu Manchu.

'Ridiculous!' he sniffed. 'Manchu is the name of a people, not of a person! The Manchu are – or were – the last Imperial dynasty.'

I noted that he had a scholarly aversion to adding an English plural -*s* to Chinese words.

'As I understand it,' I said diffidently, 'it is not really his name, but a *nom de guerre*. He is, apparently, a Manchu, and the word *Fu* signifies something like "valorous."'

Thereupon came the inevitable question.

'Can you write it?'

'I'm afraid not,' I confessed, a trifle shamefacedly. 'But Nayland Smith has shown it to me – it was appended to a letter which Fu Manchu once wrote to the Reverend J. D. Eltham – and I think I might recognise it if I saw it again.'

'This one?' asked Professor Davies, and scribbled rapidly on the tablecloth with his forefinger.

* Nickname of the Empress Dowager Tz'ŭ Hsi. [Ed.]

I laughed, unable to help myself.

'How can I tell, when you haven't written anything I can see?'

'Follow the stroke order.'

'But I don't *know* the stroke order!'

'Oh! Well, then . . . ' He fumbled in an inner pocket for a pen and notebook, opened the latter to a clear page, and carefully drew a Chinese ideograph. 'Is that it?'

'Yes,' I replied, nodding. 'I believe it is.'*

'That's right, then. It means "militant" or "warlike," you might say. Evidently it is used here as a descriptive title of respect, such as "Alexander the Great" or,' the professor added, with a grin, 'Davies-the-Heathen.'

He picked up a bottle of Chinese wine from the table, offering to top up our glasses, but we refused politely. No doubt it was a rare vintage, but it had a somewhat sharp taste, and neither of us liked it very much. Morgan Davies refilled his own glass, and continued with alacrity – glad, I think, of having some students to lecture.

'You tell me that this Dr Fu Manchu often wears a yellow robe – which he is not entitled to do, unless he is over eighty, like me, or a member of the Imperial family. Perhaps he is. In that case, he is not, ethnically speaking, Chinese.'

'Not Chinese?' I queried.

'Not *han-jen* – that is to say, not Chinese in the same way that the Normans were not English. The Manchu are a people from the north, who conquered China in 1644, ever since which they have furnished the Imperial dynasty, and most of the ruling caste. They had their own language – which was written with an alphabet – and their own customs. Dr Fu Manchu does not, I imagine, wear a pigtail?'

'No. He does not.'

'He wouldn't – naturally. It was the Manchu who

* For any who are interested, this is how it appeared on Eltham's letter. [P.]

251

forced the *han-jen* to wear their hair in this absurd fashion to distinguish themselves as subjects.'

'But the Manchus are pretty well assimilated by now, are they not?' put in Sherlock Holmes.

'Not so completely as you might suppose,' answered Professor Davies. 'The rank-and-file soldiery have mixed with the indigenous inhabitants, and been largely absorbed. But the privileged class always kept themselves separate. Peking, you know, is divided down the middle by a broad avenue. The *han-jen* live on one side of it, in what is known as the Chinese City. On the other side is the Tartar City – a huge, square-shaped area, enclosed by a fortified wall. Most of the people there are Manchu, and within that again is the Forbidden City, surrounded by a moat, which houses the temples and palaces of the Imperial court. All that will change soon – is already changing. But we are still close enough to the old days to regard the Manchu as a numerous and powerful enemy, desperate to regain their supremacy at any cost. If they have found a leader such as this so-called Dr Fu Manchu, it is not surprising.'

He talked easily and with authority, like a professional lecturer. I thought that he had probably been a good one. As I listened, it occurred to me that here was an invaluable chance to obtain expert opinions which, before long – for my faith in Sherlock Holmes remained unshaken – I should be able to pass on to Smith.

'Fu Manchu seems to have held mandarin's rank,' I remarked, 'and is said to have administered a province. Have you any idea as to his real identity?'

The professor considered carefully before replying.

'I can't tell you who he is,' he said at length, 'but I can hazard a guess as to *what* he is. I think he was probably one of the officials who sided openly with the Boxers in 1900, when the old Empress Dowager gave them her blessing to go out and murder all the foreigners. Afterwards, when the revolt failed, she disowned them, of course, and Dr Fu Manchu no doubt had to flee for his life – likely enough going into hiding in the wilds of

Sinkiang.' He turned towards Holmes. 'You mentioned, I believe, that the Si Fan is apparently made up principally of elements from all over the Middle and Far East, rather than exclusively Chinese?'

'Yes,' said Holmes. For a rarity, paying attention to his meal, he reached out and scissored a fried shrimp neatly with his chopsticks. 'We have recently encountered a Korean and two Mongols. In the past, Dr Petrie has chiefly had to do with Burmans, Hindus, and Arabs.'

'Then I shall venture to do some more guessing,' said Morgan Davies. 'Do you know much about Sinkiang?' We both answered in the negative. 'Well, gentlemen, Sinkiang lies on the western borders of China. I have never been there myself, but I can assure you that it is nothing like your probable impression of a Chinese province. It is largely desert country, lying between the Tien Shan and Kunlun ranges, with a mixed population of Uigurs, Kazakhs, Mongols, and Chinese Moslems. India and Afghanistan are directly to the southwest, and Mongolia on the northeast.'

He paused to take a sip of wine, and, as neither of us interrupted, continued:

'I suggest, simply as a tentative theory, since I had never until now come across this secret society, the Si Fan, that, at the time of Dr Fu Manchu's visit, it existed merely as an old-established group of thieves and robbers in the district of that name. Quite possibly, the society then had no official name, but its members, who were known and feared in the locality, were generally referred to as "the men from Si Fan." You tell me that Fu Manchu is a man of tremendous personality and extraordinary knowledge. Therefore, I think it would have been easy for him to gain control of this loosely knit organisation, and use it as the nucleus of something far more ambitious, by giving its adherents an identity and a purpose – the struggle of East against West. . . .'

When we could literally eat no more, our sumptuous repast concluded with jasmine tea and raisin-flavoured *lichee* fruit preserved in syrup. Afterwards, we withdrew once more to the library. Yang and Yin came running out with their tails erect, mewing raucously in feline Siamese, and followed Chao Hsing back to the kitchen. As Far Eastern cats, they were presumably rice-eating.

We re-seated ourselves in the same armchairs, and Holmes brought out his calabash pipe – which he smoked only in moments of ease – while our generous host insisted on serving us with whisky and soda.

'I hesitate to presume further upon your hospitality, Professor,' said my companion, gravely, 'but we have nowhere to stay to-night, and, in any case, I am frankly unwilling to leave you alone here, in the present situation. Would it unduly inconvenience you to provide us with a shakedown somewhere?'

Professor Davies laughed. 'You may have the choice of fourteen bedrooms, but none of them very well aired, I'm afraid.'

He summoned his manservant by means of a thoroughly Western bell push, and instructed him (I assume) to make arrangements for our accommodation. Since we were now to remain overnight, it was necessary also to find accommodation for the car. After more unintelligible conversation, I followed Chao Hsing outside and was directed around the building, with many smiles, unhelpful Chinese words, and much gesticulating, to a former coach house. This, I was surprised to observe, had been converted into a garage, although there was no vehicle in it. I gathered, later, that the professor sometimes had visits from academic friends, and, in fact, still went occasionally up to Aberystwyth to give a lecture at the university.

I returned to the library to find Holmes and Morgan Davies once more discussing the diary of Li Lien-ying, which, throughout dinner, had remained unceremoniously stuffed into a side pocket of the professor's Norfolk jacket.

'How long will it take you to translate it?' Holmes was asking, as I came in.

'About three hours, I should think,' replied Professor

Davies. 'It's not very long, but I still need to be careful about the names, and I shall have to make a lot of notes, if the information is to be of any use. Well, I will do it to-night, if you insist, after you've gone to bed.'

'That will keep you up rather late, won't it?' I asked solicitously.

It was already past ten o'clock.

'Not unusually.' Morgan Davies shook his head. 'I always work at night. It's the best time for thinking, when everything's quiet and you've got the world to yourself. And somehow I find that the older you get, the less you sleep, and the less early you feel like it.'

But, since he considered the work to be of no literary interest, he was obviously not anxious to begin. For the next hour, we sat around indolently and talked. The two cats rejoined us, licking their whiskers, and immediately resumed their curled-up position on the settee.

'In a way, you may say that I am accustomed to being under fire from the Manchu,' said our host, 'since I lived for over ten years in a city held by the T'ai Ping rebels.'

As the old are wont to do, he spoke mostly of his youth, telling us of the vanished glories of Nanking, established in the fourteenth century as the new capital of the first Ming emperor, whose bones still lay beneath a tumulus outside the city, approached by a long avenue of colossal stone images. The remains of his 'modern' successor, the self-styled T'ai Ping emperor – who had poisoned himself to escape capture – had been less reverently treated. Torn from the tomb by the victorious Manchu, they were dismembered and thrown to the beasts.

The China of Professor Morgan Davies was a barbaric state different again from the disorderly but 'civilised' China of Nayland Smith. His first memories of Shanghai were of severed heads exhibited in bamboo cages – his last memories of Peking, a tumultuous city thronged with street vendors, beggars, and fortune-tellers, among whom wild-eyed victims of Manchu justice groaned and implored sustenance, their necks surrounded by huge

255

square collars of wood, or one hand shackled to the opposite foot.

This, I reflected, was the China into which Dr Fu Manchu had been born. . . .

Though, as the time passed, the professor seemed to grow more lively, both Holmes and I were feeling distinctly sleepy by eleven. I found it difficult to suppress a yawn and Morgan Davies, noticing, smiled indulgently.

'You have had enough of listening to an old man's tales,' he said. 'Go to bed, then, and I will have your translation ready for you when you get up.'

Holmes hesitated. I could see that he was all for remaining on guard, but the professor would have none of it.

'I can't bear to have people sitting around me while I work,' he declared. 'Go along with you both. I shall be perfectly all right down here.'

'You will work in this room, I take it?' asked Holmes, standing up reluctantly.

'Yes, I always do.' Morgan Davies crossed to a small bureau, pulled down the writing-table top, and deposited the diary of Li Lien-ying upon the leathered surface. 'I don't for a moment suppose anything will happen, but, if it does, I'll sing out. Your rooms are directly above.'

'Very well,' answered Holmes, yielding. 'But at least take elementary precautions. Remember you are a marked man. You are in greater danger here than you ever were in Nanking.'

He strode across the room to inspect the two floor-length windows opening upon the terrace and make sure that they were locked.

'Neither of them has been opened for six months,' said the professor.

'No matter. Have your man go around the house and see that every door and window is fastened; there must be a hundred of them! Do you possess any firearms?'

'Only that.' Morgan Davies pointed to a double-barreled shotgun standing upright in a corner. 'Now and then, I do a bit of shooting in the park.'

'Hardly a convenient weapon,' muttered Holmes. 'Load it, anyway, and put it beside your chair.'

'Anything else?'

'Yes. Lock the door, pull the curtains – and don't sit in line with a window!'

Chao Hsing appeared and guided us upstairs to our rooms.

'In fact, Petrie,' commented Holmes dryly, as we ascended, 'men such as you and I should *never* sit in line with a window. . . . '

The bedrooms made ready for our use were situated, with a bathroom in between, on the same side of a corridor lighted by an oil-lamp, which stood upon a small table at one end. Since the house had no electricity, similar lamps had been left burning in all three rooms. Holmes, standing with his hand on the doorknob, after Chao Hsing had left us, detained me a moment longer.

'I don't like it,' he said darkly. 'But the professor is our host, and we must respect his wishes. . . . '

'You think that an attack may be imminent?'

'I know no more than you do! We have got here in advance of the Si Fan, thanks to Kâramanèh, but if Dr Fu Manchu should have found out that she warned us, he will speed up his plans.' Holmes frowned, gnawing at his lower lip in palpable uncertainty. 'Well, we must make the best of it, and try to be ready for anything. Usually, I sleep like a cat, but I don't know if I can do it to-night when we have been eating more like hogs. Lie down and sleep – but don't get undressed, lest we should have to turn out again in a hurry.'

On that we retired – as we hoped, for the night – into our respective rooms. I turned the lamp down low, but left it alight. Then, obedient to Holmes's instructions, I took off my coat and my boots, loosened my collar, and lay down on the bed, covering myself with a thin eiderdown.

Used as I am to the life of cities, I was immediately

conscious of the silence – a silence like that of the great Sahara, so profound that it can be listened to. Even in Cardiff and in Swansea, there had been sounds – sounds of some sort. Here there were none. In my overtired state, it depressed me, and my first thought was that I could not sleep. But this was an illusion, for sleep I did, and almost at once.

Sleep is timeless. I dreamed, and again had the illusion that my dreaming was immediate. These days, there was every reason that I should dream, and that my dreams be nightmares re-woven from the fabric of anxieties and strange events through which I lived. Yet, in the light of later events, I have often thought that in those bizarre fantasies of the night lay some hint of stranger and more terrible happenings yet to come.

What I dreamed was this:

I stood bound to a marble pillar in a hall so vast that I could see neither walls nor ceiling. Before me – the only object within my view – rose the perforated ivory screen which I had seen in the ruined cottage, and between me and the screen danced Zarmi the Eurasian, adorned only with a long string of flashing emeralds draped around her neck. She moved sinuously, swaying like a snake dancing to the reed pipe, her dark eyes fixed upon me in a hypnotic gaze of vicious enjoyment. Closer she came and closer, holding the string of emeralds in both hands and swinging it from side to side, tempting me and taunting me in my helplessness. She stood only inches removed and leaned forward, her lips almost touching mine – then, crossing her hands, threw the string of emeralds over my head and tightened it round my throat. I felt the sharp facets of the stones cutting into my flesh, strangling me – fought to draw breath, and felt my lungs bursting. My senses reeled; sunbursts of light blinded me, and there was a great ringing in my head like the pounding of a Chinese temple bell. . . .

I choked, gasped air into my lungs, and jerked bolt upright on my bed. For an instant, sleeping and waking were confused; I saw the room about me, and within it, as it seemed, the lithe, undulating form of my tormentor shimmering and slowly dissolving into stardust. I swung my feet to the floor and sat for a moment on the edge of the bed, my heart thumping painfully. The dream had been so vivid and so horrible that I felt no desire for further sleep just then. My head ached and there was a singing in my ears. I groaned, recognising the symptoms of a cold and the result of sleeping on one's back.

Standing up unsteadily, I moved to the chair upon which Chao Hsing had placed my overnight bag, and extracted my small medicine chest. A glance at my watch showed me that it was two-thirty. I had slept heavily and dreamlessly for three hours before being awakened by that ghastly nightmare, induced by inflamed sinuses. The silence of the house and its surroundings was penetrated only by the distant hooting of an owl. I searched for and found a phial of aspirin, opened the door into the corridor, and went into the adjoining bathroom.

Two tablets are standard, but three, I estimated, would be needed to cope with that headache, which was acute. You may safely extend the dose to four. I shook them out into my palm, scrunched them one by one between my teeth, enduring the vile flavour so that they should work more rapidly, and washed them down with copious draughts of water. I finished, turned to go back to my room, and was startled to see Sherlock Holmes standing in the doorway in his shirtsleeves.

'What! You too, Petrie?' he exclaimed. 'I was just coming to you to see if you had any aspirins. I have an abominable headache.'

'And a singing in your ears?' I asked.

He nodded. I passed him the phial, rinsed out the glass which I had used, refilled it, and handed it to him.

'I am afraid,' I said mournfully, 'that we have both caught cold.'

'Very likely,' he growled, and, making a wry face, bolted an aspirin. 'After driving all over Wales for two days in an open car, what can you expect?'

'No,' I said. 'A good, honest breeze does no harm to

anyone. It was more likely the draughts in the broken-down cottage where we had tea with Fu Manchu – Good Heavens! was it only yesterday? – and as for Kâramanèh, I am afraid she may get pneumonia!'

Holmes grunted, and returned the phial to me.

'I shouldn't worry,' he said. 'She has the services of a first-class physician.'

Stung by his indifference, I glared at him and began an indignant retort – which was suddenly and dramatically cut short. From somewhere below, a scream echoed through the house. For an instant, we stood aghast, staring at each other.

'God in Heaven!' I burst out, voicing the thought that was in both our minds. 'They have got him!'

Holmes said no word. None was necessary. Acting with one accord, we raced along the corridor and down the stairs to the library, our headaches forgotten.

The door was locked, and pounding upon it produced no result. From within came the sound of a low, continuous moaning. Temporarily, we stood baffled. Then:

'Look!' snapped my companion. 'The door!'

I turned, following the direction of his glance across the wide, dimly lighted hallway, and saw, as he had seen, that the front door stood wide open. We ran to it neck-and-neck, out upon the terrace, and alongside the house to the point where lamplight streamed out from the two long windows of the library. As we approached, I observed that the nearer – which I had seen Holmes check – now likewise stood open.

We reached it and halted on the threshold, seeing more or less what we feared to see. In the middle of the big room, Chao Hsing, still in his Chinese dress, crouched upon hands and knees, wailing and beating his head upon the floor, while outstretched on the carpet beside him lay the inert form of Professor Morgan Davies.

23

A ROUND OF HEADACHES

We hesitated, appalled, then rushed into the room. Chao Hsing, seemingly unconscious of our presence, continued his noisy lamentations, bowing his forehead repeatedly to the floor, like a Moslem at prayer. Ignoring him equally, we passed around the huddled body and bent over that of the professor.

He lay face downwards, with both hands raised above his shoulders, as though to shield his head at the moment when he fell. We turned him over, and I knelt quickly beside him – gasped, and recoiled in shock. The gentle features of Morgan Davies were contorted in a fixed spasm of agony, lips drawn back from his teeth, and eyes screwed shut – but even more horribly and inexplicably, the whole of his great, hairless cranium was suffused down to the temples in reddish-brown patches. Two thin trickles of blood ran from his ears.

'Is he dead?' demanded Holmes.

I took the limp wrist in my fingers, and bent my head to the fallen man's chest, though one look at the tortured visage and hideously discoloured skull was sufficient to make further examination unnecessary.

'Yes,' I said dully. 'But he died only a short time ago. That scream – '

'It was not he who screamed,' interrupted Holmes. 'It was Chao Hsing, when he found out what had happened. Professor Davies was struck down so rapidly that he had no chance to cry out.' He frowned, shaking his head perplexedly. 'Good Heavens! Can he have had a stroke?'

'It might almost seem so,' I said slowly. 'But I have never seen a cerebral haemorrhage of such extensive proportions. Every blood vessel in his brain appears to be ruptured.'

Holmes snapped his fingers irritably. 'He was murdered! Of course he was! But, in Heaven's name, how did they do it?'

He turned aside, stared at the bureau behind us, and swept a comprehensive glance around the room.

'It is gone!' he said angrily. 'They have taken both the Chinese diary and his translation – there is nothing on the desk now. The fool!' He pointed an accusing finger at the shotgun in the far corner. 'He did not take the gun, and he left the curtains open. How can I protect people when they disregard my advice? Though,' he added in a milder tone, 'I am not sure that it would have helped him much.'

Chao Hsing, exhausted by the vehemence of his mourning, lay bundled up in a heap, no longer wailing, but sobbing uncontrollably. If ever I had thought of the Chinese as an unemotional race, I thought so no longer, and, despite my earlier suspicions, found it impossible to believe that his grief was assumed.

Holmes, I noted, had returned to the open window by which we had entered and was bending to examine it.

'I thought as much!' he announced, straightening up. 'One of these small panes of glass has been cut out, so that the assassin – let us call him that – could reach through and turn the key in the lock. I would have removed it earlier, but it was rusted and I could not get it out.'

'Then how could it be turned?' I asked.

Holmes smiled mirthlessly. 'They came prepared for such an eventuality. The whole lock has been drenched with oil.'

Conscious of cramped muscles, I stood up stiffly, and, as I did so, my stockinged foot – for we had left our boots upstairs, and brought no slippers with us – brushed against something cold and hard. I glanced down quickly and saw the whisky bottle from which we had been served after dinner, unstoppered and lying upon its side, so that most of the contents had flowed out and soaked into the carpet. A second glance, inspired by the first,

262

showed me an empty glass, overturned, and now half hidden by the professor's body.

'Look at this!' I burst out excitedly. 'He was drinking when he fell! They have poisoned him!'

Holmes left the window and came back to where I stood. He frowned down, unspeaking, then picked up the glass, sniffed at it, held it up to the light, and tested it with his finger.

'No,' he said quietly. 'He was not drinking, but about to drink. This glass has never been filled. It was not this which killed him, but at least you have found something which helps us to reconstruct the scene. He got up from his desk, having finished his work, or leaving it partially finished, to get a drink from the Ming cabinet – we know that was where it was kept. He had the bottle in one hand, and the glass in the other, when the blow fell – something which occurred painfully and suddenly, like a knife in the back. He dropped both bottle and glass, raising his hands to his head, and spun around – '

The confident, clear-cut details of his reconstructions tempted me to think sometimes that he supplied them from his own imagination.

'How do you know that he turned?' I inquired critically.

Holmes's eyes flashed, and I realised that I ought to have known better.

'Use your intelligence!' he retorted. 'Professor Davies was not left-handed! As he lay when we first found him, the bottle was on his left, and the glass on his right. Therefore, he had turned after dropping them. Anyone other than a left-handed man pours a drink with the glass in his *left* hand and the bottle in his *right*!' I looked crestfallen, and his fierce expression relaxed. 'Never mind, Petrie! You were obviously not born to be an investigator.'

I was inclined to agree with him, and felt a little thankful that I was not, when I recalled the escapades and tight corners into which my participation in the investigations of others had all too often landed me.

'It was done silently,' continued Holmes, 'so that no alarm was raised, and the man waiting outside on the terrace had ample time to break in afterwards. The professor was afflicted in such a manner that he was unable to shout for help – the effect, however produced, was that of an apoplectic stroke – and since the carpet is thick, his fall could not be heard outside the room.'

'Certainly, we heard nothing,' I said. As I spoke, my gaze wandered aimlessly, and, with a vague feeling of surprise, I saw the familiar ball of fur curled up on the settee. 'Why, even the cats were not aroused – '

I stopped short, and, with a sudden apprehension, walked quickly across the room and peered down.

'Oh, my God!' I said unsteadily. 'This is uncanny! They are both dead – and they died as he did!'

A bright rivulet of blood exuded from the ears of both animals.

Holmes, with a terse exclamation, came over to join me.

'God knows what it is!' he muttered.

He took two or three paces back towards the open window – with what object I was uncertain – then stopped, clapping his hands to his trouser pockets.

'Confound it! I have left my pocket lamp upstairs in my coat.'

Walking with quick, nervous strides to the door leading out into the hallway, he unlocked it and again turned back into the room, glancing down at the bowed figure of Chao Hsing.

'Get him out of here, Petrie!' he said softly. 'You have the bedside manner and can deal with people in distress better than I. The poor fellow is in no state to answer questions, and since we have no common language, we cannot ask them.'

He went out into the hall. I crossed to where Chao Hsing knelt, took him gently by the shoulders, and endeavoured to raise him up. He turned his face towards me, and, saying a few quiet words which I hoped he might understand from their tone, I inclined my head towards the door. The aged manservant made no resistance. He stood up shakily with my help, and tottered out. I accompanied him to the door, and would have gone farther with him – for he could hardly walk – but he pushed away my hand and, with the travesty of a smile, shuffled off alone.

I stood in the doorway, watching him disappear around the angle of the staircase, and wondering in a hopeless fashion what was to happen to him – an old man past seventy, friendless in a foreign country and unable to speak a word of the language. Not for the first time in my medical experience, I realised that the greatest tragedy of death is for the living.

At the far end of the hall, the front door of the house remained open, since neither of us had yet thought to close it. I crossed to it automatically and thrust it shut.

Sherlock Holmes came hurrying down the stairs, having put on his jacket and carrying mine, also my boots. He handed them to me.

'The Si Fan have beaten us at the post,' he said sourly. 'They have killed our man, and taken his papers – leaving us with nothing but the bleak satisfaction of finding out how they did it. Well, we must do our official duty, I suppose. There is a telephone somewhere in this house. I must look for it and inform PC Parry, since he will have to take charge here until they can get someone out from the town.'

I nodded, and went inside the library, leaving him to search. Sitting on a chair while I laced up my boots, I stared across at the body of Morgan Davies, feeling a sharp sense of loss and a great anger at the fiends who had cut short the few remaining years of his life. This was an affair which had touched me more deeply than the deaths of other eminent men whom I had seen murdered by Fu Manchu – for none of them had been one with whom I had sat at table and learned quickly to like.

After the passage of only a few minutes, Holmes rejoined me.

'It was on the other side of the hall,' he said, 'in a sort

of alcove. I have got the constable out of bed, and he will be riding over here on his bicycle. Well, we have twenty minutes or so to pursue our investigations unhindered before he comes bumbling around.'

While I continued to sit looking on, he strode quickly to the open window, half closed it, and re-opened it. The hinges responded with a rasping screech.

'Chao Hsing has sharp ears,' he remarked. 'It must have been this which brought him running around outside the house, to see what had happened.'

'Why, where was he, then?' I asked.

'Sitting outside the door of this room, of course!' Holmes regarded me severely. 'You saw that he was fully dressed. Did you not also see, when you went out in the hall just now, that a chair had been moved close to the door? Chao Hsing was as anxious about his master as I was, so he determined to remain outside the room and mount guard, as best he could, till the professor had safely completed his work.'

'In that case,' I ventured, unable to dispute this logical suggestion and vainly attempting to add to it, 'do you not think that he may have heard the noise of the professor's collapse, and, unable to get in by the door, come out upon the terrace – that it was *he* who broke the window?'

'Chao Hsing does not carry a glass-cutter and an oilcan!' said Holmes acidly.

Switching on his electric torch, he went outside and stayed there for some minutes, playing the beam upon the paving stones. Momentarily, he passed out of sight, and I saw his light moving against the other window, which was still closed and locked. I heard him muttering to himself and making grunting sounds. Then he reappeared at the broken window.

'H'm!' he commented. 'This is a little odd. I cannot find the pane of glass which was removed. The man seems to have taken it with him, for some reason. But, apart from that, he has been at no pains to cover his tracks. He has left some excellently muddy footprints – obviously, he had been hiding among the bushes. He wears neither shoes nor socks, and judging by the separation of the toes, is a savage who is unaccustomed to wearing them.'

'That sounds to me unpleasantly like a dacoit!' I said.

'You may well be right.' Holmes sat down opposite me, his brows creased in thought. 'Who or whatever he is, it was his purpose to recover the diary after the professor had been killed. Whether or not it was he who also did the killing, I am not yet in a position to say, since I still fail to see how it was done. Poison, of some kind, it must have been. But what? This time, Petrie, Dr Fu Manchu has used something outside my knowledge.'

I stood up, crossed to the body of the man whom we had sought, and failed, to save, and again knelt. A second and more careful examination added nothing to my first.

'I suppose,' I said wearily, 'that we are not looking for subtlety where none exists? Suppose the dacoit burst in, after breaking the window, and struck Professor Davies from behind. . . . No doctor may be exactly sure of the results of such a blow, in the case of a man over eighty years old – '

I stopped, aware that my companion was regarding me silently, with an arch smile. Holmes is right: I shall never be an investigator. A thought comes to me, and I blurt it out without pausing to consider its relevance.

'No, of course not!' I exclaimed, flushing at my own stupidity. 'The cats!'

'Just so – the cats!' said Holmes. 'And more than that, perhaps. How is your headache?'

'My headache?' In the events which had followed our hurried descent from upstairs, I had forgotten that I ever had one. 'It is gone,' I replied.

'So is mine – and I do not think it was the aspirin. I do not think that we have colds.' He pointed meaningly to the still form at my feet. 'I believe that we have been subjected to a mild dose of the same thing.'

I started violently, such a possibility not having previously crossed my mind.

'Good Heavens! Was it, then, something that we ate at dinner? But, if so, why was the effect upon us so little? Was there anything of which he ate a great deal more than we did?'

'So far as I recall,' said Holmes slowly, 'we all ate about the same amount of everything.'

I thought furiously for a moment, searching my memory.

'The wine!' I burst out suddenly. 'He had most of it. We did not like it – '

'The cats did not drink the wine!'

Standing up again, Holmes began to pace restlessly about the room, glancing here and there, occasionally picking up things and putting them down again, but making no attempt at the kind of detailed examination which I had first seen him conduct at our rooms in Fleet Street.

'It was not done at dinner,' he said finally. 'It was in nothing that we ate or drank. Something was introduced into this room, after we had gone upstairs – something which, almost instantly, killed every living thing in it. Some kind of gas, perhaps? But, if so, why is there no trace of it in the room now? Even if it is odourless, we have been in here for a considerable period, and yet we feel no ill effects.'

I saw from his expression that he was not talking to me, but merely thinking aloud, and I did not interrupt.

'As to how it was introduced,' he went on, 'I see two possibilities. The glass may have been cut from the window while the professor was still alive. It would have been difficult to do this quietly enough to avoid disturbing him, but not impossible, perhaps. The only other means would have been the chimney – '

I watched him go to the Adam fireplace, in which a fire still burned, and stoop to examine the embers. He raked out some of the ashes with the poker. Then, as if all at once remembering my presence, he turned, addressing me directly.

'There are poisons which are released by combustion –

poisons such as that fiendish stuff with which Watson and I once nearly killed ourselves, the Devil's Foot root. But most of it would have surely gone back up the chimney, if they had dropped some such thing down. Perhaps they could have driven it into the room by placing a cover on top, but then the room must have been full of smoke – '

For the second time that night, and in the same manner, conversation was abruptly terminated by a wild, despairing cry from outside – a summons even less anticipated than the first.

Holmes dropped the poker with a crash, and bounded to the door. I was not a yard behind him as we burst into the hall.

'My God!' I gasped, and snatched at my pistol.

At the remote end of the wide, lamplighted space before the staircase, the front door of the house again stood wide open – and there, upon the very threshold, old Chao Hsing was struggling desperately with a lean, brown man who wore nothing but a loincloth.

24

THE TESTAMENT OF
CHAO HSING

My pistol was useless; the old man had his back to us, shielding the body of his opponent.

We hurled ourselves across the hall towards the doorway and the patch of lamplight beyond, in which the two figures struggled. But the contest was hopelessly ill-matched. While we were yet ten paces distant, the dacoit broke loose – a leaf-bladed knife flashed in a vicious, chopping stroke, and I saw Chao Hsing go reeling back against the doorpost.

The brown man cleared the terrace at a bound and leaped over the low stone balustrade – not so adroitly as his Korean counterpart, but neatly enough. We heard his feet crunch upon the gravel below, and, as we rushed past the stricken man in the open doorway, had a brief glimpse of a sinewy form, glossy like that of a snake, ere it was swallowed up in the impenetrable dark of the thick foliage. Leaning out over the parapet, I fired shot after shot blindly into the bushes.

'Useless to go after him!' said Holmes savagely.

Turning back to the house, I saw Chao Hsing leaning against the doorframe, his face grey and the breath whistling between his teeth. His left hand was clutched to his midriff, compressing the loose folds of his Chinese clothes into a tight wad, and, at the sight of the bright arterial blood dripping through his fingers, I knew the worst. I hurried to his side, the dacoit forgotten.

'*Wo bu shing lur!*' he whispered – words of such clear and terrible significance that they stuck in my memory.

'Is he badly hurt?' snapped Holmes.

I nodded grimly.

From the direction of the driveway came a crash and a shout.

'Great Heaven!' exclaimed my companion. 'He has run into the constable!'

He took a quick pace towards the steps, then halted, irresolute.

'Parry must look after himself,' I said tersely. 'We have a dying man on our hands. Help me to get him inside the house.'

I knew that it was futile, but we could not leave him there to die on the doorstep. Holmes, seeming content to follow my lead, answered with a nod. Supporting Chao Hsing between us, we re-entered the hall, again making for the library. We did not know where else to take him, and, from the direction of his faltering steps, this appeared to be where he wished to go. Arrived there, we had some thought of laying him down upon the settee – with what purpose I cannot say, for I knew that we could do nothing to staunch that dreadful wound – but he shook his head slowly. We allowed him to guide us, assisting him as well as we might, and he turned towards the bureau in the corner.

The long skirt of his robe was already blood-soaked to the ankle, and a ghastly trail extended over the carpet. With his left hand still clenched below his ribs, Chao Hsing sat down in the chair last occupied by the professor. He reached out over the desk top, took a plain sheet of paper from one of the compartments at the back, and laid it before him. Then, lifting the cover from a flat cedarwood box, he disclosed an ink-stone.

'He is trying to write something!' cried Holmes.

Spellbound by a horrible fascination, we watched the slow, deliberate movements of the man sitting at his master's desk. From a small silver vessel shaped like a tiny kettle, he poured a few drops of water into the shallow well at the base of the flat stone, then took up a stick of solid ink and rubbed it until the minute quantity of liquid became black. He picked up a writing brush.

Lifting his hand, and holding the brush perpendicular to the paper in what seemed to me a peculiarly awkward and difficult fashion – between the second and third fingers and upraised thumb – he began to write. It was a task which called for a steady hand, but the ancient hand of Chao Hsing never wavered. Now, in the last moments of his life, he became young.

One glance he gave me, and I saw his eyes burning like coals of fire. I remembered our host's tales of Nanking, and saw Morgan Davies seated on a great pile of silks and cushions (under which was the youthful Chao Hsing), placidly reading the verses of Po Chü-i while the Imperial soldiers stormed through his house, searching for T'ai Ping rebels. Now their adventures had been shared to the last.

With great deliberation and infinite care, Chao Hsing traced a line and a half of Chinese characters vertically upon the sheet, then laid aside his brush. He picked up the paper and handed it to Holmes, who took it. Chao Hsing smiled, said a word in his own language – and fell forward across the desk top. Taking his wrist, without otherwise disturbing him, I found no pulse and knew that I had witnessed a triumph of mind over matter: only an indomitable will had postponed death till that moment.

'He has tried to leave a message for us, in the only way that he could!' said Holmes, staring at the paper. 'We may never know just how he came by his death, but he must surely have seen, or heard, that fiend out on the terrace and gone out to tackle him. But why? Why did the man come back?'

'Why, indeed?' I echoed. 'What more can they want here? They have murdered the professor, and taken that accursed diary. Better for him that he had never received it – '

'What's going on here?' shouted an excited voice in the background.

We turned quickly to see P C Parry in the doorway. There was mud on his trousers, and he held his helmet in one hand by the chinstrap, while using the other to dab at a small cut on his forehead with a handkerchief.

'There's a naked devil running wild!' he went on, as

though hardly expecting to be believed. 'He charged full tilt into me, and pitched me off my bike! I went after him, but I couldn't catch him – '

'As well for you, perhaps, that you could not!' said Holmes shortly.

'I don't understand this!' announced PC Parry, rather unnecessarily. 'And what's happened to old Davies?' His inquiring glance passed from the body of the professor to that of his servant slumped over the writing desk, and he started visibly. 'What! The both of them? Oh, Lor'! The inspector isn't going to like this. . . . '

'Chao Hsing has been killed by the man you saw,' I explained.

'And the professor?' Constable Parry approached the corpse of Morgan Davies, peered at the bloodshot skull, and gulped. 'Oh, Gospel Bells! He's burst his brain! Well, you can't wonder at it, can you, now. . . . '

'He, too, has been murdered,' said Holmes, 'but we do not yet know how.'

The village constable muttered something incoherent.

'Let me see to that cut on your forehead,' I offered. 'It wasn't done with the man's knife, was it?'

'No, sir. I hit my head when I fell off my bike.' Parry looked at me askance. 'I didn't know he'd got a knife!'

'Well, he has,' I said, 'and it could take your head off. I know the kind of knives these people use. He is a Burmese dacoit.'

I went upstairs to get my medicine chest, thinking as I did so that I was having my fill of doctoring to-night – and, it seemed, all the excitement was not yet over. What did the Si Fan want? How had Chao Hsing known that the dacoit would come back, and what was the meaning of the cryptic message he had tried to convey to us?

As I came back down the stairs, I noted that the front door of the house, which we had left open, had again been closed and secured, by either Holmes or the constable.

In the library, I found Holmes sitting on the end of the settee farthest from the two dead cats, and frowning over

Chao Hsing's message, as though by dint of sheer concentration he might be able to read it. I took a candle from the mantelpiece, lighted it, and made PC Parry hold it to shine directly upon his face while I examined and dressed his superficial wound.

'Come and sit down over here, Petrie,' said Holmes. 'And you too, Constable.'

There was little enough laughable in that night's affairs, but his face was, I thought, unusually grave. We seated ourselves as directed, and waited.

'I think you should understand our situation,' he continued. 'There is an armed assassin outside, and, for all we know, there may be a dozen. The men from Aberystwyth will not arrive before dawn. Meanwhile, we are under siege. There is something in this house which the Si Fan mean to have, and they are armed not only with knives but with something else – something with which they can kill us all without even entering, as they killed him.'

He gestured towards the corpse of our murdered host, and Constable Parry shifted nervously in his chair. Holmes, leaning over to me, held out the paper in his hand.

'We must learn what this means!'

I stared down at the futile message. Unlike the scribbled characters of Li Lien-ying's lost diary, the last words of Chao Hsing were neatly and clearly written, though they remained unintelligible to us. They consisted of fourteen ideographs – four in the first line, and ten in the second – which, re-arranged from left to right, appeared as follows:

請查原稿
老師一直用本國語寫出

'We lack the knowledge to read it,' I said, 'but no doubt we shall later be able to find someone who can.'

'We cannot wait!' declared Holmes. 'He used the last of his strength to write it, and it is urgent. We must know *now*!'

'But it is impossible! We cannot read Chinese.'

Holmes sniffed contemptuously. 'Nonsense!' he said stiffly. 'If I solved the riddle of the Dancing Men, I can solve this.'

'But this is not a cipher,' I protested. 'These things are not letters, but words!'

'Precisely! Do you think that I cannot find the meaning of fourteen words, in a room filled with reference books and dictionaries?'

'That is all very well,' I said, still unconvinced, 'but since you do not know how they are pronounced, how can they be looked up?'

'There must be some established way of doing it,' he replied, shrugging, 'and these books will tell me what it is.' He stood up, glancing around the bookshelves. 'It may take me some time, of course, and I should prefer to be well guarded while I work. I shall want you outside on the terrace, Petrie.'

'Very well,' I said, and, in turn, stood up.

Constable Parry, looking utterly out of his depth, but making a brave effort, came to his feet also.

'What shall I do, sir?' he asked.

'I shall be obliged if you will sit in the chair which you will find placed outside the door, and keep watch in the hall. The front door has been left open for some time, and it is possible that there are men already in the house. You are not armed, I suppose?'

'I've got my truncheon, sir!'

'That will be little use against a dacoit's knife,' I said. 'You had better have my pistol. Since I am to be outside, I will take that.' I pointed to the shotgun in the corner.

'Good!' said Holmes. 'There is a box of cartridges on one of the shelves beside it.'

His words reminded me that my Browning was no

longer fully loaded – I had fired five shots. Slipping out the magazine, I recharged it from the spares which, in these days, invariably added weight to my jacket, then handed the pistol to Parry.

From the way in which he took it, I guessed that he was quite unfamiliar with such weapons.

'Leave the safety catch released,' I said, 'or you may forget to do it, if there is an attack – but keep your finger off the trigger. In the event of an emergency, don't hesitate to shoot. These fiends are quick on their feet.'

Constable Parry swallowed audibly, nodded, and went out into the hall, holding my pistol gingerly, with the muzzle pointed at the floor.

'It will be about as much good to him as a truncheon,' remarked Holmes wryly.

I took up the heavy shotgun and broke open the breech, thinking again of Morgan Davies. Eighty-odd, and he had said that occasionally he still used it! I pushed two cartridges into the chambers, and, as an after-thought, put two more in my pocket.

'With that cannon, you should be able to blast any-thing within range,' commented my companion, with a grim smile. 'I am giving you the honour of the more dangerous position, Petrie. Pah!' he added with disgust. 'This place is like a charnel house, but I must work in it, because of the books.'

'I fear that you may find it an impossible task,' I said pessimistically.

Holmes shook his head, glancing down again at the paper.

'The Chinese language has no system of grammar, as we know it,' he answered. 'If I can discover the separate meanings of these ideographs, the total meaning may be deduced. Leave me, now, to get on with it.' He laid down the sheet on one of the barrel stools used as side tables, and turned to begin a search of the bookcases. 'I shall reverse the instructions which I gave to Professor Davies. I shall leave the door unlocked, so that Con-stable Parry may get in quickly if I call, and the windows uncurtained, so that you may look in from time to time to see if I am still alive. But do not stand in front of them, where you will make too easy a target for a shot or a knife thrown from the bushes. Stay in the shadows as much as you can.'

I went outside, closing the window behind me; but Holmes did not lock it, for the same reason that he had left the door unlocked.

Beyond the yellow spill of light from the library, the terrace was shrouded in darkness. In the severe Georgian façade of the house there were no projecting buttresses or recesses to provide me with cover. With the gun balanced in the crook of my arm, I took up my position, leaning against the balustrade at a point where it was crowned by a large stone urn, offering a modicum of concealment from below. There was little I could do to protect my back, but the steps leading up to the terrace lay in front of me, so that the enemy could not easily come at me from behind, unless they climbed over.

I wondered how many there might be. So far, we had seen only one, but I knew that the dacoits usually worked in pairs, so that there was likely to be another. This was not the first time that I had been in a household besieged by the Si Fan. I thought of our adventures, early in the fight with Fu Manchu, at Eltham's place in Norfolk – but then there had been five of us (including his daughter), and servants in the house. Here we were but three.

Remembering my advice to Parry, I hefted the shotgun and pulled back both the hammers ere settling myself as comfortably as I could, my eyes fixed on the windows of the room where Sherlock Holmes pored over dictionaries, with two dead men and two dead cats to keep him company. I felt reasonably satisfied that he was well protected. No one could approach unseen, and the small, square panes of glass into which the windows were divided by regular glazing bars made it almost impossible for any object to be flung through from a greater distance. So long as I was vigilant at my post, he must surely be safe.

The night was less dark now than when we had arrived, the cloud layer having dispersed some hours previously. Pinpoints of light shone down from the vault of heaven, though there was no moon, providing a wan illumination in which I could see the black wall of the shrubbery and the tall, straight shapes of the poplars along the drive rising above it like an avenue of obelisks. All was silent, save for the mournful voice of the lonely owl, still hooting monotonously in the distance.

I am not superstitious, but I derived no comfort from the reflection that exactly a month had gone by since my homecoming from the north – and, in that ill-fated year, Friday the thirteenth came twice in succession.

Estimating that ten minutes had elapsed, I made my first visit, creeping along the front of the house like a thief, past the closed door and beyond it to the nearer of the library windows. Flattened against the wall, I peered around the edge of the frame and saw Holmes seated in an armchair which he had placed so that he could not be seen from any other position. He had a writing pad on his knee and a stack of books on the floor beside him. Reassured, I crept back to my station at the balustrade, repeating my visits at roughly guessed intervals of ten minutes.

An hour passed without alarm, yet, as the time lengthened, I became the less easy. I have too lively an imagination to make a good sentry. Each breath of wind rustling through the leaves made me jump; repeatedly, I found myself glancing over my shoulder into the bushes. My night vision is good and, now that I had been outside for some time, I could discern the shapes of individual clumps which stood out from the rest. My wayward imagination turned them into monsters lurking in the darkness. One in particular seemed to me like a mammoth-sized toad, and each time that I looked, I found it increasingly difficult to convince myself that it was not nearer than it had been before.

278

Making my seventh or eighth visit to the window, I was relieved to see Holmes still hard at work. Earlier in his efforts, he had relaxed his interdiction on smoking at the scene of a crime, and the weight of the great, bell-mouthed calabash clamped between his teeth caused his jaw muscles to stand out like whipcord. The solution of Chao Hsing's cryptogram was clearly one which demanded tobacco.

All seemed as it had been. I returned to my post, feeling by now a little chilly and wishing that I had put on my overcoat. For a moment, my thoughts wandered to such personal trivialities – and then, as I least expected it, came a sound from below which brought me stiffly upright, the short hairs prickling on the nape of my neck like the hackles of a startled mastiff. It was a low, eerie ululation, inaudible from the house – a sound which I had all too often heard – the cry of a dacoit.

It had come from somewhere in the bushes. Then, as I listened, tense in every nerve, it came again – closer. I turned, raising the twin barrels of the shotgun above the parapet, and leaned over, peering into the darkness. Strain my eyes though I might, I could see nothing. I persisted, striving vainly to penetrate the formless barrier of foliage – till suddenly I realised with a shock that for a good twenty seconds or more I had switched my attention away from the library windows.

I spun around and, careless of caution, hurried towards them, my heart racing with apprehension. Nothing seemed changed in their appearance; the lamplight flowed out across the flagstones as before, casting a latticed pattern – but, my perceptions sharpened by anxiety, I saw now that there *was* a difference. Halfway up the nearer window, the regular pattern of the lattice was interrupted by an opaque disc, large enough in diameter to obscure almost the whole of one pane. Two more paces brought me level with the steps, and, at the same instant, I saw him kneeling upon them in the angle of the balustrade – the dacoit, bending double over a square box from which a T-shaped rod projected, the bar grasped in his hands.

I take no credit for my actions. The scene before my eyes . . . half-forgotten scraps of scientific reading . . . the face of the dead professor . . . the enigmatic phrases of Smith's letter – all combined in a flash of inspiration to which I reacted with no conscious thought. The gun leapt to my shoulder as though of its own accord, and I fired – not at the dacoit, but at the window. The crash of the heavy weapon echoed around the estate like a thunderclap.

It was answered from the steps by a scream like that of a jungle beast. With the gun still to my shoulder, I turned and saw the dacoit bounding towards me, the curved blade swinging above his head, his eyes dilated and his lips flecked with foam. I was aware of no fear – only a cold, deadly rage. He was hardly six feet from me when I pressed the second trigger – too near for the charge to spread. The whole force of it took him full in the chest, literally hurling him backwards.

I lowered the shotgun and turned again, thankful to see the shattered window standing open and Sherlock Holmes on the threshold.

'Are you all right?' I asked tremulously.

'Yes,' he said. 'But some of those pellets came uncomfortably close. Why – '

PC Parry came rushing through from the library door, brandishing my pistol in an alarming manner, and wordless with shock. He stared down, gasped, and shone his police lantern on the mangled corpse of the dacoit.

'*Duw*! There's horrible!' he faltered.

'Come inside,' I said to Holmes, my voice still trembling.

He obeyed without a word, and, putting down the gun, I searched briefly at my feet among the carpeting of splintered glass – sought for and found a large rubber suction cup attached to a yard or so of broken cable. Inside, at the base of it, was a tangled mass of fine wires and metallic discs.

280

'It was not *thirty thousand bicycles*,' I said, 'but *thirty thousand megacycles* – a supersonic wave, incredibly beyond the range of human hearing. The study is only in its infancy, but we believe that if such frequencies could be produced, they would be destructive to life.'

Holmes nodded, took the device from my hand, and examined it.

'Fu Manchu is primarily a chemist and a poisoner. But with his team of captive scientists, he is fifty years ahead of us in all branches.' He broke off, thought for a moment, then nodded again. 'Ah! I see now why I could not find the pane of glass from the window. They cut around this thing after it had done its work, and used it to withdraw the glass from the frame, so that it still adhered to it when they took away their apparatus. The reason why you fired at the window, of course, was in order to destroy it?'

'Yes,' I replied. 'I had no time to think, but, somehow, instinct warned me not to fire at the dacoit, in case he should fall across his infernal machine and so set it in motion.'

'It was a sound instinct,' said Holmes warmly. He peered closely at the intricate mechanism, and prodded it with his finger. 'I take it that this contrivance is irreparably damaged?'

'I think so. There is probably nothing much in the box out on the steps but a hand-operated generator.'

Holmes smiled, threw the object down roughly on the floor, and set his heel upon it.

'Thank Heaven!' he said seriously. 'If events in Europe take the course which Fu Manchu predicts – and I fear they will – I would not like to think of such a thing even in the hands of our own Government.' He turned back to the terrace, where Parry was still pottering about outside. 'Come in, Constable! You can do no good out there, and there may be more dacoits around.'

Constable Parry rejoined us, his honest face set in an expression of self-disbelief.

'I can't think what the inspector's going to say!' he muttered uneasily.

'Bother the inspector!' said Holmes shortly. 'Confound it! I have dropped my pipe on the floor and burnt the carpet. Oh, well – never mind. After to-night's doings, the room is in poor shape, anyway.'

So much was sadly evident. Furniture and bookbacks were torn and pocked with shotgun pellets. Holmes picked up the calabash, re-lighted the unspilled remainder of the contents, and threw himself down into an armchair. His narrow escape from death seemed not to have affected him at all.

'To you go the honours for solving this one, Petrie,' he said magnanimously, 'for you had the answers before I did. My contribution has been only the solution of this somewhat elementary problem. . . .'

He searched among the tumbled books beside his chair, and held up a writing pad.

'What!' I exclaimed incredulously. 'You have read the Chinese ideographs?'

'Of course. It was a while before I could find it, but the indexing system is a simple affair based on commonly recurring elements. The chief difficulty was that most of these characters have several meanings, and it was sometimes not easy to choose the right one. But, in the end, I managed well enough, and had only to write out a fair copy when you fired your salutary shot. However, you will be able to make out my final notation, I think.'

He passed the pad to me and I saw that, on the top sheet, he had written numbers to represent each ideograph, with English equivalents alongside. I glanced at the first four.

1. PLEASE   3. ORIGINAL
2. SEEK   4. DRAFT

'Yes, that seems clear,' I said. 'We are to look for the professor's manuscript – his translation, I suppose.' I hesitated. 'But I cannot make much of the second group.'

5. OLD	10. BASE
6. MASTER	11. COUNTRY
7. ONE	12. WORDS
8. CONTINUOUS	13. WRITE
9. USING	14. OUT

'But it is child's play!' cried Holmes impatiently. 'Apart from the fact that the verb comes last, as in German, it is plain English! Obviously, there are cases where two Chinese words are necessary to represent one in our language. I assume that "one continuous" stands for "invariably" and that "base country" may be read as "homeland." Don't you see? It means that Professor Davies always translated first into Welsh!'

'Good Heavens!' I said, staring. 'What an extraordinary procedure!'

'Not at all,' he replied, shaking his head in reproof. 'The professor told us that he came from a Welsh-speaking family. He could speak and write both English and Chinese fluently – but he could not easily translate directly from one into the other, since *both* were foreign languages to him!'

Standing up quickly, he thrust his pipe into his pocket.

'Now to find the manuscript!'

He strode across to the corner where the bureau stood, and where Chao Hsing still sat in the chair before it, his head down upon the desk top, peacefully, like a student who has fallen asleep over his work, save for the dreadful crimson stain which had spread out over the carpet. I shuddered slightly. Holmes, ere commencing his search, again paused and turned back to address us.

'Professor Davies, having completed his draft, may either have intended to re-translate it, or leave us to have that done by someone else,' he said. 'At all events, he had laid it aside somewhere and left his chair to get a drink when he was struck down. As to what followed, I see now that my first impressions were

283

inaccurate. The dacoit was in here longer than I thought. Chao Hsing was shielded from the lethal sound wave only by the thickness of the heavy oak door, and I believe it rendered him unconscious.'

'It must have been at the same moment that we both awoke with a headache!' I exclaimed.

'Quite. So the dacoit was here, searching, while we were talking in the bathroom upstairs. He soon found the Chinese diary, and must have known sufficient English to be able to identify a translation. But all the professor's papers proved to be written in Welsh! Short of taking or destroying everything in the room, what was he to do?'

I thought of our first terrible night together in Sussex, and shivered reminiscently.

'It would have been a suitable occasion for one of those hideous Stromberg globes,' I commented.

'No doubt. But, luckily for us, he did not have one handy. He would very likely have set fire to the place, but before he could make up his mind, or take steps, Chao Hsing came to his senses and began knocking on the door. Failing to obtain a reply, he hurried round by the terrace, while the dacoit fled, fearing that he might have all three of us to face.'

Constable Parry, who sat listening with a stricken look on his face, ventured a question.

'Then – how was the old Chinaman killed, sir?'

'Afterwards,' said Holmes briefly. 'Chao Hsing could not be sure whether the manuscript had been taken or not, and could not ascertain, since he himself did not understand Welsh. When he had somewhat recovered from his grief at the professor's death, he realised what the position might be, but he had no way of telling us. Therefore, he watched to see if the dacoit would return, and, in doing so, lost his life.'

He hunched his shoulders in a kind of shrug, as though to indicate that his exposition was complete, and turned away, staring down at the bureau and the body of Chao Hsing.

'There are drawers underneath,' he muttered, 'and it may be in one of those, but I am loath to disturb him. . . . Perhaps it will not be necessary. Ah! This looks likely!'

He pointed, and, hurrying impatiently to join him where he stood, I saw, piled up on a chair directly beside the bureau, a stack of fifty or sixty ordinary school exercise books of a sort which could probably be purchased for a penny in the village shop. Holmes picked up a few and opened them at random. Each was partially filled with small, neat handwriting in Welsh.

'Yes – almost certainly!' he declared. 'These are his drafts, and, logically, the one we want will be the one on top.'

'But how can we tell?' I inquired vaguely. 'We cannot read Welsh either!'

Holmes laughed shortly. 'On the contrary – one of us can!' He swung around, facing back into the room. 'Come here, Constable, and earn your share of the credit!'

He thrust the exercise book into the hands of the sadly bewildered policeman.

'Read some of this,' Holmes directed, 'and tell us if it has to do with the employment of secret agents to hinder a revolution against the Imperial government of China.'

Parry thumbed obediently through the pages, scowling at them, and clearly understanding little of what he read. But, eventually:

'Yes, sir,' he said. 'It does.'

'Excellent!' said Holmes, taking the book from him. 'We have it! I doubt if there will be any further attack to-night, since they have now lost their devil's contraption. But I think we will all go upstairs and make ourselves secure in one of the other rooms till the officers from Aberystwyth arrive.' He looked at me and smiled, but his clear grey eyes were more than usually solemn. 'We have won this round, after all, and gained an advantage over the Si Fan. But we have paid a heavy price for it in the lives of two great men – for you know, Petrie, in his own simple way, Chao Hsing was as great as his master. . . .'

25

BETWEEN TIDES

During the rest of that night we were left in peace, but there had certainly been other agents of Fu Manchu on the premises – for next morning we found that the box on the steps was gone. I confess that I had thought no more about it till that moment, and I rather suspect that Sherlock Holmes had deliberately allowed them an opportunity to take it.

I prefer to draw a discreet veil over the scene which ensued when the police investigation team at length turned up. PC Parry's nervous apprehensions as to what the inspector would say proved justified. What the inspector said was much, and little of it was complimentary.

It was borne home to me in no uncertain fashion that one does not shoot dacoits in Wales as freely as rabbits. I may say with pride rather than shame that he was not my first, but he caused us trouble. Among other stupidities, it was observed that I had no licence for the shotgun, and that the constable had no legal right to borrow my pistol. I was politely but firmly told that an inquiry would be needed to determine whether I had committed an act of justifible or criminal homicide. In the meantime, a triple inquest must be held and all of us would be required to give evidence.

We spent most of that day in Aberystwyth, and did not get back to Swansea till later the next, arriving there under something of an official cloud. Superintendent Gribbler was embarrassed – sympathetic, but helpless. We got in touch with Weymouth at Scotland Yard, and, through him, certain steps were taken, resulting in a postponement of the inquest, but, until my own position was resolved, I was not supposed to leave the district.

Holmes was furious. Both of us felt it vital that we should be free at any instant to take up the trail and follow it whither it might lead us. Yet, ironically, the restrictions now placed upon us were no hindrance, for, though we could not know it, we were about to begin a further ten days of maddening inactivity.

The dearly bought manuscript of Professor Davies was translated into English, copies made, one despatched to the Foreign Office, and the rest deposited in three separate banks till we were sure that it had reached there safely. Even in Swansea, we still feared a last-minute attempt by the Si Fan to regain their secret, but nothing happened. Fu Manchu, acting in character, accepted his loss philosophically and sought no revenge.*

Holmes withdrew once more to his bedroom and shut himself up with his books, to the disgust of the hotel staff; occasionally, he emerged at mealtimes. I saw little of him, nor did I make much attempt to cultivate his society. When we were not actively discussing business, his table conversation was invariably on abstruse topics ranging from Elizabethan shorthand to wildlife in New Guinea. He had, as I recall, once shocked Watson by declaring that he believed the capacity of the human brain to be limited, and that he would put nothing in his which he did not need – but I found it hard to imagine any useful application for the studies on which he chose to spend his off-duty hours.

Sad to say, during all the weeks we spent together, he told me nothing of himself, and, save for a few oblique references, said nothing of the affairs which he had handled in the past. I became the recipient of no fascinating case-histories unrelated by Watson. Only once that I remember did I succeed in getting any personal information out of him.

* The loss was a major one. Fu Manchu's activities were curtailed in his own country, and the Si Fan remained dormant for fourteen years. [P.]

'By the way,' I said, 'to clear up a long-standing mystery, was Dr Watson wounded in the shoulder or in the leg?'

Holmes looked at me as if I were prying into family secrets – which, perhaps, I was – but he answered.

'There is no mystery,' he said shortly, 'other than in Watson's neglect to make himself clear. Watson went down in a hail of bullets at the battle of Maiwand. One struck him in the left shoulder, another in the thigh, and a third nicked his ribs. The one in the shoulder had shattered the bone, and was still causing him a good deal of pain when we first met. But the bullet in his thigh had lodged in the muscle, so that it could not be extracted, and it was this which continued to trouble him years after his other wounds had healed – in fact, it still does.'

The second day after our return to Swansea, our spell of fine weather was interrupted by a rainstorm of tropical intensity. It blew up from across the bay in a dark pall, visible an hour beforehand, and teemed down till well past nightfall, turning the long slope of the high street into a river, and flooding the lower sections of the town. No one who could avoid doing so went out. The wheels of the lumbering, maroon-coloured buses churned up water-spouts across the pavements, and the ramshackle train which skirted the edge of the bay round to the lighthouse suspended service, its tracks deluged in bursts of spray.

Next morning, it was sunny and as warm as before. At breakfast time, a telegram arrived for Holmes, in response to which he once more begged leave of absence to go up to London on the 'personal' business about which I had agreed to ask no questions.

'While I am there,' he said, 'I will take a little time to drop in at Whitehall and see if I cannot do something to extricate us from this tangle of red tape. Nayland Smith has special powers, conferred upon him by the Commissioner, at the direct request of the Home Secretary. Unfortunately, I do not know either of those gentlemen, but perhaps I can do as well. I have an occasionally useful brother, who is an *i*-dotter and a *t*-crosser in a Government department.'

He departed and was gone for a full three days, counselling me before he left to avoid involvement in any further misadventures, and, in particular, to shoot no more dacoits.

His advice proved unnecessary, since I had no such chance. With nothing more urgent to do, I turned my attention westwards again, still stubbornly determined to pursue my explorations of that rockbound coast as far as possible. There, we believed, Smith had been brought ashore. Holmes did not dispute the possibility that he might still be held there, in some isolated cottage or farmhouse, but, small though the area looked on the map, there must be a thousand such, and we could not obtain search warrants for each and every one – to say nothing of the caves with which the place was honeycombed.

Thinking at first, to pick up my tracks at the point where, earlier, I had turned inland, I learned that this was impossible. No path existed around the face of the cliffs beyond, which became progressively steeper and higher. At the summit, I came to a wide grassy plateau covered with gorse bushes and soft, springy turf upon which cattle and horses grazed. Keeping my steps turned persistently to the west, I crossed it and, in another hour, found myself looking down into the biggest bay I had so far seen.

It was fantastic – yet the whole vast expanse of clean golden sand was utterly deserted, save for a wandering sheep dog. A great spur of rock ran down the centre, terminating in three saw-toothed peaks, and pierced through from side to side by a natural arch, while, rearwards, a serpentine stream meandered in a continuous series of S-bends through a broad, wooded valley, to pour ultimately across the sands into the sea.

This was surely a scene from the pages of Robert

Louis Stevenson.* (High on the sandhills to the east, there was even a ruined castle!) But, as I sat there gazing down in wonder at this realisation of a novelist's fantasy, I knew that it was Fu Manchu country.

Shielding my eyes against the sun, I stared out beyond the spur which, at half tide, divided the bay into two equal segments, to the far extremity where the waves lapped at the base of a towering three-hundred-foot pinnacle of grey limestone. What lay beyond, still farther to the west? Distantly, I could make out the glimmer of yet more sands – a long, dark green promontory reaching far out to sea. . . .

This, I resolved, it should be my business to determine the following day. But, as it transpired, the following morning brought me a telegram from Sherlock Holmes, giving the time of his train, and asking me to meet him at the station. I obeyed, wondering what this summons might mean, and was astonished to discover that it had no meaning. My heart went out to him as he stepped off the train, looking desperately tired, and I realised that all he had wanted was to have someone waiting for him on the platform.

I took his bag without a word, and together we walked the few steps to our hotel. I saw that his business in London – whatever it might be – had taxed him to the limit. He craved the warmth of human companionship, and, even though I knew that, in the end, it would bring us no closer, I gave it to him gladly.

As we sat in the hotel lounge after dinner that night, I told him of my wanderings in the Gower peninsula, while he listened and smiled tolerantly.

'You should really see it for yourself,' I urged.

Holmes took out his pouch and crammed a prodigal amount of tobacco into his ruminative calabash.

'I imagine,' he replied gravely, 'that I shall be called upon to do so in the end – for it is almost certainly there

* This is Three Cliffs Bay. Dr Petrie's impressions may be verified at the expense of a two mile walk from the nearest bus stop. [Ed.]

that the Chinese ship will come. We know now that the Si Fan is closing down its operations in Europe. The stores which were taken from the mine at Nant Gareth are not to be used, as we first supposed, for furnishing some new headquarters, but simply to be taken home. In the interim, if you have the urge to wear out your bootleather, go ahead – spy out the land.'

The next few days passed very much as the preceding. Encouraged to go on with my exploring, I did so, working my way doggedly around the coast – a summer paradise reserved for the energetic few who would tramp through the woods and scramble down cliffs to reach it. It was healthy exercise and worth every moment of it for the glorious prospects with which my eyes were rewarded; but when I saw and realised the vast number of sites from which boats could slip out unobserved to the Chinese ship waiting offshore, I felt near to despair. They would be gone and away before we could do anything to prevent them.

In one respect alone was the situation eased. I had asked Holmes nothing about his trip to London, or if he had been able to do anything about our legal affairs, as I might term them. However, one morning he came into the breakfast room with an official-looking envelope which he had collected at the desk, and tearing it open, glanced at the contents with a brusque nod of satisfaction.

'Good!' he announced. 'We shall hear no more about the dacoit.'

He waved his letter under my nose and put it away again without giving me a chance to read it – but not before I had seen the name 'Asquith' written at the bottom. Noting my start of surprise, he smiled.

'He owes me a favour,' he said, shrugging.

Whilst I toiled and fretted, Holmes continued quietly to amuse himself in his own scholarly fashion and was not, I am sure, sorry to have exchanged Cardiff for Swansea. At no great distance was Craig-y-nos Castle –

the retreat of the seventy-year-old Adelina Patti, whose voice he had admired in his youth, and, through the good offices of Superintendent Gribbler, he managed to obtain an invitation to one of the rare recitals staged in her private theatre. I drove him out there, but, being less attracted to the twilight performances of ex-prima donnas, chose not to accompany him. Waiting to bring him back, I spent my time pleasantly enough at a nearby hostelry, talking to the locals, who told me of caverns extending miles underground, deep, narrow ravines winding through the hills, and stupendous waterfalls so difficult of access that few had ever seen them. Again it was impressed upon me that this, as much as the coast, was Fu Manchu country.

I mentioned these facts afterwards to Holmes, but his only comment was that, personally, he had some reason to dislike waterfalls.

It was now five weeks since we had left London, and, though there was no sign of the unseasonal heat wave mentioned by PC Jones as an occasional phenomenon, Spring was well advanced. I had good weather for my walks. Everywhere, the trees were budding and in blossom. The marshland behind the long, sandy beach which I was currently exploring was bright with wild iris and alive with bird-calls, some of which I did not recognise – one a high, piping note, and another like the hammering together of two small stones. The town, too, was taking on a festive appearance, with a good deal of tidying and repainting going on in preparation for a forthcoming state visit by the young Prince of Wales, whose investiture had taken place only three years previously.

The suggestion was made, again by Gribbler, that, if we were still in Swansea at that time, Holmes should be presented – a distinction which my companion contemptuously dismissed.

'What have I to do with kings and princes?' he demanded with a sniff, and added: 'I knew his grandfather, and I did not like him.'

Tuesday passed very much as Monday and the days before. Dusk was falling when I returned to our hotel, having spent most of the afternoon in an unsuccessful attempt to find a path through the dense woods of Oxwich Point. I went up to my room, changed into more respectable clothes, and then, remembering that I had scarcely set eyes on Sherlock Holmes over the past forty-eight hours, went to knock on his door. His high-pitched, querulous voice bade me enter, and, doing so, I discovered him seated cross-legged on his bed in a cloud of tobacco smoke, his eyes boring like gimlets into a book of basic Chinese ideographs, which he had filched from Professor Davies's house. He looked up at me standing in the doorway, and shook his head dismally.

'One can never be sufficiently prepared,' he observed. 'If only I had been able to speak, or even to write, Chinese, Chao Hsing's life might have been saved.'

'Perhaps it was better that way,' I said sadly. 'He was old, and I think it pleased him best to die with his master.'

'Stuff and nonsense!' retorted Holmes. 'You are an arrant sentimentalist!'

I smiled, making no attempt to argue the point and, instead, asked him when he had last eaten – to which he replied that he did not remember. I therefore proposed that we should dine together, and, at my insistence, he yielded.

'Oh, very well, then!' he said ungraciously. 'Give me a few minutes to make myself acceptable in the dining room, and I will join you downstairs.'

I went down into the lobby and waited, smoking a cigarette. Nothing at that moment seemed conspicuously different from any other – but it was just then that I heard the telephone bell ring, and, a few seconds later, the desk clerk calling out to me.

'Call for Mr Holmes, or Dr Petrie! Will you take it, sir?'

I stood up, walked across, and picked up the instrument. The voice which answered me was only vaguely familiar, and until the speaker had identified himself, I did not recognise it as that of our old acquaintance Sergeant Hughes of Brynamman – he who had been responsible for our inconclusive visit to Carreg Cennen – now sounding very excited and very Welsh.

'It's that old Chinese doctor, sir! There's no knowing what he'll do next, and now he's done it!'

'What *has* he done?' I demanded.

'Well, sir,' stammered Hughes. 'it's the sheep business again. Only now it's a man!'

Out of the corner of my eye, I saw Sherlock Holmes descending the stairs.

'Just a minute,' I said. 'You'd better speak to Mr Holmes.'

I beckoned to him, and, with a quick word of explanation, passed over the receiver. Eager and impatient, I watched him standing there at the desk, one elbow thrust up on it as he leaned forward to the candlestick mouthpiece.

'Yes . . . yes . . .' I heard him say. 'Where? It is called *what*? Spell it!'

He snapped his fingers at the desk clerk, snatched a pencil and pad, and began to write. A few more minutes passed while I listened to the one-sided conversation, making nothing of it; then Holmes put down the telephone and turned towards me, his steely grey eyes once more bright and alert.

'Tighten your belt, Petrie!' he snapped. 'Dinner is off! Can you find your way up to Carreg Cennen in the dark?'

'What?' I exclaimed. 'We are going there to-night?'

'Immediately. We will pick up Hughes in Brynamman, and he will guide us around to an unpronounceable place a mile or so on the other side of the castle.'

Holmes thrust the notepad into my hand, and, glancing down at it, I saw the pencilled notation, 'Sarn-y-Rhednwyddwr.'

'The body of a farm labourer has been found there,' he continued, almost jubilantly, 'in the same condition as Mr Garman's sheep. Your hell-bird is out again – and this time, there is a man who saw it!'

26

THE SMUGGLER'S CAUSEWAY

'Then there *is* such a thing!' I burst out excitedly. 'I was right!'

'At least you have a witness,' replied Holmes, shrugging. 'But his credibility may be another matter. I gather that he was so unnerved by what he saw – or thinks he saw – that he is now fortifying himself in the local public house and intends to stay there till they throw him out. Let us not waste time. We must get up there before the place closes.'

I hurried up to my room and changed back again into my now sadly used clothing. Within fifteen minutes, we had the car out of the garage, the headlamps lighted, and were upon the road once more, forging up towards Pontardawe. This was a route which I now knew fairly well – the same which we had covered on our first visit, and the same which I had followed more recently when taking Holmes up to the concert at Craig-y-nos. Even at night, I no longer found it difficult.

'Hughes is a good man!' shouted my companion. 'I must really see that something is done for him. But for him, we should know nothing about this – and but for that stupid inspector of his, who thinks he can take care of everything in his own district, we should have known about it this morning.'

I devoted my attention to the road, driving as fast as I dared, and, for a while, asked no questions. Apart from the vocal hardship of contending with the engine and the wind, I was still too inexperienced for discussions at the wheel. But before we had proceeded very far, curiosity spurred me to the effort.

'The sheep were taken more than a fortnight ago,' I

said. 'If this predatory creature really exists, why has it been inactive until now?'

'Well – judging by its behaviour,' answered Holmes, with a dry chuckle, 'it appears to be insane! But there may be another reason. Wait a minute. . . .'

I was aware of movement beside me as he fumbled inside his coat. Then his pocket lamp was switched on, and I saw him turning over the leaves of his notebook. He scrutinised them carefully, then switched off the light.

'Yes, I think I am right,' he announced. 'It works by moonlight. On the night when it attacked the sheep, the moon was four days past the full, and visible all night. Since then there has been a new moon, and, until recently, insufficient light for it to operate.'

Now that the road was familiar, it seemed shorter. Sooner than I expected, I had found my way to Ystrad-gynlais (though I still did not know how to say it) and, immediately on entering the town, turned off to the left. The cottage lights of a string of intervening villages flashed past in quick succession, and, soon after, we were in Brynamman. Here, as arranged over the telephone, Sergeant Hughes was waiting for us at the bus stop, and I observed that, once again, he had changed into plain clothes.

Holmes jumped out and greeted him warmly. 'You are off duty now, I suppose?' he asked.

'Yes, sir – till midday to-morrow. I phoned you as soon as I left the station.'

'Good! Then you may join us in a private investigation.'

Directing Hughes to sit in front with me, where he could act as navigator, Holmes climbed into the back, took out and looked at his watch.

'We can afford five minutes before we leave,' he said. 'Tell us something about this impossibly named village we are going to visit.'

'Sarn-y-Rhednwyddwr. Well, it's a bit of a queer place, sir.'

'That's what you said about Carreg Cennen,' I reminded him.

'It's *all* queer places around there, sir!' replied Hughes, grinning. He slewed round in his seat to talk to Holmes. 'It's just an inn and a dozen or so houses on one side of a marsh, which is about half a mile wide. Over on the other side, right opposite, there are two or three farms, and in between, there's an old stone causeway that goes right across the marsh. That's what the name means, sir – the Smuggler's Causeway. Of course, I think it's only a legend, sir – I mean, I don't see where they'd be smuggling anything from. It's probably an old dike, or something. But they call it that because it leads straight to the inn, and when the reeds are up, you can't see it, so that it looks like there's no way over. The men who live in the farms often walk across it when they want a pint, since it's a good two miles round by the road.'

'Isn't it dangerous?' I asked.

'Oh, no, sir!' Hughes glanced back towards me. 'It's ten or twelve feet broad. There's been a few drunks fallen off now and then and got themselves a wetting, but nobody's ever been killed – '

'Until last night!' added Holmes darkly. 'This was the place where a man was seized and carried off like the sheep, wasn't it?'

'Well – we *think* he was, sir,' said the sergeant cautiously. 'Nobody actually saw it.'

'I thought you said somebody did.'

'No, sir. He only saw the thing that did it.'

'Very well,' said Holmes, in a rather disappointed tone. 'Precisely what happened, then?'

Hughes persevered, and his evidence was soon given. Shorn of his nervous trappings, it amounted simply to this:

Iowerth Williams, a farmhand employed at one of the farms mentioned, had left the inn ten minutes before closing time, to walk home via the causeway, happy but not drunk. He failed to arrive. At the tearful insistence of his wife, the police were informed, but nothing could be done till the morning, when a search was begun, on the assumption that he had tumbled into the marsh and been drowned. Whilst the search was still going on, the body of the unfortunate man was found independently on farm premises a mile to the north. He had apparently fallen from a great height through the tin roof of a barn, and been killed instantly.

And, in the meantime:

Wyn Crumlin. likewise a farm labourer, but at a different farm, had left the inn shortly after Williams and slightly inebriated. Halfway across the causeway, he had seen something monstrous in the sky and bolted back to the inn, where he was denied re-admission, since it now lacked but three minutes to closing time. His later attempts to tell his story to the police, after the fate of Williams became known, had been scornfully dismissed, and he was currently at the same public house, endeavouring to gain a sympahetic hearing.

'Time is up!' declared Holmes, looking again at his watch. 'If we wish to interview this man we must be on our way. We have ten miles to go, and over bad roads.' As I re-started the engine, he leaned over to address Hughes. 'This is the second time that we have been indebted to you, Sergeant. I hope that you and your family are not too deeply attached to Brynamman, for I think you will soon be offered the post of inspector elsewhere.'

Sergeant Hughes flushed and began to stammer incoherent thanks, which were lost in the roar of the engine. The car jerked forward as I slipped badly into gear, and then we were off again, plunging through leafy tunnels of blackness towards the mysterious realm of Morgan le Fay. Hughes shouted directions in my ear, and I followed blindly, my thoughts in a turmoil. What was the meaning of this grotesque fairy tale of flying monsters and lost sheep?

It was hard to understand how Fu Manchu could have a hand in it – yet harder still to believe the earlier appearance of Wang Lo no more than a coincidence.

What unthinkable creature had he loosed upon this peaceful farming community? Granting even its incredible size and strength, this was no ordinary bird of prey – for it did not feed upon its quarry, but hunted seemingly for the vicious lust of killing. Granted its existence, where did it live, and how had it been brought here?

Lapsing into Gothic fantasy, my fertile imagination conjured up a winged horror hatched and nurtured in the stygian catacombs of Nant Gareth, which flew up the shaft at night to plunder the countryside. . . .

Without Hughes to pilot me, I should have been hopelessly lost only minutes after leaving the town. The narrow, winding lanes straggled endlessly across a patchwork of hills and valleys, where landmarks were few by daylight and now invisible. I had little idea where we were till, presently, the wheels splashed through a ford, throwing up a sparkling cascade into the glare of the headlamps, and I knew that we must be near the village of Trapp. Hereafter, relying upon memory, it seemed to me that we were retracing the route which we had taken in the company of the disgruntled sheep farmer. A few more moments afterwards, we came to a point where, to the right, the land lay more open than before – where, I thought, we had left the car and crossed fields to the riverbank. I glanced sideways and saw that I was right.

In the near distance, the imposing mass of Carreg Cennen loomed up black against the sky, the hard outline of the castle wall and one round tower clearly distinguishable at the summit. I stared up – then, with a sharp exclamation, jammed on the brakes and, as the car ground to a halt, leaned out.

'What is it?' demanded Holmes, from the rear. 'Why have we stopped?'

'I saw a light up there!' I said breathlessly.

All three of us sat staring upwards, but there was no light now to be seen, and, though we watched for some minutes, it did not re-appear. Holmes, I thought, would surely say that I had imagined it. But, surprisingly, he did not.

'What kind of light was it?' he asked sternly. 'Was it steady, or moving?'

'Moving, I think, and it flashed on and off three or four times.'

'Like a signal?'

'Not exactly. It was more like . . .' I hesitated, then recaptured an elusive memory. 'I know! It was carried by somebody walking past the window openings in the passage that leads down to the cave.'

A silence followed, during which I sensed Holmes's indecision. But at length:

'It is useless to go back and climb up there now,' he pronounced. 'No one will be there by the time we arrive, and we shall miss the man we have come to see. We must go on.'

Under the guidance of Sergeant Hughes, our interrupted journey was resumed. Once more the woods engulfed us, and the castle was lost to sight as we plunged into territory we had not previously visited. For another ten minutes, it was all uphill and downdale work through a pall dark as the Vale of Avalon, and I could see nothing but the grey ribbon of the road unwinding beneath our wheels. Then, to the left, there appeared what seemed to be a meadow stretching away to a distant horizon, and, to the right, an erratic line of low-roofed, white-walled cottages with smoking chimneys and lights glowing in tiny, deep-set windows.

'This is it, sir!' said Hughes. 'The inn is just ahead – where you see the signboard.'

I pulled up alongside, climbed out, and extinguished the headlamps. Above our heads, the inn sign swung and creaked funereally in the wind – a square board bearing the painted letters 'Ddraig Goch' and an evil-looking representation of the Welsh dragon. Holmes came to join me, and, standing with our backs to the building, we stared out for a moment across the marsh which I had first mistaken for a grassy plain.

It was, as Hughes had said, a queer place – eerie, perhaps, even in more cheerful circumstances, the whole surface covered with a dark thicket of reeds but not yet grown high enough to hide the Smuggler's Causeway. Bathed in moonlight, and composed of some light-coloured stone, it extended in a dead straight line from almost opposite the doorway of the inn, narrowing in the distance till it was lost against the wall of trees on the opposite side.

'Anyone who walked across there would be visible for a hundred yards or more,' I commented. 'The thing has enough light to see by tonight.'

'More than enough,' agreed my companion. 'An owl could manage with a lot less. Whatever this creature is, it is evidently not fully adopted to hunting by night.' He turned towards Hughes and pointed in the direction of the inn. 'I take it that the castle lies back that way? How far would it be – in terms of flying distance?'

'About a mile, I should think, sir,' said Sergeant Hughes doubtfully. 'You think that it comes from up there, sir? Where Dr Petrie saw the light?'

'If it does,' answered Holmes, shrugging, 'it is obviously controlled. Birds do not light lamps. Well, let us go inside now, and see what we can make of our witness.'

27

THE HELL-BIRD

Closing time was still forty minutes off. We entered the taproom of the Ddraig Goch to find it in a state of uproar, which, according to Hughes, was its usual condition. Like the inn at Pentrefdu, the place consisted of a single room and might even have been smaller, though is appeared the larger by reason of the fact that it was less crowded. The clientèle was made up of some twenty to thirty men in rough farming clothes, their faces reddened, their manner boisterous but untinged with the desperate gaiety of the miners. I doubted if Zarmi would have been equally able to play her tricks here.

Hughes shoved his way through quickly to the bar and ordered drinks for us with an eagerness which told me that his grandchildren would hear the story of how he had once bought a pint of beer for Sherlock Holmes.

We did not need to ask for the already notorious Wyn Crumlin. A few steps farther down the counter from where we stood, a hot debate was in progress, centred around a rat-faced little man in his late fifties. From time to time, others joined in from various quarters of the room, while two men intent on a game of darts ignored it completely. As Hughes received his change, a hoarse yell broke through the bedlam at our backs.

'I seen it! I seen it! A bird as big as a 'ouse!'

The landlord, who was evidently not a supporter, glared ferociously and shook his head. He was a huge man with shirtsleeves rolled up on arms like gnarled tree trunks and a black patch over one eye, which lent him a piratical appearance – assumed, possibly, to add colour to the legend of the smuggler. Turning away from serving us, he bent across the counter and bawled into the speaker's face.

'Go 'ome to bed, you old fool! There's daft as a brush, you are!'

'I seen it! I seen – '

The piratical landlord straightened up, glancing at us.

'Don't take no notice of 'im, gen'l'men,' he advised. ''E's as bad as old Griff Penry, what come tearing in 'ere three years back, with 'is face like a bed-sheet, saying 'e seen the 'Eadless 'Orseman riding 'is 'eadless 'orse – and three doubles 'e 'ad, straight off, 'fore anybody asked who was to pay for 'em!'

'I wouldn't do that!' complained Wyn Crumlin, in an injured tone.

'You tried!' said the landlord.

A thin man with a warty face rose to the defence.

'Ho!' he roared. 'Then what took 'im? Answer us that! What took Iowerth Williams?'

'I reckon 'twas a whirlwind,' said a gruff voice behind us, 'like as took the roof of Denzil Simon's hen-house, and it come down two mile away and killed a cow.'

'That was before you was born!' shouted someone else.

Holmes turned towards the previous speaker, injecting himself quietly into the conversation.

'There was no gale last night, was there?' he asked.

'No,' admitted the gruff-voiced man. 'But it was blowing, same as it is to-night.'

'Always is!' said the landlord.

We moved in upon Mr Crumlin and, at the price of a further pint, easily obtained his story, but it was disappointing. All he could say was what he had said many times already – that he had seen a great winged shape soaring up above the trees at the far end of the causeway.

Holmes looked thoughtful.

'You left here only two or three minutes after Williams, didn't you?' he inquired.

'That's right – no more'n three minutes.'

'But you did not see him walking ahead of you on the causeway?'

'No, I never . . .' said Wyn Crumlin slowly, as if this were a thought which had not previously occurred to him. 'No, that's right! He weren't there!'

Pressed for some further description of the creature which he had seen, he proved unable to furnish any. We asked him if he could draw it. He was doubtful, but we gave him a piece of chalk, taken from the scoreboard, and he sketched very roughly on the counter top something which looked to me more like a giant bat. Curious faces peered over our shoulders.

'There ain't no such thing!' declared the landlord.

'There was once!' countered a new voice. 'I seen pictures in my young-un's school book – like half a bird and half a crocodile. A peter-o-dactill, they called it. Who knows, there might be one left somewhere.'

'Aye!' said the man with the warty face. 'Flew over from Ireland, I reckon.'

One of the dart players broke off from his game long enough to express his opinion that it was the Devil.

We withdrew, leaving the argument going on, and seated ourselves on a high-backed settle in a remote corner.

'I will admit an outsized condor, if I have to,' murmured Holmes impishly, 'but not a pterodactyl!'

I observed that, though the horrible and unaccountable death of Iowerth Williams had produced a commotion in the neighbourhood, there was nothing like a panic. No one had yet heard of the assault upon Mr Garman's sheep, on the far side of Carreg Cennen. But the few who regularly crossed the fatal causeway had prudently decided to stay at home to-night, with the exception of Wyn Crumlin – who announced his firm intention of walking the two miles round by road.

Holmes took out and lighted his pipe. I noted that the leisurely calabash had been superseded by the businesslike briar. His brows were creased in thought, but he showed no sign of the irritation which I had rather expected. So far as I could see, we were no nearer to the heart of the mystery than we had been before. Sergeant

306

Hughes, evidently thinking the same, tentatively asked if we wished arrangements to be made for us to see the body, which had been taken to Brynamman, but Holmes declined.

'It is unnecessary,' he said shortly. 'Williams is of no interest.'

In moments when his thoughts were elsewhere, Holmes had a tendency to appear somewhat inhuman.

'You put it a trifle harshly,' I reproved. 'But I see what you mean. The Si Fan could have no more interest in a farm labourer than in the sheep.'

'Precisely! That is the solution!'

I stared at him wonderingly. 'The solution?'

'The solution to what lies behind all this.' Holmes fixed me with a steely glance. 'Don't you see, Petrie? Both of these meaningless attacks were *experiments* – to ascertain if it would work, and perfect their technique. They began with the sheep; then, when conditions were right, transferred their operations here and staged a dress rehearsal. For the moment, let us not concern ourselves with the means. Their real target is some person who is in the habit of walking across that causeway. But who is he? Who is there in a community like this who could possibly be an object of interest to the Si Fan?'

It seemed to us, both then and afterwards, that he entered on cue. No sooner were the words spoken than the door opened to admit a man who, as Holmes remarked later, 'stood out like a camel in a cornfield.' Perhaps thirty-five years of age, and slenderly built, he was neatly dressed in a well-cut fawn overcoat, and limped slightly, leaning on a stick. He was hatless, revealing flaxen-coloured hair, and his sharp ascetic features were combined with the distant, slightly vapid look of a scholar. Evidently he was well known in the district, for, as he crossed to the counter, the pirate behind the bar greeted him with an affable nod.

'Evening, Mr Randall! The same as usual?'

'If you please, landlord.'

'Right you are, sir! Double Scotch and one jigger of soda.'

The innkeeper took bottles and a measure from the shelves and compounded the mixture with the care of a dispenser.

We stared at each other, the effect produced upon all three of us so marked and unanimous that no discussion was required. Holmes stood up quickly.

'Get a chair, one of you,' he ordered, 'while I go and capture him.'

I watched him shoulder his way through the crowd, in the direction of the newcomer. Like most such establishments, there was little to sit on in the Ddraig Goch. Sergeant Hughes left my side, stole a chair from under a man who had just gone up to the bar for a further drink, and brought it back. Almost at the same moment, Holmes re-appeared, with the flaxen-haired man in tow.

'Mr Philip Randall,' he introduced briefly. 'Dr Petrie . . . Sergeant Hughes . . .'

We installed him in the chair facing us, while we sat side by side on the settle.

'Now, sir,' said Holmes briskly, 'you know what my profession is, I think. May I ask what yours is?'

Philip Randall hesitated an instant – not, I thought, that he was hesitant by nature, but that he was not yet recovered from the surprise of being buttonholed by the fabulous Sherlock Holmes and invited to sit with us. I wondered just what Holmes had said to him.

'I – er – am a lecturer in mathematics, at the university.'

I noticed that the musical Welsh accent to which I was now accustomed was conspicuously absent from his speech.

'Ha!' exclaimed Holmes, in a tone of satisfaction. 'You are a man of science, then. At the university, you say – that would, I take it, be at Aberystwyth?'

'Yes, Mr Holmes – at the University of Wales.'

'Did you perhaps, know the late Professor Morgan Davies?' I asked eagerly. 'The Chinese expert?'

'No, I fear that I did not. He was there before my time.' Randall looked at me strangely. 'But you refer to him as "the late." He has died, then?'

'He was murdered nearly two weeks ago,' said Holmes grimly, 'by a gang of Oriental fanatics who may now have it in mind to murder you!'

'You alarm me, Mr Holmes!'

'I intend to alarm you. If I fail to do so, I have little hope of saving you.' Holmes peered at him thoughfully for a moment. 'As a mathematician, what is your particular branch of study?'

Philip Randall laughed, a trifle self-consciously. 'Well, if I have any special study, you might perhaps say that it is in the field of complex or imaginary numbers. But I really fail to see – '

'The Si Fan – the secret society we are talking about – ' I said, 'directs its efforts chiefly against specialists in obscure subjects.'

'But I am not a specialist!' cried Randall. 'My position at the university is not a high one. I have published nothing, and I am engaged in no sort of research. I give my lectures, and that is all!'

'Nevertheless,' insisted Holmes, 'your field of study is a rare one.'

'Comparatively so – yes. But there must be at least a dozen men in England who can deal with it as well as I can, and no doubt better.'

Again it seemed that we were making little progress. As closing time approached, the tumult at the counter grew more fervid and vociferous, topped by a plaintive howl.

'I seen it! I seen a bloody bird – '

'Let us shelve the question of motive,' said Holmes, changing his tactics. 'You are some distance from Aberystwyth here. I note that your stick is of the surgical variety, well used, but fairly new, and you no longer need to rely upon it to any marked extent. I presume, then, that you have recently suffered some injury, and, as this is the only inn hereabouts, you are now con-

309

valescing at the home of a relative – probably by marriage, since you are an Englishman.'

The trivial display of deductive reasoning had its desired effect, for Randall looked surprised, smiled, and nodded.

'You are perfectly correct,' he replied. 'I am staying at my brother-in-law's farm, on the other side of the causeway, and I have been there three weeks.'

'How did you come by your injury?' I asked.

A blush spread over the mathematician's austere features.

'I miscalculated the height of the top step,' he confessed shamefacedly, 'fell, and dislocated my right hip. I was in hospital only a short time, but there were complications. The joint remains stiff and painful. As regards my presence here – well, sir, I am a bachelor and my rooms in Aberystwyth are situated on the fourth floor. I was, therefore, grateful for my sister's invitation to come here and recuperate.'

'And,' added Holmes, 'due to the condition of your leg, you do not go out very much.'

'No, Mr Holmes – not much. I take the precise amount of exercise recommended by my physicians. I walk around the farm for half an hour each afternoon and walk across here in the evening for a drink before going to bed.'

'Always at the same time?'

'Within two or three minutes – yes.'

'Dear me!' remarked Holmes. 'You seem, if I may say so, to be a person of singularly rigid habits.'

'I prefer to call myself a person of rigid principles,' answered the other with dignity. 'Let me tell you something in confidence, Mr Holmes. After graduating, I taught at a high school where the work was boring, and became addicted to drink. I missed my classes, and was in danger of becoming an alcoholic. But I realised the situation in time and, since Man is really no more than a machine, that my salvation lay in applying the precision of mathematics to my own behaviour. Thus, without

310

completely denying myself the pleasures of alcohol, I was able to continue with my studies, obtain my Master's degree, and, three years ago, secure the university appointment which I now hold. I limit myself strictly to one glass of whisky, and come here never earlier than twenty minutes before the inn closes, so that I may be relieved of any temptation to buy another.'

I exchanged surreptitious glances with Hughes, finding that I was not overly attracted to Mr Randall. He spoke with a dry, self-righteous complacency, and I could not help but remember my own high school days, when there was nothing we would have liked better than to see our teacher of mathematics carried off by a hell-bird.

'Regardless of your motives,' said Holmes seriously, 'the plain fact is, then, that it would be easy to launch an attack upon you while you are crossing the causeway, and difficult at any other time. You are aware, of course, of the tragedy which took place here last night?'

'I am. The man worked at my brother-in-law's farm, and the police have been in and out all day.' Philip Randall vented a contemptuous sniff. 'The locals believe there is some kind of gigantic eagle roaming the vicinity. Pure rustic superstition! It would be mathematically impossible for such a creaure to lift its own weight, let alone that of a man.'

'H'm! I believe,' commented Holmes, with a twinkle in his eyes, 'that it has also been shown to be mathematically impossible for a bumblebee to fly. However, it seems that bumblebees do not know about this. Iowerth Williams fell upon the corrugated iron roof of a barn with sufficient force to break through it. How would you account for that?'

'I suppose,' said Randall, somewhat uncomfortably, 'that he fell out of a tree.'

Sergeant Hughes, who had thus far contented himself to listen in silence, was roused to a mild protest.

'No, sir,' he said quietly. 'There are no trees anywhere near the barn.'

'Well?' demanded Holmes. 'The fact is that a man

disappeared while walking across the causeway and, some time not long after, came to a violent end at a spot situated more than a mile distant. Have you, then, no mathematical explanation for this?'

Randall shifted awkwardly and glanced around as though for a way of escape.

'You force me into the unknown territory of scientific speculation,' he said, with a notable lack of confidence in his tone. 'But even that is preferable to a biological anomaly. There have been many unexplained disappearances. If space-time is curved, as some believe, it has been suggested that an object might fall through a gap and emerge at some other point in the continuum.'

'Dear me!' said Holmes sardonically. 'Rather like thrusting a knitting needle through an orange? But, in that case, would not the man have come up through the floor of the barn, rather than down through the roof?'

'No, no!' protested Randall indignantly. 'You are confusing the curvature of space-time with the curvature of the earth!'

Clearly, he had no sense of humour.

The landlord jangled a cow-bell and bellowed, 'Last orders!' in a voice calculated to carry through a typhoon. Philip Randall drained the precise fifteen millilitres remaining in his glass and stood up.

'That is my signal to depart,' he said. 'I thank you for an interesting conversation, gentlemen, but now I must say good night. It has been a great pleasure to meet you, Mr Holmes.'

'You intend to walk back across the causeway?' inquired Holmes, standing up also.

The other nodded. 'Yes. I am grateful for your concern, but, really, you have failed to show me any convincing reason why my life would be threatened.'

That, I thought disconsolately, was no more than true. Unless the man was keeping something back from us – and he did not seem to be that kind of individual – there was no apparent reason why he should be of any greater concern to Dr Fu Manchu than the unfortunate Iowerth

Williams. Holmes, however, persisted in following him to the door, and, Hughes and I trailing after, we all stood for a moment longer under the creaking sign of the red dragon.

'I do not know if they will strike again so soon after last night,' observed Holmes, laying a restraining hand upon the man's arm, 'but there are lights in Carreg Cennen castle, and we believe they work from there. You will not take my advice and go round by the road?'

'In the present state of my leg, it would be unwise.'

'We have a car here,' I said quickly. 'There is no need for you to walk. We will drive you home.'

Randall turned to me with a smile. 'Thank you for the offer, Dr Petrie. But if I accept it I shall miss my prescribed amount of exercise. No, thank you – I will go back the same way that I came.'

We stared out across the dark surface of the marsh and the narrow pathway glittering white in the moonlight.

'In that case,' said Holmes, breathing hard, 'we shall accompany you to your door.'

'Really!' exclaimed the obstinate mathematician. 'I assure you that such an escort is unnecessary, but if you wish to put yourselves to the effort of a mile's walk, there and back, I cannot very well prevent you.'

'Take the lead, Sergeant!' ordered Holmes, pausing to argue the matter no further. 'I will bring up the rear.' He glared at Philip Randall. 'We will do our best to get you home safely to-night, but after that you must please yourself. I can give you no reasons, but if you wish to resume your lectures after the Easter recess, you will return to Aberystwyth to-morrow – or, better still, go to London!'

Randall shrugged and said nothing. We crossed the road, descended a steeply shelving embankment, and set foot upon the causeway. It was less broad than Hughes had estimated, and in places less than six feet, where the stones had fallen away. Prudence dictated that we should go in single file.

'Conditions are ideal for them!' muttered Holmes in

313

my ear. 'If they strike now, there is no chance for him – unless they take one of us by mistake!'

It was anything but a comforting thought. Sergeant Hughes, who had brought his police lantern with him, went first, sweeping the light before him, though it was hardly necessary, since the cold radiance of the moonlight was more than sufficient for our needs. Randall followed in his tracks, whilst I walked behind him, trying to keep as close as possible; but, because of his limping gait, it was difficult to do so without treading on his heels.

Beyond the yellow glare of the oil-lamps and the din of the taproom, the marsh was a lonely place, the reeds reaching up to a foot or so below the level of the causeway. Frogs croaked, and, once or twice, I heard the weird call of a bittern. The surface upon which we walked was formed of massive, rough-hewn blocks laid end-to-end without mortar. I doubted if it had been designed as a road; more likely it was a part of some ancient fortification, some outwork connected with the castle.

Out here, with the moon at our backs and the spectral shapes of our own distorted shadows dancing ahead of us on the stones of forgotten history, reality was the world of Merlin and Morgan le Fay – the causeway a precarious bridge stretched across the formless gulf of infinity. The wind whispered constantly through the rushes and, listening, I knew that I listened for another sound – the flapping of gigantic wings. It was easy to tell myself that what I feared was the macabre fantasy of an Arthurian legend – yet *something* had taken a man and two sheep.

Philip Randall limped stolidly on, never looking back – a scientist of the academic school, who would deny the evidence when it presupposed the impossible. We covered a hundred and fifty yards in safety. Then:

It came silently and without warning save for a momentary darkening of the path, blotting out our shadows. In the same instant that my eyes registered it, came a shouting from behind me and the deafening crash

314

of Holmes's pistol. Something hit me violently across the shoulder blades, hurling me down upon the stones. Ahead of me came a second shout and a splash – a despairing scream, curiously attenuated. . . .

I struggled up on hands and knees, dazed and bewildered. There was no one on the causeway in front of me, and above the trees on the far side of the marsh, I saw a great winged shape soaring up black against the sky.

28

THE TURNING POINT

Almost before I could convince myself that I had seen it, the thing in the sky dipped below the line of the treetops and disappeared. I scrambled to my feet, gasping.

'Snatched from under our noses!' said Holmes savagely. 'I hit it, but there was little chance of doing any damage. There is nothing we can do for him now.'

From below and to our right came a confused sound of floundering and cursing.

'Hughes is in the marsh,' he added. 'Lend me a hand to get him out.'

We approached the edge of the causeway and found Sergeant Hughes standing upright in three feet of mud and water. He had been struck in the back by the flailing feet of the victim, as he was dragged from the ground. He reached up, and, seizing him by the wrists, we hauled him up beside us.

'For God's sake – ' he panted.

'Never mind that now!' snapped Holmes. 'Our first concern is to get you out of those wet clothes, or we shall have another casualty on our hands.'

Hughes was a sorry sight, plastered with mud from head to foot, and soaked to the skin. Now, long after dark, the temperature of the water was icy, and his teeth were chattering. We hurried him back to the inn and found the doorway surrounded by a noisy cluster of the erstwhile customers, alarmed by the pistol shot. Answering no questions, we thrust past them, but were temporarily baulked on the threshold by the landlord.

'It's past closing time!' he grumbled.

Holmes shoved him impatiently aside. 'You are permitted to serve spirits for medicinal purposes,' he said curtly. 'This man is in need of them.'

We entered and a number of others crowded in at our heels, evidently feeling that, in the circumstances, the same dispensation should be extended to them. Sergeant Hughes, shaken and shivering, rose nobly to the occasion and faced them belligerently.

'I am a police officer!' he shouted. 'All of you get out of here, if you don't want your names took!'

They retreated sullenly. Holmes slammed the door and put up the bar with his own hands. The landlord, offering no further opposition, splashed whisky into a glass and handed it to Hughes.

'Get hot water,' directed Holmes, 'towels, and blankets.'

The landlord nodded and departed, leaving us alone in the taproom. Hughes collapsed limply into a chair, dripping water upon the sanded floor, and gulped a little of the raw spirit.

'In the name of Heaven, sir,' he whispered. 'What kind of a bird was that?'

'Bird?' exclaimed Holmes. 'It is not a bird but a kite! The Chinese have been masters in the art of kite-flying for more than a thousand years. There are traditional records of man-carrying kites having been used in mediaeval wars, and I have heard of the same things in Tibet.'

'But, surely,' I said doubtfully, 'a kite is flown from the ground, by means of a string?'

'Only in order that the user may get it back again. It will fly better without the string.'

Holmes walked around behind the counter and appropriated two glasses from the shelves.

'If Sergeant Hughes will refrain from taking our names,' he remarked, 'I think that we also might partake of a little medicine.'

He poured whisky into the glasses and handed one to me. I took it gratefully, shuddering as I thought of Philip Randall. I had not liked the man, but to think of him swept up before our eyes to be dropped to a hideous death – as a thrush drops a snail upon the stones to shatter its shell – was horrible in the extreme. What offence had he committed, I wondered, to deserve such a fate?

Holmes, seemingly unmoved by any similar reflections, sat down on a chair and re-lighted his briar.

'I had a suspicion that we might be dealing with a contrivance of this nature,' he said. 'But I could not be sure until I had seen it. I really know very little about it, but I understand that the hardest part is to get it in the air. Therefore, they launch it from Carreg Cennen, which is three hundred feet above the valley.'

'But can it be manoeuvered?' I asked.

'Obviously so, since you have just seen it done! In theory, I suppose, it operates much in the same way as a ship sailing upon the ocean. That is to say, it requires both favourable winds and an expert hand.'* Holmes puffed thoughtfully at his pipe, staring up at the ceiling. 'Wang Lo is the kite-flier. By the accounts of him we have had, he is a man of great strength, but horribly deformed. I suspect that he has been at this for some years, had some bad spills, and broken quite a few bones.'

A door to one side of the counter banged open. The landlord reappeared, followed by a fat woman in dressing gown and curl papers, who rushed past him, bore down upon the bedraggled Sergeant Hughes, and hustled him out through the same door, directing a continuous stream of invective at her husband, as if it were all his fault. The piratical landlord, looking somewhat less piratical, gave us a sheepish glance and went out after them.

'The astonishing thing is,' went on Holmes, ignoring the interruption, 'that he could bring his kite so close to the ground and get it aloft again with a double weight. He actually passed about ten feet above our heads, and used some kind of trailing device with jaws which closed

* Wang Lo's kite appears to have been something more in the nature of what we now know as a hang glider. [Ed.]

automatically upon the victim. It was this which struck you and knocked you down. Of course, it was difficult, and I do not think he had tried it until now – '

'Hence the sheep and the farm labourer!'

'Quite so. For practice. The sequence of events which first brought us out here is now clear. Wang Lo made two successful assaults on Mr Garman's sheep, but, in a third run, or on his way back from the second, he came to grief in the woods. He was injured, and the kite was badly damaged. Therefore he burnt it, this accounting for the fire which the local constable was called out to investigate. Since then – apart from unsuitable lighting conditions – he has needed time to recover and to build new equipment.'

'I think you have covered nearly everything,' I agreed. 'But it is still a little surprising to me that he could see well enough to identify his victim.'

'In the case of the sheep and the labourer, identity did not matter. Randall could be easily identified by his stick. It is also more than likely that, on these occasions, he dilated the pupils of his eyes with atropine. That might further explain how he failed in his initial attempt to stab PC Meredith – the light of the constable's lantern blinded him.'

Holmes knocked out his pipe against the heel of his left boot, and immediately refilled it.

'This is a victory for Dr Fu Manchu,' he said wearily, 'and all the more irksome because we still have no idea what his object was. I should have taken a lesson from you, Petrie, and armed myself with a shotgun before we went out on that causeway. But I cannot honestly say that I feel much responsibility for our failure to protect Randall. I warned him as best I could, and the fool insisted on walking to his death. His body will probably be found somewhere on the other side of those trees.'

But it was not found. In the morning, a number of police officers came over from Brynamman, and, with the help of men from the farms, a search was conducted. Holmes and I joined in. All that day, we searched through the woods and the fields beyond, but we came upon no trace of Philip Randall. Either he had been carried farther than we expected, or his remains lay concealed in some overgrown patch of brambles which we had neglected to probe. As to the motive for his slaying, we came to no better conclusion. We interviewed the sister with whom he had been staying, but succeeded only in confirming what he had already told us. He was a moderately clever, totally undistinguished man without much ambition, who had never been abroad, spoke no foreign language, and had no friends outside his narrow academic circle.

At nightfall, when the search was abandoned, we drove back to Swansea, while Sergeant Hughes went home to Brynamman, the poorer by a suit of clothes, and the richer by his one and only experience of working with Sherlock Holmes. We dined and spent a tranquil night making up for lost sleep, having had little the night before, and a strenuous day of open-air exercise afterwards while we combed the countryside in our futile quest.

A new day dawned and passed without significant event. As a matter of course, we related our adventures to Superintendent Gribbler, who said he thanked Heaven that Carreg Cennen was in Carmarthenshire and it would not be his job to draw up a report. Late in the afternoon, we got in touch with Brynamman, and learned that, despite further search, the body of the murdered man had still not been found.

'Not altogether surprising,' remarked Holmes. 'In country like that, there are a hundred odd corners where it might lie undiscovered for weeks – nor will it assist us much when they do find it. We know how he was killed. What we wish to know is *why*. And why was so fantastic a method chosen? Fu Manchu has a typically Chinese taste for the dramatic, yet that alone could hardly justify such complex preparations, when it would have been perfectly simple and equally effective to shoot the man while he was crossing the causeway. I wonder . . .'

But he did not tell me what he wondered.

It appeared to me that once again we had come to an impasse, and I looked forward with dismay to a further period of helpless inaction while the two persons who meant most to me in the world remained captive in the hands of Fu Manchu. Little did I realise that we had already entered upon the final phase of the business which had brought us from London.

Holmes did not come down to breakfast the next morning, and, with no instructions to do otherwise, I decided to make the next of what he sardonically called my 'sightseeing trips.' Having previously failed to penetrate the woods of Oxwich Point, I drove around to the opposite side, where I discovered another sizeable bay, adjacent to the village of Port Eynon. This, however, proved of lesser interest to me, since it was clearly unsuitable for the purposes of the Si Fan. It was easily accessible by road, and the houses came down close to the shore.

There was a lifeboat stationed there. I struck up an acquaintance with the coxswain, and spent a part of the afternoon with him, listening to tales of smugglers and wreckers, which, in this area, were something more than romantic legends. I was told of a lofty cave, 'just around the corner,' the entrance walled up like a fortress – when and by whom no one knew – within it a staircase cut in the rock, said to lead to a secret passage running miles inland. But I was also told that any further exploration of the coast westwards would mean an eight-mile walk along the tops of stark, unscaleable cliffs which, thereafter, plunged down into the sea in a sheer rock wall, extending all the way to the tip of the peninsula.

The prospect of such an expedition failed to deter me. Yet I was fated never to make it. On returning to the hotel, early that evening, I found, a little to my surprise, that Holmes was not in his room, and, coming downstairs again, discovered him in the lounge, his pipe going like a furnace, and an expression of expectancy on his face.

321

'You have missed some excitement,' he said, his eyes gleaming. 'We have their motor van.'

'It has been found?' I exclaimed. 'When? What has happened?'

'The Lord has answered our prayer for an astute constable,' he replied, smiling. 'Sit down, and I will tell you about it. Do you know where Clyne Common is?'

'Yes,' I said, taking a seat beside him. 'I was driving across it only an hour ago.'

'Two hours too late!' Temporarily laying aside his pipe, Holmes went on talking in the rapid, satirical fashion which he usually applied to the experience of others. 'At about three o'clock this afternoon, PC Lynchcombe was riding his bicycle across the common, on his way to the village of Murton, where he was to serve a summons on a certain Mr Joseph Enderby, in connection with the non-payment of his dog licence. On such trifles does the fate of nations rest, Petrie! Less than a mile from his destination, Lynchcombe was passed by a heavy motor vehicle, which he immediately recognised from the circularised particulars. Being an officer of some intelligence, he had taken due note that this was a matter concerning graver issues than an ordinary car theft, and had carefully memorised the description of the van together with the registration number. He knew at once that this was it, and, impossible though the task was, endeavoured to give chase. But, even if he managed to keep the vehicle in sight, he had obviously little chance of himself remaining undetected by the driver.'

'Zarmi?' I suggested.

'Yes, I think so – though the constable thought she was a boy. The spectacle of a rather overweight policeman crouched over his handlebars, with his legs pumping like piston rods, was one hard to miss, and she soon saw him, of course. She increased speed, and began to draw quickly away, but, before she had outdistanced him completely, found her way obstructed by a heavily loaded milk float pulling out of a side turning. She swerved to avoid it, lost control, and piled up the van

322

against a telegraph post. The radiator was crushed, and the front axle broken – '

'Good Heavens!' I cried, memory coming back to me. 'I saw it! I remember now – there was a breakdown truck and a wrecked vehicle out there when I came past!'

Holmes favoured me with a saturnine smile.

'Nevertheless, you failed to recognise it as the one which you saw after our tea party with Dr Fu Manchu – in which respect you show yourself less observant than the constable. Zarmi, apparently, was unhurt. She leapt out and took to her heels across the common. PC Lynchcombe jumped off his bicycle and tried to follow, but, after his recent exertions, he was in no condition to do so. She had a hundred-yard start and easily escaped him. But, at least, we have the van and its contents.'

'What did it contain? The boxes from the mine?'

'No. I imagine they have long since been delivered to the spot at which they are to be embarked. As a matter of fact, in proportion to its capacity, the van contained very little – merely a somewhat large consignment of tinned goods and groceries, purchased from several different stores in Swansea.' Holmes paused, shaking his head at my failure to show much reaction, and added: 'I have asked for a detailed inventory, and expect to receive it at any minute.'

'Why do you want that?' I inquired, looking and feeling as blank as ever.

'Precisely what Superintendent Gribbler asked me!' he murmured.

Seeing that he did not intend to enlighten me, I contained my curiosity in patience. The incident was encouraging in that it proved the Si Fan to be active in the vicinity, but disappointing in that it did not seem to have much additional significance. I was so much in the habit of thinking of Fu Manchu's servants exclusively in connection with murder and kidnapping that it seemed odd to reflect that they needed everyday supplies like other people, and that somebody had to go shopping for them. I wondered what Holmes expected to gain from this information. However, I was not left long in doubt, for, hardly had he picked up and re-lighted his pipe when a page boy entered with an envelope bearing the crest of the Swansea police department.

Holmes took it and ripped it open.

'Now,' he remarked, 'if we were to be shown a housewife's shopping list, we could deduce from it the number of members in her family, their tastes, their income, and, doubtless, many other such items. Let us see what we have here.'

He glanced briefly at the neatly typewritten sheet, nodded, and passed it to me.

'Well?' he challenged. 'Look first at the quantities.'

'Too much for any normal family,' I said, attempting to follow his reasoning. 'Supplies for the ship, perhaps?'

'No. Too little for ship's stores. These are provisions to sustain either a few people for a long period, or a more sizeable group for a short period. Which do you think it is?'

'How can we tell?'

'By the goods themselves, of course – and it is the latter. How long would ten pints of milk remain usable? Two or three days, perhaps. And how many persons would it require to consume it in that time?'

'Yes – I see what you are getting at,' I admitted. 'Can you deduce any more from this?'

'A little, perhaps.' He took the list back from me, and frowned down at it. 'Most of these things are tinned or dried products – not because they are to be stored for a long time, but because the users have no elaborate cooking facilities. Here, too, we have twelve pounds of rice – sufficient to enable a British housewife, who has no other use for it, to make rice puddings for several years. These people are Orientals, and, since there are various kinds of meat included, but no pork or bacon, most of them are probably Moslems. I think there are about a dozen of them, and these supplies will last them for perhaps a week. In other words, Petrie, the Si Fan is now installed in force in the premises from which they will be taken off by the Chinese ship.'

'And it is on the south side of the peninsula!' I burst out excitedly, prompted by a flash of inspiration. 'The road across Clyne Common goes nowhere else!'

'Just so,' said Holmes, nodding. 'I am glad to see that your wits have not completely atrophied during the past couple of weeks.' He folded the paper and put it away in his pocket. 'Well, they are where we thought they would be and when we expected them. The south coast was always more likely than the north, which consists chiefly of sands extending almost to the opposite shore. And, of course, we have known for some time that the ship would come for them next week.'

This casual observation left me speechless and I stared at him foolishly.

'We – we have *known*?' I stammered.

It seemed to me that this was just what we had *not* known.

'Certainly!' said Holmes absently, occupying himself with matches, and apparently unconscious of my surprise. 'We knew that they had hired the motor van for a period of two months, which ends next Tuesday, and there was no reason why this should not have been a perfectly legitimate arrangement. They had no intention of stealing the vehicle. Thus it was reasonable to assume that they were scheduled to leave shortly afterward.'

'You are right!' I said wonderingly, and, at the same time, felt a surge of indignation. 'But why on earth have you never mentioned this before?'

'What!' exclaimed my companion, staring at me with an expression of genuine astonishment. 'You mean that it was not obvious to you?'

I could find no adequate answer. When Sherlock Holmes outlined the process of his reasoning, it always seemed to me less that he was phenomenally clever than that the rest of us were phenomenally obtuse.

29

THE SEA MONSTER

Perhaps it was Holmes's confident predictions that the end of our quest lay within sight, but I felt a wave of excitement such as I had not experienced since the day we left London. I thought that I recognized that landslide of events which usually presaged the climax of a bout with Fu Manchu.

Gone was all thought of further expeditions, while we waited for something to happen. After breakfast the next morning, I accompanied Holmes into the lounge and sat there with him, content to remain all day, if need be, so that I might be on hand when the call to action came. As yet there was nothing for us to do, but while we were idle, others worked for us.

'Gribbler has every available man out searching the coast for a group of Orientals,' said Holmes reassuringly. 'They are lying low, but somebody must have seen them, and the police have the manpower to ferret them out.'

The trust which he placed in our official allies contrasted oddly with the low opinion which he had often expressed in the past, and I could not help smiling. Weymouth had been right: in ten years, the name of Sherlock Holmes had become a golden key which unlocked to us the full resources of the law, and I was glad to see that he appreciated it.

'You would not always have described the police in such terms,' I said.

'That is true,' he confessed, 'but you cannot altogether blame me. When Watson and I first entered our rooms in Baker Street, the police force itself had existed only fifty years. The Scotland Yard which I knew then was the original group of buildings on the site of the old palace of the kings of Scotland. The uniformed officers were honest but ignorant men – little more than public bodyguards, employed to keep law and order, when *order* ranked equally with *law*! The art of detection was unknown: if a man could not be taken red-handed in his crime, there was no means of catching him afterwards, and, since I believe that what I did then helped to change that situation, I am happy to admit that Britain now has the finest police force in the world.'

As if to confirm – or, perhaps, to qualify – his words, the page boy entered at that moment with an impertinent grin on his face.

'The p'lice wants Mr Shylock 'Olmes on the phone!' he announced.

'Gribbler!' said Holmes, grinding his teeth.

He sprang up and walked swiftly out of the room. I glanced at my watch, and saw that it was ten o'clock: we had not had long to wait. Less than five minutes passed before Holmes was back again and I saw from his expression that action was in the making. But his news was anything but what I had expected.

'Get your coat!' he said tersely. 'Philip Randall is in the local hospital.'

'*Randall*?' I exclaimed. 'Good God! He is not dead, then?'

'By no means. Apart from a few bruises about the body, where he was clutched by the contraption which lifted him off the ground, he is not even hurt!'

Postponing further discussion, we collected our coats, and, since the hospital was within easy walking distance, set off on foot. On the way, Holmes consented to add a few details.

'Randall was found early this morning, wandering on the upper slopes of Cefn Bryn,' he explained. 'He is in a state of shock, and suffering somewhat from exposure. But I fear we shall get little out of him. From the time when he was drinking with us at the inn, his mind is a complete blank!'

I nodded. Cases of partial amnesia among victims of Fu Manchu were not uncommon.

'Cefn Bryn is a high ridge not unlike your Sussex Downs,' I said, 'and not far from where I was yesterday. How did he come there from Carreg Cennen? Wang Lo could not have carried him all that way, surely?'

'No, no – of course not. Even under ideal conditions, I doubt if the kite could fly more than five or six miles. But the business begins to make a trifle more sense. The intention was not to murder him, but simply to abduct him. They could have murdered him a dozen different ways, but without literally snatching him off the face of the earth, it was difficult to seize him, since he never left the house other than to walk across that causeway – and even then, there might have been others crossing at the same time.'

As he spoke, I remembered his rather peculiar attitude of the previous day, which had puzzled me at the time.

'You suspected this,' I said, 'when we failed to find the body.'

'Yes, but I hesitated to say anything because I could not see how they might have landed him safely. Moreover, there is still the unsolved problem of motive.'

Our walk had brought us to the centre of the town, where a bustle of weekend shopping was in progress – for it was Saturday morning. We threaded our way through, Holmes punctuating his speech with terse apologies as we jostled against housewives, cannoned into bulging carrier bags, and dodged perambulators.

'After yesterday's mishap,' he remarked, 'the Si Fan will be on short rations. If they are wise, they will put up with it. Every grocer's shop in Swansea has been asked to notify the police of any stranger who buys even so much as a pound of rice.'

On the long, straight road to the hospital, the pavements were less congested, and my thoughts turned again to the man we were going to visit.

'I wonder where he has been, these past three days,' I said, 'and I wonder still more how he managed to escape.'

'He has not escaped. They have had what they want of him, and he has been set at liberty because Dr Fu Manchu does not commit wanton murder.'

'But what *did* they want of him? All he had was some competence in the field of higher mathematics, and he insisted that there were at least a dozen men in England who could do as much.'

'Yes,' said my companion thoughtfully, 'but perhaps he was the only man who could do it in Wales – or the only man they could find. . . .'

At the hospital, we found Philip Randall put to bed in a private room, under the personal care of Mr Lennard, the energetic young house surgeon. The patient's face was haggard and as pale as the pillows upon which his head rested. Although we were allowed to see him, he was under sedation, drowsy, and unable to respond to our questions.

'Green eyes . . .' he murmured. 'Green eyes . . .'

'He has seen Fu Manchu,' said Holmes. 'And he has been drugged and hypnotised.'

In the absence of any useful information from Randall, we retired to the house surgeon's room and remained there talking with him while a pretty nurse brought in cups of coffee. I glanced around at the glass-fronted cabinets and shelves of medical books, and felt a pang of nostalgia, suddenly remembering how far my concern with the Si Fan had side-tracked me from my proper business.

Mr Lennard – a shining example of white-coated efficiency – showed an interest in Dr Fu Manchu and his methods which came suspiciously close to professional admiration.

'There is nothing wrong with Mr Randall,' he declared, 'other than that he has somehow lost three days out of his life.'

'Which he is no doubt better off without,' commented Holmes dryly, 'for if he could recall his experiences during that period, it would probably unseat his reason.'

'You might even say that he is better off physically,' said Mr Lennard, with a short laugh.

'How do you mean?' I asked.

'Your Dr Fu Manchu – whom I should very much like to meet – is a master surgeon, even if unorthodox. He has performed a feat of osteopathic manipulation which the doctors at Aberystwyth were unable to do, and Mr Randall's hip joint no longer pains him in the least.'

'A typical gesture,' I said, looking at Holmes. 'Fu Manchu usually awards some compensation for the services which he requisitions.'

'Quite!' he snapped. 'But for what has the man been compensated? What fresh piece of devilry has he assisted him to carry out?' He turned towards the house surgeon. 'Where, and in what circumstances, was Randall found, Mr Lennard?'

Mr Lennard considered carefully ere replying.

'I understand,' he said at length, 'that some farm workers came across him at about six this morning on the open land not far from the prehistoric dolmen called Arthur's Stone – a rather weird piece of work which archaeologists say is a tomb, but which looks more like a Druidical altar. He was completely disoriented – imagined that he had suffered some sort of alcoholic collapse, and believed himself to be in the neighbourhood of Carreg Cennen. He was taken to the village of Reynoldston, where a local doctor was called and an ambulance later summoned to bring him to this hospital. His clothes, by the way, were in a terrible state. They had apparently been soaked in water and afterwards dried, but not pressed. Also, and which was somewhat remarkable, his trouser legs were stained with a considerable quantity of blood – but it was not his, since he had no injury.'

'Where are they?' demanded Holmes.

'His clothes?' Mr Lennard looked surprised. 'We have sent them down to the laundry.'

'Let us have them up here before they are laundered. They may prove more informative than the wearer.'

The house surgeon nodded, pressed a bell, and issued the necessary instructions. For the time being, Holmes had nothing further to inquire, and Mr Lennard, turning to me, took the opportunity to ask eager questions about Dr Fu Manchu, none of which I could answer. Holmes sat silent, frowning, and chewing on the mouthpiece of an empty pipe.

'You can smoke here, if you like,' said our host.

'Thank you,' said Holmes gloomily, 'but I find that an atmosphere of iodoform does nothing to improve the taste of tobacco.'

A bundle of creased and soiled clothing was brought into the room. Holmes seized upon it with alacrity and whipped out his pocket lens.

'He had no overcoat?' he queried.

'No, he had not.'

'H'm! He has lost it, then. He was wearing one when we last saw him.'

Holmes shook out a sports jacket, fingered the material, and examined it closely through his lens.

'Not sea water,' he muttered. 'No traces of salt . . . Ah! of course!' He looked up, regarding me with a wan smile on his lips. 'I am becoming dense in my old age, Petrie! Why did I not think of it before? I know now how they brought him safely to the ground after his flight. They dropped him in a convenient lake, and fished him out!' He turned his attention to the trousers. 'As for these mysterious bloodstains, they seem to have been made a good deal later, after these things had been dried.'

The telephone on the desk rang, and Mr Lennard picked it up.

'Yes?' he said. 'All right – put him through here. He laid the instrument down on the blotter and addressed Holmes. 'It's Superintendent Gribbler.'

'Again?' grunted Holmes, still occupied with Randall's clothes. 'What does he want now? You take it, Petrie!'

I took up the telephone obediently, and listened to the slightly fatuous voice of the superintendent.

'Is that you, Peter?' There was a peculiar hollowness in

331

his tones, as though he did not really believe what he was saying. 'You two better come over here on the double! There's been a ghastly murder out on Gower – ghastly!'

I had yearned for action, and now I was getting it with a vengeance! Gribbler was unable, or unwilling, to say more on the telephone. Holmes, who hated to be diverted to a fresh line of investigation before he had finished with another, was frankly disgusted.

'I cannot imagine why there should be any more killings at this stage!' he said crossly. 'Our worthy superintendent has got the bit between his teeth, and now believes that every death in the vicinity is the work of Fu Manchu. We shall probably find that some drunk yokel has been beaten over the head with a bucket and robbed for twopence-ha'penny.'

He threw down the patent-leather boot which he had been examining, and put away his lens reluctantly.

'These things are intriguing,' he added, 'though they tell us nothing conclusive. I should very much like to know where the man has been. There are grass seeds and thorns, which might come from almost anywhere, and specimens of soil from at least three different places, including some dry, powdery stuff such as I should not expect to find on Cefn Bryn. There is no sand, so he has not been on the beach, but his boots are scratched and cut about in a manner which suggests a considerable amount of scrambling over jagged rocks. Well, well – I suppose we shall come back to it in due course, and, in the meantime, we must go and see what is upsetting Gribbler.'

A taxi was called for us, and, in a matter of minutes, we had exchanged Mr Lennard's antiseptically odorous premises for the big, untidy room of the police superintendent. Gribbler shook hands rather limply, his manner less cordial than usual, and collapsed heavily into the old-fashioned swivel chair behind his desk. His florid cheeks were pale and his eyes round with a comic expression of incredulity.

'Who is the victim?' demanded Holmes, without preamble.

'We don't know,' replied Gribbler, in a dull, disbelieving voice. 'The body was found wedged in between some rocks at the foot of the cliffs, a couple of miles this side of Rhossili. Been in the water about twenty-four hours, they say. He wasn't a white man, nor a black man either. Some coffee-coloured sort of chap, with no clothes but a rag around his middle, and a funny mark on his forehead – '

'A dacoit!' I exclaimed.

The superintendent turned weary eyes in my direction. 'Might be,' he said heavily. 'If I knew what a dacoit was.'

'The dacoits are organised groups of thieves and robbers operating in Burma and India,' I told him.

'But not in South Wales!' exploded Gribbler, showing sudden animation. He glared indignantly. 'What are these fellows doing here? What – '

'As I have told you before,' snapped Holmes, 'they are members of the Si Fan. But, in this case, it seems that the dacoit was the victim. How? Was he drowned?'

'He was drowned all right. But worse than that – much worse . . .' Superintendent Gribbler's voice sank to a horrified whisper. 'Both his hands had been chopped off clean at the wrist!'

'Good God!' I muttered, momentarily shocked almost as much as he.

I must do justice to Gribbler, even though Holmes could never forgive him for the 'Shylock.' Two years short of retirement, he was a man who had run his administration in a lax, easy-going fashion, guided by good nature and the rule of common sense. Major crimes and savage outrages of this kind had never come his way, and now he experienced the betrayed feeling of a father deceived by his family.

There was a hushed moment of silence, almost as though all of us sat paying tribute to the memory of the deceased. Then:

'This is the end of some poor devil who has rebelled against his master,' said Holmes sombrely.

I shook my head, experience for once allowing me to speak where he was ignorant.

'No,' I said. 'It is not that. Fu Manchu punishes disobedience with severity, but rarely with death. Kâramanèh would not otherwise have survived as long as she has. This is the fate of one who has committed the unpardonable offence of making a mistake! In such cases, he is more ruthless with his servants even than dealing with his enemies.'

'I stand corrected,' acknowledged Holmes, with a tight-lipped smile. 'Your point is well taken, Petrie. Yes – horrible and fantastic though they may seem, it is only by such Draconian methods that Fu Manchu can control his organisation. His fighting men suffer from no lack of zeal, but they are recruited from among some of the most notoriously inefficient people in the world. Small wonder that he cannot afford to condone errors! You are right – this miserable dacoit has done something stupid and paid for it with his life.'

Superintendent Gribbler cleared his throat and eyed us sadly, his patient affability struggling with the pent-up wrath of a Celtic temperament.

'It's not that I don't like you,' he began apologetically, then, as the barrier gave way, went on with a rush, 'but, damn, I'll be glad to see the back of you, and there's the truth of it! We never had anything like this, and now it's chaos! Jars of poisoned honey, policemen chasing motor cars on bicycles, damn' great vultures carrying people from Carreg Cennen to Cafn Bryn, and bloody corpses floating about with no hands!' Stemming the tide with an effort, he drew out a handkerchief and dabbed at his forehead. 'It's more than I can cope with, and that's a fact. I think I'd better call in Scotland Yard and have another talk with inspector Widemouth.'

This was the last straw even for Sherlock Holmes, who turned his head aside and choked.

'I think that would be a good idea,' I said placatingly.

Another, and lengthier, silence followed, while Holmes sat with his pointed chin sunk in his chest, evidently considering. Finally, he looked up.

'Superintendent Quibbler – ' he said absently.

'Gribbler!' amended the superintendent hastily.

'Oh, yes – of course! Gribbler.' Holmes gave him a wickedly innocent look. 'I think you said that the body was discovered near Rhossili?'

'Well, not exactly near. Two miles down the coast, beyond the big cliff called Thurba Head.'

'There are eight miles of them,' I said, remembering my talk with the lifeboat coxswain, 'with no villages and not even a farmhouse anywhere near the edge.'

'Quite. Our nearest point of contact, then, will be at Rhossili, which, if I remember rightly, lies at the extreme end of the peninsula.' Although he had not accompanied me on my excursions, Holmes had done his exploring on the map and seemed to know all the principal names, together with their locations. 'It is, I believe, a very remote place,' he added, 'with less than sixty houses and a population of about two hundred and fifty.'

'Yes,' replied Gribbler. 'We have no constable out there at the moment. If you are going, the man for you is the coastguard at the lookout post. He's the one who told us about the body.'

'Are we going?' I asked, turning towards Holmes.

'Yes, I think we must.' He nodded and stood up, glancing afresh at the superintendent. 'Matters are coming to a head, and the next few days may be rather hectic, I am afraid. But, with your valuable assistance, we will do our best to get Dr Fu Manchu off your hands. Thank you again, and good morning, Superintendent Scribbler!'

We emerged quickly into the street before Gribbler could think of a rejoinder. Holmes shot a swift glance up at the clock above the entrance.

'Half-past eleven,' he announced. 'Back to the hotel! How long will it take us to drive out to Rhossili?'

335

'About ninety minutes, I think,' I answered, a little uncertainly, 'if the last part of the road is no worse than the rest.'

'Then we will have an early lunch – for I don't know when or where we shall eat next – and start as soon as possible.'

'You want to see the place where the body of the dacoit was washed up?'

'Perhaps. What I really wish to do is to see the coastguard and any others who know about the tides and the currents – who may be able to give us some idea of where he was thrown in. He may have been cast overboard from the ship, if it is already here, or more likely hurled off some point on the cliffs. Judging from the copious amount of blood on Philip Randall's trouser legs, I think it possible that he was close by at the time.'

'You think he saw it?'

'Yes. He is the stubborn kind of fool who would probably refuse to do what was demanded of him unless he was confronted with some such demonstration.' Holmes spoke in a flat, disapproving tone. 'I do not like mathematicians,' he added irrelevantly. 'The late Professor Moriarty was one.'

In the dining room of our hotel, he hurried me through lunch, gobbling his food in the manner of a man stoking a furnace. I believe that he had the digestion of an ostrich. He paused only once throughout our meal, holding knife and fork poised above his plate.

'For all your foot-slogging, I fear you did not go quite far enough, Petrie,' he remarked. 'The Si Fan have ventured farther afield than we expected. Yet they seem to have become singularly careless. By dumping Philip Randall on Cefn Bryn and allowing the dacoit's body to be found near Rhossili, they have given us a rough idea where they are.'

Refusing coffee, he chased me up to my room.

'Pack a bag,' he directed. 'We shall probably not come back here tonight – perhaps never.'

When I came downstairs, he was waiting for me in the

lobby, attired like a gamekeeper in knee-breeches and leggings, and with his antique deerstalker – which I did not know he had brought with him – crammed down over his ears.

'Good!' he said shortly. 'Let us be off!'

This was a route which I now knew well, though it was new to my companion. Out past the suburbs, we crossed the southern tip of Clyne Common, where a scarred telegraph post, leaning at a drunken angle, marked the spot at which the Si Fan had lost their vehicle, and only minutes later we were passing through the beautiful wooded stretch leading down to Parkmill, where the branches of tall trees met overhead. Weaving from north to south, to link the scattered villages, the road followed roughly the line of the coast, but rarely approached within less than a mile of it, so that we had only occasional glimpses of the sea.

Holmes sat silent at my side, looking straight ahead and stoically enduring the interruption of his eternal pipe smoking. Our journey was without event. The car ran well, leaping up the hills and bounding down into valleys, the powerful throbbing of the engine acting upon my spirits as the thundering hooves of their mounts must once have incited the hordes of Jinghis Khan. It was a fine piece of engineering, and, despite modern improvements, I sometimes wish that I had it still.

An hour from our starting point, we skirted the high ridge of Cefn Bryn, where Philip Randall had been found, turned away, and drove on to a point not far from Port Eynon, where the road forked off right-handed into unknown territory. The nature of the terrain changed again. Here we were crossing a wide green plateau – a huge expanse of open land across which the wind blew ceaselessly in a fierce, thirty-mile-an-hour gale, impeding our passage. The needle of the speedometer slipped back, and I had to put my foot down hard to bring it up to twenty. Nowhere, now, were there trees of any size – only a few bent and stunted specimens with their branches streaming back landwards, testifying to a stiff onshore breeze which never changed. I looked out to the left. Distantly, the horizon ended at eye level in a serrated edge of cliffs, and I felt puzzled – for I had long since made up my mind that the Si Fan would choose one of the secluded coves of Oxwich, where the woods came down close to the shore.

'There is nowhere for them to base themselves out here,' I said doubtfully. 'They would have a hard time getting down those cliffs, and even if they could, the ship would be unable to come close in. There is a submerged reef running parallel most of the way, and more than a hundred vessels have been wrecked on it.'

Sherlock Holmes shrugged and said nothing, reserving judgement.

We were nearly at our destination. A group of houses came in sight, then the road turned sharply to the left and became a lane descending in a steep slope. At the foot, it turned again, forming a corner, at the angle of which stood a church set among tombstones, the short, square tower crowned by a pitched roof like that of a shed – a weathered structure of such crude simplicity that it fulfilled my mental impression of some place in the Outer Hebrides. It was difficult to conceive a spot so rugged and desolate within twenty miles of the populous streets of Swansea.

A space in front of the churchyard offered a convenient parking place, and I pulled into it. No one was present to greet us, but we anticipated no difficulty in finding the coastguard station. A few minutes' walk along the lane brought us to a farm gate, and, passing this, we found ourselves on the verge of black, ominous cliffs, higher and more precipitous than any I had yet encountered.

I stopped, staring down at the vast sands of a bay which spanned the whole tip of the peninsula from north to south. Nothing appeared above their surface but the wooden ribs of some anciently wrecked ship, like the skeleton of a whale. Shorewards, the cliffs ended abruptly, and the bay was bounded only by sandhills, rising

338

to a broad shoulder of sparsely cultivated land and a steep, grass-covered hillside. Seawards, the long Atlantic rollers broke far out in wave upon wave of surf, and, seen from above, curiously resembled the scalloped fringe of a lace curtain.

'Come along!' said Holmes impatiently. 'They are not down there. There seems to be only one house' – he pointed to the roof of a solitary property, conspicuous by its isolation, just above the sandhills – 'and I do not suppose they are in that.'

He turned his back upon the bay and set off walking rapidly eastwards. There was no longer any path, but a line of wooden poles supporting a single telephone wire pointed the way to a small building situated precisely at the point where the bastion cliffs turned sharply, heading back towards Port Eynon.

'There it is,' he said tersely, 'and it looks as if we have a mile to walk!'

I doubt if Holmes ever really enjoyed walking for its own sake, regarding it merely as an emergency means of reaching his destination. For myself, I found our current exercise pleasant rather than otherwise. The strong breeze blowing across the clifftops was healthful and invigorating. A small herd of black, long-horned cattle – more common here than our dark red Sussex breed – regarded us incuriously and ambled out of our way.

I had thought that this wild and deserted coast of deep, landlocked coves and dramatic seascapes held no more surprises for me – yet another was in store. As we drew nearer to our objective, my gaze was caught and held by what seemed to be a line of rocks stretching far out to sea in a caricature of some colossal prehistoric monster. The nearer rose high above the waves like a humped back, joined by a long, saurian neck to the farthest, which reared up like a raised head. Distance plays tricks with perspective, and it was with a sense of shock that I suddenly realised they were not mere rocks but a chain of islands, more than a mile in extent and a mile out from the shore.

Even Holmes seemed to be impressed, for he halted briefly, shading his eyes.

'It looks to be rough out there,' he said. 'That pinnacle must be two hundred feet high, if it's an inch.'

The sea appeared calm, but, as he spoke, I saw a white cloud of spray burst out from the side of the dark tower of rock, not far below the summit.

For a further ten minutes we walked on, finding, at close quarters, that the so-called coastguard station consisted simply of a hut built of rough-hewn stone, with a broad, stoutly glazed window on the seaward side. Nearby stood a tall mast, with a storm cone now resting at the foot. As we passed in front, a man seated before the window raised his hand to us, stood up, and came to open the door.

'I am Sherlock Holmes,' said my companion.

The coastguard nodded and smiled. He was a powerfully built man with the windburned skin of a seaman, his eyes puckered in crow's feet at the corners, and wore a double-breasted navy jacket.

'Ah!' he said. 'Mr Holmes, is it? So you're the man who's had me cooling my heels out here for the last six weeks! We don't usually staff this place, unless there's a gale warning.'

We passed into the hut, which proved to contain no furnishings but a single chair and a bench set before the window, several wooden lockers, a signalling lamp, and an outsize pair of binoculars mounted on a stand.

'My name's Trevor Bennett,' said the coastguard.

'You have been keeping watch for the Chinese ship?'

'Yes – but never a sign of her I've seen, nor hardly any other ship. There's not much comes out this way. To tell you the truth, sir, we're wasting our time. There aren't that many of us, and we're a life-saving service, not policemen. We don't have a fleet of patrol boats, or anything like that, you see.'

I moved across to the bench, idly noting that there was a chart spread open on it, and stared out of the window. From this viewpoint, the distant chain of islands looked more than ever like some primaeval denizens of the deep, ready at any moment to dive beneath the surface. Bennett gestured to a heap of books piled up at one corner of the chart.

'I've read everything in the village,' he said mournfully, 'from *The Three Musketeers* to the Bible, and gone near cross-eyed keeping one eye on the print and the other on the horizon.'

'At least, you have a remarkable view,' I commented, 'though I suppose you might get used to it in time. That is the strangest-looking island that I ever saw.'

'Yes,' he said glancing out. 'That's what most people say, sir. Only it isn't an island. At low water, it's joined up with the shore.'

'Really?' I exclaimed. 'That looks impossible!'

The coastguard laughed and shook his head.

'You'll see it happen about six-thirty, and you can walk all the way out to the end, if you like – only not to-night, because it's a lot farther than it looks. It's a kind of Z-shape, and you can't see the middle bit from here.' Taking a short, black pipe from his pocket, he searched behind the books for a tin of ship's tobacco, and went on blandly, 'We call it The Worm.'

341

30
THE ENEMY AT BAY

For a long moment, Holmes and I stood gaping foolishly
at one another while Trevor Bennett, blissfully unaware
of the sensation he had produced, went on placidly
loading his pipe.

'. . . *They are using the worm* . . .' I said slowly.

'Confound it!' burst out Holmes. 'It wasn't marked on
the map!'

'The official name is Worms Head,' said Bennett,
glancing at us curiously. 'But that's a bit misleading,
because "Head" means "headland" – not a *worm's* head.
So far as the shape goes, it's the whole darned insect – or
reptile – whatever a worm is.'

'Vermiform invertebrate,' murmured my companion
automatically.

'The Si Fan – ' I began, but he interrupted me.

'Let us have some more facts first.' He turned back to
the coastguard. 'Give us an idea of the geography of this
place.'

He joined me at the window and peered down.
Bennett scratched his head, frowning.

'Well, sir,' he said awkwardly, 'it's in three bits. Call
them islands, if you like. You can't see the middle one.
It's joined up to the big one by slabs of rock about
twenty or thirty feet high, and all jumbled together like'
– he hesitated for a simile – 'well, rather like a staircase
tipped over on its side. That's the roughest part, if you
go out there. There's an easy path over the next island,
and then you come to the Devil's Bridge.'

He bent to the big binoculars on the stand and
adjusted them, then stood upright, beckoning to
Holmes.

'You can see it through here, sir.'

Holmes put his eyes briefly to the lenses, and invited me to take his place. Doing so, I was able to make out a bright patch of daylight, as though a window had been pierced through the dark wall of rock. Even with the powerful magnification of the instrument, I could discern no details, but I realised that I was staring at a natural bridge suspended a hundred feet or more above the sea, linking the two islands.

'It appears somewhat risky!' I said.

'Not so bad, if you've a good head for heights,' answered Bennett, smiling. 'It's wide enough, and you've no need to fall off, unless there's a gale blowing. Beyond that, there's another easy path out to the end, and you can climb right up to the top without any trouble. It looks rather grim from here, but when you're out there it's just like a rockery, and, at this time of the year, all over flowers, pink and yellow, like a garden.'

'It is uninhabited, of course?' inquired Holmes.

'Yes – excepting for about a million gulls, and a lot of other birds. You want to watch yourself in the nesting season, because those big herring gulls can be dangerous. They can break your arm, or knock you off the path.'

'Do people often go out there?'

'Not so often. A few visitors do, in the summer, but mostly they're afraid or too lazy. The locals don't have any reason to go. Earlier in the year, it's only some kids, maybe, or one of those crackpots who like staring at birds, because there are all sorts there that can't be seen anywhere else.'

'I take it then,' said Holmes, 'that no one is out there now?'

'Well, as a matter of fact there is, sir,' replied Bennett, looking slightly puzzled. 'There's a Boy Scouts' camp – '

'What!' I exclaimed, so violently that he started and recoiled.

'You didn't ask me till now!' he said defensively. 'It's the first time I've known them do it – not many people stay out there, unless they get caught by the tide. But you know what boys are, sir. They like a bit of hardship. Damn, I ran off to sea when I was fifteen, and I wasn't the only one. This scouting thing's been going five or six years now, and they get everywhere. . . .'

'Incredible!' I muttered, looking at Holmes. Clear as the inference was, it seemed too ridiculous to entertain. 'The Si Fan disguised as Boy Scouts?'

'Would they have to be?' he snapped, and looked again at Bennett. 'Did you see them go out?'

'Yes, Mr Holmes, I did. They went out a week ago, just after midday, and I was up here then. About a dozen of them, there were, carrying a lot of gear, and I wondered then if they were going to stay. . . .'*

'Quite! But from this distance you could not see they were scouts!'

'No . . .' admitted Bennett, somewhat unwillingly. 'But that's what I heard in the village. I suppose somebody saw them.'

Holmes moved to the binoculars. 'Where are they encamped?' he demanded.

'On top of the Inner Head – the big island, that is. I don't think you can see their tents, but I've seen their campfire after dark. . . .'

While Holmes fiddled with the eyepieces, I peered once more from the window at the serpentine shape below – black and forbidding, and the last place, I thought, that anyone would choose for a camping ground.

'On top of *that*?' I said incredulously. 'It looks like a precipice!'

'It is, on the other side,' answered Bennett, grinning again at my ignorance. 'But on this side it's just a steep hill, covered with grass, and as wide as a football field on top. I don't know how they're getting on for water – there isn't any there – if it comes on to blow, they'll have to come down. . . .'

---

* In these days of permits and regulations, such a haphazard proceeding might be difficult. But I have known one hardy customer who camped out there for a week, undisturbed and unnoticed by anybody. [Ed.]

'The scoundrels!' said Holmes, bristling with indignation. 'They have put up a flagpole and hoisted the Union Jack!'

He sat down upon one of the square wooden lockers, took a half-smoked pipe from his pocket, and lighted it. Bennett, who had filled his but forgotten to light it, took his cue to do likewise, his weatherbeaten features creased in perplexity.

'I'm sorry if I've missed something, sir,' he said apologetically. 'But I didn't have any instructions about this. My orders were just to watch out for a Chinese ship, and I don't even know why – whether it's smuggling, or what it is.'

'No, it's not smuggling,' replied Holmes. 'We will give you the full story when there is time. For the moment, let us say only that there is a gang of criminals who have set up a secret rendezvous with this ship. Would it be possible for them to join it out there?'

'No, sir,' answered Bennett promptly. 'You're thinking, maybe, it looks something like a pier. But there's nowhere even for a small boat to make a landing – it's all just rocks and boulders. The only way to get out there or back is by the causeway.'

'Which is open when, and for how long?'

'Approximately one hour and forty-five minutes either side of low water, sir, which is at intervals of twelve and a half hours.'

'H'm!' grunted Holmes. 'Somewhat complicated!'

'Well, sir,' said Bennett helpfully, 'with the Spring tides making it a bit longer, say four hours open, and an hour later every day.'

My companion nodded abstractedly and, for some moments, remained lost in thought, drumming his fingers irritably upon his knee. At length:

'About the body which was found near here this morning . . .' he said, reminding me with a start that I had completely forgotten the sanguinary business which had brought us. 'Supposing that the man had been thrown off The Worm, might it have been carried to the spot where it was found twenty-four hours later?'

'Likely enough,' answered Bennett. 'There was one of those bird-watching idiots who got climbing about out there, nearly six weeks ago, and slipped. His body was found more or less in the same place.'

'Very well, then.' Holmes stood up and glanced in my direction, as if suddenly recalling my existence – rather, I thought, in the way one looks around for a dog. 'I don't think we will bother ourselves any further with the dacoit. We shall have to stay here to-night, and perhaps longer. But there seems to be no inn. . . .'

'Some of the houses in the village take in boarders,' volunteered Bennett. 'That's usually in the summer. But I daresay they'd be glad of somebody. If you think I can go off duty, I'll walk back with you and help you get fixed up.'

'Thank you,' said Holmes. 'That is an excellent idea.'

We returned by the way we had come, and, with the coastguard's recommendation, were able to obtain accommodation at the first house we came to – a long, low cottage set back from the lane and sheltered below the level of the roadway, so that one walked down steps to reach the entrance.* Overlooking the bay on one side, and close to the gate leading out upon the cliffs, it was ideally situated for our purposes. Our Standard tourer had to share a large shed at the back with several cows, but I doubted if they would interfere with each other.

By the time we were unpacked and settled in, it was four-thirty. We reclimbed the hill to the corner, where there was a small general store and post office, together with the only congregation of houses, the rest being strung out at long intervals all over the cultivable land. For an hour or more, we wandered about, striking up brief acquaintanceships – Holmes could be very soci-

---

* It was later converted into a guesthouse, and is now a modern, fully licenced hotel. [Ed.]

able when he chose – and endeavouring to learn more about the campers on The Worm.

Here, however, we soon found ourselves up against one of the unsolved mysteries of village life. Everyone knew that a party of Boy Scouts had arrived in a motor van the previous Saturday. Everyone had heard it from someone else; no one could be found who had actually seen them. Through the same grapevine of hearsay, we were likewise informed that several of the scouts had, on various occasions, come ashore and passed through the village, but without staying there.

'The Si Fan will certainly have three or four short-stature members who can pass for boys,' observed Holmes. 'People from the Far East frequently look ten years short of their age, and in this case, even if they were obviously Orientals, it would not matter. The scouting movement is international. It gives youngsters a chance to play at soldiers, and has gone through the world like wildfire. They might easily be from our own colonies – which, in fact, some of them are.'

After six, though twilight was approaching, curiosity drove us out once more to the coastguard station, to see for ourselves the incredible parting of the waters. The shore was invisible from the hut itself, so we passed below it and sat on the edge of the cliff, where the sheer face gave way to a steep green slope leading downwards to the fringe of the restless waves.

The sun sank below the horizon and, that evening, I saw such colours in the sky and upon the sea as I had never seen elsewhere. The heavens were a deep orange, shading upwards to yellow and a hint even of pale green, while the waves became literally purple – an ocean of fire – deepening gradually to violet. The contorted shape of The Worm writhed across it in stark black silhouette, awesome and menacing – an unreal scene, not of this earth, but some modern painter's impression of a Martian landscape.

Imperceptibly, as we watched, the tide was receding to right and left. When the opening of the way came, it was

347

dramatic – not as the waves rolled back to give passage to the Israelites. One by one, isolated rocks broke the surface – irregular black shapes which, minute by minute, expanded into islets. Flat dark patches appeared above the water, broadened, joined up with one another, and grew to a wide shoal extending in all directions.

Very faintly, borne on the persistent wind, came the notes of a bugle, as the campers lowered their stolen flag.

'What shall we do?' I asked breathlessly.

'Nothing,' replied Holmes tartly. 'Do you propose that we go blundering out there in the dark, and have our throats cut?'

In twenty minutes, the bridge had stretched out from the shore almost completely to the linked islands, but the light was nearly gone. The dull glow of a campfire showed on the crest of the high ridge a mile distant.

'I wonder what they are using for fuel,' said Holmes thoughtfully. 'There can be nothing out there but a few pieces of driftwood.'

But I scarcely listened to him.

'They are there,' I said, trying vainly to keep the emotion from my voice. 'And Smith . . .'

'Quite probably – and Heaven knows what we are going to do about it!' Holmes jumped up impatiently. 'We must go back. We have left it too late already, and we shall have trouble finding our route.'

Darkness overtook us ere we were halfway to the village. Thankful that the moon was up and near full, we completed our journey stumbling through the short, wiry grass and stubbing our toes on unseen stones. Glancing rearwards, I had a last glimpse of The Worm – an evil, reptilian form swimming in a sea of molten silver. The lighted windows of the cottages on the hill guided us, but on the last hundred yards up to the gate we were obliged to go slowly and use our pocket lamps, for here we came so close to the edge of the cliffs above the bay that if we strayed from our proper course, a single false step would be fatal.

Holmes was pensive and taciturn over dinner that night, leaving me to make conversation with our hosts, and soon afterwards retired. But before doing so, he paused for a word of caution.

'Make sure that your window is fastened,' he said. 'The Si Fan will certainly have agents left ashore, and we cannot go around asking questions in a place like this without being noticed.'

He went up to his room and I was not long in following his example. The strong sea air of the cliffs was heady, like wine – stimulating but soon conducive to sleep. I noted, however, that Holmes had not gone to bed, for I heard him pacing about the room next to mine until I fell asleep. The cottage in which we were now staying was a notably solid affair, built by a retired stone mason to withstand the Atlantic gales, and though the small, deeply recessed windows gave one rather the impression of being in a cell, they also conveyed a feeling of security. I slept soundly, wakening to early morning sunlight and the hoarse cries of a herdsman driving cattle down the lane.

According to my calculations, the next scheduled opening of the causeway was for 7.15 a.m., but Holmes , saying that it could serve no useful end, had refused to get up early enough to witness it. We breakfasted at the more reasonable hour of eight, and subsequently, by tacit consent, went out again upon the cliffs to resume our vigil – though what we expected to gain by it, I myself was none too sure.

Coastguard Bennett, who had no relief, was already back on watch at the lookout post. We waved to him as we passed, but, without going in, went to sit down on the grass at the same spot that we had occupied the previous evening. Below us, the causeway now lay open to its full extent – not such a causeway as we had walked upon across the marsh, but a broad plain of uneven rock, the veritable sea bed itself, scattered about everywhere with stones and boulders, as though by a giants' game of ninepins. As it appeared now, it was difficult to believe that it could ever be submerged, and easy to understand how unsuspecting visitors might find themselves marooned.

The Worm, now slightly less grim and foreboding, lay bathed in sunlight, and, whereas it had formerly seemed black throughout its length, I could make out a covering of green on the near side of the Inner Head. I experienced a sense almost of elation: We knew where they were – we had them at bay. But Holmes seemed far from elated. He sat frowning and silent, his lantern jaw set in an angry, baffled expression.

'They are trapped!' I said exultantly.

'Trapped?' he retorted. 'Of course they are not! The coastguard may say there is nowhere to land a boat, but they have some way. I am sure of it. It is we who are trapped, not they! They may slip off quietly after dark to-morrow or the next day – perhaps even to-night. And how are we to hinder them?'

This was a point which, in my excitement, I had not really thought about till now.

'Their ship is lying hull-down over the horizon,' he went on morosely, 'or will be before long. They are in touch with her by wireless, and they have emergency communication with both the ship and the shore by means of the kite. It can be launched either from out there or from any of these cliffs. That is why they brought it – not to kidnap Philip Randall.'

He fell silent again; then, evidently prompted by the same thought, continued speaking, more to himself than to me.

'They took him *there*. His boots were damaged while climbing over the rocks between the big island and the next. Why? What could they want with him?'

To my dismay, Holmes produced his malodorous cherrywood, which he had not smoked since the commencement of our adventures. I watched him fill and light it, knowing the mood which it signified.

'Complex numbers . . .' he muttered. 'Complex numbers are algebraic absurdities which have no solution –

but, somehow or other, they are used in mechanics and electricity. . . .'

After that he said no more, and, knowing better than to break in upon his thoughts, I kept my eyes fixed upon the causeway. While I watched, I saw several men go out armed with poles to search among the rocks for lobsters; but none of them went very far. Holmes sat as unmoving as a statue, save for frequently re-lighting his pipe and littering the ground about him with a score of spent matches.

In this fashion, an hour went by while, slowly and inexorably, the returning tide encroached upon the causeway from both sides, each temporary recession of the waves leaving pools and lakes till, presently, the whole dark plain began to split up into an archipelago of islets and atolls, as seen upon a map. Then, all at once, as if reaching a decision, Holmes changed his position, knocked out his pipe, and stuffed it into his pocket.

'This is no good,' he said quietly. 'We may sit here forever and come to no solution. We know they are there, but the difficulties of getting at them are almost insuperable – both materially and legally.'

'Legally?' I cried, regarding him in amazement, and he nodded brusquely.

'Yes – legally! Do you imagine any magistrate will give us leave to raid a camp of Boy Scouts because we *think* they are members of the Si Fan?'

Standing up, he pointed dramatically at The Worm, now once more almost isolated.

'They are as good as entrenched on a fortified island! Anyone who goes out there can be seen from the moment he leaves the shore. If you or I go, we shall not come back. If anyone else goes, what will he find? A Boys Scouts' camp! He will see only one or two of the *boys*, and very likely they have some renegade Englishman to play the part of the scoutmaster. If a stranger should go there and, by chance, find something incriminating, they will make away with him. You heard what

351

the coastguard said about the bird-watcher who lost his life six weeks ago.'

'My God! You think they were there then?'

'They had at least a caretaker. They have been setting up these arrangements for weeks.'

Holmes turned aside, and began walking up towards the coastguard station, leaving me to follow.

'We have the police behind us,' he said, as I fell into step with him, 'but the police have no ships, machine guns, or artillery. They could be armed only by an order from the Home Office. In order to cope with this, we need the co-operation of Trinity House, the coastguard service, the lifeboat institution, and the Admiralty! And, in a bureaucracy such as ours, are we likely to get it? We have had inquiries out for that Chinese ship ever since we first learned of her existence from Smith's letter – and the results up to now have been exactly nil.'*

'What are we to do, then?' I asked blankly.

'Absurd though it seems, and undoubtedly is,' said Holmes, with a wry smile, 'the final moves in the game will have to be made across many desks, and I shall have to make them. I must go back to Swansea, and see the Chief Constable. In all probability, I shall need to go up to London to secure the necessary papers. In the meantime, you must hold the fort on your own, Petrie. I can only pray that I may not be too late – for I am no longer certain how much time we have.'

We stopped at the hut and held a brief conversation with Trevor Bennett, the upshot of which was that I was to dine with him and his wife, Megan, that evening and give him a full understanding of what our strange business was about. He lived at Middleton, a suburb of Rhossili – if such a place could be said to possess a suburb – half a mile down the road, from which a track led across the cliffs directly to the lookout post.

---

* Indeed, it was not until weeks after it was all over that we had this information. The S.Y. *Chanak Kampo* had landed Ki Ming and his entourage openly at Liverpool, and, during our sojourn in Wales, made a leisurely cruise around the coast of Ireland. [P.]

'He will be our principal ally from now on,' observed Holmes, as we continued on our way to the village. 'In fact, he is our only ally in these parts.'

Pausing at the cottage only long enough to pick up his things, he took leave of our hosts, who were surprised and a little disappointed to see him depart so soon. It was suggested that we should remain for lunch, but Holmes was anxious to be back in Swansea without delay, so we declined. I got out the car and we drove uneventfully and pleasantly enough through the awakening countryside, arriving in the town just before two. Here, as a matter of course, we descended at the hotel near the station, where we had formerly been accomodated, and where our rooms were still kept, though we did not go up to them.

Holmes continued to refuse lunch, but consented to drink a cup of coffee with me in the lounge before hurrying off on the first round of his official negotiations, and in order to give me any last minute instructions that he might think of.

'How long do you think you will be away?' I asked.

'I have no idea,' he said, shaking his head rather wearily. 'I shall try to be back as soon as possible. It will certainly not be to-morrow, but the next day, I hope. Meanwhile, you must occupy yourself as best you can.'

'What should I do!'

Again Holmes shook his head. 'If I knew that, I should not be going! You will have to use your own initiative. I suppose that you will spend some time watching the causeway, and if one of those alleged Boy Scouts comes ashore, you may try to follow him – though I doubt if you will succeed. But promise me one thing.' He looked at me sternly. 'Whatever happens, you will not go out on The Worm.'

'Very well,' I said reluctantly. 'I promise.'

Holmes nodded his approval, picked up the sugar tongs, and absentmindedly added a knob to his coffee.

'That is the third time you have sugared it!' I told him.

'Dear me! Is it?'

With the cup in his hand, he glared at the sickly brew, glanced around, and began to push back his chair.

'For Heaven's sake,' I said hastily, noticing his eyes light upon the glass front of a large aquarium close beside us. 'Not in the fish tank! Just leave it for the boy to take away, and let me pour you another.'

I collected an empty cup from an adjacent table, and filled it from the silver pot standing between us.

'Thank you,' he murmured, with more than a hint of sarcasm. 'Really, I don't know what I shall do without you, Petrie.' He stirred thoughtfully for a few seconds. 'But you, at least, will not be entirely without companionship,' he continued. 'I hear from our farmer friends that you are to have a fellow boarder, either to-night or to-morrow.'

'Indeed?' I inquired, a little surprised. 'They said nothing about it to me.'

But, as I spoke, I remembered that Holmes had been talking with them whilst I got out the car.

'Yes,' he said slowly. 'They are not too happy about him, but he appears to be vouched for by people whom they would rather not offend. He is a professor of zoology, from Munich.'

'A professor? You think that he might be another victim of the Si Fan?'

'Well, he is certainly liable to become one, if he goes poking his nose out there – which is evidently his intention. It seems that he is one of the bird-watching fraternity, of whom Coastguard Bennett takes a poor view – and whose opinion I am somewhat inclined to share. I fail to see why anyone should wish to pry into matters of so little concern to human affairs.'

I smiled, unable to help it. Holmes was grossly intolerant of all tastes which did not match his own.

'You watch bees!' I remarked. 'It takes all sorts to make a world.'

'So they say,' he agreed dryly. 'And look what kind of

world it is! Anyway,' he added, more seriously, 'you had better keep an eye on this itinerant Bavarian – and don't forget that he may equally well have been sent by the Si Fan to keep an eye on *you*!'

31

ISHTAR ARISES

My dinner engagement with the Bennetts was for eight o'clock, and as I walked up the garden path to the coastguard's house, the wind gusted into my face with such violence that it literally took my breath away.

'Aye, there's a bit of a breeze!' agreed Bennett, exerting some force to shut the door behind me.

I wondered about the Si Fan in their exposed position on top of the Inner Head, but he shrugged and said that it was nothing much. In times of a genuine gale, he added, he had sometimes had to crawl back from the lookout hut on hands and knees, to avoid being blown off the cliff.

Dinner followed, and it was not until afterwards, when the coastguard and I were ensconced in armchairs with our pipes going, that I found a chance to carry out my mission. This, however, proved easy enough.

'If it's Fu Manchu we're fighting,' he declared, 'you can count me in!'

Like most of his colleagues, Bennet was an ex-navy man, and like most seamen who had been cheated and robbed in half the ports east of Suez, he had decided ideas about Orientals.

Megan (as she insisted on being called) returned from the kitchen, drying her hands on her apron, and the talk turned to more pleasant topics. Time passed quickly, and it was after ten when I finally dragged myself away to complete my journey down the hill to the farmer's cottage overlooking the bay.

Here, having manoeuvred the car into the cowshed, to the marked displeasure of its lawful tenants, I entered the parlour to find my hosts, Mr and Mrs Gwynn, conversing in hoarse whispers. I gathered that the eminent Herr Dr Hans Reinhardt had arrived some twenty minutes previously. He had hired a taxicab to bring him all the way out from Swansea, and immediately gone up to his room. True to his word, he came armed with an introduction from the owners of the Penrice estate, to which half the peninsula belonged.

Gwynn and his wife knew no more of him than this, but were convinced, firstly, that they did not like him, and, secondly, that he was mad.

I did not see the professor that night, but I heard him. He occupied the room originally prepared for Holmes, and long after I had gone to bed, I was rudely disturbed by the sound of his stamping about the floor, coughing, clearing his throat, and, now and then, shouting Teutonic imprecations. Nor, to my surprise, did I see him the next morning. On coming down to breakfast at eight, I learned that he had arisen at an unearthly hour, breakfasted, and left soon after seven, presumably to cross the causeway as soon as it became practicable. With Germanic attention to detail, he had provided himself with a monthly tide-table, issued by the Swansea Docks and Waterways.

It seemed that Holmes's tentative suggestion of keeping an eye on Dr Reinhardt would be difficult to put into practice.

I finished my meal quickly, hurried out to our former vantage point on the cliffs, and sat down to scan the causeway with an excellent pair of field-glasses loaned to me by Coastguard Bennett. The way was already open, but as yet narrow and winding, and I could see no one upon it. Later, some fishermen went out, but, as before, stayed relatively close to the shore.

Fortunately for my comfort, the morning was sunny and warm. The wind had dropped to its customary level, brushing back the grass so that it had the sleek appearance of a well-combed head of hair, but at no time was it ever quite still. Day and night, it blew ceaselessly onshore, moderate or violent, and not the least of the local curiosities was the only tree in the village – a tough and ancient survivor, which, at the height of a few feet above the ground, bent and grew *horizontally* across a farmyard.

Time drifted with the tide as events – or, should I say, a lack of any – followed the pattern of the previous morning. No one came ashore. After eleven, as the sea closed in once more to claim its own, I raised my borrowed glasses again and studied the returning fishermen with their poles and baskets, but if Dr Reinhardt had indeed gone out there, I was unable to distinguish him from them.

No more was to be seen that day. I stood up slowly, easing cramped limbs, and walked rather stiffly to the lookout post. Here I found Trevor Bennett, back on duty since dawn, and more alert than before, now that he knew what the battle was all about.

'If the Si Fan don't get clear to-night,' he said cheerfully, 'they won't do it to-morrow. We're having the coastguard cutter round in the morning.'

It was clear, then, that Holmes's diplomatic efforts were beginning to bear fruit. I returned to the cottage with an improved appetite for lunch. But Dr Reinhardt, who was on a bed-and-breakfast arrangement, did not put in an appearance.

Now that the causeway was closed and must remain so for the next eight hours, there was no point in resuming my watch from the clifftop. Hence, after a leisurely lunch, I turned my steps in the opposite direction, and descended the long, winding track behind the cottage, which alone gave access to the bay.

Seen from this side, where the escarpment came down sheer into the water, the stark outline of The Worm looked more sinister than ever. Again, as on the night of our arrival, I saw the great burst of spray fan out from the dark tower of the Outer Head – a final touch of the dramatic, produced not as I had first supposed by the angry waves leaping up and rebounding from the pinnacle of rock but, even more strangely, fountained out

358

through a funnel-shaped cavern beneath with a small opening at the top.

I did not go all the way down to the beach, but turned off and walked along the shoulder of cultivated land between the dunes and the green rampart of Rhossili Down. The shrill voices of children playing on the sands drifted up to me but were soon lost in distance. Far ahead, nothing moved upon the bow-shaped curve of the beach – a simple paradise unsullied by the sordid amenities of deck chairs, ice-cream stalls, and bathing machines, lacking only palm trees and a tropic sun to lend it an aspect of the South Seas.

My purpose was to visit the solitary house which Holmes and I had seen from above. This, I had since learned, was inhabited by the rector of Rhossili and Llangenydd, who, as the incumbent of both parishes, had a long walk to either. Other than by footpaths, there was no communication between the north and south coasts of the peninsula westwards of Reynoldston. But, I thought, in its isolated position, the house was an ideal point from which any suspicious phenomena might have been observed.

To that extent, I was right. I was fortunate enough to catch the clergyman at home, and, as I had anticipated, found him a lonely man, happy to receive a visitor. Without revealing the exact nature of my interest, I had only to lead the conversation in the right direction, and he soon confessed that, several times during the past few weeks, he had seen furtive lights out to sea. These he concluded to be due to the goings-on of smugglers, adding, with a sad smile, that prices being what they were and human nature what it was, little else was to be expected.

He was unwilling to let me go: gave me tea, and told me stories of the locality – how, in times of heavy snow, it was sometimes cut off from the town for as much as a week; how it had been the home of Edgar Evans, a member of Scott's ill fated expedition which had come to a heroic end in the Antarctic only two years ago. It was late when I left, and the light was already growing dim as I toiled up the last part of the track on my way back.

But, late as I was, Dr Reinhardt was later. Dinner time passed without sign of him and when, by nine o'clock, he had still failed to appear, my genial hosts commenced to feel some anxiety. Unless one had friends to visit – which as far as we knew, he had not – there was nowhere to go in Rhossili after dark. The locals must all have been teetotallers, since it was the only village I ever visited which had no tavern. I began secretly to wonder if he had already fallen foul of the Si Fan, and Mr Gwynn thought it likely that he had been cut off by the tide.

However, while we were discussing the possibilities, in he came, and I had my first sight of him – a stoop-shouldered, comically absurd figure clad in leather shorts which did little to enhance either his bony knees or his grossly protuberant stomach. His bushy black beard and moustache grew wild and untrimmed, giving his face the appearance of a feather-duster, and he wore a battered Tyrolean hat jammed on his head like a flower-pot. A bulky leather case hung from a strap around his neck.

Giving no greeting, and offering no explanations, he plodded across the room, heading straight for the stairs. But, with the bold familiarity of fellow visitors to a foreign land, I jumped up from my chair and hurried to intercept him.

'Good evening!' I said. 'I am Dr Petrie.'

He turned, standing with one foot on the bottom step and his hand on the rail, glared at me, fierce-eyed, then grudgingly inclined his head in a quick jerk.

'Hans Reinhardt!' he growled, in a harsh, rumbling voice.

'You have come here to watch birds?' I asked inquisitively.

'*Bitte*?'

'Birds!' I repeated, and made flapping motions with my hands.

'*Ja, ja*!' he said. 'I go. I see. *Die Vögel.*'

'But you cannot watch birds at night!' I protested.

'Ja!' said Dr Reinhardt. 'I go. I see. *Nachtvögel*.'

He clumped up the stairs and slammed the door of his bedroom. A silence followed his going. Then:

'You know,' said Mrs Gwynn darkly, 'it's my belief that man's a spy!'

I nodded thoughtfully. At this juncture in history – and, as later events proved, with good reason – we were inclined to feel suspicious of Germans who wandered about the coast with 7 × 50 binoculars.

Soon afterwards I retired, lighting my way to bed with a candle and feeling, not for the first time, that I had moved back into the Middle Ages. Next door, the professor was repeating his performance of the night before, emitting oaths and unpleasant noises at odd intervals, but neither his uncouth behaviour nor my continuing anxieties could keep me from sleep after my daily overdose of strong sea air and energetic walking. I slept dreamlessly and, for the third time in succession, woke to sunlight, feeling rested and refreshed.

No longer depressed, but eager to see what this new day would bring, I washed and dressed hurriedly – the latter posing a minor problem, since I had left London with no clothes suitable to the conditions I was now experiencing. I felt disinclined for a collar and tie, but had brought no tennis shirts with me. In this climate, one needed clothing which was windproof rather than heavy, so, finally, I compromised by pulling on a light cashmere sweater and putting a sports jacket on top.

A clatter of crockery from below informed me that a meal was already on the table, but this morning the opening of the causeway would not take place until after nine, so that I did not expect the elusive Dr Reinhardt to outdistance me. I hastened down and found him shovelling into a huge breakfast, while disputing loudly and incomprehensibly about his coffee, which he seemed to want neither black nor white. My embarrassed hosts looked at me in mute appeal.

'Pliss!' said the professor desperately, glancing up also. 'Vot is, *auf Englisch, Schlagsahne*?'

I did not know, but he made an urgent, stirring motion with one finger, and, by a happy chance, memories of German habits came back to me.

'Give it to him four times as strong as usual,' I said, turning to Mrs Gwynn, 'with a teaspoonful of whipped cream.'

She departed, relieved, and I sat down opposite Dr Reinhardt, feeling that, since he had begged my aid in the matter of his coffee, I now had some right to question him.

'You have been out on The Worm?' I inquired.

'*Bitte?*'

'The Worm!' I repeated, and tried to draw a serpent in the air.

'*Ach! Der Wurm!*' he said. '*Ja, ja.* I go. I see.'

'Did you see the Boy Scouts?'

'*Bitte?*'

'The Scouts!'

'Scoots?'

'Boys!'

'*Ja, ja.* I see. *Die Jungen auf der Wanderschaft.*'

This was a conversation which could obviously not be long continued to much purpose, and I gave it up sadly. Dr Hans Reinhardt consumed his Germanic coffee noisily, gobbled three more slices of toast, and finished his meal before I was halfway through mine. Standing up, he adjusted his ludicrous, cross-strapped braces, slung the binocular case over his shoulder, and walked out.

Determined not to lose him, I guped down my coffee, abandoned the rest, and was out after him in two minutes. He had taken the direction I expected, and was out upon the cliffs, but well ahead of me, his duck-footed gait carrying him over the ground at a surprising speed. I strode off in pursuit, keeping him in sight, but making no attempt to catch up.

Looking to neither right nor left, Dr Reinhardt made straight for the coastguard station, passed below it, and disappeared over the brow of the cliff. A hundred yards to the rear, I reached the same spot, to find that he had already descended the slope and vanished behind the rampart of boulders at the base. I watched anxiously till, presently, I saw him emerge on the other side. The causeway was not yet fully open, but he started out upon it immediately, confident that it would clear before he reached the end.

I could follow him no farther – Holmes had forbidden me – but I knew where he was going. For the fourth time seating myself on the grass, I took out my borrowed field-glasses and focussed them upon him. So far, no one else was out there, and it was easy to keep track. For half an hour, I watched him making minor detours, this way and that, skirting the larger pools and jumping over the smaller, till at last his stooping figure was lost against the tawny background of the Inner Head. Though I continued to watch, he did not reappear, and I could safely presume that he had climbed up to the path which led across it.

Relaxing – for now there was no more to do but duplicate the process of the last two days – I opened my tobacco pouch and lighted my first pipe of the morning, using my coat as a windshield, and managing expertly enough now with the expenditure of only three matches. The results of my surveillance had been inconclusive. I still did not know what to make of Dr Reinhardt – whether he was an agent of the Si Fan, an agent of Imperial Germany, or a harmless bird-watcher. He had gone where he was supposed to go. The question was, rather, where did he go when he came back?

The next hour passed as it had done the day before and the day before that. I trained the glasses on The Worm, swept the whole visible length of it, and peered till my eyes were weary. I could see nothing to indicate that the Si Fan were there – that they had ever been there. Then, just as I turned my head aside, a flash of light caught my eye and there, on the highest point of the Inner Head, appeared the unmistakable dot-and-dash of a heliograph. On and off it winked for twenty or thirty seconds, while I wished helplessly that I could know what it meant and to whom they signalled.

They were there! A surge of elation ran through me and died as swiftly. I groaned. Boy Scouts were trained in signalling by heliograph and other such means. We were sure – and yet what real evidence did we have that they were *not* Boy Scouts?

The signal was not repeated. Another half hour elapsed, during which all was as it had been – during which I sat and stared at the macabre chain of islands, hating and fearing it. A poet would have called it beautiful – an onyx jewel set in an azure sea – but, to me it was menacing and terrible, a sea monster of Arthurian legend, petrified by the hand of Merlin. . . . A shout from behind me woke me to my senses and I turned quickly.

Coastguard Bennett was standing outside his hut, beckoning to me. I stood up and went to join him, noting as I approached that his hands were clenched and his face was like thunder.

'The cutter won't be coming,' he said tersely. 'There was an explosion in the engine room, ten minutes after she put to sea. One man badly hurt.'

'My God!' I exclaimed. 'They knew – even about that!'

Bennett shrugged listlessly. 'They were expecting it. What else could we have sent?'

I was silent for a moment. Then:

'Did you see the signal from The Worm?' I asked.

'Yes,' he said. 'I saw it.'

'Could you read it?'

'No. It wasn't Morse. God knows what it was!' He shook his head grimly. 'I've got to go over to Port Eynon and report to the station. They're hopping mad about the cutter.'

He locked the door of the hut and strode off angrily towards his house, leaving me to my fruitless vigil. I sat down again, shocked by his news but not really surprised. Fu Manchu had foreseen our every move and was

364

ready to counter it. And yet, I felt, something was wrong in all this. Why these elaborate arrangements to stage and to cover a retreat which could be so much more easily accomplished? There was a score of secluded points around the coast better suited to their purpose; if they chose, they could run a boat in anywhere, after dark, on the deserted, four-mile shore of Rhossili Bay. What was the true secret of The Worm?

It was eleven o'clock – nearly two hours to go before the causeway closed. I shifted my position slightly and yawned. One of the big herring gulls touched down on the grass a few yards distant and regarded me with a baleful eye. They were ugly brutes, twice or three times the size of our southern seagulls, with a wickedly curved bill, and varied the mewing cry of their species with a tittering sound which, in the present circumstances, I found distinctly irritating. Through the field glasses, I could see droves of them wheeling about the Devil's Bridge and the Outer Head, suggesting activity going on in that quarter.

The causeway did not run in a straight line from the shore but in an L-shape, adding an extra convulsion to the zigzag shape of The Worm. I studied it again carefully, searching in vain for something new; the gull looked at me and tittered. Halfway out, I saw the men with their hooked poles probing holes in the rocks for crabs and lobsters, one man standing at the edge of the water with rod and line. But presently, as I watched, I became aware of a solitary figure farther out but heading shorewards – one who had come down, apparently, from the Inner Head. As he came closer, I saw that he was dressed in shorts, and supposed that it was Dr Reinhardt, returning sooner than I had expected. But, as he came closer still, I saw that it was not, and my heart gave a bound.

It was a 'scout,' making one of their rare trips ashore. Breathing more rapidly, I followed his approach through the lenses, and, to my renewed excitement, discerned that he wore a blue turban in lieu of the usual wide-brimmed hat. Twenty minutes after I had first discovered him, he reached the foot of the track below and began to ascend. I jumped up and withdrew to the coastguard's hut, concealing myself behind it.

His turbanned head appeared above the cliff edge, and then the rest of him. He was a dark-skinned, good-looking lad, ostensibly about fourteen, and no doubt in his early twenties – not, I thought, a regular member of the Si Fan, but probably one of those outside helpers whom Sherlock Holmes described as conscripts. With no suspicion that he was observed, he set out for the village and I followed at a discreet distance, finding it no longer possible or necesary to remain in hiding. I had never seen him before, and I doubted if he had seen me. His high, straight turban looked like that of a Sikh.

I was anxious to learn where he went. If he had business ashore, it would scarcely be possible for him to return ere the closing of the causeway made return impossible. He led me back by the way I had come, to the gate, and up the lane to the church. The open space in which Holmes and I had parked the car on our initial arrival was now occupied by a motor bus – one of the infrequent service which, I believe, had only recently replaced the daily horse bus from Swansea. It was empty, but evidently due to start soon, for a small group of people stood beside it awaiting the coming of the driver and conductor from their mid-morning cup of tea in a nearby cottage.

My quarry ranged himself behind them and I took my place boldly behind him, determined that if he boarded the bus I would do likewise. Several minutes went by, during which two or three villagers walked past and, seeing the foreigner in his neat uniform, called out a cheerful 'Good morning!' to which he responded politely but with a thick accent. Then, while we continued to stand there, I glanced up the road and, to my astonishment, saw a *second* scout descending the hill towards us.

Attired identically with the first, he was so alike in appearance that they might have been brothers. I won-

dered where he had come from. Since he had certainly
not come off The Worm, he must either have spent the
night in the village or, perhaps, arriving by the same bus,
descended from it at the corner to make some purchase
at the general store. Drawing level with us, he halted,
and the two exchanged greetings – not in Hindustani, but
in colloquial Egyptian Arabic. I listened intently, striving to catch the meaning.

'*Râyeh feyn?*'

'*Arûh el-medînah ashtiri lahm. Etfaddal weyyâya!*'

This was clear enough, but disappointing. The newcomer had asked where the other was going, been told
that he was going into the town to buy meat, and invited
to accompany him. But the response left me gasping.

'*La! Lâzim a'abil 'ârib el-Hakkîm.*'

I could scarcely believe my ears. I knew that Fu
Manchu's Arabic-speaking followers invariably referred
to him as *el-Hakkîm*, and what the newcomer had said
was this: 'No – I must go and meet the Doctor's boat.'

Losing interest in the youth whom I had followed to
the bus stop, I turned away and, as his comrade walked
on down the lane, set off after him. It seemed almost too
good to be true – yet, as even Holmes admitted, it was
upon such mere chances as this that great issues rested.
These two junior assistants of the Si Fan were rank
amateurs, who could not distinguish one European from
another – who had never dreamed that a European
might understand their speech.

For the second time within fifteen minutes, I passed
the gate, and came out again upon the cliffs, deliberately
allowing my new quarry to increase his lead till he was a
hundred yards ahead. Heading only roughly in the
direction of the coastguard station, he passed well
behind it and continued on east. There were others out
walking, and, even if he looked back, there was no
reason why he should notice me. But he did not look
back.

It proved to be a remarkably long walk, but I followed
doggedly, determined not to lose him even if he should

lead me the entire eight miles back to Port Eynon. Distantly, to the left, I saw the houses of Middleton, where Trevor Bennett lived. We came to a minor valley, leading down to some lesser bay which I had not visited, and were compelled to make a lengthy passage inland before we could cross it. As I descended the nearer side, I saw the scout climbing up the farther. At the top, he turned seawards again till we were close to the cliff edge.

Glancing behind me, I noted that there were now no others in sight. Only the more dedicated lovers of exercise came out so far. The Worm had long since vanished, hidden beyond the ragged outline of the cliffs. Now I must trust entirely to luck that my pursuit might remain unsuspected, for out here there was no cover of any kind – not a tree, not a rock. Holmes had cast doubts upon my ability as a tracker, but, short of disguising himself as a cow, I do not see how he could have done better.

The sun was at zenith, and, despite the open nature of the land and the eternal breeze, it was warm work. I took off my sports jacket and slung it over my arm as I walked, always intent upon my quarry, but unable, now and then, to resist a glance at the spectacular prospect hard upon my right. These, which I now saw for the first time, were unlike the grey-green Pennard cliffs farther east, which stretched out to sea like a line of fangs, one behind the other. Here they plunged vertically from a height which I estimated at well over three hundred feet to a foaming line of surf – the stupendous outer wall of an impregnable fortress. Halfway down, I saw the black shape of a cormorant perched upon a crag, immobile till presently its sharp eyes detected the glitter of scales and it plummeted like a stone to snatch a fish from the water.

I did not look at my watch, but it must, I think, have been well over an hour before our way was once more interrupted by a ravine, narrower and steeper than the preceding. Again the scout turned inland, as if to skirt it, still seemingly unaware of my pursuit, but continued only a short distance ere descending. Quickening my pace as he disappeared from sight, I scrambled down the steep slope in his wake, forcing my way through spiky gorse bushes and undergrowth. There was no path till, at length, I reached the bottom and came out upon a narrow, stony track running down to the sea.

I stopped, staring all about me, but could see no sign of the scout. If he had gone up the opposite slope he might still be hidden in the dark screen of vegetation, but, though I waited for some minutes, he failed to emerge at the top. I was forced, then, to conclude that he had gone down to the shore. I turned and took the same direction, proceeding cautiously now.

If, as I had interpreted his words to mean, Dr Fu Manchu was to make a landing at some unsuspected point along the cliffs, I meant to be there to witness it – a foolhardy venture, and one of which Holmes would doubtless have disapproved, but I was committed to it. If I could remain unobserved, I might learn something of Fu Manchu's plans – more even than that, perhaps. My pistol was ready in my pocket. I might take him by surprise . . . capture him. . . .

Step by step, I followed the seaward course of the ravine as, gradually, it grew wider and the enclosing slopes yet more precipitous. The path shelved deeply and, at length, brought me into a landlocked cove strewn with boulders. I paused, baffled. The place was empty of occupant: nowhere was there any sign of the youth whom I had followed.

Before me was a yellow strip of sand, at which the waves lapped lazily, on either side the great wall of cliff, extending far out into the deep water. Sheltered from the wind, it was an enchanted spot unlike any I had previously seen, patched here and there with porous, spongelike rocks which, save for their lighter hue, resembled lava. At the fringe of the tide, I saw the bright orange shapes of stranded starfish, while all about lay seeweed of a dozen different varieties, some of them quite unfamiliar. But not so much as a footprint marked the smooth surface of the sand.

I stood still, irresolute and wondering. Had my quarry discovered me, and eluded me by hiding among the bushes while I followed a false trail? Search as I might, I could see nothing, hear nothing but the mournful clanging of a bell-buoy set to mark the submerged reef where, in the days of sailing ships, so many lives had been lost. Minutes passed and then, as I was about to give up hope and retrace my steps, a new sound reached my ears – the sputtering note of a petrol engine. A boat appeared around the headland to my left, and turned, heading inshore.

Dropping my jacket from my arm, I fumbled urgently with the case-strap of the field-glasses, lifted them quickly to my eyes. She appeared to be a fishing vessel of fair size, thirty feet, perhaps, from stem to stern, but badly in need of repainting. I could not make out the name written on her bows. She approached to within two cable-lengths; then the noise of the engine ceased abruptly, succeeded by the rattle of an anchor chain.

So far as I could see, no one was on deck. I watched, aware that my pulse was well above normal. They could come no closer. If a landing was to be made, how was it to be effected? It seemed to me that an eternity went by while I waited for the next development, and, when it came, it caught me unawares. A plume of white appeared against the hull, and I realised, incredulously, that someone had dived off the side.

Despite the warmth of the sunlight, this was not such a morning as I would have chosen for a swim. Forgetting the ship, I turned my attention to the swimmer, but all I could see was the dark dot of a head, as he struck out powerfully shorewards. I watched, fascinated, till at last it dawned upon me – too late – that my own position was untenable. I had no reason to fear a solitary swimmer, yet, if I was discovered, the purpose of my pursuit would come to nothing. Searching all around, I saw to my alarm that the beach offered no means of concealment – a fact which Sherlock Holmes would doubtless have taken into account minutes before.

The hardy swimmer was already close to the shore. Dodging within a maze of boulders, I came up to the wall of the cliff and flattened myself against it, trying to squeeze into a crevice. It was poor cover, but all that was available. If the swimmer looked about him when he gained the sand, he must surely see me. Who was he? What was his object, and what had become of the scout whom he came, presumably, to meet? For a moment, the wild idea occupied my mind that this might be none other than Nayland Smith – Smith who had seized the chance to throw himself overboard in a reckless bid for liberty. But there was no outcry aboard the boat.

I was not left long in doubt. Less than fifty yards from where I crouched against the rock, the swimmer reached the shadows and stood up, and, before my amazed eyes, a dusky Aphrodite rose from the waves – no, not Aphrodite, but Ishtar, her Babylonian sister, her barbaric loveliness clothed in a halo of sunlight . . . Zarmi the Eurasian.

32

THE UNHOLY ALLIANCE

No one was there to meet her, but Zarmi strode confidently ashore. Reaching the sand, she *waved*, headed straight towards me, and my heart sank as I realised that it was *I* whom she came to meet! I had walked into an ambush.

Standing there flattened against the cliff, I was only making myself ridiculous. I stepped out boldly and faced her as she halted less than six paces from me, resting her hands on her hips. Her full lips curved in a derisive smile.

'Now you see all of me!' she said.

This impudent observation was superfluous, since she wore nothing. But if she expected to embarrass me, she had forgotten that I was a doctor. I stared at her coldly, as I might have stared at a subject in the dissecting room.

'Call your followers!' I said curtly. 'I am armed and ready for them. Let them try to take me, and I will shoot you there and then.'

She laughed, and shook her head violently, as a dog shakes itself, showering me with icy drops.

'Nobody is here,' she answered softly, and took another step forward, 'Ahmad gone back after he bring you. We are alone. Why don't you kiss me?'

I turned away deliberately and seated myself with my back to the cliff, feigning indifference, but still watchful. To my horror, I remembered that my pistol was in the pocket of the sports jacket which I had dropped halfway up the beach when reaching for the field-glasses.

Zarmi regarded me silently, frowning. She sat down on the sand, picked up a piece of seaweed – a weird thing, composed of a thick stalk and a cluster of long, ribbonlike streamers – and toyed with it idly, tearing off the leaves till nothing remained but the tough, rubbery stem.

'You are angry with me, because I make a fool of you last time,' she said petulantly. Her eyes blazed. 'All right! I don't have a knife. This time, your turn!'

Springing, catlike, to her feet, she flung the plant stem across my knees, spun on her heel, and, to my astonishment, threw herself face down upon the sloping shelf of rock, with such force that I heard the smack of it against her flesh. She gasped, jerked back her head, and glared at me over her shoulder.

'Hit me!' she demanded.

I stared at her blankly, making no move to avail myself of the invitation, though God knows, I had reason enough. She was a priestess of evil, conjuring up all that is primitive and wicked in mankind. Shameful thoughts ran through my mind, confusing reason, while she lay sprawled upon the rough stone surface, as if offering herself for sacrifice on the altar of some pagan god, every sinew of her lithe frame tense and expectant – provoking and daring me to strike her. But as still I neither moved nor spoke, she straightened up slowly and turned again to face me.

'You are afraid,' she said scornfully, 'afraid if I scream.'

She stooped, snatching up the whiplike stem, and brought it down viciously across her thighs, raising a livid mark on her ivory skin.

'See?' she hissed. 'I am strong! Nothing make me scream – ever!'

'You have a strange way of amusing yourself,' I said hoarsely.

'Feel anything is good.' Zarmi frowned again and hesitated, finding the concept too difficult for her limited English. 'Feel happy – feel pain . . . Feel nothing is death. *Ya selám!*'

She shuddered, and spat hastily over her left shoulder to discourage any *Ifrít* which might have crept up on her – a futile gesture, I considered, since she was anything but a devout Moslem.

'What do you want with me?' I asked impatiently.

Zarmi smiled mysteriously.

'It is not enough because I come to you?' she murmured. 'Look at me! Be careful, my big, strong sailorman! Maybe I do something for you.' She stood silent for a moment, wringing the water out of her hair. 'I think about it. Give me a cigarette.'

It was hardly an answer to my question. I did not suppose that she had lured me here and swum a quarter mile out from her boat to ask for a cigarette. But her request was opportune.

'I have some in my coat,' I said, trying to speak casually. 'Will you hand it to me? It is there on the ground, behind you.'

If I went to get it myself, she might suspect . . . She glanced back, saw my jacket lying on the sand, and shrugged.

'I think you want to see me walk when I don't have skirt!' she said mischievously.

She turned and walked across the beach, swinging her hips insolently, picked up my coat by the collar, and, to my profound relief, brought it back to me, holding it up to her throat in a mockery of modesty. I took it from her thankfully, gave her the cigarette she wanted, lighted it for her, and folding the garment carefully, laid it beside me with the gun butt close to my hand. But now that I had it, I was not quite sure what I was going to do with it. Against my better judgement, I was half convinced that she spoke the truth: I was in no immediate danger of attack. I could take her prisoner, perhaps – but the prospect of a two-mile walk back to Coastguard Bennett's house with Zarmi clad solely in my jacket defeated my imagination.

For a longer period, she was silent again. She studied me with narrowed eyes, as though trying to make up her mind. Then, at last:

'Be nice to me,' she whispered, 'and I will save Smith!'

I gazed at her in amazement and open disbelief.

374

'You don't believe me,' she said reproachfully. 'All right. Wait. I show you.'

Holding the cigarette between her lips, she reached up under the dark masses of her hair. Wet, and hanging about her shoulders in long, straight strands, it lent her features a more dignified appearance than the frizzy style in which she usually wore it. I was conscious – more conscious than I wished – that she was wickedly attractive. Withdrawing her hands from her hair, she displayed a tiny glass phial of the kind used for medicines, corked and sealed with wax.

As she broke the seal, I watched her suspiciously, nervous of such objects in the hands of one who served Fu Manchu, and wondering what she might let out of it. Opened, it proved to contain only a rolled scrap of paper. She took it into her palm, unrolled it, and handed it to me without a word.

It was a page torn from a notebook, scribbled with several lines in the small cramped handwriting of Nayland Smith! Staring down at it incredulously, I read:

Petrie – I have only a minute, no time to explain. Zarmi will help me to escape. For God's sake don't fail me – Smith.

If it was a forgery, it was one more clever than I could believe possible. I knew Smith's handwriting as well as my own. It was his writing – his style. I looked up wonderingly at Zarmi.

'Why?' I asked, in an odd, unnatural voice.

She hesitated, licking her lips.

'I don't want to go to China,' she said sullenly. 'In China, woman is nothing. I want to stay here – have big motor car, pretty clothes, many men buy me things.'

Her reply left me speechless. I could not – dared not – believe her. Yet, the longer I thought about it, the more possible it seemed. Her reason was simple and ingenuous, uncomplicated by any attempt at subtlety. Zarmi was waiting eagerly, it seemed, for my answer.

'Still you don't trust me,' she muttered, 'don't believe I will be your friend. All right – try! I tell you anything – do anything you want. Try!'

I made no immediate response. Given the offer, I found that I did not know what to say. But the first question which came to my mind was neither of Smith nor of Fu Manchu.

'Where is Kâramanèh?' I asked.

'Always you ask of *her*!' Zarmi scowled, and bit her lip. 'Never mind. I tell you, like I say. She gone now – back to London on train. Very sleepy.'

My disappointment was alleviated by a sense of relief. Though beyond our reach, Kâramanèh was not, then, to be taken aboard the Chinese ship until after the meeting of the Seven.

'And Nayland Smith?' I said quickly. 'Where is he? Is he in the camp on The Worm?'

'Not yet. They bring him to-night.'

'Where is he now, then?'

'Don't know. We have many places here. I know of some of them. Not all.'

'How do you go out there?' I inquired, with some curiosity.

'Sometimes walk. Sometimes go in boat.' Zarmi inclined her head towards the fishing vessel lying at anchor. 'You see now. Very dirty boat, but very strong engine.'

'But you cannot land there!' I said, remembering what Trevor Bennett had told us.

'Don't know what you say. How you mean, land?'

'There is no beach,' I said trying to put it more simply. 'The boat cannot go close to the rocks.'

'No. Cannot do. Go up rope.'

I did not fully understand, but I doubted if she could explain more precisely.

'How many of you are there?' I pursued.

'Must think. *Wâhid, itneen* . . .' She counted on her fingers, bending them inwards, one by one, in the Asiatic fashion. '*Ishreen!*'

The reply startled me. Twenty! That was altogether more than we had expected.

'So many?' I said. 'I thought there were only a dozen.'

'First, yes. More stay after bring things from the big ship.'

'Bring things? From the Chinese ship?'

'Yes. Come three times.'

I was puzzled. From her words, it appeared that they were landing further supplies instead of loading them. I realised that we were still far from penetrating the secret of The Worm.

'Why?' I insisted. 'What is Fu Manchu doing there?'

Zarmi tossed the stub of her cigarette into a shallow pool between the rocks, where it expired with a hiss and a curl of smoke. She laughed and shrugged gracefully.

'How I should know that? Nobody ever know what he do.'

'You are staying out there too?' I asked.

'I stay there one week.' She laughed again, and her eyes sparkled. 'Sometimes I wear boy's clothes – very good for show my legs. But best like this, eh?'

Locking her hands behind her neck, she pirouetted slowly in front of me. I drew a deep breath, suppressing an angry retort. Nothing was to be gained by antagonising her.

'Give praise to Allah,' I said, 'who has seen fit thus to create you.'

That much I could say truthfully. But my grudging compliment produced altogether more of a response than I had anticipated. She clapped her hands delightedly.

'That is the first nice thing you ever say to me!'

Turning swiftly about, she sat down beside me with her long legs extended straight in front of her, and leaned up against me. Even the sea water had failed entirely to wash out the perfume of her hair – a hot, narcotic scent like the atmosphere of a Burmese temple, or such as I imagined it to be, since I had never been inside one.

'Be nice to me!' she repeated.

I looked sideways at her, still wondering. In an abstracted fashion, I noted that there was a large purple bruise just above her right knee, below the red mark of her self-inflicted injury.

'How did you get that?' I inquired.

Unthinkingly, and with professional detachment, I touched it lightly with my fingertips. But it was all the encouragement she needed. She reached over and covered my hand with her own, pressing it against her.

'Hurt myself, when I smash up truck,' she said cheerfully. 'When I see the fat policeman chase me, I laugh so much I can't drive straight.'

She bent forward, whipped my arm over her head and around her, and trapped my wrist under her elbow.

'Hold very tight!' she directed. 'Now we will be friends.' Resting her cheek against my shoulder, she turned up her eyes to my face. 'Smith is gentleman?' she asked anxiously. 'Always keep promise?'

'If Smith has promised you anything,' I said firmly, 'he will do it.'

'All right. Then I help.' Zarmi settled herself comfortably into my reluctant embrace. 'Afterwards, he make all right with police – give me money.'

It was plausible, I thought. Smith might have bribed her. But, under the present conditions, it was difficult to think clearly about anything. Zarmi sighed, slipped her right hand behind me, and, insinuating it neatly under my sweater, ran questing fingers up my spine.

'To-day, no shirt!' she murmured. 'Good!'

Her sensual teasing would have upset the composure of a Trappist monk. I gritted my teeth.

'Tell me how you plan to help Smith,' I said sternly.

'To-night there will be chance. To-night, I am boss. Everybody do like I say, while *el-Hakkîm* is asleep.'

'Asleep?'

'Not sleep like you and me. He is in *samadhi*.'

This I took to be a Sanskrit word meaning that Fu Manchu was in some sort of mystic trance. Zarmi's voice

378

sank to a husky purr, and, to my further discomfort, she alternated the caressing movement of her fingers with sharp digs of her pointed nails, in the manner of an affectionate but misguided cat. Everything about her was feline. With my arm around her, I felt the ripple of hard muscles under a skin textured like velvet.

'There is an old house on the big hill above the sea,' she went on dreamily. 'Nobody live in it. To-night they bring him there – bring Smith. Two men, I think. I will send them down to the beach to wait for boat. But boat don't come, because I don't order. I show you where to bring motor car, and make signal when men gone. Three flashes. Then, you come to the house – '

'Why?' I asked suspiciously. 'Why can't you bring Smith out to the car?'

'Cannot do alone. I don't see him since last week, but I think he still can't walk so good. Something gone wrong when they bring him from London. For too long time he is like dead man.'

I nodded. It was horrible to think of Smith in such a state, but this, at least, checked with what Kâramanèh had tried to tell us.

'Very well,' I said. 'I will come and help you. And then?'

'We go very quick to town, and you put me in lock-up. I don't mind lock-up. I stay there till they are all gone back to China.' Zarmi shifted suddenly, detached herself, and sat up, looking at me with a hint of fear in her lustrous eyes. 'Must be very careful. Only you and me. If you try to bring policemans, they know. I think somebody in village is watching you.'

Again I nodded. I did not much like the idea of acting alone, but she was probably right.

'Maybe somebody watch me too,' she said, and shivered. 'I take big chance for you. If *he* catch me, you know what he do to me?'

She put her lips to my ear, and whispered unspeakable things which brought the hot blood to my cheeks, and which, I thought, would have shocked Dr Fu Manchu.

379

'You need have no fear,' I said stiffly. 'I will come alone. How shall I find the house?'

'Easy to find. Presently, I draw map for you.' Zarmi gave a long sigh, and fell back across my lap, raising her knees at an acute angle. 'First we do kissing – just like you kiss *her*. . . .'

I stared down into her beautiful, evil, face, remembering her savage temper, and wondering what Sherlock Holmes would have done. She was a temptress skilled in the arts which have made Man the plaything of Woman since the days of Eve. But if Nayland Smith's freedom was to be had at the price of a few kisses, had I the right to refuse? She stretched up her arms to me, and a certain amount of diplomacy became necessary before the conversation could be usefully resumed.

At length, picking up my jacket, I furnished Zarmi with a sceond cigarette, then took out a pen and notebook.

'Draw your map for me,' I requested.

'Plenty of time. I don't have to go back yet.'

I made no reply, and she gave me a long, sad look.

'You are a big, strong man,' she said scornfully, 'but you are a fool!'*

When Zarmi had returned to her boat as she had come, I made my way up through the valley and began the long trek across the cliffs, my thoughts in confusion. Once out of her bewitching presence, I was already assailed by doubts. She had answered all my questions frankly and without reserve. Yet, when I came to think about it, had she told me anything that could be useful to us? Dared I trust her?

She was utterly faithless – I knew that – but, in the last resort, she might be equally faithless to Fu Manchu. The brief note from Nayland Smith was compelling evidence, if it was not forged. Could he have been made to write it under hypnosis? Knowing my friend's iron will, I did not

* Dr Petrie ends this scene somewhat abruptly, leaving the reader to wonder if he *was* such a fool! [Ed.]

believe that he *could* be hypnotised, even with the aid of drugs. In the final analysis, it was not really a question of whether or not I dared trust Zarmi, but a fact that while any hope of rescuing Smith existed, I dared not distrust her.

In my present state of mind, I took no account of time, and, when I ultimately reached the village, I was startled to observe that it was five o'clock. My adventure had occupied far longer than I thought, and I found my hosts anxious about me because I had missed lunch. I explained briefly that I had been out walking on the cliffs and lost my way. Mr Gwynn gave me a dubious glance and remarked that I looked as if I had been dragged through a hedge backwards, which was not far from the truth. What with battling my way through gorse and brambles, scrambling over rocks and boulders, and fooling about on the wet sand with Zarmi, my light clothes were soiled, torn, and minus a few buttons.

I went up to my room, changed into cleaner and tougher things, and, refusing the offer of an immediate meal, went out again. I had less than two hours daylight in which to survey the ground which I must cover after dark. Zero hour was ten o'clock.

It was unnecessary to take the car, although I should be doing so later. The distance was not great. I walked up the steep hill to the corner where the post office stood and where I was now more or less on a level with the high ridge overlooking the bay. With the aid of the sketch map in my notebook, I soon located the lane, and followed it for some way till it terminated in a rickety gate. A hundred yards beyond, the property which it had once served was plainly visible, standing alone on the brow of the hill – a tumbledown cottage, surmounted by the remnants of a thatch like the worst nest that any bird ever made.

It was obviously deserted, and looked to have been so for half a century. Up here, the wind blew more strongly than ever; cultivation of any sort must have been difficult in so exposed a spot – which, perhaps, was why the place had been long since abandoned. One small, square window faced the gate where I was standing, and, using the field-glasses, I noted that it appeared to be boarded up on the inside. Zarmi had suggested that I should come up and see it, so as to be sure of my way later, but cautioned me against going any nearer, in case my movements were covered.

I wondered who, if anyone, could be covering me, and thought again of Dr Reinhardt. He, however, seemed more anxious to avoid me. A new idea crossed my mind. Fu Manchu had kidnapped Randall, the mathematician, and presumably made use of him. Might not Dr Reinhardt be some scientist in league with the Si Fan, who had been summoned to assist in their nefarious operation?

Now that Holmes had left me to my own devices, I was appalled to discover how much I had come to rely upon him. Wishing urgently that he might return in time to counsel me, I retraced my steps to the cottage, told Mr and Mrs Gwynn that I should be leaving after dinner, and went upstairs to pack. If all went according to plan, Nayland Smith and I would spend the night in Swansea; if all did not, I reflected grimly, I should probably need no accommodation anywhere.

I dined without appetite, too excited to notice what I ate, and eating only in order to fortify myself for the night's work. Still there was no word from Holmes, and at eight o'clock, I took my leave, somewhat to the regret of my hosts, who did not fancy being left for the rest of the week with Dr Reinhardt. I gathered that he was booked to stay till Saturday, but, as on the previous evening, he remained mysteriously absent and I saw no more of him.

Coaxing the car out of the cowshed with some difficulty in the dark, assisted and misdirected by the encouraging shouts from Mr Gwynn, I made an ostentatious departure, the engine waking the echoes as the Standard roared up the hill. This was intentional. If Dr Reinhardt was lurking about somewhere with his formidable night-glasses, or if some other watched, I was anxious to give the impression that I had gone back to Swansea. Passing the entrance to the lane which I was later to visit, I drove as far as Middleton and stopped at Coastguard Bennett's house.

I intended to disregard Zarmi's instructions to the extent of taking one companion with me – if I could find one – and, in the absence of Sherlock Holmes, Trevor Bennett was my only hope. But I was doomed to disappointment. Megan informed me that her husband was still at Port Eynon and had telephoned to say that he would be home late. Now I was really alone. I dared not attempt to get in touch with him, or with Superintendent Gribbler, for I felt sure that the solitary telephone line out from the village would be under surveillance.

Megan Bennett, knowing something of our problems, and curious to know more, invited me in. If she had not done so, I should have asked her, anyway, since I needed an advance base from which to operate. I accepted a cup of tea and gave her a brief outline of my intentions. The result was that I had a hard time to dissuade her from accompanying me herself – she insisted that she could sit in the car and wait as well as her husband – but I was adamant. The idea of involving the coastguard's pert blond wife in an adventure of this nature was beyond justification. I pointed out cunningly that she could not drive, and would not be able to make a quick retreat if I failed to return, which she reluctantly agreed to be true.

Ten o'clock drew near, and I stood up resolutely. Megan accompanied me to the door, gave me a chaste peck on the cheek, and wished me good luck. I thanked her and told her that if I had made no further contact by midnight, she should call the police – a natural but useless precaution, for, if the plan misfired, a bullet or a knife in the back would doubtless have settled my affair in a matter of seconds. Henceforward, I must depend entirely upon the ingenuity and sincerity of Zarmi.

I drove back slowly down the road to the lane and

turned into it, hoping that my advent from this direction might escape the notice of any who had seen me leave the village. Good timing was essential. I must not arrive before Smith's captors had been sent down to the beach, nor arrive too long after they had gone. Reaching the gate at the end, I succeeded in turning the car – an awkward business, since the lane was narrow and unsurfaced – got out, and extinguished the head-lamps. Anyone who had seen them from the cottage should, I reasoned, be deceived into thinking that someone had entered the lane by mistake, and, on finding a cul-de-sac, driven out again.

A glance showed me that a light now burned in the cottage. The window had been unlocked, and it shone out also through the gaps in the roof – a bright, yellowish glare which flickered oddly, that of neither a candle nor an oil-lamp, and I wondered how it was produced. But so far, so good.

I took off my overcoat, not wishing to be burdened with it, and threw it into the back of the car. Inconspicuous in dark slacks and a heavy sweater, I stood by the gate watching intently, my electric torch ready in my left hand and the Browning pistol thrust into my hip pocket – a conventional place for it in fiction, but highly uncomfortable in practice. My heart beat wildly while I waited impatiently for the expected signal. Zarmi's plan had the virtue of simplicity. The only fault I could find with it was that the two men who had brought Smith might see no logical reason why both of them should go down to meet the boat. But, against this, as Holmes had often said, was the fact that Fu Manchu's servitors were more accustomed to obey orders than to reason. Probably, it would never occur to them to question her orders.

Why did she not give the signal? She must have seen the headlights of the car, must know that I was ready at my post. Were the others still there, or had they failed to arrive? Five minutes passed, seeming more like fifty – and then, at last, it came. The light from the window was blotted out as something was draped in front of it, uncovered, and blotted out again – three times.

I pointed the torch towards the cottage and pressed the switch once for the agreed answer. The gate creaked under my fingers, and I strode rapidly across the grass. I did not need the torch to guide me. The moonlight was brilliant – too brilliant, if an enemy should be watching. I had only a hundred yards to cover, and was halfway there when, like an astral warning, the doubt entered my mind, so suddenly that I almost pulled up short in my tracks.

If, as she had told me, Smith was scarcely able to walk, how had they brought him here? They could not have carried him far over the footpaths which alone crossed the open expanse of Rhossili Down. They must, then, have brought him by the same road that I had taken. But, in that case, where was their vehicle?

Slowing my eager steps, and wary again of a trap, I approached cautiously, making a wide detour to avoid being seen from the lighted window. The door of the place proved to be on the adjacent side; it stood ajar, outlined by a vertical streak cf light. I pulled out the pistol and thumbed off the safety catch. Nayland Smith had long ago told me how to enter a suspected premises. I took the last twelve paces at a run, kicked the door violently inwards, so that anyone standing behind it might have the full benefit of it in his face, and burst into the room beyond.

Garishly lighted by a naptha flare, like those used in a fairground, it was a ruin of fallen laths and plaster, and there, face down upon the littered floor, lay Zarmi, wearing the striped skirt which I had seen her wear in, Pentrefdu, and some sort of flimsy undergarment which left her shoulders bare. Her hair was spread out in a cloud and her face turned away from me.

I started towards her with a cry. But ere I had taken six steps, my ears caught a soft sound behind me, and a heavy blow across my wrist sent the pistol skittering into a corner. It went off as it fell, and the bullet whined

385

dangerously close to my head. I spun around and leapt back.

Before me stood a grossly fat man, olive-skinned, exotically garbed in baggy trousers and a kind of waist-coat. One glance was sufficient, and I *knew*. This was 'Ali of Istanbul, the torturer of women, and between his outstretched hands he held the deadly instrument of his office – the bow-string.

33

FLIGHT

Retreat was impossible. 'Ali stood between me and the open doorway, through which he must have entered silently behind me, and in his beady, coal-black eyes I read my death sentence. I was to die, swiftly and ignominiously, as hundreds had died in the Osmanli dungeons.

He moved ponderously, ominous, but slow on his feet, and I met his advance with a hard left and right to the body, half expecting him to collapse like a pricked balloon, but nothing of the sort happened. It was like punching a feather pillow, and about as effective. I side-stepped, and tried for a straight left to the chin – but the man *had* no chin! My fist sank harmlessly into the rolls of fat joining his head to his body. I side-stepped again, and, simultaneously, Zarmi, whom I had thought dead or unconscious, bounded to her feet with a harsh laugh, struck me behind the knees and sent me reeling up against my opponent.

My deception was complete. I battered at him furiously but helplessly. This was 'Ali, who had punished Kâramanèh, cruelly and expertly, for her attempt at escape – the fiend whom I had longed to meet, and now that I did so, I knew the mortification of finding myself outmatched. In a trice, the bow-string was thrown about my neck and drawn tight – a thin, devilish thing, no thicker than a pice of twine, cutting deep into my skin with the burning agony of a knife.

Zarmi seized my arms above the elbow, dragging them behind me, needlessly to hinder my resistance. To say that I gasped for breath would be inaccurate; so neatly did the eunuch perform his dreadful task that not even a gasp was possible. My lungs fought to draw in air, to expel the air that was in them. One does not last long like that. My eyes wide open and streaming, stared up into the lurid glare of the hissing naptha flare and were blinded.

There was a sullen roaring in my ears and, as conscious slipped from me, I re-lived that strange, prophetic dream – of Zarmi strangling me with a string of emeralds. . . .

Re-awakening came first with an awareness of pain, then of my own identity, next a feeling of surprise that I was still alive. Reason returned more slowly with the knowledge that I could not have been senseless for more than a few minutes: strangulation to unconsciousness is quickly followed by death. An acrid stinging in my nostrils suggested that some crude restorative such as ammonium hydroxide had been administered. My eyes were watering and my inflamed throat was paining me so acutely that it was difficult at first to make out where I was or in what condition. I was no longer inside the house but in darkness – a darkness which gradually resolved itself into moonlight – and somehow caught up in a swinging, thudding movement.

The fresh air helped to revive me and when I realised the truth I was hardly surprised that I had been long about it – for I was being carried, slung head downwards across a man's shoulder, my wrists fastened behind my back, and my ankles lashed together. Bearing my weight with no apparent effort, he was walking towards the steepest part of the hill, a few hundred yards beyond the cottage. Later – much later – it occurred to me that he was probably the tall man who had assisted in the abduction of Nayland Smith, and whom we never identified.

He halted, and I was thrown down roughly upon the ground. Though I could breathe now, it was impossible to think clearly, each rasping intake of breath being accompanied by excruciating pain in my swollen throat. A horde of half-seen, half-clad figures swarmed about me in the semi-darkness – dacoits. I suppose that there

388

could have been no more than four or five, but they came and went rapidly about their business, flitting in and out of my vision like shadows out of hell, so that they seemed numberless. They clutched at my body, rolling me over, and began to swathe me from head to foot like an Egyptian mummy, in thick, strong bandages.

The purpose of this strange operation was not apparent and the insane thought flashed though my mind that I had been resuscitated only in order to be buried alive. I had a glimpse of a more distant figure, so grotesquely hideous that it might have been that of the dwarf-god Bes – an apelike creature with the head cocked sideways on a giant's shoulders, one held above the other. Then he moved out of sight.

Winding a turban of bandages about my head, but leaving my face uncovered, my captors bound me yet again, with some kind of harness, drawing the straps so tight that breathing was still further restricted. Nightmare became one with reality. Outspread above the hard edge of the skyline I saw the wings of a gigantic, batlike shape, and knew the truth, succeeded by a wave of sheer, cowardly terror.

I was to be carried out to The Worm by means of the kite!

In my preoccupation with Smith's danger, I had forgotten my own – ignored the warning of Dr Fu Manchu. '*If I find that I can acquire your services without inconvenience to myself, I shall do so.*' For a brief moment, wounded pride overcame panic, and I felt a surge of indignation prompting me to struggle against my bonds, though I could not move a finger. I was considered as nothing but an extra item of luggage, picked up, contemptuously, at the last minute.

Hands seized me again and hauled me across the grass. By straining my eyes upwards to the limit, I could just make out the great black silhouette of the kite looming above and behind me – twenty feet or more from tip to tip, and now less like the wings of a bird than like the triangular sail of a yacht, shuddering in the wind.

The canvas, or whatever it was made of, flapped and vibrated, emitting sharp popping sounds; a network of ropes held it to the ground. I heard what I took to be the voice of Wang Lo, shouting orders, but I could not see him.

Zarmi appeared beside me, casually trailing from one hand an embroidered blouse which, typically, she had not yet troubled to put on. I suppose that she had removed it to add a touch of dramatic colour to her treachery. The moonlight gleamed on her arms and shoulders as she bent over me.

'Fool! You think kisses make promises?' she hissed. With no slightest provocation, she slapped me hard across the face and laughed. 'Never mind – I make it up to you when we go on the big ship. Bye-bye!'

I was conscious of a shout, a tremendous jerk at my body, as Wang Lo launched himself out into space. Then I was free of the earth and falling. I saw the beach and its rushing waves – then, miraculously, the kite lifted and soared up into the night. It is still a mystery to me how he could sail it *into* the wind. Those who understand these things have tried to explain that it was necessary to get the kite aloft, but I could never see why it was not simply blown backwards. Suffice that it was not.

I did not think about it then. All thought was impossible. In the years since, I have flown in aeroplanes and smiled at the nervousness of my fellow passengers – for the horror of that first flight will be with me all my life. Swinging back and forth on the harness to which I was attached, I was neither more nor less than the tail of Wang Lo's abominable kite. Higher and higher it rose – a thousand feet, two thousand, I do not know – till all sense of height was lost. For the most part, nothing was visible but the sky and the stars. When chance enabled me to look downwards, the sea was like a relief map, frozen and unmoving.

We were heading straight out across the bay, and, though logic told me that I was being kidnapped, I could not rid myself of the fear that at any instant I might be released and cast down to destruction, like the sheep and the farm labourer. An age seemed to pass while Wang Lo explored the upper couches of the atmosphere, no doubt searching for some current of air which would take him in the direction he wished to go. From my pendent position, I could not look directly upwards – could not see the kite itself. I seemed to be floating alone in the firmament.

When the turn was made, I was unaware of it, but presently I saw the serpentine shape of The Worm – and, beyond it, the grey outline of the Devon coast, and the flashes of the lighthouse on Lundy Island. Though, in fact, it was no less swift, the descent from so great a height appeared gradual till the last few hundred feet. Then, all at once, we were hurtling down with the speed of an express train towards the Inner Head and I saw it as I had never seen it before – a perpendicular wall worn smooth by wind and sea, glittering like polished obsidian, the waves seething about a saw-toothed line of rocks below.

Again I was conscious of the wind upon my face, and a new fear took possession of me: we should be dashed against the cliff. But, at the last moment, we passed smoothly above it and then struck the ground with a shock adequate to break my legs, but for the protective wrappings. I rolled over and over, dragged across a hard, grassy surface, and came to rest more dead than alive.

Hands snatched at my body, unfastening the harness. Two men – dacoits – were kneeling beside me, parting the mummy-like bandages with deft slashes of their murderous knives, swiftly but so neatly that not a scratch was inflicted upon me. Turning my head sideways, as movement became possible, I saw the luminous wedge-shapes of half a dozen tents with lights burning inside. There were none of the big, round sort usually seen in a Boy Scouts' camp; it was more like the camp made by hunters on a safari.

I felt the chill of steel upon my wrists and looked down to find my hands manacled in front of me with handcuffs of an unfamiliar pattern, linked by a six-inch chain. The dacoits hauled me upright, and holding me under the arms – for I could not walk – frog marched me towards the group of tents, my feet trailing uselessly. They ducked under the flap of the nearest, and flung me down upon a camp bed. Breathing remained difficult, and swallowing almost impossible. Half choked and hovering on the verge of unconsciousness, I was dimly aware of an angry altercation conducted in a language which I could not identify – though one of the voices seemed curiously familiar.

My head swam and I think I lost my senses again – for my next impression was of a figure bending over me, and I looked up into the anxious eyes of Nayland Smith.

'Smith!' I whispered.

'Don't try to talk,' he said, restraining my efforts to sit up. 'It's not so many weeks since I had a strangler's cord around *my* throat, but at least I was spared the bowstring. Here – ' He raised his hands, which, I saw, were chained like mine, fumbling awkwardly with a glass-stoppered phial, and succeeded in extracting some pale green tablets. 'Slip one of these things under your tongue; it will ease your throat. Lie still and relax.'

I followed his direction. The sub-lingual tablet had a pleasant flavour, reminiscent of lime juice and honey, and a subtle, soporific perfume in which I suspected a trace of opium. Pain gave place to a sense of lethargy, and my eyelids closed. A short period of natural sleep usually follows an unconsciousness induced by drugs or injury – it is Nature's restorative.

It seemed to last only a minute, but when I re-opened my eyes the tablet had dissolved and my throat was no longer constricted. I could breathe normally, and though my neck still smarted with the burn of the bow-string, I was in full possession of my senses. Nayland Smith sat on a canvas stool beside me, attired in the same grey suit which he had worn in London, and which still looked surprisingly fresh.

'How long have I slept?' I asked.

'About thirty minutes,' he replied. 'Better?' And, as I nodded: 'Dr Fu Manchu's remedies are as effective as his poisons, fortunately. I have had a few of both.'

I struggled upright and swung my feet to the ground, experiencing a momentary nausea which passed off rapidly. The slanting roof of the tent was just high enough to enable us to sit without bending.

'Smith!' I said again, grasping his hands. 'Thank God you are alive and well. That she-devil told me you were ill!'

'So I was!' he rapped. 'Up to a week ago.' Although slightly hoarse, his voice had lost nothing of its incisive quality. 'She lied to you – but a good liar sticks mostly to the truth.'

'She tricked me,' I said bitterly. 'She had a note which I could have sworn was in your handwriting – '

'It was! I wrote it for her last week.' He looked at me strangely and with a trace of embarrassment. 'I *helped* them to trap you! But I don't think you will blame me when you know the circumstances. You have seen the Wire Jacket used on a man. Can you imagine its effect upon a woman?'

For an instant I stared at him uncomprehending, then drew a quick breath.

'Oh, my God!' I said unsteadily. Kâramanèh?'

'They had it on her, Petrie.' The grim set of his lips softened to a smile. 'Oh, don't worry! I capitulated before the screws were tightened. What else could I do?'

'Nothing,' I said, and added fervently, 'Thank Heaven that you did!' I shrugged, endeavouring to appear more nonchalant than I felt. 'Well, it is not the first time we have been captives together.'

Smith laughed – a short, mirthless bark. 'The fifth, I fancy – but it may well be the last. Three times, it was Kâramanèh who came to the rescue; once, Ryman and his river police. But Kâramanèh has been sent back to London, and this is far from being the Thames.'

'Nevertheless,' I said hopefully, 'we may not be entirely without help. There are others on the shore, who know where we are. And Sherlock Holmes is here – '

'Yes, I know.'

'You knew?'

'Three weeks ago!' Smith smiled again, though his eyes remained grave. 'I was in the room on the other side of the ivory screen, when you had your meeting with Fu Manchu.'

Save for that slight hoarseness, as though he suffered from a cold, his voice was as strong as ever. But, studying him and taking stock, I saw that his clothes hung loosely upon him. He was lean to the point of emaciation, and though nothing could bring pallor to that tropically bronzed skin, his clear-cut features were as sharp and angular as those of Sherlock Holmes.

'You are as thin as a rake!' I said anxiously. 'For Heaven's sake – what have they done to you?'

'Oh, I have had the best of treatment – the very best, in fact.' The wry smile hovered, unquenchably about his lips. 'Really, I have nothing to complain about – apart from a lack of anything to smoke.'

It was my turn to force a smile. 'Perhaps I can do something about that,' I said, and, delving into my left trouser pocket – awkwardly, because of the manacles – fished out his cracked and blackened briar. 'I have been carrying this around with me ever since Holmes and I left Fleet Street.'

Nayland Smith took it with an amazed expression on his face.

'Petrie, you are incredible!' he murmured. 'Who else in the world would have thought of such a thing? Now, if you happen to have some tobacco on you . . .'

Luckily, I had. I found that I had left my matches in my overcoat, but having filled his pipe, Smith contrived to light it by raising the glass of the hurricane lantern attached to one of the tent poles.

'Tell me what has been happening to you,' I urged.

'Since you have Holmes on the job,' he replied, 'you may well know more about that than I do! You know, of course, how I was attacked and taken from our apartment?'

'Yes, we found out that much.'

'It was a good fight while it lasted, till one of the devils got a hypodermic needle into me, and that was the end of it.' Smith looked down at his hands, flexing his fingers in a curious fashion, as though testing them. 'When I woke up, I was lying on an iron bedstead, tied hand and foot. I stayed there, more or less in the same state, for five days, looked after – if you can call it that – by a hideous old hag like the Witch of Endor, who never spoke a word. I guessed that I was still in London, because, sometimes, I heard the sound of traffic – motor horns. Apart from the bed, there was nothing else in the room, but there were bars on the window, and I thought it had very likely been a nursery, on the top floor of one of those old Regency houses, somewhere north of Hyde Park. Probably it was the same place that you were taken to, when you saw Ki Ming, and which Weymouth is looking for – unless he has already found it, that is.'

'No. Not yet.'

'Well, if it was, it must not be too far off Portman Square. They were anxious, evidently, to prevent me from shouting for help. They couldn't keep me gagged the whole time without suffocating me, but they had a better way. Every night, the old witch hung a queer-shaped lamp over my head – a damnable contrivance which burnt with a blue flame and produced a vapour which robbed me of the power of speech! One of Fu Manchu's less pleasant devices. I wondered why they didn't dose me immediately with his cataleptic stuff, but, later on, I found out. . . .'

Listening to his narrative, I had almost forgotten that we were prisoners. Smith, puffing contentedly at his pipe, was as calm and seemingly unconcerned as if we had been comfortably seated in our rooms in Fleet Street.

'I don't know how or when they finally administered it,' he went on, after a moment, 'and, as to what happened later, I know only what Dr Fu Manchu has chosen to tell me. It appears that a victim of *F. katalepsis* may be under its influence for only a relatively short period. Kâramanèh's brother was subjected to it for some months, but, as you no doubt remember, revived at regular intervals. The ship in which, apparently, I was brought here was delayed, and I went two days past the safe limit. They had a devil of a job to restore me to consciousness, and, when they did so, I was paralysed!'

'Good God!' I muttered.

'I could see and hear – nothing more.' Nayland Smith spoke quietly, but the horror of the experience was reflected in his eyes. 'Fu Manchu was solicitude itself; he exercised all his skill. Oh, I am not that valuable!' He laughed shortly. 'He has taken me only to spite Ki Ming, but you know his colossal pride, Petrie. If it suited him, he would murder me as readily as he has often tried to do in the past, but he could not bear to have me die by accident! For nearly three weeks, I was treated daily with injections, and with some kind of electrical apparatus. It was almost impossible to keep track of time. In fact, I am still not sure . . .'

'It is Tuesday,' I said. 'The last day of March.'

Smith shook his head dazedly. 'It's been seven weeks, then, since I was last a free man! Yet, by the change in the weather, I thought it might have been even longer. . . .' He hesitated, then continued: 'Fu Manchu had to keep me with him, in order to give me his personal attention. We travelled a good deal, in a motor van which was half an ambulance, with a cot bolted to one side like a ship's bunk. The number and the variety of the places which he has available is remarkable. Once we were in a crypt, and once in a cave. . . . Eventually, though I can't say I was conscious of any change, he seemed satisfied and I was transferred to a sanatorium – a bona-fide establishment, staffed by doctors and nurses who have no idea that it is financed and controlled by the Si Fan! Li King Su brought me there as his patient, acting in the rôle of a visiting physician.'

Outside the tent, visible through the open flap, I saw one of the dacoits squatted upon the ground, rocking himself gently back and forth – chewing something and, at the same time, mumbling a monotonous refrain. England seemed far distant. With the low canvas roof stretched above our heads, it seemed to me, rather, that Smith and I sat in some encampment among the Shan hills.

'I was kept in that place for another week,' he went on, 'and when recovery came at last, it was swift. I woke one morning to find that I could move my hands. An hour later, I could move my arms up to the elbow, and by nightfall all my limbs were under control. My first thought, naturally, was of escape. I dared not wait till Li King Su made his next examination. Though I was watched all the time, I took them by surprise, and burst out of the room – and I almost made it. But before I could get out of the building, I was seized and restrained by the regular staff, who thought I was mad! By the most ironical trick of Fate, I could use my arms and legs, but I was still unable to speak!'

Smith broke off long enough to refill his pipe, though it was still hot, twisted a page of his notebook into a spill, and ignited it from the lantern.

'It may add something to your medical knowledge to learn that a man paralysed from top to toe can still feel a craving for tobacco!' he remarked. 'Ah! That's better! Well – after that, there was no further chance, of course. They shifted me again, next day to a farmhouse, and a couple of days later – a week ago, to be exact – brought me out here in a fishing boat. Or, rather, something disguised as a fishing boat.'

'I have seen it,' I said, thinking of Zarmi.

'Oh, have you? It's a shallow-draught vessel, very fast – something like the craft used by up-to-date slavers – and packed with equipment which would be worth a fortune to the navy. They can bring her in within two hundred yards of the big cliff at the seaward end of this thing – the Outer Head, as they call it. They work mostly in the dark, but they have some sort of supersonic device which tells them both the depth and their distance off the rocks.'

I nodded, and shivered slightly, remembering that I had encountered other supersonic devices less beneficent in the hands of Fu Manchu.

'But how do they land?' I asked.

'Roughly by the same gear used for rescuing people from a ship stranded close to the shore. In the remote face of the cliff – which can be seen only from the sea – there are two small caves, one somewhat above the other, and about halfway down to the high-water mark. They have a light, but permanent, line running down from the upper cave and underwater to a small buoy – a glass float filled with some phosphorescent material, so that they can find it easily. By this means, they haul up a heavier line, and fix up a ropeway. And then, up you go! It's an uncomfortable and somewhat undignified business, swaying about in a sort of canvas sling, but it works. Above that, they've rigged up a framework of those crazy bamboo scaling ladders which they use in the Far East, going up to the top of the pinnacle.'

'Smith,' I said earnestly, 'what are they doing here? What is the secret of The Worm?'

My friend looked at me long and gravely before replying. Then:

'I don't know,' he said slowly. 'All I know is this: They have something here – something of such power that even Dr Fu Manchu is afraid of it – and they plan to use it to-night. . . .'

34

THE DEVIL'S BRIDGE

Nayland Smith stood up, folding himself neatly beneath the pointed roof of the tent like a man used to living under canvas.

'Let us go out for a short walk,' he suggested. 'The air will do you good.'

'Will our captors allow us?' I asked doubtfully.

'Yes. They will follow us around, of course – and cut us down at a second's notice, if we attempt anything – but otherwise we are free to do as we please.'

He stepped outside. The dacoit raised his head, baring his teeth like a watchdog. With his wild eyes, his unkempt, matted hair, and the brand of Káli burned upon his brow, he looked as bestial a creature as any who had ever trod the hills of Wales in the pre-dawn of civilisation.

Smith spoke to him curtly in his own language, with the authorative tone of an Anglo-Indian addressing a servant. The dacoit rose and moved aside. Another appeared silently out of the shadows.

'What did you say to him? ' I inquired.

'Merely that we wished to take a stroll,' he answered, laughing at my surprise. 'These brutes will obey orders from anyone who can give them in Burmese, so long as they do not conflict with those of Fu Manchu. Just ignore them, and you will come to no harm – but avoid sudden actions, or they may set upon us.'

He moved off, turning away from the camp, the dacoits following at our heels. Now that at last I stood upon it, I saw that the razor-edge of the Inner Head – as it appeared from the shore – was a broad, flat table-land, not dissimilar from the clifftops upon which I had walked earlier in the day, save that here there were no bushes.

The cold glare of the full moon glittered on the thick carpeting of tough sea grass, making it appear like spears of blue-green glass.

'Look!' said Smith, and pointed. 'It will not be long now. We are the only ones up here.'

No lights were burning in any of the tents but that which we had left.

'Where have they all gone?'

'To the Outer Head, to await the awakening of their lord.' Smith spoke in a flat, factual tone, as though fearing disbelief. 'He is out there now on the top of the pinnacle, sitting on a great upright chair like a throne – as he has sat for the past forty-eight hours, muffled up in an overcoat and an astrakhan cap, in a sleep nearer to death than to life . . .'

I started, recalling what Zarmi had told me. Yet such ascetic exercises seemed to me scarcely consistent with what I knew of Fu Manchu.

'Why?' I asked puzzled.

'Because he is not, in his own eyes, a criminal but a messiah! His gods are the immutable principles of the universe, as Chinese philosophy perceives them – the supremacy of left over right, male over female, East over West. He wishes to assure himself that his motives are tinged with no human frailty or personal ambition, for to-night he will tamper with cosmic forces.'

'In Heaven's name, what does he intend to do?'

'I have no more idea than you, Petrie.' Smith shook his head. 'But I can form some estimate of the power which he has at his command. The upper cave, where the ropeway terminates, is like the interior of a gigantic wireless set. It is filled to the last inch with racks of huge storage cells – not the kind which we use in our pocket torches, but the other type, which will release all their energy in a single burst. You have seen the Blow Hole, I take it?'

'You mean the cavern where the sea is forced out through an opening high up in the rock?'

'Yes, that is it. Well, I believe that he has found some

400

way of harnessing that force to charge these things, like an enormous generator. It has been running, night and day, for weeks, till now he has the power of lightning itself stored up there. When it is released, it will all go in a few seconds to some apparatus which he has in the lower cave – which I have not seen – and what it will do, I tremble to imagine.'

As we walked unhindered across the grass, the illusion of freedom was almost complete, bringing back memories of nights when we had strolled over the common opposite my old premises in South London. But the chain swinging between my wrists reminded me otherwise, and, glancing back, I noted the lean, shadowy forms of our dreadful escort, their knives ready.

'Philip Randall!' I said suddenly. 'He had a hand in all this!'

'Eh?' jerked Smith. 'Who?'

'Randall – the mathematician. The man they brought out here. Did you see him?'

'Oh! Yes, I did. But it was hardly an occasion for introductions.' Smith lapsed into silence for a moment. 'A grotesque episode,' he muttered, 'absurd and, at the same time, horrible.'

'What happened?' I persisted.

He looked at me, the old, ironical smile plain upon his lips in the brilliance of the moonlight.

'It doesn't affect the issue, but I will tell you, if you like. It was the second day after I came here, and I suppose that Dr Fu Manchu must have come afterwards, for I didn't see him when I arrived. In fact, I have seen him only twice. He stays on the Outer Head, since the passage over the rocks is too much for him. At all events, on that particular morning, I was summoned into his presence, where I found this man – Randall? – in a hysteria of rage and terror. He had been kidnapped and brought here as the result of a trivial accident more than a month previously, which had jeopardised the whole success of their operation. One of the dacoits had dropped a box containing a sensitive instrument and damaged it.'

401

'Could not Fu Manchu repair it himself?'

'Oh, yes! He could, and he had. But he could not *reset* it, since even Dr Fu Manchu cannot be in two places at once! It was some kind of wireless affair, linked with another device aboard the Chinese ship, and the two parts could only be correlated by two operators, each of whom must have a working knowledge of higher mathematics.'

'I see!' I said slowly, wondering, as often during the past few weeks, why so simple an explanation had never occurred to me.

'Dr Fu Manchu politely requested me to assist him in explaining the situation and persuading Mr Randall to do what was required of him,' went on Smith, 'and, for his own sake, I did so. Still he hesitated, and it was then that the absurd became horrible. The wretched dacoit who had dropped the box was dragged forward, his hands struck off with a sword, and he was thrown from the pinnacle. The blood splashed on Randall's clothing, and he fainted. I didn't see him again afterwards, but I don't think he gave any further trouble.'

I glanced around again at the sinister figures trailing in our wake, and found it hard to repress a shudder.

'How can they serve a fiend who handles them in such a fashion?' I wondered aloud. 'They are fanatics!'

'It is not fanaticism in quite the sense you mean it,' answered my friend quietly, 'although it is true that blood lust is probably the only emotion which really arouses them. You do not understand the minds of these people, Petrie – and what European does? Even the word "identity" means to them oneness with something else. They have – and desire – no more will to control their own actions than my little finger.'

Regardless of our captivity and our danger, Nayland Smith seemed oddly more at home in this weird No Man's Land than he had ever done in London. He talked easily and confidently, as though he were showing me around some remote part of his territory north of the Chindwin River.

We had come to the landward extreme of the ridge, where the ground fell away steeply, marked with a clear path down to the sea level.

'We can go no farther,' he warned, halting and laying a hand on my arm. 'One step on that path, and we shall have them on our backs.'

Twelve hours had elapsed since I had last sat staring across the causeway from the opposite side. Now the wide L-shaped shoal lay revealed once more, stretching all the way over to the dark mass of the Rhossili cliffs – a highway to freedom, if we might but set foot upon it. But, as we stood and watched, I saw that the tide had already turned.

'We have less than two hours to get away from here,' I said urgently, 'but even by moonlight we could make the crossing in thirty minutes.' I looked back over my shoulder at the two dacoits, ranged one to either side of us and a few paces in the rear. 'There are only two of them . . . What do you say? Shall we make a run for it?'

'Impossible!' snapped Smith. 'They would have us before we could cover fifty yards. Man for man, in a fair fight, I think we might get the better of them. But while we have our hands fastened and they have their knives, we don't stand a chance.'

Anxious moments passed while he remained lost in thought and absent-mindedly tugging at the lobe of his left ear – the old, familiar habit now curiously awkward since he had to raise both hands in order to perform it.

'Time is running short!' he murmured. 'At any minute, he may send for us. He will wreak the havoc he has planned – whatever it may be – and make his escape. Zarmi has gone to take charge of the fishing boat. She will bring it round to take us out to the Chinese ship, and once we are aboard, we are done for. We shall be drugged out of our minds and turned into work slaves of the Si Fan. If we cannot find some way to free ourselves before then, there will be no hope later.'

I stared out helplessly at the distant shore. Out here, beyond the restless line of the surf, the ocean was as tranquil as the Mediterranean. Left and right, it scintillated in the moonlight, rippling across the boundaries of the causeway like the tidal waters of two great lakes. Above the sombre wall of the cliffs, no sign of human habitation was visible, save a solitary pinpoint of light – some isolated cottage, I thought, till, all at once, it dawned on me that it appeared where no cottage existed, and my heart skipped a beat.

'Do you see?' I exclaimed. 'There is a light in the coastguard's hut! Something is going on! No one is ever there after dark. Holmes has succeeded! He is back, and he has brought a raiding party with him!'

Now that I looked more closely, straining my eyes, I was almost sure that I detected other firefly lights coming and going about the brighter light in the lookout station.

'If so,' rapped Nayland Smith, 'he is leading them into a death-trap, unless he has a regiment of soldiers at his back! You know very well what an assault on any Fu Manchu's places can mean, and this is the most formidable stronghold he has ever had. God knows what his defences are! All the more reason why we must do something for ourselves . . . if we can – '

His speech was punctuated by a thin, piping note like the call of a night bird. I turned quickly, startled, and traced it to a small, square pendant hung around the neck of the man standing closest to me – an object which I had vaguely noted before and thought to be some amulet, like the *hegáb* of the Moslems. He looked at us, growled something in his strange language, and gestured fiercely with his knife.

'It is the signal,' said Smith tonelessly. 'Fu Manchu is calling us to join him.'

Hot rebellion welled up within me and I hung back for an instant, clenching my fists. But Smith gripped my arm, urging me into step with him.

'Come along, old man,' he said quietly. 'Let's choose some better moment to get ourselves killed. Fu Manchu has discharged his obligation to me, and given me fair

404

warning. If we resist, he will do nothing further to protect us.'

We had been in some tight corners, but none tighter than this, or more bizarre, I reflected, as we walked back towards the deserted camp, our footsteps dogged by savages who hated to wear more than a loincloth, who carried barbarous knives – and had telegraphic equipment beyond the knowledge of Western engineers.*

'They know their business,' observed Smith, with a glance over his shoulder. 'They are keeping just far enough back to make sure that we don't rush them before they can use their weapons.'

He said no more until we had reached the tents. Then:

'Are you game to stake everything on a single throw?' he demanded.

'Yes!' I said fervently. 'What do you suggest?'

'Our only chance – such as it is – will come when we cross the Devil's Bridge. Neither of us is afraid of heights.' Smith spoke calmly but tersely, clipping his words in the staccato fashion which he always adopted in moments of tension. 'There we shall go in single file. I shall go first. One of the dacoits will follow behind me, and the other behind you. Slow down, as far as you can, and try to get some distance between us. You understand?'

'Yes. And then?'

'When I give the word, double up and throw yourself backwards into the man's legs! You will knock him over, and with any luck, he will lose his knife. Fall on top of him, and keep him down. If you can do that, it will be enough. I am more used to this sort of thing than you are, and if I can dispose of my man, I will come to your assistance.'

It was a desperate plan, but clearly the only one which offered.

'The success of our attack will depend entirely upon speed and weight,' went on my friend, after a moment.

* At least, in 1914. [Ed.]

'We must use the technique of Asiatic swordsmen. You have seen how they fight? They watch each other for minutes, neither of them moving, till one springs at his opponent with a howl like a wild animal and strikes with the speed of a cobra.' Smith's voice took on a grimly humorous note. 'You needn't bother about the howl – one will do for both of us. But it is a sound, scientific part of the game, not just a warcry. It shocks the nerves, even when anticipated, and may give the attacker the split second that he needs to drive his blow home. So don't think I have gone berserk, and be ready for it. My yell will be your cue to act.'

'I shall be ready,' I promised.

We passed the last of the tents, gained the far end of the ridge, and, heedless of the two who came behind us, paused to look down at the remote half of The Worm. Few, I suppose, have first seen it under the chilly radiance of a full moon – none in such circumstances as ours. For all my preparedness, it was bigger – much bigger – than I had visualised it. The long mole of jagged rocks which we had first to traverse ran in a wide quarter circle to the outer islands, of which there now appeared to be three, though only two were visible from the shore. Seen from this side, the pinnacle no longer looked like a smooth-sided tower, but was more like a ruined pyramid, rising in three unequal stages to a queerly tip-tilted summit.

Smith raised both arms and pointed. 'There it is!'

He was pointing to the Devil's Bridge, which, hitherto, I had seen only through Coastguard Bennett's outsize binoculars. Outlined stark against the sky it linked the nearest island with the next, poised a hundred feet above the water, and, at a guess, fifty or sixty feet in length. At close quarters, the name ceased to be fanciful. A geologist would have described it as a natural arch, but there was nothing of the arch about it. The fearsome space beneath was harsh and angular, like the four sides of a box bent out of shape, giving it a peculiarly hellish appearance. Even in broad daylight, it would have been awesome, and my spirits quailed at the thought of staging a life-and-death struggle on that fearful catwalk, but I knew that we had no alternative.

We were allowed to linger only for a moment. The dacoits shouted and waved their knives threateningly, driving us down the steep slope to the rocks below.

'Watch your footing!' warned Smith.

Now we were upon that part of the way which Trevor Bennett had likened to a staircase on its side, or, I thought, a stack of dominoes scattered so that their edges lay in steps. It was not particularly dangerous, but exhausting, the going rendered harder beause of our fettered hands. Here we were at the lowest point – the long, scaly neck of the sea monster – with the incoming tide slapping and gurgling about the base of the rocks twenty or thirty feet beneath us. The dacoits, scrambling over with simian agility, did nothing to help – they were gaolers, not guides – and, in the half light, some caution was necessary. Here and there we were obliged to step over fissures, no wider than a broad pace but deep and treacherously hidden in shadow.

Already my legs were aching with the constant up-and-down work, and I wondered ruefully how my calf muscles would feel next day – then laughed insanely to myself as I remembered that, for me, there would very likely be no next day. In thirty minutes or less, the issue would be decided – and with that thought came another. Even if we succeeded in overcoming our captors, could we return before the causeway closed? The arduous passage across the tumbled rocks was taking far longer than I had estimated.

It was with a feeling of thankfulness that at last I looked up to see the first of the islands outstretched before me, even though I knew that each passing second brought me a step nearer to destiny. The uneven surface of the rocks gave place to solid earth and a reasonable path leading gradually upwards across a long green slope. The island beyond rose higher to a peak, shaped oddly like a volcano, concealing the

Outer Head, where Fu Manchu and his assembled forces waited.

'Take it easy!' ordered Smith, again grasping my arm. 'Get your breath back. In a few minutes more, we shall come to the Devil's Bridge.'

'What do you think of our chances?' I asked.

'Roughly, three to one against us.'

'Well,' I said, trying to muster such courage as I possessed, 'we have taken longer odds than that.'

The dacoits let us proceed at our own pace, no doubt deeming us Western weaklings incapable of sustained effort. We walked slowly, harbouring our strength. The path snaked up to the farthest and highest point of the island, from which the Devil's Bridge spanned the gap to the next. The hill hid it from our sight until we reached the top and saw it only yards in front of us, so placed that the sea beneath was invisible. It leaped across space, the right-hand side forming a horizon with the sky, the left terminating in a black cavern where the waves boomed hollowly, hinting at awful depths below.

Nayland Smith stepped out upon it, and, as he did so, one of the dacoits shouldered past me to range himself behind. Mindful of my instructions, I hesitated and drew back till the seond man, thinking me afraid, snarled something viciously in my ear and gave me a push forward. Despite its diabolical appearance, the bridge was wide enough for comfort, but too narrow for two to walk safely abreast. I moved obediently and looked back. The dacoit was directly behind me and closer than at any time before, the curved, swordlike blade swinging in his hand. Had they but had the sense to place the points of their knives at our backs, we should have been helpless, but, as I knew, their favoured style was to cut rather than to thrust.

Smith was a dozen paces ahead. My pulses raced, sending the adrenaline coursing through my veins, as I nerved myself to react instinctively to his lead. Now I, too, must think like a dacoit – think only of what I must do, careless of the result. I was halfway across; Smith had almost reached the end. I counted the seconds. But for the fact that I was ready and waiting for it, the hoarse, animal cry which burst from his throat would have frozen me in my tracks. I started, and converted my start into blind action – jack knifed, and catapulted myself backwards into the dacoit.

We went down together in a heap, and, to my intense relief, I heard his knife clatter upon the stones. I turned, still on top of him, pinning him down under my superior weight – clenched my hands together and tried to bring them down upon his forehead, but he twisted his head aside, snapping like a dog, and seeking to bury his fangs in my wrist. He was as slippery as an eel. I clutched his throat, seized the leather thong which held the signalling device slung around his neck, and attempted to draw it tight, to serve him as 'Ali had served me, but the steel fetters prevented me from parting my hands widely enough. The dacoit clawed at my eyes. I jerked my head back. He wriggled half from under me, and we rolled over.

Now he was on top, but I clutched again at his throat and secured a hold. In my new position, lying on my back, I could see the far end of the Devil's Bridge and the encounter taking place there. Smith had been less successful in his assault. He was down on his knees, and the dacoit upright, the leaf-shaped knife still gleaming in his hand. I saw it swing upwards and flash down in a savage, chopping stroke. But even as my heart stood still, Smith threw up his hands and caught the edge of the blade upon the chain stretched between his wrists – fell backwards and shot up his legs. His feet took the dacoit squarely in the midriff, hurling him back. The man staggered, tried vainly to regain his balance, and with an unearthly scream, pitched headlong into the abyss.

My opponent writhed to one side, sprawled half across me, his fingers digging into my arms as he sought to break my hold upon his throat. I held on but, suddenly, with a chill of horror, felt my feet flailing on space; I was nearly off the path, with my lower legs over the edge!

Smith came running towards us, bent – and checked himself, irresolute, realising the truth in the same moment that I realised it myself. It was only the dacoit's grasp upon my arms which prevented me from slipping down to destruction. If he tore the man from me, or knocked him unconscious, I should be precipitated into the void.

A timeless instant of terror followed, interrupted in so strange a manner that even terror was suspended. A wordless cry of fury rang out across the scene – so sharp and unexpected that all three of us turned our heads sideways.

There at the foot of the Devil's Bridge, stood Dr Fu Manchu, attired in his yellow robe, his arms raised above his head like a magician commanding the elements, and the moonlight glittering upon the coral ball which ornamented his black skullcap.

35

THE CATACLYSM

Never have I beheld a figure of such fiendishly supernal authority. The moonlight shimmered on the silken robe, bathing him in an aura of Satanic majesty, the wind whipping the thin material wildly about his gaunt frame.

Involuntarily, my fingers relaxed. The dacoit tore himself loose and stood up, facing his dread master. Panic returned as, inch by inch, I felt myself slipping, but Smith dived instantly, seizing my arms. Without his aid I had been lost, but with it, I was never in any real danger. It was unnecessary for him to drag me to safety; he had only to support me while I drew up my legs, gained purchase, and hauled myself up. Occupied with our own affairs, we took part in the conclusion of the drama only as spectators.

The dacoit stood crouched with his hands dangling, staring like a man hypnotised. Slowly and deliberately, Fu Manchu lowered his arms to shoulder level, till his extended fingers pointed straight at him, then jerked them downwards in a peremptory gesture. With the moonlight shining upon him, I saw a shadow of fear cross the man's face, succeeded by an expression which I can only describe as one of religious ecstacy.

'Si Fan!' he screamed – and turning, leapt far out from the bridge to join his comrade on the rocks beneath.

'*God in Heaven! They are maniacs!*'

It was a low, horrified cry in the voice of Sherlock Holmes – but it came from the man in the yellow robe! He hurried towards us, and as the light fell upon his features, I saw that they were not those of Dr Fu Manchu.

'Holmes!' I cried incredulously.

'I meant only to make him kneel, so that I might have

a better chance to disable him,' he muttered, his voice still tremulous with horror. 'But he interpreted my gesture to mean that he should destroy himself!'

'The Sheikh al-Jebal exercised the same power over the *Hashîshîn*,' said Smith evenly.

Holmes seemed by an effort to regain control of his emotions.

'Ah!' he said. 'Mr Commissioner Nayland Smith, I presume?'

They shook hands solemnly.

'I had long hoped to meet you,' murmured my friend. 'But I never thought I should be so glad to see you as I am now!'

In times such as this, Smith possessed the faculty of allowing nothing to surprise him. But I did not.

'Holmes!' I stammered. 'How in Heaven's name – '

He smiled. 'You were once kind enough to point out that I bore a superficial resemblance to Dr Fu Manchu. With the light behind me, I thought it might serve, if only for a moment.' He glanced down again into the gulf where the sea boomed over the common grave of the two dacoits, and shuddered. 'Quickly, now! Let us get away from this hell-begotten spot before we have the whole tribe of them after us.'

Suiting the action to the word, he strode off briskly up the slight acclivity to the crest of the hill. We topped the rise and commenced to descend the slope on the other side. A hundred questions boiled in my brain, but I had no immediate opportunity to ask them.

'Nothing has gone right to-night,' went on Holmes irritably. 'I have tried to do too much, and ended by doing too little.'

'But how – ' I began.

My query was cut short by an attack of an unexpected nature. A grey steak shot past me, and a tiny monkey sprang upon Holmes's shoulder, biting and scratching at his face. He uttered a short cry of pain and alarm, grabbed the creature by the scruff of its neck, and hurled it from him. It bounded up the slope to one side of the

412

path and turned at a safe distance, gnashing its teeth, whistling and chattering.

'Upon my word!' exploded Holmes, fingering his cheek. 'Is this damnable island infested with mad monkeys?'

'It is Fu Manchu's pet marmoset,' I said, remembering then that he had never seen it, 'and it knows that you have stolen its master's raiment.'

'Oh!' he snapped. 'Well, God forbid that it has the intelligence to go and tell him so! These ridiculous things have served their turn anyway, and it is time to get rid of them.'

He threw aside the skullcap and tore off the yellow robe – revealing beneath it the leather shorts and cross-strapped braces of Dr Hans Reinhardt. I stared foolishly.

'What!' I exclaimed. 'It was *you*?'

'Of course it was I!' he retorted. 'Did you not know? I dared not take you directly into my confidence – you are no better at keeping up a deception than Watson – but I gave you every chance to guess.'

We hurried on down the slope, leaving the enraged Peko bouncing up and down, and screaming vituperations, but, to my relief, making no attempt to follow us. Holmes's absurd shorts now looked doubly absurd, gathered about his waist in makeshift pleats, and, although I felt annoyed at the trick he had played upon me, I could not help laughing.

'You have lost some weight since we last met!' I said sardonically.

'Girth, but not weight,' he replied. 'One may obtain an interesting variety of stomachs by suitably tying a balloon. But it can be highly embarrassing if it bursts at the wrong moment.'

Returning more rapidly than we had come, and in vastly improved spirits, we arrived in a matter of minutes at the point where the path led out upon the rocks. Here, however, Holmes halted us once more.

'We shall make better time if we first get those chains

off your wrists,' he said, and directed us both to sit down. 'If I cannot do it in five minutes, I have lost my skill.' He thrust an electric torch into my hand. 'Hold the light for me, Doctor!'

It was the first time that he had called me 'Doctor' since we had been in the train from London, and again I found it hard not to smile at this queer Victorianism whereby he plainly meant to indicate that, from the moment of my reunion with Nayland Smith, our temporary partnership was dissolved. Holmes produced a large pocket knife and fanned out a useful selection of picklocks.

'An excellent implement,' he remarked, 'bestowed upon me by a true gentleman in his profession, who said that he would have no further use for it where he was going. . . .'

While I trained the light on my friend's hands, Holmes set about the locks, and, by a few deft turns, dealt with each in less than sixty seconds, then performed the same office for me. I breathed a sigh of relief as the cuffs fell from my wrists, knowing now what it felt like to be a freed slave – not that our freedom was as yet by any means assured.

'It will be touch-and-go,' observed Holmes, as we began the descent. 'The causeway is due to close at one-fifteen, and it is already long past midnight. All Fools' Day! Well, well – it still remains to be seen who will be the fools.'

'Keep over to the left,' advised Smith. 'The going is easier higher up.'

The long wearisome scramble had now to be negotiated in reverse. But how different were my feelings! I scarcely noticed my tiredness, though the effort was equivalent to climbing the three hundred and eleven steps of the Fire Monument. By this time, Fu Manchu would surely wonder why we failed to appear, and would send others to find out. Now and then, I glanced back anxiously; but, so far, there was no sign of pursuit.

On the outward journey, the Inner Head had lain

behind us, so that I had had no view of it from this point. Now it loomed high above us, the length of it hidden, the shorter side appearing as a blunt-pointed triangle with the precipitous scarp falling vertically seawards. As we approached more closely:

'I take it that no one is up there now?' queried Holmes, turning to Smith.

'No. They have left the camp empty.'

'Good! Then we have nothing to fear from that quarter.'

We ascended thankfully from the rocks, but did not go up over the top, for the more regular path – which I had not previously traversed – skirted the base of the slope, only a few feet above the level of the causeway.

'I am sorry that I broke my promise not to come out here,' I said dryly, 'but I had no choice in the matter.'

'Quite so! I witnessed your arrival,' answered Holmes, 'though I could not be certain then that it was you. Well, you may claim a place among the pioneers of aviation, if only as a passenger. But I am not sure that I envy you the experience.'

The immediate and lengthier part of our return along the foot of the ridge entailed no more hardship than walking across a field, so that normal conversation again became possible. Holmes, feeling, perhaps, that he had mystified us sufficiently – and me, in particular – consented to give us some account of himself, talking rapidly as we strode along the path below the steep green hillside.

'When we left here, I told you the truth,' he said. 'But I knew that it was impossible to secure the official assistance we needed, and I did not mean to try. It was a job for one man working in disguise. I had to disappear. Our presence in the village was already known, and, in any case, Fu Manchu has always seemed able to discover our whereabouts whenever he chose.'

'Yes,' said Nayland Smith quietly. 'He could.'

Holmes paused, glancing at him a little strangely, but asked no question.

'Since then,' he continued, addressing himself to me

rather than to Smith, 'I have told more lies than Ananias. Our hosts, Mr and Mrs Gwynn, knew that we were detectives. I mean,' he amended hastily, 'they knew that I was one, and they thought you were. If I could not entrust you with my secret, I could obviously not entrust it to them.'

I smiled, feeling grateful at least for that consideration.

'Therefore, I made sure of my accommodation by telling them that Dr Reinhardt was a German spy, for whom we had set a trap.' He gave me a slightly apologetic look. 'I did not like leaving you to draw the enemy's fire – you have a peculiar genius for getting into mischief – so I did my best to keep you out of harm's way by also telling you to watch Dr Reinhardt. But, unfortunately, you always allowed me to escape you too easily.'

'How did you manage to assume your new identity and return here so quickly?'

'Oh, I was not particularly quick! It was about three o'clock, if you remember, when I left you in Swansea, and I did not come back here till ten. After we parted, I made a few telephone calls and raided the wardrobe of the Palace Theatre. I then bought a ticket for London, secured a carriage to myself, and got off the train at Cardiff – having, in the meantime, become Dr Reinhardt – after which I simply walked across the platform and took the next train back.'

All of this was new but not very informative to Smith, since I had told him nothing of the Dr Reinhardt episode.

'What have you been doing since?' I inquired.

'I made my first reconnaissance the next morning, in my guise of the earnest bird-watcher. The Si Fan did not interfere with me, but I was not permitted to cross the Devil's Bridge. As soon as I reached there, I was met by a very English scoutmaster, who assured me that it was dangerous to go farther. You have seen this man, I suppose?'

'I have,' replied my friend grimly. 'Not only here, but

also in Moulmein and Shanghai. He is the younger son of an earl – a dope smuggler, a gun runner, and one of the worst blackguards ever sent down from Oxford.'

Sherlock Holmes nodded. 'When I pretended not to understand, he soon came out with the words *gefährlich* and *verboten*. I did not venture to argue – his German might have been better than mine! I sat down on the rocks and spent the rest of my time studying the place through my field-glasses. This morning – or yesterday, if you prefer – I repeated the procedure. On my way back, I came up over the top of the Inner Head, and walked right past their camp – which created something of a panic, I believe.'

'Ah!' said Smith. 'So that's why I was confined to my tent with a dacoit's knife against my throat!'

'And to-night?' I prompted.

'To-night I was ready to put my plan to effect – or as much of a plan as I was able to devise. I got rid of my inconveniently bushy whiskers, but retained the Dr Reinhardt costume, and came out here after dark, as soon as the causeway opened. I did not know if they kept a watch on it at night, but I took no chances. I have spent some time in the United States and picked up a few tricks from the North American Indians. Going mostly on all fours, and with the aid of a rubber groundsheet, I masqueraded as a boulder – and it took me an hour to cover the distance. My observations had convinced me that the Si Fan were doing something on the Outer Head, and I knew of the two caves situated on the face, since I had meanwhile consulted people who have been out there. I was convinced that they had some large and elaborate mechanism concealed in one of them.'

'Do you know what it is?' snapped Smith.

'No, I do not. It is an engine of death – but more than that I cannot say. Whatever it might be, my intention was, firstly, to put it out of action, and afterwards to rescue you.' Holmes turned his face towards me. 'You remember Cliff Langley, who accompanied us into the mine at Nant Gareth?'

417

'Yes, indeed!'

'I telephoned him after my first trip out here on Monday. One cannot buy explosives at the general store. He met me this afternoon at Port Eynon, bringing me dynamite and an alarm clock, with which I was able to construct a suitable device – '

From somewhere far behind us came a long, wailing cry, followed by another and another.

'The dacoits!' said Smith. 'They are out searching for their fellows.'

'Yes,' agreed Holmes, unperturbed. 'But they will not catch up with us before we reach the causeway. Whether we can cross it is another matter. Well, we will see when we get there.' Calmly, he resumed his story. 'I was afraid to use any of the normal paths, and I had to perform almost the whole journey clambering over the rocks, which took me a second hour. It is possible to by-pass the Devil's Bridge by making a wide detour – at least, at low water – and it was as well that I did. Not long after I had seen the arrival of the kite, seven or eight men came down from the camp, and I was obliged to lie low till they had passed. I saw that they had no prisoners with them, and assumed that you were still up there. But a general exodus seemed to be taking place, and I thought it likely that whatever had been planned was planned for to-night.'

'Yes!' interjected Smith. 'It is!'

'Holmes shrugged resignedly. 'Well, we can do nothing about it now but try to get ashore and warn them – though of what we are to warn them I am still not at all sure . . . Getting around the base of the pinnacle to the caves was a wicked job, but I have always been a good climber, and I had climbing irons with me. All the same, working by moonlight and in unknown territory, it was the worst thing I have tackled since Reichenbach. Eventually, I found myself near the lower cave. But, just as I was approaching it, I saw two men coming down the arrangement of ladders which they have fixed up above. I was in an exposed position. I had to make a quick retreat, and, in doing so, I met with disaster. I slipped, and went down twenty feet or more before I could check my fall.'

'Good Heavens!' I muttered.

'I was unhurt, but all my gear was contained in a small knapsack strapped on my back. It was torn open, and nearly everything went into the sea – including my bomb! The two men had entered the cave, and the worst of it was that I could not be sure they would ever come out again. There I was, clinging on like a lizard, with the waves dashing against the rocks beneath me, drenching me with spray, and there I had to stay for the next half hour. But, at last, by the grace of God, the two of them went back up the ladders, leaving me free to climb up. I did not know quite what I could do, having lost my equipment, but to make sure that I should not be interrupted for a while, I went up a little higher and cut down the lowest of the ladders – they are fixed together with straw ropes. Then I went inside the cave – '

'What did you find there?' demanded Smith impatiently.

'A machine – as I had expected – but I could make nothing of it. It was unlike anything I had ever seen, and there was little that I could do to damage it. I had only a few minutes. Above me, I heard some of the Si Fan coming down again, and there was a tremendous fuss when they found the ladder gone. While they were bringing another down and getting it into position, I looked around quickly, and came across Fu Manchu's robe and cap.'

Nayland Smith laughed boyishly. 'I daresay he intended to put them on before playing his masterstroke. He has a Chinese love of the ceremonial – and there will be a hue and cry when he fails to find them!'

'No doubt! I took them, thinking that they might be useful when I went up to the camp to get you out – if you were still there.'

'How did you propose to do it?' I asked curiously.

'If there had been only two or three left on guard, I

would have held them at pistol point – and if necessary, shot them. If there were more, I intended to set fire to the tents and assist you to escape in the resulting confusion.' Holmes shook his head in distaste. 'Dear me! I shall be thankful to have done with this business, for I believe I am becoming as murderous-minded as the rest of you. However, such tactics proved unnecessary. I was nearly up to the Devil's Bridge when I saw you on the opposite side. I retreated and put on Fu Manchu's things, hoping to make the two dacoits turn back, and then take them from behind. I had no idea, of course, that I should find a battle in progress when I returned.'

We had come to the end of the path, and I stared anxiously across the causeway – or what was left of it. Fully ninety minutes had gone by since I had stood atop the ridge with Nayland Smith and looked down upon it. Now it was broken up again into an intricate maze of islets and, from our present elevation, it was impossible to se if it remained open all the way to the shore.

'Can we make it?' I asked doubtfully.

'We must!' rejoined Holmes. 'We are literally between the devil and the deep!'

'Quickly!' added Smith, assisting me to clamber down. 'We have a good start on them, but those fiends can climb like baboons. It won't be long now before they reach the camp and find us gone.'

The stony surface was uneven, someimes slippery and carpeted with molluscs. Everywhere there were rock-pools, mostly small in diameter, but often more than a foot deep. In the moonlight, they appeared only as dark patches of shadow, and it was difficult to avoid stepping into one. Stumbling rather than walking, we made the best time that we could, but progress was necessarily slow.

We had covered less than a hundred yards when something hissed viciously past my ear and struck upon the stones with a dry, clattering sound.

'Arrows!' snapped Smith. 'And no doubt poisoned!'

'H'm!' said Holmes thoughtfully. 'I imagine they have

firearms, but it seems they prefer not to make a noise. Well, hurry up, and we shall soon be out of range.'

I glanced back but could see no sign of our pursuers.

'At least,' I said thankfully, 'they are not coming after us.'

'An ill omen! They are convinced that we cannot reach land!'

Indeed, it seemed doubtful whether we could. The causeway was by no means level, so that the returning tide left lakes and channels between which we were forced to weave an erratic route. Time passed inexorably while we blundered on through a nightmare wilderness strewn with boulders and ancient scraps of wreckage encrusted with barnacles – at one point, a ship's anchor.

No more arrows were fired – or, if they were, fell short – but we had achieved only a third of the way when Smith gave a sharp cry of warning.

I turned and looked again at The Worm, to see the sinister shape of the kite rising above it. It soared, veered, and came swooping down towards us – now trailing beneath it a spiderweb of cords armed with a multitude of glittering steel barbs.

'Down!' shouted Holmes.

We threw ourselves flat, and only just in time, as Wang Lo's fearful contrivance swept above our heads. The kite rose, turned in a wide circle, and seemed for an instant to hang motionless on the apogee of a second sweep. Holmes sprang to his feet and stood boldly upright. Grasping his pistol in both hands, like one shooting at a target, he fired four shots.

The kite staggered in the air, pitched sideways, crashed into the steep side of the Inner Head, and disappeared.

'Got him!' cried Smith jubilantly.

Holmes shrugged, thrust the pistol back into his pocket, and strode purposefully on, continuing to lead, since he alone of us had been this way before. No further attack was launched against us, but now it appeared likely that where Fu Manchu had failed, Neptune would

421

succeed. As we passed the halfway point, and drew closer to safety, we came into danger more imminent, as ever it became more difficult to find a path through the labyrinth – a labyrinth in which the passages closed before and behind us with every passing minute, barring access and cutting off retreat. It was like trying to navigate a course across a madman's chessboard where the black spaces expanded shapelessly over the white.

Increasingly, we were compelled to splash through streams and shallow lakelets, where the icy water was ankle deep. The terrain underfoot was painful and treacherous, like a stony beach, the pebbles welded into one vast conglomeration of hard, irregular shapes, slimy with seaweed and knobbed all over with the polished oval shells of a million tiny marine creatures. Rarely was there any point flat enough to put a foot down squarely. Reeling like drunkards and avoiding falls by a miracle, we forced our way yard by yard closer to the cliff face now towering above us till at last we found our escape blocked by an unbroken line of surf foaming between us and the shore, still more than a hundred paces distant.

We hesitated an instant, then plunged into it in a desperate bid to wade across, for no alternative remained. As yet, the water was not deep – it rose only just above our knees – but the meeting of the tides set up cross currents, swirling fiercely about our legs and dragging us off our feet: a maelstrom in which it was possible neither to walk nor to swim. I managed a dozen steps, lost my footing, fell, and struggled up, soaked to the skin, with the taste of salt water in my mouth.

'My God!' I panted. 'We are finished!'

'Not quite!' said Holmes, between his teeth. 'Back! Back!'

His bony fingers closed hard on my arm and he hauled me back to the fast-disappearing patch of dry land which we had just quitted. Smith followed unquestioningly, though I wondered what purpose it might serve. In ten minutes or less, our refuge would be covered. The highest point was a scant two feet above the tide.

Holmes tore open his shirt and, from beneath, snatched out a cylindrical object. Holding it aloft in one hand, he tugged at it with the other. There was a loud, plopping sound, and a snake of fire arced up into the sky to burst into a yellowish flare which drifted slowly down, briefly illuminating the panorama of sea patchworked with shoals and atolls, and the white barrier of surf.

Coincident with its extinction, a score of lights appeared on the slope descending rapidly to the shore. A dozen burly men came barging through the water, bringing with them a lifeline – tough seamen who were fresh where we were spent. They seized us and passed us along the human chain, shouting boisterously to each other, and *laughing*. Rough hands took charge of us as we reached land, pushing and sometimes half-carrying us, as they helped us to climb over the boulders and up the slope to the clifftop.

All was happening so quickly, that I had no time to question or to wonder. In a dreamlike state, my limbs responded to the direction of others. We reached the summit and, with the vague astonishment which one feels in dreams, I saw the coastguard station surrounded by a crowd of men carrying lanterns, pitchforks, and shotguns – in the background, three farm wagons with sleepy horses dozing between the shafts.

'These are my Welsh Irregulars!' said Sherlock Holmes in my ear. 'I have been raising an army!'

At the end of my resources, I could not even venture an answer. I did not lose consciousness in the medical sense, but the next few minutes passed in a confusion which left no clear impression. My overtaxed brain registered nothing more until, presently, we were seated in the coastguard's hut, gulping down spirits, and clad in an odd selection of dry clothing subscribed by the men outside. (My blessings go to the generous unknowns who contributed their trousers.) Trevor Bennett sat on one of the lockers opposite me.

'The Lord be praised!' he said. 'Megan was frantic. . . . I was watching you all the way through the glasses. I saw the bird thing go out for you on the causeway!'

I stared stupidly at the lanterns moving about on the cliffs outside the window, still trying vainly to sort fact from fantasy.

'I have nearly sixty men here from points as far afield as Llangenydd and Reynoldston,' said Holmes, answering my bewilderment. 'Where official action was wanting, I knew that I could depend on the Celtic imagination and stout-heartedness which, more than a century ago, vanquished the Napoleonic invasion.'

His bland observation, made as calmly as if we had not minutes before been fighting for our lives in the surf, had the desired effect of restoring me to my senses. I smiled, thinking that, for all his out-of-the-way knowledge, Holmes was weak on history.

'But there was no Napoleonic invasion!' I said. 'French soldiers never set foot on British soil.'

'Oh, but they did!' he replied, matching my smile with one of his own. 'The Martello towers of the Channel coast were never called upon to display their effectiveness, but fourteen hundred Frenchmen landed in Pembrokeshire. They were met and promptly defeated by farmers armed with agricultural tools, and happily assisted by a crowd of female spectators, whose red cloaks the French mistook for the red coats of British soldiers!' Enjoying my discomfiture, he added: 'On Monday afternoon, I bought a bicycle and began touring the countryside and the public houses, searching for recruits. I told them that The Worm had been occupied by the advance force of a Chinese invasion!'

Nayland Smith uttered a short bark of laughter.

'I'm afraid they will be furious with me because I did not, after all, lead them into battle,' went on Holmes regretfully. 'I intended to summon them to the attack after I had rescued you, but I was half an hour too late. I dared not give the signal and risk having them trapped out there on the causeway.'

Taking up his briar from the assortment of personal

articles laid out beside him, he detached the stem from the bowl, blew down it violently, squirting out sea water, and accepted a fill of ship's tobacco. For a few minutes, he said nothing, the pipe crackling and hissing. Then:

'In my capacity as a professional investigator,' he said slowly, 'my case is concluded. I was commissioned by Dr Petrie to inquire into the abduction of Mr Nayland Smith and secure his release. This I have done. The further affairs of Dr Fu Manchu are really none of my concern. But, for what it may be worth, I will give you my report.' He looked up, not at Smith, but at Bennett. 'In the lower of the two caves on the face of the Outer Head, Fu Manchu has some kind of weapon. It is surrounded by coils and insulators, mounted and shaped like a naval gun – '

'A gun!'

'Yes – but one which fires no such projectile as we know. It has no breech, and the barrel is a rod of solid quartz! Above it, and evidently connected with it, is a second apparatus, consisting of a hooded glass screen upon which a thread of light appears, reflected in three small mirrors set at different angles.'

My eyes met Smith's and we both shook our heads. Bennett appeared equally baffled.

'I do not know what this thing is or what it does,' continued Holmes gravely, 'but I will make a suggestion. I believe that the thin line of light represents and invisible beam extending between The Worm and the Chinese vessel, somewhere far over the horizon, like an alarm wire. When another ship crosses it, a signal will be registered on the screen – and it is Fu Manchu's purpose to destroy that ship – '

Trevor Bennett leapt to his feet, his face suddenly pale.

'Christ!' he shouted. 'It's the battleship *Hindustan*, with the Prince of Wales aboard!'

Bennett ran his fingers through his hair in a gesture of exasperation at our lack of immediate understanding, glaring at us wild-eyed.

'The *Hindustan* is the ship in which he once served as a cadet,' he explained hoarsely. 'She is coming round from Dartmouth, to cruise westwards around the coast on a series of state visits to the Welsh ports, starting with Cardiff. My God! Don't you read the newspapers?'

'I do not read the columns devoted to announcements of that sort,' answered Holmes stiffly.

'. . . *and set an example which this arrogant island shall remember* . . .' I whispered.

The picture of Fu Manchu in that ruined cottage with the ivory screen and the two huge Mongols at his back returned to me vividly, and now I knew what he meant: a savage affront more shocking even than the assassination of the reigning monarch, aimed at England's hope of the future – the destruction of the heir to the throne, a battleship, and all her crew, at the very moment when we stood on the brink of war. It was a demonstration of his power – his contempt – for which no redress could be sought, no government held responsible. . . .

'She will pass too distantly for us to see from here, but sometime to-night,' said Bennett, in a low, horrified voice, 'perhaps in the next few minutes!'

'They must change course!' rapped Smith. 'A wireless message . . .'

'Yes,' muttered the coastguard, and I saw that his hands were trembling. 'But we have no wireless here. I must get in touch with the station – '

He snatched up the telephone and jerked the receiver from the hook – but no sooner had he lifted it to his ear than he was forced to take it away again. A buzzing, sputtering sound emanated from the instrument. Still holding it in his hand, Trevor Bennett stared at it blankly.

'What on earth – ' he began.

Simultaneously, I became aware of a startled outcry from outside, and, with one accord, we rushed out from the hut, where Holmes's allies stood pointing and mur-

426

muring. The solitary telephone wire stretching all the way back to the village was alive with an eerie, coruscating glow of St Elmo's fire.

'He has energised the coils, and set up an electrostatic field,' said Holmes tersely. 'We have no communication – and it would be too late now if we had.'

We turned and stared out again at the monstrous shape of The Worm, jet black on a silver sea. Never had it appeared more menacing, for we knew now what was there. It seemed to me that a faint, bluish-green nimbus hovered about the dark tower of the Outer Head, but I could not be sure.

'This is a deed which will gain him the unquestioned leadership of the Si Fan,' said Smith, clenching his hands. 'He regards it, perhaps, as a reprisal for the death of the young Kuang Hsü emperor, which he blames on Britain – as he blames us for everything that has happened in China.'

'Can he do it?' I asked wonderingly. 'Has he really the power to strike at a ship so far off that it cannot be seen?'

'The power of lightning!' snapped Smith.

'Yes,' said Holmes soberly. 'But this will be no artificial bolt of lightning. It will be converted into some other form of energy – a shaft of heat, perhaps, or some such supersonic wave as that by which he killed Professor Davies.'

Minutes of suspense passed while I stood there helpless on the clifftop with Holmes on my left and Smith on my right – between those two great leaders with whom I had shared so many adventures – while all of us waited breathlessly for the tragedy which we were powerless to avert.

'Is there nothing we can do?' I groaned.

Smith shook his head, and it was Holmes who answered.

'Nothing now,' he said, and hesitated. 'But there is still a chance. When I was there in the cave, I could see no way to damage that machine sufficiently to be certain

427

it could not be repaired. But I have strong fingers. I have bent each of the three mirrors a fraction out of position – '

And then it came – silently, and with such results as we had never envisaged. An intense light, bright as an electric arc, burst out from the far side of the pinnacle, throwing it into high relief – but not, as we expected, a tight, deadly beam aimed at the horizon. It fanned out and struck downwards, impinging upon the waves three miles distant from its source – and where the light fell the sea vanished! Great clouds of vapour boiled up into the sky, as the unknown force instantly disrupted water into its constituent parts of hydrogen and oxygen. A chasm opened up, hundreds of yards across, and reaching down to the bed of the ocean – a chasm whose walls were of water, held back by the unearthly light which destroyed every drop pouring in to fill it. For ten seconds or more, the phenomenon persisted, the gulf widening and deepening till it seemed to me – rightly or wrongly – that the sea bed itself disappeared.

'Almighty God!' cried Smith. 'He is off target – and he cannot stop it!'

For a further ten seconds, the incredible scene lasted. Then the light went out, succeeded by a natural spectacle as awful as the unnatural spectacle which had preceded it, as the outraged sea rushed in to close the gap. The waves rolled out, contrary to the tide, till half of the submerged causeway reappeared. Half-blinded by the brilliance of the destructive light, for a moment I saw nothing, then, as vision returned, saw a white wall of water – a wave such as no British coast had ever seen – foaming towards us, driven by all the weight and fury of the Atlantic.

It struck against the pinnacle – thundered on, and, for a moment, engulfed the whole length of The Worm in a seething torrent – raced on, and struck with a dull shock against the base of the cliffs upon which we stood. For a space of seconds, the waves lashed angrily back and forth, white-capped and furious.

Then all was quiet and tranquil as it had been before.*

* This was evidently a prototype device built on plans stolen from the Norwegian Henrik Eriksen, who was himself abducted by the Si Fan not long afterwards. The future Duke of Windsor never knew how near he came to destruction. [Ed.]

36

A POSTSCRIPT

The lifeboat came round from Port Eynon, but found no survivors. Dog tired, but still reluctant to leave our post, we slept that night on the floor of the coastguard's hut, rolled up in blankets brought from the village, and too near exhaustion to notice the hardness of our couch.

Soon after dawn, four bodies were reported washed up on the broad sands of Rhossili Bay, where the tidal wave had run up to the dunes, splashing the windows of the rectory. It was well after ten before the causeway again became practicable, but as soon as it was so, a search party went out – the three of us still weary but refusing to be left behind. My leg muscles had stiffened, and at first I could scarcely hobble, but the stiffness wore off.

Bathed in sunlight, the hellish plain across which we had stumbled the night before took on an aspect of fairyland, the dark holes which had threatened and impeded our passage now limpid pools of delight in which tiny fish darted. We ascended to the top of the Inner Head, but nothing remained to indicate that a camp had ever existed. Again we scrambled over the rocks, crossed the Devil's Bridge – though not without a shudder – and, for the first time, I climbed the Outer Head. As Coastguard Bennett had said, it was like a giant rockery – a riot of colour with wild anemones springing from every crevice.

We scaled the pinnacle, but I did not go down to the caves. The ladders were gone. Two experienced climbers descended by means of ropes, and found only a few twisted fragments of wreckage. On the way back, we came across two more bodies among the rocks – both of them those of dacoits. Whether or not they were the men who had died in the fight on the Devil's Bridge, we could not determine.

'It will take more than a tidal wave to kill Dr Fu Manchu!' said Smith grimly.

Twenty men had been out there on The Worm when we left it, but we had found the corpses of only six. It was hard to believe that all of them had perished in that devastating but brief inundation and vanished without trace – that every vestige of the Si Fan's occupation could have been destroyed so completely. It was my belief – and Smith's – that Zarmi had brought in the fishing vessel and taken off the survivors long before the arrival of the lifeboat.

When we returned to the shore, we went up the hill to the lane, where I was relieved to discover the Standard tourer just as I had left it. A visit to the cottage yielded nothing informative – it had clearly been used only in setting their trap for me. As an afterthought, I searched in the rubbish for my fallen pistol, but it was not there. I thought that I had lost it, but, as a matter of fact, it had earlier been found by children playing in the ruined building, and I got it back a few days later – together with a very unpleasant letter threatening me with proceedings because I had failed to notify the authorities of its loss.

An hour afterwards, we got into the car and I drove it for the last time – back to Swansea.

Next morning, while I continued to laze in bed, Sherlock Holmes and Nayland Smith went over to police headquarters and delivered a report which very nearly drove Superintendent Gribbler out of his unremarkable mind. As usual, however, it was decided in the end that a full disclosure of the facts would not be in the public interest. The local papers devoted only a few lines to a phenomenal spring tide at Rhossili, which had drowned a band of gypsies encamped on The Worm.

Thus the official side of our escapades was brought to a conclusion. Grouped together in the hotel bar that night over an early bedtime drink, we all looked a trifle

431

the worse for wear – particularly Smith, still lean and haggard from his long captivity. Holmes had a cross of sticking plaster on his right cheek, concealing the scratches inflicted by Fu Manchu's marmoset; while I wore a bandage around my throat, lending me a certain resemblance to a clergyman.

We were all rather silent for a while, till, presently, Holmes looked across at Smith.

'There is still one feature of this affair upon which I should welcome some enlightenment,' he remarked. 'When we were out on The Worm, I commented on the fact that Fu Manchu seemed always able to discover our whereabouts, and you implied that you knew he could. May I ask how he did it?'

Smith hesitated momentarily. 'I'm afraid,' he said slowly, 'that you will think it rather fantastic . . .'

'Everything about this case has been fantastic. Pray proceed!'

'Strictly speaking, it is Dr Petrie whom he can find.'

I started, and Holmes, too, looked surprised.

'How do you mean?' I asked.

'Let me tell you another story first.' Smith faced us with a curiously shy smile. 'I have a native servant in Rangoon, who has looked after me from the time I first went out there. My duties require me to be away a good deal – sometimes only for a few days, sometimes for months. I never advise him of my return, but, whether my absence has been short or long, he is always there to greet me at the quayside. He cannot tell me how he does it. All he can say is that, on a particular day, he *knows* I shall be there – and he is never wrong.'

Holmes nodded impatiently. 'I have heard such tales before – they are common enough in the Orient, and I do not suppose that all of them are false.'

Nayland Smith half turned in his chair to address me. 'You remember how it was,' he said, 'in the old days – when Kâramanèh often appeared in the least likely places? How did she find you that night in New Oxford

Street, when she could not possibly have known that you would be there? She has an instinct which *tells* her – not where you are but in what direction, and, insofar as nothing stands in her way, she will walk straight towards you.'

'Good Heavens! Is it possible?'

'It is unconscious, of course. If she tried to do it consciously, she would probably fail. When Dr Fu Manchu wishes to locate you, he first places her under hypnosis – which he is easily able to do, having had her in his service since she was a child. She is then taken to some open space and told to go to you.' Smith turned again towards Holmes. 'I saw this done, on the day that you met Fu Manchu. The direction that she takes is carefully noted and the experiment repeated at a second site. Two lines are drawn upon a map, and the point where they intersect shows the whereabouts of Dr Petrie. In other words, Fu Manchu employs her much as a surveyor might employ a prismatic compass! Accuracy depends not upon Kâramanèh's instinct, which seems to operate irrespective of distance, but on the scale of the map. Sometimes it is possible only to pinpoint a town, at other times a street, or a house.'

A lengthy silence ensued while Holmes digested this astonishing information.

'It would be didactic and foolish to deny that these powers exist,' he said finally. 'The human mind is an unexplored storehouse of potentials which may one day need to be taken into account in the art of detection.'

He stood up and went to bed.

At nine the following morning, while Nayland Smith and I were partaking of a late breakfast, he rejoined us, neatly attired in the well-cut suit which he had worn on our departure from London. I noted, as he sat down at our table, that his dark tie was ornamented with an exceedingly handsome emerald pin – a decoration so unusual for Sherlock Holmes that I congratulated him on its possession.

'I wear it only upon special occasions,' he answered.

'As you know, I am not sentimental, but it was a gift which I value highly.'

'From a lady?' inquired Smith, smiling.

'Yes. A very gracious lady.'* Holmes leaned over and laid a plain office folder beside my friend's plate. 'Here,' he said, 'are my notes concerning the Fu Manchu case. I hope they may be of some service to you. I am leaving for London on the midday train.'

'You will not continue to assist us, then?'

He shook his head, slowly and gravely. 'Fu Manchu is your adversary,' he replied, 'as Moriarty was once mine. I have my own fish to fry. Now it is up to you to continue the pursuit and to set Dr Petrie's fiancée at liberty.'

But of how we accomplished that I have written elsewhere.

Midday came. We accompanied him to the station, saw him comfortably settled in one corner of a first-class carriage, and put his suitcase up on the rack. He thanked us and shook hands. Then the guard's whistle shrilled and the train drew away from the platform, carrying him out of our sight and out of our lives – an odd, lonely man who risked his life for strangers and feared to make friends. Of his subsequent doings I know no more than the rest of the world. I have heard only that when Watson's wife died (his second, or his third? – for he was never lucky with his wives), Watson came at last to share the villa in Sussex – that he died in his friend's arms, and Sherlock Holmes wept.

Nayland Smith and I stayed on in Swansea for a few days more, but by the weekend we were back in our rooms in Fleet Street. Only forty-eight hours later, I was off again to complete my interrupted work on the tangled affairs of my eccentric relative.

* Queen Victoria. (See *The Bruce Partington Plans*.) Our current Government was less generous. Holmes, I regret to say, never received a penny for his services in the Fu Manchu affair, the War Office contending that he was employed full-time on the Von Bork matter. [P.]

The business being terminated – and in a manner financially satisfactory to myself – I discovered that with luck I could just catch the fast train back. . . .*

* *The Hand of Fu Manchu*, Chapter XXX.

ACKNOWLEDGEMENTS

In conclusion, let me propose a cordial vote of thank to Sir Arthur Conan Doyle and Sax Rohmer for the creation of those two immortal characters Sherlock Holmes and Dr Fu Manchu. To Sax Rohmer I owe also a more personal debt of gratitude, for many years of friendship and painstaking instruction in the art of writing a good story.

To the best of my beliefs, I have contradicted nothing which may be found in the original sagas. For additional material, I have adopted the dates and details suggested by W. S. Baring-Gould in his imaginative biography, *Sherlock Holmes of Baker Street*. As regards the Welsh settings, readers who feel tempted to follow in the footsteps of Dr Petrie will, I am afraid, search in vain for the Smuggler's Causeway, but will find the rest very much as it is here described.

Among the many who have furnished me with advice and much needed encouragement, I should particularly like to mention Robert Briney, editor of the *Rohmer Review*; John Carroll, of the Baker Street Irregulars; Jack Torrance of the Torrance Detective Agency; Ciaran Murray, late of the *Irish Times*; Sally Richards, of the *South Wales Evening Post*; Mr and Mrs Heller, proprietors of the Worms Head Cottage Hotel; Dr 'Ali Hassan el-Samni, and Miss Teng Wei Kwang.

Cay Van Ash,
Department of Literature,
Waseda University
Tokyo